Forgotten
Love

Forgotten Love

Kara Hunt

Horizon Publishers

Springville, Utah

ISBN: 978-0-88290-821-2

Published by Horizon Publishers, an imprint of Cedar Fort, Inc., 2373 W. 700 S., Springville, UT, 84663
Distributed by Cedar Fort, Inc. www.cedarfort.com

Cover design by Nicole Williams
Cover design © 2007 by Lyle Mortimer
Typeset by Kammi Rencher

Printed in the United States of America

10 9 8 7 6 5 4 3 2

Printed on acid-free paper

Dedication

To Jeff—I'd do it all again.

Acknowledgments

I'd like to thank Jackie Howa and Wilma Rich, my fellow writers, critics, cheerleaders, and dear friends, without whom this project would have remained in the top of my closet. And I'd like to thank my mom, Marilyn Van Wagoner, for typing the first rough draft from illegible scribbles.

I'd also like to thank my editor, Kammi, for her great ideas and hard work.

Chapter One

The steady downpour seeped into the cracks of the creek bed and melded the sections of dried mud together like a gigantic jigsaw puzzle. Dark clouds blocked the afternoon sun, and distant red cliffs hid behind a blanket of gray. Indian summer was over in this remote part of southern Utah.

Sagebrush and junipers dotted the plains, and then disappeared where a deep ravine gashed the earth. On the side of the steep embankment a young woman lay sprawled across the saltgrass and sandstone, her torn jeans and sweatshirt red with dirt and blood. On one foot was a mud-caked tennis shoe, the other, only a sock of indistinguishable color.

A groan escaped as the girl opened her eyes. Stringy blonde hair blocked her vision. Pin pricks stabbed her chilled fingers as she brushed the hair away.

"Ohhh," she groaned. *Pain everywhere.* Her arm plopped back in the mud. Raindrops stung her eyes, and she squeezed them shut against the onslaught. Tiny rivers of rainwater ran down her temples and settled in pools in her ears. She scratched her ear, and then looked at her finger. Was that blood or water? *Hard to tell with red mud.*

The girl sucked in a gulp of air and tried to clear the fogginess in her head. Where on earth was she? What had happened to her? How long had she been lying in the mud and the rain?

Her legs seemed petrified when she tried to move them, and her head felt as if it were impaled on a metal stake. She looked from side to side. There was not much to see. A steep slope. Sagebrush. Mud. Nothing . . . *nothing* was familiar.

How did she get here? Where was her car? Was she alone?

A lizard sat motionless and stared at her with unblinking eyes from under a lip of rock.

"What are you looking at?" she croaked. Her mouth opened wide to let the cool rain trickle down her parched throat. *That feels better. Head hurts. I wonder if I can move it off this stake?* Thoughts tumbled in her head.

She rolled her head to one side, and a white-hot poker seared the base of her skull. Lights exploded behind her eyes, and consciousness ceased.

ಬಲ

A chill wind whipped at the young woman, and she again became aware of her surroundings. She moaned as heavier raindrops pelted her. *I'm dead. Dead and in hell. And it's not hot.*

Grit drizzled in her eyes when she tried to open them, so she wiped them with her grimy sleeve, and then howled in pain as the granules ground into her eyes. She squeezed her eyes shut and let tears wash them clean. The lizard continued its vigil.

How long have I been out? What is this place? Her teeth chattered, and violent tremors shook her body. *What am I going to do?*

Gotta get up. Thoughts of searing pain at her last attempt to move caused her head to throb worse. *Maybe I'm not alone. Someone else might be out in this mess, and they can help me. Maybe a house is nearby with a hot bath, warm bed, and food.* Her stomach churned, and bile rose in her throat. *No food.*

She eased onto her side. The pounding in her head increased, but she didn't black out this time. *Maybe someone else is hurt, too. Maybe they need my help. Maybe . . .*

Wait. A deeper chill crawled from her toes to her scalp and made every hair follicle stand at attention. *Who? Who needs me?*

Who knows I'm out here? Her guts twisted into knots.

Who am I?

A scream broke from her throat and split the air. The searing pain in her head choked off further screams as bile bubbled up into her throat. Nausea rolled over her, and she retched as her whole body trembled and her head threatened to explode. She retched again and again, until her insides felt ready to detach. White knuckled, she gripped clumps of saltgrass and gasped for air. When her breath returned, she fell onto her back and let the rain wash her face. Tears mixed with the rainwater as sobs shook her soul.

I don't know who I am. I'm cold, and hurt, and I don't know who I am. Hopelessness pervaded to her core.

She looked at the lip of rock. The lizard was gone. *I'm all alone. Nobody's going to come. I'm going to die here all alone, and no one will know.*

The storm increased its fury as the girl softly whimpered, her sobs spent. *Why aren't I dead yet?* Death had to be better than this numbing cold and relentless rain. *Get it over with.*

Her eyes roamed to the overhang where the lizard had been. Maybe she'd fit under that. At least she'd be partially sheltered. Carefully, she turned over onto her stomach, and then pushed herself to her hands and knees. The scenery swayed. Or was it her? Darkness swirled behind dancing pinpoints of light as she began to crawl. Streams of mud oozed around her and cascaded down the ravine. She reached the overhang and surveyed the crevice. Perhaps it was big enough. What choice was there?

A grunt escaped her as she wedged herself between the sandstone slabs. Her head throbbed, and she gulped huge breaths to avoid nausea. Curled into the fetal position, she rested her head on her arm, relieved to be out of the barrage of rain.

The tension in her body gradually eased, as the smell of cedar trees filled her nostrils. A great smell. And familiar, somehow. Where were the images to go with it? Her eyes scrunched as she tried to picture something, anything, but a steel door had been closed in her mind as tight as a safe, and she didn't know the combination.

The rain pounded out a steady beat. Lulling . . . lulling. Her face relaxed, and her lashes rested on her cheeks. She'd sleep now. Maybe when she woke up she'd remember . . .

The wind howled. A tear slipped across the bridge of her nose and splashed on the sandstone. Thunder resounded in the distance.

Thunder? Her eyes flew open. That was no thunder.

Where had she heard that sound before? Her flesh crawled, and every nerve in her body tingled. The premonition of immediate danger pulsed through her veins and screamed to her mind.

Flash flood!

I've gotta get out of here! Scrambling from her shelter, she tried to stand up but slipped in the mud and sat down hard. Lights exploded in her head. Nausea and blackness threatened to overpower her. She pressed the heels of her hands against her temples and fought to remain conscious. *Hang in there. Hang in there. Don't lose it now. You don't want to die.*

Her teeth ground against the pain, and her vision cleared enough for her to take a look around. The rim of the ravine. So far. So very, very far. *Who am I kidding?* A deep rumble snapped her into action. If she were to be swept away, she wanted to climb, not sit and wait for it to happen.

With great effort, she rolled onto her hands and knees. Her head swam and her eyes blurred. *No time. Gotta move.* She focused on a spot a few feet up the hill and began to crawl. Inch by inch, she worked her way up the slope to the spot. Warm blood trickled down the back of her neck.

Another goal: a huge sagebrush. *Not so far.* Fingernails dug into the mud as her feet slipped and slid. Her hands grasped a patch of rabbitbrush. The sharp edges sliced her palms as she pulled. It loosened, but held. She grunted as she hauled herself up. Now she used the brush as a foothold. It was slippery, but not like the mud. The cold was forgotten as beads of sweat formed on her forehead.

The rumble bellowed louder now, but she reached the

sagebrush and pushed past to a new destination. Determined to succeed, she ignored the constant pounding in her head and the stream of sticky warmth trickling down her neck.

She clutched a rock, but it came loose and plunged down the decline. *That was close.* A few more inches to her next goal. Her nails were cracked and bleeding, and her clothes and hair clung to her like wet wallpaper. Rain ran into her eyes and blurred her vision. Another clump of green. *Good. Brush is more solid than mud.* Her hand reached up and grabbed hold. *A cactus!*

With a yelp of pain, she let go and tumbled back down the hill.

"No!" The word tore from her throat in a desperate cry but was lost in the roar of the approaching flood.

Over and over she plummeted until she smashed into the huge sagebrush she'd passed earlier. Both hands clutched it. She screamed as the quills of the cactus plunged further into her flesh. Tears streamed down her face, but she didn't dare let go.

"God, please help me." Her prayer was shouted into the wind, her head thrown back as rain spilled over her face.

God exists. He has to.

"Please, please help me." The shout turned to a whimper as her head flopped forward in defeat.

A different warmth crept over her, like a soft blanket that enveloped her body and soul. Her sobs quieted, and new strength surged through her limbs. Her chin lifted, and she brushed the hair from her face. *I can make it. I won't die.*

"I will not die!" she yelled at the storm.

Her jaw clamped shut as she dragged herself to her hands and knees and began to climb. This time, she churned through the mud, grabbing anything within reach, ignoring the pain, the wind, and the driving rain. Her sights locked on the rim of the ravine. Mud flew in all directions. Rocks gave way and bounced down the slope. The flood roared in her ears like an enormous beast crashing toward her, devouring everything in its path.

Lord, help me. Please help me. Precious inches were lost, and she clawed at the earth when her footing gave way and she slid backward. Blood oozed between her fingers and slid down the backs of her hands.

A glance over her shoulder showed a gigantic wall of water. The huge wave pushed an icy blast of wind before it. The wind dashed her in the face and tore at her clothes.

Her desperate gaze sought the rim and found it. Her fingers jammed into a crevice, and she pulled with all her strength. *If I can just . . . get . . . hold of that cedar tree on the edge . . .*

Got it. Hand over swollen hand, she heaved while her feet floundered in the mud. Her remaining shoe and her socks were sucked from her feet. Chunks of earth broke off and hurtled downhill.

Momentum. I need momentum. She gripped the spiky branches of the juniper, and seconds before the gargantuan wave roared past, she pulled herself over the edge and rolled away.

The twisted remains of a red Jeep churning in the flood and the chilling spray of water on her face were the last things she remembered.

Chapter Two

A bright ball of light danced behind shimmering waves. *The sun? No more rain. Why is everything swaying? Aah, warmth. Must be day. Wait, where'd the sun go? My head is pounding. Will this pain ever stop? The light again. Why doesn't it hold still? What's that smell? Not cedars. Smells more like . . . rubbing alcohol.*

"Jack . . . Jack. Come quickly. She's waking up," an excited voice whispered nearby.

What? Who's that? Who's there? I'm not alone. Help at last. Maybe they have food. The young woman's stomach rolled. *Forget food.*

"Darling . . . darling, can you hear me?"

That voice again. Minty breath fanned her cheek. *Why did she call me darling?*

The girl turned her head to the side. Plastic tubes tugged at her nose. A blurry, blue dress beneath dark hair swayed before her. *Who is that?*

"Hello, sweetheart. We've been so worried about you."

Eyes won't focus. Have I heard that voice before? Her mouth opened to speak, but nothing came out. She licked her lips and tried again.

"Where am I?" Her tongue was dry and swollen, her voice a hoarse whisper.

"Jack, hand me that cup of ice chips," the woman said.

A man moved into view and handed the woman a cup. *He's tall, very tall. Wish I could see him clearly.*

A blue arm moved, and something cool was placed against her lips. Ecstasy. Her mouth opened to allow the ice to slip onto her parched tongue. Little slurping noises escaped as she closed her eyes to relish the moist trickle down her throat. The woman spooned ice chips into her mouth until she clamped her lips shut and carefully shook her head.

"That's enough. Thank you." Her tongue was more pliable now, and when her eyes opened, she saw the woman clearly. *Handsome features.* Black hair with streaks of gray framed a face that looked like it had been hand-painted by an Italian master. An older woman. Who was she?

The woman smiled at her, and the girl looked away, embarrassed that she'd been staring. Details of her surroundings caught her attention. A sink stood against the far wall next to a door that stood ajar, allowing a glimpse of white porcelain in a darkened room. *Bathroom. Critical element.* Her inspection continued along the light green walls to the dingy gray window framed by off-white, vertical blinds.

With raised eyebrows, she glanced back at the woman by her bed.

"You're in the hospital, dear. You gave us quite a scare, but the doctor says you're going to be fine." The woman took a hesitant step forward and reached for the girl's hand but was refused contact when the young woman pulled back and turned her head away.

The girl looked at the IV hanging from a pole. Clear liquid dripped from a plastic sack suspended on a hook and disappeared under a bandage on her arm. Fingertips with cracked nails poked out of thick bandages. She looked at the woman again.

"What happened to me?"

The woman's eyebrows shot up, and her head jerked back.

"Don't you know?"

The girl scrunched her brows and concentrated a moment before answering.

"All I remember is waking up in the mud with rain pelting me . . . not able to move . . . cold . . . pain . . . black . . ." Her eyes closed, and tears slid from their corners as more images crowded her mind.

This time the girl didn't pull away as the woman sat beside her and took one of the bandaged hands between her own. Warmth crept through the bandages and began to thaw her heart.

"Go on, dear."

Words tumbled from cracked lips. "I woke up again . . . lost . . . so lost. Had to get out of the rain. A flood came . . . had to climb the hill . . . so much pain . . ." Her words ended in a sob and she covered her eyes with her arm.

"There, there now, sweetheart. You're safe now. Everything's going to be all right." A soft arm slipped around her shoulder.

Wiping her face on the sleeve of her hospital gown, the girl looked into the obsidian eyes of the woman sitting beside her on the bed.

"Who are you?"

The eyes bulged, and painted lips moved up and down wordlessly.

"Darling . . ." she clasped the girl's bandaged hands, her eyes wide with shock and hurt. Then she looked at the man, who gave the girl a worried glance, shook his head, and shrugged at the woman. Then he stared at his feet, hands clenched in front of him.

The woman turned back to the girl, who watched her through narrowed eyes.

"Oh, sweetheart . . ." she began again. "Why, we're your parents."

The girl's jaw dropped and panic blossomed within her. Her eyes shot from one parent to the other.

No. Not possible. She felt no spark of recognition. For a frightening moment she was back on the hillside, clawing her way through the mud. To what? This? To not know her own parents?

Her mother's grip tightened on her hands until the girl gave a small yelp of pain. She glanced down and saw the color return to her mother's knuckles as she released her grip. Their eyes met.

"I'm so sorry. I didn't mean to hurt you. You frightened me." The black eyes shone as the woman sat up and clasped her hands beneath her chin.

Emptiness replaced panic. The girl bowed her head as tears slid down her cheeks. She'd thought . . . she'd hoped . . . darn the blackness!

"Oh, honey . . ." the woman tentatively placed a delicate hand on her arm. "Don't you remember anything?"

Her chin and shoulders dropped as she barely shook her head.

"Jack, she doesn't remember us." The woman's stunned whisper echoed through the empty chambers of the girl's mind. She stared at the sheet while great drops fell from her eyes and made ever-widening circles on the material.

"Esther, for heaven's sake, tell her our names." The man's voice rumbled from his chest. The young woman's eyes met his misty blue ones, and the compassion she saw there filled her heart with hope. Quiet strength emanated from his tender smile. An image flashed through her mind of silver hair bending over her while coolness trickled down her throat.

The woman broke the spell.

"What do you mean, tell her our names? She knows our names." The woman glared at the man, and then turned her attention back to the girl, her grip tightening on her arm.

"Andrea, darling, you must remember us."

Andrea? Who's Andrea? Her brow furrowed. Nothing.

"I'm sorry . . ." The girl's bottom lip quivered and her head pounded. She grimaced.

"Oh, sweetheart, you must be in terrible pain." The woman stepped to the bed and pushed a button on the armrest.

"Nurse's station," a voice squeaked over the intercom.

"My daughter needs a pain killer. And send something to help her sleep, too." The authoritative tone surprised the young woman, and she stared at the person claiming to be her mother. Was it possible? The smile that greeted her was sweet and full of compassion.

"They'll be right in, darling. Then you can rest." She picked a strand of hair from the girl's forehead and tucked it behind her ear. The man cleared his throat.

"Our names . . ."

The woman's shoulders rose and fell as a sigh escaped her lips. Her eyebrows lifted as she gazed at the girl, who shrugged and shook her head.

"Very well, although I feel ridiculous introducing myself to my own daughter. I'm Esther, and this is Jack." She indicated the man with a wave of her hand. "Esther and Jack Kensington, at your service," she added with a twinkle in her eye. "And you, of course, are Andrea, our darling daughter." The woman chewed her lip and reached behind her while her eyes remained riveted to the girl's face. The man stepped forward and clasped her hand in both of his.

Andrea. Me? Esther, Jack . . . Her thoughts dove into the blackness but came up empty. A landscape painting of green hills dotted with cows and bluebells captured her attention. Car horns and sirens in the distance seemed incongruous.

Andrea . . . Andrea . . . The name rattled around the emptiness in her mind. A sigh that started from her toes rumbled through her soul. *Why me?* Silence palpitated through the room until Esther cleared her throat. Andrea tore her gaze from the cows. Her attempt at a smile felt like a grimace.

"So what now, Esther and Jack?"

Esther's thin lips broke into an enormous smile.

"Well, for starters, you can call us Mother and Father."

Andrea's chin quivered. She bit her bottom lip. *Be brave. It's okay. They're nice people. You'll remember.* The tips of her fingers below the bandages fiddled with the edge of the sheet.

"Mother . . . Father," she whispered. The words felt strange on her tongue.

A touch of sadness etched the blue depths of her father's eyes as he looked at her. She ached to be held. Maybe if they held her, the nightmare would go away. Esther seemed to read her thoughts and stroked her forehead. The corners of Andrea's mouth turned upward, but her eyes filled with tears. Her head hurt. Her heart hurt. Not even her mother's touch was familiar.

The clock on the wall ticked.

A thought leapt to her consciousness, and Andrea reared up in bed, gulping to force down the bile that rose in her throat.

"Where's a mirror?" Her voice was excited for the first time. Why hadn't she thought of it before? If she saw herself, she'd remember.

Her parents glanced at each other.

"Well, honey, there's not much to see right now," her mother stammered. "Just bandages. You had to have some surgery on your face . . ." Her mother let the words trail off, and two tiny lines appeared between her brows as she peered at Andrea.

Andrea eased back onto her pillow and fingered her face. Did she look that bad? A large bandage covered her nose. When had she hurt her nose? There'd been so much pain . . .

She reached up farther. Her head was bandaged too. It still hurt. That, she remembered. Where was the nurse with her pain pills?

"How long have I been asleep?" She still had so many questions. Maybe talking would take her mind off the pain.

"Three days. Four with the surgery." Esther answered, but Andrea watched her father. He smiled. A funny little half smile. Andrea returned the smile.

"Where are we, anyway?" Her question was directed at him.

"L.A." Short, but sweet. Is he afraid to talk?

Wait a minute. L.A.? But she'd been so alone . . . deep ravines . . . sagebrush . . . cedars? In L.A.?

"How did I get here?"

Jack started to speak, but the door burst open and a mountain of a woman lumbered into the room.

"Look who decided to join us. Not feeling so good, huh?" Her gravelly voice grated on the young woman's ears. "Would you like some broth before goin' back to sleep?"

Andrea shook her head.

"Well, then, honey, I'll just check your vital signs and get out of your way. Tomorrow we'll go for a little walk."

Andrea groaned. Sitting up had been agony. How was she supposed to walk?

"That's what they all say," the nurse said as she chuckled.

She changed the IV sack, and then checked Andrea's temperature and blood pressure readings.

"You're doin' jus' fine," she said. Esther and Jack watched the proceedings in silence.

"We'll have you out of here in no time, chil'." The nurse smiled and nodded at Andrea's parents, and then moved to the end of the bed where she scribbled on a chart attached to a clipboard. Then she waddled over and injected something into the IV in Andrea's arm.

"Night-night." White teeth gleamed from her dark face as she patted Andrea's hand. Then she turned and waddled from the room.

"We'll leave you alone too, dear, but I'll be back first thing in the morning." Esther took hold of Jack's arm. They both seemed to sway and become blurry at the edges.

"Okay," Andrea smiled. Everything was hunky dory. *I'll just float around the room for a bit before I go to sleep.*

"Goodnight, darling." Esther and Jack moved closer, and Esther placed a gentle kiss on Andrea's forehead. The floating stopped for a second, and tears welled up in her eyes again. She gazed at her mother. Such love in her eyes. Why couldn't she feel that love? How does one forget love?

Her head rolled and swayed. Jack patted her foot and gave her a sweet smile, and tugged at Esther.

"Come on, dear. See you tomorrow, Andrea."

Andrea closed her eyes. Her mother's heels clicked beside her father's heavy footsteps as they crossed the room. The door opened and closed. She was alone.

"Dear Lord . . ." What? How should she begin? Ask him to give her life back? He had, hadn't he? Her parents were here. She was safe now. That wasn't enough. Relationships were meaningless without the memories behind them. Where were the memories? Lost in a black void. Maybe she'd join them . . .

Chapter Three

Andrea stabbed at the grayish gruel. The spoon felt cool and smooth between her fingers and thumb. Her stomach growled. Breakfast? They must be joking. Her appetite had returned with a vengeance this morning, and this wasn't exactly what she'd had in mind. *I wonder if cows like mush. Spoons make great catapults . . .*

Tap, tap, tap. Someone was at the door. It opened a crack, and Esther's dark head peaked around the edge.

"Oh good. You're awake." Esther flounced in the room, followed by Jack and the scent lilacs.

Andrea smiled at the image of sunshine Esther portrayed. Her bright yellow suit matched her shoes as well as the hat perched on shiny black hair pulled back in a bun. Netting from the hat partially covered her eyes but didn't hide their sparkle. Black hose and a white silk blouse finished the outfit.

"Good morning, darling. How's my angel doing?" Esther kissed Andrea's forehead.

"Starving. I feel like I could eat Louisiana, but all they gave me was the swamp."

Esther's laughter tinkled through the room, and Jack's smile added crinkles to the corners of his eyes. He pulled a starched, white handkerchief from the jacket of his dark gray suit and wiped the lipstick from Andrea's forehead, and then patted her on the shoulder.

"You're looking much better this morning, Andrea." He stepped behind Esther, his face flushed.

Andrea shook her head as she smiled at him. He had such a commanding presence with his height and broad shoulders and that thick head of silver hair. Why the reserve?

"Well, let's see about getting you some decent food, shall we?" Esther took over.

She set her handbag on the stand by Andrea's bed, picked up the phone, and began punching numbers. Her long, red fingernails clicked on the railing of the bed while she held the phone an inch from her face and waited.

"Let me talk to Sam." The clicking continued, and then stopped as she stood straighter.

"Sam? Good. You know who this is, right? Okay. Listen, I want some Belgian waffles with boysenberry syrup, real butter and whipped cream, hash browns, bacon, and orange juice sent over to the Los Angeles Community Hospital, room 203, right now. Got it? No, no, just one person, but bring plenty."

She clamped down the receiver and smiled at Andrea.

"There now, dear. We'll have some real food here shortly."

Andrea pushed the gruel away.

"Sounds great, but are you sure they won't mind?"

"Who are 'they,' darling? We don't let our lives be run by the 'theys' of this world."

"I mean, the hospital staff. Is it all right for me to have solid food now?"

"Yes, yes. By all means. You've had enough liquid piped in through tubes. It's time to put some meat back on those bones."

Esther flitted about the room, smoothing a wrinkle here, wiping a speck there. Andrea watched, a smile tugging the corner of her mouth. What a bundle of energy Esther was this morning. Maybe that's why Jack was so subdued. Who could keep up?

Jack cleared his throat.

"Uh, I hate to leave so soon, but I have a meeting. I hope you'll forgive me, Andrea." He bent over and kissed the air above her bandaged head.

"I'm really glad you're feeling better. Have a nice visit with your mother." His smile came from somewhere deep inside. Andrea felt warmed. Her hand raised in farewell as he stepped through the door. She watched it close behind him, and then stared at the fire escape plan posted there until she realized Esther was speaking.

"Well?" Esther slid a chair next to the bed and sat down, her arched, painted eyebrows raised as she looked at Andrea.

"Well, what?"

Two lines appeared between the brows.

"I asked if you remembered anything more today."

A cloud descended on the room. Andrea bowed her head.

"No." The whispered word carried a sorrow so intense Andrea felt she'd be crushed beneath it.

Esther made no reply, and the room remained silent as Andrea tried not to think of a lifetime lost in a void.

The nail clicking began again, and Andrea met Esther's intent gaze. Esther's solemn look burst into radiance.

"Well, never mind about that. I'm here for you, sweetheart, for as long as you need me. I'll tell you anything you want to know." She clasped Andrea's bandaged hands, elbows leaning on the bed.

Andrea's head swam. Where to begin?

"I'd . . . I'd like to know what I look like. I mean . . . am I so hideous you're afraid I'll go into shock or something?"

Esther laughed.

"Of course not, darling. But you have looked better, and I didn't want to worry you when you had so much else on your mind."

Andrea winced.

"Oh, I'm so sorry. I didn't mean . . ." Esther's words trailed off, and her grip tightened until Andrea yelped.

"Sorry, again." Esther released her and picked up the purse she'd dropped on the nightstand.

"I have a mirror in here somewhere." She rummaged through the contents.

Andrea held her breath while she waited. An earlier attempt

to make it to the bathroom had ended when she'd swung her legs off the bed and tried to sit up on her own. Stars had danced before her eyes, and her head had sought the pillow of its own volition. She hadn't tried again, and frankly, hadn't wanted to. What if she was truly awful? Besides, the sight of her own face was the last hope she had of triggering a memory. What if it didn't?

"Here it is. It's not very big, but . . ." Now Esther held her breath.

Andrea took the mirror, and closed her eyes as she slowly brought it in front of her face.

Please, God . . .

Her eyes eased open. The oval frame was filled with the white of her bandage. Tilting the mirror, she glimpsed her face. Numbness crept through her veins as she examined the purple circles under turquoise eyes, separated by a big, white bandage that ran down her nose and halfway across her cheeks.

Blank. The face of a stranger stared back at her.

Her head turned from side to side, and up and down. Strands of greasy, blonde hair stuck out from a turban-like bandage on her head. Small, colorless lips pressed into a thin line.

Nothing in the room moved. Sounds, smells, time . . . all disappeared as she studied the face. Her face. The eyelashes were blonde, as were her eyebrows, and with the pastiness of her skin, the brilliant blue-green of her eyes was the only color reflected in the image.

Her hands sank to rest on her lap, and her eyes glazed over as tears rolled down the bandages. The cow painting shimmered.

"Andrea . . ." Esther's voice was satiny against her ear, but she continued to stare at nothing. The warmth of a hand seeped through the thin sleeve of her hospital gown.

"I don't remember. Not even my own face." She turned to her mother.

Esther's eyes grew moist. Her bottom lip quivered as she tried to smile.

"It'll be okay, darling. Really. We'll take you home soon, and everything will be okay. You'll see."

Andrea's eyes bore into Esther's.

"If only I knew what you know."

"We'll work on it, sweetheart. I'll be here every day. I'll tell you every moment of your life."

A knock on the door made them both jump. Esther squeezed Andrea's hand and went to answer it. A teenage boy wearing oversized jeans and a sleeveless basketball shirt carried a tray covered with a white cloth into the room.

"Señora Kensington?"

"Yes, Jose." Esther brushed past him and cleared the remains of Andrea's hospital breakfast from the table over her bed.

"Set it down right here."

"Gracias, señora."

A thick silver chain with a big crucifix clanked against the tray as he set it down.

He grinned at Esther, then Andrea, and then flicked the white cloth from the tray, tossed it in the air, and laid it across his arm.

"Your breakfast, señorita."

Andrea gasped, and her stomach responded with a loud rumble. Esther's high heels clicked across the floor as she retrieved her purse. Andrea picked up a fork, cut off a huge bite of waffle, and shoved it in her mouth. Her eyes closed in ecstasy.

Andrea heard the snap of a wallet being opened.

"Here you go, Jose. Tell Sam thank you. He did well," Esther said.

"Gracias, señora. I'm glad señorita like the food. Adios." Rubber squeaked on tile, the door opened and shut, and he was gone.

Andrea took a drink of orange juice, and then cut into the second waffle.

"You'd better slow down, or you will make yourself sick." Laughter bubbled beneath Esther's words.

"This is wonderful. Thank you so much," Andrea mumbled through the food in her mouth.

Esther laughed. "You're welcome. I think."

The door lurched open, and Andrea yelped when a nurse whisked the tray off her table. She stabbed at some hash browns with her fork, but the nurse was too fast.

"I thought I smelled something besides oatmeal. What do you think you're doing, young lady? Do you want to spend the rest of the day worshipping the porcelain god?"

"I . . ." Andrea's disappointment was too acute to think of a reply.

"It's my fault, dear," Esther stepped in. "You didn't really expect her to eat that . . . that . . . whatever it was, did you?"

"It was oatmeal, and yes, as a matter of fact, I did. She hasn't had solid food in nearly a week. She has to start out slowly."

"It's okay, Ma . . . Mother. It was good while it lasted. I might make it 'til lunchtime now. What's for lunch?"

Esther and the nurse looked at her and laughed.

"She's going to be just fine," the nurse said and chuckled as she carried the tray from the room.

Esther sat in the chair next to the bed and took Andrea's hand in hers.

"Now, where do you want to begin?"

Chapter Four

"What?" *Impossible.* Surely Andrea hadn't heard Esther right. "A fire?" Perfect. Not only was her memory wiped out, but also all memorabilia. Her past was gone.

"I'm so sorry, sweetheart. Maybe I should have waited to tell you." Esther stopped pacing and clutched the silver rail at the end of Andrea's bed, her knuckles turning white.

"I wish I had pictures, something, but everything's gone . . ."

Andrea stared, eyes blank.

Esther let go of the bed and straightened so quickly she had to take a step backward to keep from toppling.

"Except for . . ." she hustled around the bed, picked up her handbag, and dug through it. Her fingers curled around a dark green alligator-skin wallet, which she snapped open, while the bag landed with a thunk on the nightstand.

"All except this . . ." Esther pulled a scrap of paper from its plastic cover and handed it to Andrea. One corner was bent, another ripped. The edges were yellowed and worn. An image of a little girl peeked from between creases in the old photograph. A plaid skirt showed beneath a dark overcoat. White tights led to shiny, black shoes that buckled on the side and had a bow on each toe. A teddy bear with matted fur and one eye missing hung by its arm from the girl's tiny fist. Her other hand was by her face, index finger in her mouth. The eyes were light in color, as was the mass of curly hair. A beret perched at an angle on top of her head.

Andrea let her fingers trace the shape of the girl.

"This is me?" she whispered, her attention riveted on the picture.

The bed creaked as Esther sat next to her. "Yes, dear. I cherish that photo. It's all I have left of when you were small. I had it with me in my wallet when the house burned down, or it would be gone too."

"How old was I in the picture?"

"You were three." Esther patted her arm and let her study the picture in silence.

The background of the photo was blurry, but Andrea saw the outline of a huge house.

"Is . . . was that our house?"

"Yes. The house you grew up in." The atmosphere in the room was heavy. Esther pushed on.

"Your father and I were vacationing in Europe, and you were away at college when it burned to the ground. We never did discover the cause. Bad wiring, probably. It was an old house." Esther's speech increased in speed.

"We moved out here shortly after that. I was so devastated that I wanted to get as far away from New York as possible. You stayed to finish your last year of school and were driving here to join us when you . . . had your accident."

Andrea still didn't speak, so Esther continued.

"Your father and I were expecting you, and when you didn't show, we got worried, so we took our plane and went looking for you. Your father's an excellent pilot. It was a miracle we found you, really. If you hadn't called on your cell phone to tell us about those Indian ruins you wanted to check out . . ."

Andrea looked up for the first time. "Huh? You mean you and Fa . . . Father found me? You rescued me?"

Esther's smile was smug. "Yes, we did. We—"

"You came on your own . . . looking for me? But where was I? How did you ever find me? What about the police? Didn't you call them?" Andrea fired off the questions in rapid sequence.

"Whoa, hold on there. One question at a time, please." Esther chuckled as she sat back in her chair. Andrea took a deep breath and waited.

"First of all, you were in Utah, and like I said, you telephoned us about some Indian ruins you wanted to explore and gave an apt description of where they were located, so it's not like we just took off, flying around the country on a whim." Esther leaned over to pat Andrea's arm, and then continued.

"Secondly, of course we called the police, but it seems they're only interested in cures, not prevention. Something drastic has to have already happened before they'll become involved, and you hadn't been missing for the mandatory twenty-four hours. But I couldn't wait that long. I knew something dreadful must have happened. Call it a mother's intuition." She smiled and patted Andrea's arm again.

"I'd tried to talk you out of your little expedition, but I never could talk you out of anything you'd set your mind to." Her smile broadened, and Andrea smiled back.

"Your father spotted you lying on the edge of the ravine. Ole' eagle eye. I always said he could spot a pretty girl from ten miles away." Andrea thought a laugh was an appropriate response, but failed, as yet, to find humor in any of this.

"But the rain . . . How could he see anything? How could he even fly?"

"Oh, everything was wet, all right, but the rain had stopped by the time we reached Utah. The landing was a little tricky, but like I said, your father's an excellent pilot." A shadow crossed Esther's immaculate features.

"It was just so awful to find you like that." Her face dropped to her hands, and Andrea thought she heard a muffled sob, so she reached out to stroke her hair.

An awkward silence followed until Andrea finally said, "It's okay. Thank you so much for rescuing me. I'm fine now."

Fine now. If only that were true. Memories of her ordeal in the ravine washed over her, and she shuddered. So cold. So alone. Terror like she hadn't known existed. And her poor hands. How they'd clawed through the mud, brush, and cactus. Andrea winced.

The twisted hunk of metal she'd seen swept away. That . . . that had been her Jeep. And with it had gone any clue to her life that wasn't burned in the fire. Was there no hope? Another tremor passed over her. Esther sat up, retrieved a hanky from her purse, and dabbed at Andrea's eyes.

"I'm sorry, sweetie. I hope I didn't upset you further. It's just that I've had to be strong for so long, and when I thought about you lying there in the mud, bleeding . . . Well, anyway. I'm sorry." She braved a smile.

Andrea took a deep breath. "I'm okay. Really." The bleakness had to pass. Time healed everything. Didn't it?

"Of course you are, darling, and we're all going to live happily ever after. Just like in the fairy tales." The sparkle was back in Esther's obsidian eyes. "Now, let's talk about happy things. Let me tell you about your old Uncle Peter . . ."

Esther droned on the rest of the afternoon, regaling Andrea with stories of her childhood and eccentric relatives, all dead now. Instead of cheering her up, it had the opposite effect. Someone telling you about your life was not the same as living it. No faces to associate with names, no colors, smells, or emotions. Just facts. It felt like studying for a history exam—an exam she didn't care if she passed or failed.

Chapter Five

The scent of orange blossoms and roses drifted through the open French doors of the balcony of a second-story bedroom. The rain had stopped, but the smell lingered and mingled with other fragrances to beckon Andrea onto the balcony. She filled her lungs with the freshly washed spring air, a precious commodity in L.A.

With eyes half closed, she breathed in the beauty of the gardens. The western sun turned gray clouds to pink. Raindrops glistened on the velvety petals of the roses that lined the cobbled, circular driveway. The manicured lawn shimmered as it rolled out to the huge, wrought iron gates. Oleanders and citrus trees sparkled in the waning sunlight, and lavender pansies gleamed in their symmetrical beds.

Heaven. Andrea's life was a fairy tale, just as her mother had promised—but where was the handsome prince?

She sighed. Esther assured her she'd had no serious relationship with a man, so why this feeling of great loss? Of course, she'd lost a lifetime of memories, but it seemed more than that.

She leaned over the rail and saw a spider web sparkling among the leaves and crimson blossoms of the oleander bush beneath her balcony. A praying mantis was caught in the crystal strands. *Serves you right, silly lady. Why do you kill your mate? Don't you get lonely?*

Andrea sighed again. Maybe she'd meet someone tonight. Someone to fill the void. Her parents doted on her, but it wasn't enough.

She straightened and walked back into the room. Her countenance brightened. This room always cheered her. Pink roses on a bed of dark green adorned the walls and curtains. Matching comforter, ruffle, and pillow shams dressed the four-poster Rice bed. The cherry-wood dresser and nightstands stood on graceful, curved legs and were decorated with brass hardware. A forest green, winged-back chair sat on an Oriental rug in front of the fireplace. A Victorian dream.

Andrea climbed the wooden steps at the side of her bed and sat down. She remembered the first time she'd seen her room. Thick, velvet drapes blocked the light from the French doors. A massive bed of dark walnut sat under a heavy, red bedspread of crushed velvet with fringe around the bottom. Red shag carpet had covered the beautiful hardwood floor. Andrea grimaced. It had been hard to come "home" to a strange place, even one as nice as this, and the oppressiveness of the room had overwhelmed her.

Her mother had seen her distress and shown her to another room. Andrea had been delighted when she'd overheard Esther on the phone with a decorator the next day. She smiled when she thought of Pierre. He'd waddled through the front door that very afternoon with an entourage of underlings loaded down with wallpaper books and fabric samples. She'd felt sorry for him when she'd seen his face turn beet red at her mother's insistence that her room be redone to Andrea's exact specifications. He'd obviously had his own ideas, and his head nearly exploded with the effort of keeping them to himself. In the end, however, he'd been most pleasant to work with, and his suggestions had been marvelous.

Andrea flopped back on the bed, arms sprawled above her head. It was nice to have memories—even if they only went back six months. A healthy portion of those months had been spent in clothing stores. A smile crept over her face, and she raised her head to peer at the enormous walk-in closet across the room.

"Your clothes were all destroyed in the accident," her mother had explained. "Even the ones you were wearing at the time."

"That's what I get for trying to drive from New York by myself," she muttered. She'd thought about a trip to New York to try to find old acquaintances, but there hadn't been time, between buying clothes and finishing her room. Besides, if seeing her own parents hadn't jogged her memory, why would friends? Her past was now one-dimensional. Esther's perceptions were all she had to rely on.

Her father was no help. He acted like he was afraid to talk to her, and she knew the servants were. Esther had strict rules about "keeping them in their place."

"Don't get too familiar with the servants, Andrea, or they'll lose respect for you." She must have heard that a thousand times since coming here.

Her attention turned back to the closet. As she surveyed the rows of gabardine slacks and silk blouses, she scoffed.

"A couple of pairs of jeans and some T-shirts would have sufficed," she mumbled.

And dresses. Why so many dresses? One or two for church were all she needed. Whoa. Where had that thought come from? They never went to church. Her forehead creased, as she looked at nothing in particular for a moment and probed her mind. Nothing. As usual. Not even a clear mental image of a church.

She shrugged and let her gaze drift downward. *I'll bet a centipede couldn't wear that many shoes in a lifetime. What a waste.*

"Guess I'd better get up." Andrea sat up, slid off the bed, and wandered to the antique brass mirror, where she'd been preparing for tonight's ball before being enticed onto the balcony.

Two tiny lines appeared between her eyes as she scrutinized her image. She still didn't remember hurting her nose in the accident, but whatever had been wrong, Dr. Melner had done a fine job fixing it. It looked like a perfect nose to her—now. She'd had her doubts when the bandages first came off, though.

Andrea took a deep breath and stood up straight. Tonight she'd promised to enjoy herself. After the past two weeks of frenzied preparations that had been made strictly for her sake, it was the least she could do.

A tremor of excitement ran through her as she thought of all the people from the entertainment business who'd be at the party. She was fascinated with anything to do with music and didn't understand her parents' reluctance to let her become involved.

"You can't hide me this time." She spoke as if they were there. They granted her every wish except her greatest one—to share her music with the world. What a lost opportunity, for her. They owned Starstream Recording Studios.

Life had begun the day she'd discovered the music room. The grand piano had begged her to sit and caress its keyboard. Music had flowed from her soul and gently spilled over the keys, her voice singing songs that seeped from behind the locked door of her mind. Why could she remember words to songs but not her own name?

She closed her eyes and slowly swayed from side to side, softly humming, caught up in the rapture of her memory. Music had saved her. Saved her from the crushing sense of loss and a sadness that all the opulence in the world didn't erase.

A knock on the door startled her from her reverie.

"May I help you dress, miss?" It was Rosa.

"No, thank you, Rosa." She didn't need a personal maid; she needed a friend. Rosa's tight-lipped refusal to make anything but perfunctory remarks eliminated that possibility. But that didn't stop Andrea from trying, regardless of what her mother said. Tonight she wasn't in the mood to try to crack Rosa's shell, and she wasn't apt at giving orders, so she'd dress herself—which she was more comfortable doing, anyway.

Her shimmering gown of misty green was draped over a chair. Andrea gently picked it up. Did she dare wear such an exquisite garment? Yes. Her skin tingled at the soft caress of the satin lining as she stepped into the dress and slid her arms into the sleeves.

She minced to the mirror as she slipped pearly buttons into loops up her back. Too late to recall Rosa. Her arms contorted behind her. What had it been like to be fat? That was one thing she was glad she didn't remember. Esther said she'd gained extra weight her first year of college but had managed to lose it the following year.

Andrea remembered her first bath after arriving home. The squiggly lines on her stomach. A lot of chocolate, that's what had caused them. A snort of disgust escaped as she thought of the permanent damage traded for momentary pleasures. Many moments.

Fumbling with the last few buttons, she breathed a sigh of relief and straightened up. A few tugs smoothed the creases in her dress.

"Wow," she said, turning sideways, then backward, straining to see over her shoulder. A slit in her dress revealed slender calves and dainty ankles. Light gleamed from cascading blonde waves as she turned to the front again. She had to smile. Small lips framed straight, white teeth. Not the same bruised girl from the hospital.

Her stomach fluttered as music drifted up the stairs. A low murmur sounded as the crowd gathered. *Tonight's the night. He'll be there. I just know he will. My soul mate.*

Andrea closed her eyes and remembered the feel of strong arms pressing her to a muscled chest. Coarse hair tickled her cheek. A wave of sadness made her stumble backward and open her eyes. A sob stuck in her throat, and she grasped a post of her bed for support.

What was that all about? A breeze from the open door caressed her face and she gulped in the fresh air, trying to regain her composure. What if he wasn't there? *No, no, can't think like that. Mother promised she had someone special for me to meet.*

Mother. That sounded strange. So formal. But Esther didn't seem like a "mom." She'd been great at the hospital, so tender and caring, but after they'd gotten home Andrea started to catch glimpses of another side of her mother. A harsher, more severe and demanding side. Sometimes, Esther exhibited behaviors Andrea even considered disturbed. Especially in the past few weeks as she'd prepared for the party. The devoted, doting woman from the hospital had been replaced by a shrill, order-barking machine who'd mowed down anyone in her path. And Jack . . . who was Jack?

Another knock.

"They're waiting for you, miss," came Rosa's clipped tones through the door.

"Thank you, Rosa. I'll be right there." Her voice sounded strangled. She took a deep breath and stood up straight. This was it. Slender feet slipped into pale green satin heels as she gave her face a final check. Her eyes had the sheen of inexplicable unshed tears.

"No more tears." With a forced smile, she turned and glided toward the door.

Chapter Six

Andrea stood at the top of the marble staircase and surveyed the scene below. Most of the guests had already arrived, and they milled about, drinking champagne. Quite an assortment, as tended to be the case in the music industry. Milling around the room were producers in tuxes with their wives or "significant others" in sequined gowns, songwriters with open collars and hair to their shoulders, and performers with no shirts at all under leather vests and hair to their waists. Andrea's heartbeat increased.

Esther and Jack waited at the bottom of the stairs. Andrea smiled and began her descent. A few people glanced her way, but most were wrapped up in their own conversations. One young man stood riveted, however. Andrea watched his gaze crawl up and down her body. His eyes had a predatory gleam. She shuddered and turned away. That one was dangerous. Handsome, yes, but creepy. Andrea felt soiled just from his look.

Her eyes scanned the room as she continued downward. The chandelier cast rainbows on the gilt-framed portraits of deceased relatives, making them seem less severe. The tinkle of crystal mixed with the strains of the Barbra Streisand tune the orchestra played. An occasional burst of laughter rose above the underlying din of conversation.

Andrea glanced at the tall blond again. He winked and licked his lips. *Yuck.* Was that supposed to excite her? Why did the good-looking ones think all females were scrambling to get in bed with them? Maybe they were. Maybe she was just out of it—maybe living like that was something else she'd forgotten.

Andrea reached the bottom of the stairs, and Esther gave her a quick embrace.

"You look wonderful, darling." Andrea felt like a beef at the county fair as Esther examined her appearance.

"Thank you, Mother. So do you." Andrea kissed her cheek.

Her father stepped forward and brushed his lips against her hair, then hopped back into place and stood at rigid attention while his gray-blue eyes darted around the room. Andrea watched until he looked at her again. He blushed when their eyes met, but the flash of warmth she saw there was unmistakable.

A slight smile tugged at the corner of her mouth. Her father intrigued her. Impeccable in his black tux, he towered above her as he shifted from one shiny shoe to the other, light dancing on his thick waves of silver hair. Why was such an imposing figure so self-conscious?

In direct contrast, her mother exuded the power and control of Hitler. Her black eyes snapped as she took Andrea by the elbow and guided her toward the blond who'd watched her descent.

"Where are we going?" A wave of dread weakened Andrea's knees.

"Remember that special someone I wanted you to meet?" The excitement in Esther's voice matched her quick pace as she dragged Andrea along.

The man watched their approach, and Andrea felt the hair on the back of her neck stand on end. Lights, music, and conversation all blurred. Only the death grip on her elbow and a triumphant gleam in pale blue eyes existed.

"Well," Esther cried, as she stopped in front of him. "Here he is." His eyes never left Andrea's face as Esther beamed at him.

Andrea felt ill.

"David, darling, so good of you to come." Each word dripped with honey.

I'm gonna be sick. Andrea grimaced while Esther continued to stare at David.

"Wouldn't have missed it for the world." David's tone matched Esther's as his wolfish gaze devoured Andrea.

She gave him a withering look, but his smile just broadened. Esther seemed oblivious to the interchange.

"Allow me to introduce my lovely daughter, Andrea." Esther tore her eyes away from David. Andrea faked a quick smile.

"Andrea, this is David Woodbury. His father owns Woodbury Studios."

I don't care if he owns Canada. "How nice."

Esther missed the heavy sarcasm in Andrea's tone. She reached for their hands and clasped them together. *This can't be happening.*

"David plays polo and tennis." Esther's voice exuded pride. Andrea rolled her eyes.

"He also graduated from Stanford in finance." Esther gazed adoringly at David as she said this. Andrea felt sure her skin must be a sickly hue by now. David chuckled in a low, menacing way. Esther must have thought this charming, because her smile broadened.

"I'll leave you two to get better acquainted." Andrea shot Esther a look of sheer panic, her eyes pleading, but Esther seemed not to notice as she faded into the crowd.

Andrea dropped David's hand like it was leprous. Laugher rumbled in his throat.

"Relax, sweetheart, I don't bite. Not in public, anyway." He laughed again. "Your ol' lady has big plans for us."

Andrea spun around and left without a word. David's arrogant chuckle followed her as she fought through the crowd, mumbling pardons as she went, her mouth dry.

A waiter with a tray of long-stemmed crystal glasses filled with sparkling liquid passed by, and Andrea snatched a glass and took a big swallow. Her eyes bulged, and beads of sweat formed on her forehead as she refrained from showering nearby guests. Champagne. *I hate champagne.* This was not going well.

She worked her way to the edge of the huge hall and set the glass down on an antique walnut table and then collapsed in the tapestry chair beside it.

What possessed her mother to abandon her with David that way? Had she missed Andrea's silent plea? And where was she now? This was supposed to be Andrea's party. She wanted to be introduced to music producers and entertainers—someone who could give her a toehold in the music world—meet the man of her dreams, and dance the night away. Instead, here she sat. Alone in a crowd.

Andrea fumed as she slumped in her seat and stared at the floor. If David was Esther's idea of a prince, she'd take a toad. *So what if he has looks and money. I'm not for sale.*

What she craved was tenderness. The word evoked deep emotion. Her eyes squeezed shut as she clutched at shadowy figures dancing behind the black shade drawn on her memories. Warm. Soft. She almost cried out at the painful emptiness in her heart.

A hand on her shoulder made her jump. Sharp words leapt to her tongue as she spun, expecting to see David's leer. But it was her father's nervous smile that greeted her.

"May I have this dance?" Relief burst through Andrea.

"Of course." Her smile stretched across her face as she stood and placed her hand on her father's arm. He smiled back and led her into the ballroom.

They floated around the dance floor, one with the waltz. The steps came easily to Andrea, as music had before. Tension drained from her body. In the half a year she'd been home, she'd never known her father to relax in her presence as he did now. His smile smoothed years from his countenance and put a sparkle in his eyes she hadn't seen before. But he still didn't talk.

Then the life drained from his face, and Andrea stumbled into him when he stopped dead. His mouth became a hard line.

"Hey . . ." she began as she regained her balance, but hesitated when she saw his look. She turned to see her mother storming toward them.

"What's her problem?" Andrea was surprised at the murderous gleam in her eyes.

"Ssh . . . She'll hear you." Jack almost smiled.

They watched Esther's approach in silence. Andrea clasped her father's limp hand. Esther stopped in front of them and impaled them with her eyes.

"May I have a word with you, Jack?" Esther hissed, and grabbed him by the arm, ignoring Andrea as she ripped his hand from her grip and marched him toward the patio.

Andrea was stunned. Wasn't her father allowed to dance? Or was it something she'd done? Was her mother jealous? *I don't get it. How sad.* Why did he put up with that kind of treatment?

Before they reached the open French doors, Esther stopped, turned, and came back alone to where Andrea still stood.

"Andrea, darling, David would love to have the next dance." She smiled sweetly, but her eyes sent a chill down Andrea's spine. Without another word, Esther turned and marched back to her husband, fists clenched at her sides.

So that was it. Her mother was mad because she was dancing with her father instead of David. This was more than a simple case of matchmaking. What was her mother's interest in that creep?

"She can have David, and I'll take my father." Andrea felt the heat rise in her face when she realized she'd spoken aloud. Alone on the dance floor now, several couples stopped to gawk at her.

"Excuse me." She sidled toward the edge of the room. The orchestra played a rock song, and the free champagne took effect on the crowd. Andrea felt like a pinball as she escaped the ballroom.

Where to now? The patio. *No, that's where Esther dragged Dad.* The thought of her mother humiliating that noble figure in public made her stomach quell. *Maybe I can help him. Or not. I wasn't much help when Esther marched him off the dance floor. I lack her pitbull quality. Maybe I should get the waltz with the unholy creep out of the way. No, not yet. I can't stomach him yet.* She opted for the banquet hall.

No sign of him. *Good.* But what a spread! She'd never seen so much food in one place. At least, she didn't think she had. Stacks of china plates with a red and gold pattern around the edge were at the end of a long table covered with white linen. Andrea took the plate and set of gold flatware proffered by the gloved servant dressed in white tails, and made her way down the table, her spirits lifting with each serving of the beautifully displayed food piled on her plate. By the time she reached the fountain with red punch cascading around an ice sculpture of a swan, her plate was heaped as high as she dared. *Probably not ladylike to pig-out, but, what the heck.*

"Nice to see a chick with a healthy appetite for a change."

Andrea's head jerked up, and she felt the heat rise in her cheeks as she met the smoldering tawny eyes and amused smile on full, sensuous lips of the most gorgeous man she'd ever seen. Her gaze roamed from the top of his shiny black mane that fell around broad shoulders, past a muscular chest covered with a pale yellow cotton shirt unbuttoned far enough to show a mass of dark, curly hair, down tight, faded jeans with a rip over one knee, to brown, scuffed cowboy boots. Prince Charming.

"Nice to see you got all dressed up for my party." Andrea nearly dropped her plate as her eyes flew to meet his and her hand clamped over her mouth. The man tipped back his head and laughed.

"Honest, too. You are a rare one, Miss . . ."

"Kensington. Andrea Kensington." Andrea thrust her hand at him. His eyes sparkled with a mischievous glint as he bowed and brought her fingers to his lips. Her knees began to shake, and the full plate of food wobbled precariously. He dropped her hand and grabbed the plate before the contents landed in a heap on the floor, then laughed again.

"Maybe you'd better sit down," he said, as he glanced around the room. "You dining alone?"

Andrea nodded.

"Seems that I am, too. Mind if I join you?"

She shook her head, so he guided her to a small, round table with two chairs, set her plate on the table, then pulled out a chair for her and saw her comfortably seated before returning to fill a plate for himself.

Andrea watched him, no longer aware of the food she'd been so interested in a few minutes before. He moved with grace and ease, despite his height and bulk. Once, he turned and winked at her while he heaped a plate of food that made hers look like kiddy portions. Soon he returned and sat down across from her.

"Go ahead. Dig in," he said with a grin, his own fork halfway to his mouth.

"Who are you?" Her question made him choke on his food. When he'd composed himself, he stared at her.

"Are you kidding me?"

"No. Why would I be kidding?"

"Oh yeah. Andrea Kensington. Your old lady's hosting this shindig. You lost your memory or something, huh?"

"That's right." Andrea lifted her chin and clenched her jaw at the painful reminder.

"I'm sorry. Did I say something wrong? It's just been so long since anyone asked me who I was . . ."

"So . . . who are you?" Again, the laugh.

"Jason Nyberg. *A votre service.*" At Andrea's blank stare, he continued. "Singer, songwriter, all around great guy . . ."

Her shoulders lifted and fell and he scoffed. "You are a refreshing change, anyway. Most young ladies fall down and offer to lick my toes before I get a word out."

Andrea laughed. "Forgive me, Mr. Nyberg. You are incredibly handsome, but I think I'd rather sample the shrimp." They both laughed and then settled into a companionable silence for a few moments while they ate.

A Greek goddess sauntered up to their table.

"There you are, Jason. I was beginning to think you'd skipped out and left me to find my own way home."

Crab salad stuck in Andrea's throat as she gazed at the vision who stood above her. The chair across from her scraped the floor as Jason stood next to the woman, slipped his arm around her waist, and placed a kiss on her cheek. A matched set. Except the woman's ensemble was straight off a glossy magazine cover. Her shimmering black dress hugged every luscious curve of her tall frame, ending mid-thigh, exposing long, long, long legs.

"Never, my love." He looked at Andrea.

"May I present my wife, Nicole."

Andrea died a little.

"Nicole, Miss Andrea Kensington. Our charming hostess."

Andrea stood and extended a shaky hand.

"H—how do you do?"

The woman clasped Andrea's hand with both of hers.

"I'm so pleased to meet you, Andrea." Her smile radiated warmth and confidence—confidence born of security in a relationship.

Nicole let go of Andrea's hand and put both arms around Jason's waist. Her gaze met his and sparks flew. *Wow. What must that be like?* Andrea's stomach leapt, and she felt like somehow, she knew.

"Excuse me," she muttered. "I really should go mingle with the other guests." Andrea tried to slip past them, but Jason grabbed her arm.

"Where are you running off to? You've barely touched your dinner."

"I, uh . . ." No words came. Andrea's glance fell on her half-eaten plate of food.

"Go ahead. Sit down and finish. I'll grab a plate and join you." Nicole's satiny voice both soothed Andrea and made her resent her all the more.

Andrea wanted to hate her, but as she looked at the warm, inviting smiles on the faces of these two beautiful people, she sat down instead. *Oh well. I hate eating by myself, anyway.*

"Good. I'll be back in a moment." Nicole kissed Jason's cheek and then headed to the food table. Jason watched her for a moment before sitting back down by Andrea.

"She's a peach, ain't she?" He grinned like a little boy with a brand new puppy.

At least. "She's beautiful. You two look very happy." Andrea tried a strawberry tart, usually a favorite, but food had lost its flavor.

"She's a singer, too. In fact, that's how we met. She auditioned to be a back-up singer for my band, and I haven't let her out of my sight since."

Andrea poked at a sautéed mushroom with her fork, her chin resting in her other hand.

"Hello, Andrea. Welcome to L.A." She turned to identify the source of the deadpan voice. An older gentleman greeted her with a frosty smile. A woman too large for her evening gown eyed her coldly as she clung to the man's arm and dragged him away.

"Hello. Thank you," she stammered at their retreating backs, feeling as welcome as a virus. *I'm not hungry anymore.*

"What's with the long face?" Jason asked. Andrea looked at him and sighed. He laughed.

"Hey, this isn't the same girl I started to chow down with. What happened?"

Men are so thick. Andrea attempted a smile.

"I don't know. I guess I just put too much stock in tonight, and things aren't turning out exactly how I planned."

"What's not turning out how you planned?" Nicole set a plate of green stuff on the table and slid into the chair between Jason and Andrea.

"I was just going to get to the bottom of that." Jason tore his eyes from Nicole to look at Andrea. "Well?" His smile was encouraging.

Andrea's cheeks burned. Was she supposed to tell this gorgeous woman she'd been fantasizing a happily-ever-after relationship with her husband before she showed up? *Think fast.*

"I . . . uh . . . This is embarrassing."

"Go ahead. I feel like we're old friends. Tell us anything." Nicole placed a soft, manicured hand over Andrea's. They really did seem like old friends. How was that possible?

"Actually, I'm an aspiring songwriter, too." Andrea glanced from one to the other. They didn't laugh, so she continued.

"I want so much to produce my music, but my parents—my mother—doesn't seem to want me involved in the business. I thought I might be able to meet someone tonight who could help me." It wasn't a lie.

Jason's brow furrowed. *Oh no. I bet he gets this all the time. He's going to think everything I've said and done has been an act, and I'm trying to use him.*

"Are you any good?" His look was serious as he studied her.

"I . . . well . . . yeah!" Andrea thrust back her shoulders. What did she have to lose?

Jason and Nicole both laughed.

"Atta girl." Nicole winked at her.

"You've gotta love her, don't ya?" Jason stood suddenly. "Come on." He grabbed each woman by the arm and pulled them to their feet.

"Where are we going?" They stammered in unison as he dragged them through the crowded dining room.

"To my studio."

Andrea halted abruptly, causing the others to do the same.

"I can't run out on my party. My mother would have my hide."

"You're right. That might be kinda rude. You have a piano in this dive?" Jason's grin was crooked and his eyes sparkled. Nicole slugged his arm, and Andrea chuckled.

"I'll see what I can scare up. Follow me." She led them to the music room and flipped on the light. A couple on the couch jumped to their feet, straightening clothes and stammering apologies. The trio turned their heads and hid smiles as the couple dashed past them and out the door, slamming it behind them.

"Anyone else?" Andrea's voice echoed through the room. "I think it's safe."

"Wow. Pretty impressive." Jason walked in circles as he scanned the room.

Andrea watched him, chin high, eyes glowing. This room was her life. His response pleased her.

An ebony grand piano gleamed in the corner, adorned with

fresh flowers arranged in a crystal vase atop a hand-crocheted doily. A Victorian settee, trimmed in wood and upholstered in a floral tapestry, reigned between two wing-backed chairs in solid, matching colors. Marble-topped end tables, also with fresh flowers, nestled between the chairs and settee.

Nicole sat on the couch and crossed her legs, her arms extending along the back of it.

"What a room."

Andrea smiled at the appreciative look on Nicole's face. These were the first people she'd truly connected with since her past had been obliterated so it gave her pleasure to share this special room with them. Her lifeline.

"Well? Let's see what you've got." Jason moved behind the piano and motioned toward the bench. Andrea joined him and sat down, shifted, and arranged her dress until she was comfortable. She lovingly placed her fingers on the keys.

What to play? She knew: a haunting love song she'd been working on began to float from the piano, then merged with her voice to fill the room with an aching sweetness that seemed to charge the air with an energy all its own. Andrea closed her eyes and swayed to the notes, her voice rising and falling in conjunction with the words.

"Where is the man I long to touch?

"Why does my heart hurt so much? . . ."

The song ended, and the room was still. Andrea opened her eyes, folded her hands in her lap, and looked at Jason. He burst into applause. Andrea's heart swelled. She hadn't expected such enthusiasm.

Shifting in her seat, she glanced at Nicole, who was crying. *Wow. This is good, right?* Jason cleared up any doubt.

"That . . . was nothing short of incredible. And I'm not easily impressed. You are truly gifted, young lady. Your parents are crazy not to take advantage of your talent. You could double their business in a matter of months."

Andrea beamed. "You really think so?"

Nicole nodded vigorously.

"Absolutely," Jason said. "If they're not going to use you, I am. Talk to them, Andrea. Seriously. A talent like yours shouldn't be 'hidden under a bushel,' as the Good Book says."

"Thank you. Thank you so much. You don't know what it means to hear you say that." Andrea stood. "Well, better get back to the party."

"No." Nicole jumped to her feet. "You're not getting off that easy." She moved over next to Jason and clasped his arm. "We want to hear more, don't we, sweetie?"

"Of course, of course. Carry on there, girl; let's see if you're a one-hit wonder."

Andrea sat back down and played several more numbers before she remembered David and one murderous mother. With a sigh, she stood.

"As much as I hate to, I really have to get back to the party. There's someone I promised my mother I'd dance with. Actually, it's more like she threatened me if I didn't dance with him." Her laugh decreased the seriousness of the last words.

"Okay. I guess we can't be selfish and keep you all to ourselves." Jason took Nicole's elbow and guided her toward the door. Andrea followed.

Jason opened the door for the ladies but stopped Andrea before she disappeared into the crowd.

Hey, Nicole and I are going to take off, but I want to thank you for a great party and a wonderful concert. It was terrific meeting you. And keep after your music. You're gonna go far. Let me know if I can steal you." He and Nicole each shook her hand.

"He's right, you know. He never misses on spotting new talent. Don't give up." Nicole's smile warmed Andrea's heart.

"Thanks again, guys. You made the party for me. Keep in touch." Andrea watched as they made their way to the front door, where they both turned and waved as the butler opened it for them. When the door closed behind them, Andrea sighed. Now to find David.

Climbing a couple of steps so she'd have a better view, she

scoured the crowd for some sign of him. *Darn. No luck. Maybe he left—wishful thinking!*

Stepping down, she weaved between clusters of people with drinks in their hands and phony smiles on their lips. Edging past the library, she heard an arrogant chuckle from behind the door. *Maybe that's him.* She pushed the door open, and froze. Her jaw dropped, then she slammed the door behind her, the sickening image of David and the brunette burned into her memory.

Andrea's stomach churned as she leaned against the door for support. David's wicked laughter drifted through the door and propelled her through the crowd. Why had her mother imagined she'd have anything to do with that creep? It didn't matter anymore. Whatever plans Esther had for David Woodbury, Andrea was determined that under no circumstances would they include her.

Chapter Seven

Matt McCandlass was sprawled across the rose-colored sofa in his home in Roy, Utah, wearing only a pair of jeans. His eyes burned in their sockets, and each blink was like dragging his lids across sandpaper as he stared at the fluorescent glow from the television. His fingers, nails bitten to stubs, rubbed through the dark, curly hair on his bare chest. *Where is she?* he wondered for the trillionth time.

He glanced around the room. Everything reminded him of her, from the blush-colored carpet to the cream and dark-green striped wallpaper with tiny, pink rosebuds. Pink and green. Her favorite colors.

Her guitar stood in the corner, behind the piano. Each instrument in turn had filled the house with music for hours on end. Both were covered with dust now. To him, they were untouchable. Even to look at them brought back the sound of her voice with such aching clarity that he'd almost choke on the lump in his throat. The love songs . . . her eyes while she sang . . . the memory sent goosebumps up and down his flesh.

She used to tease him that if he didn't behave, she was going to run away and be a rock star. He'd always laughed and told her she could never live without him. The jokes had stopped when their son was born. What if they hadn't been jokes?

He sucked in his breath and pressed the heels of his hands

to his temples, his fingers buried in thick waves of hair. His eyes squeezed shut as the air crept from his lungs. Her image danced before him. No way. They were a family, and that was the most important thing. Melody knew that. She'd taught him that. So what was the alternative? A shiver ran down his spine. His mind wasn't ready to go there.

"Why can't I find you?" His ragged whisper echoed in the darkness of the empty room. He thought of the trips back and forth to southern Utah he'd made every week for six months, searching, always searching, but to no avail. Not even a private investigator had been able to turn up any clue as to her disappearance.

"Melody," he groaned. How unfair. She was his life, and now she was gone.

"Daddy, I wanna dwink."

Matt jumped. Three-year-old Skyler stood in the doorway of the living room, tiny fists balled up in his eyes. The front of his fuzzy red footy pajamas was still smeared with the graham crackers he'd eaten before he'd gone to bed.

"Okay. I'll get you a drink." Matt forced a smile as he crouched. "But not until I get a hug."

Skyler raced across the room, stubby legs a blur of motion, and dove into his father's arms. Soft, brown curls brushed Matt's cheek. Tears welled in his eyes as he held his son. His lifeline.

"Now can I have a dwink of water?" Skyler raised his head to look at his dad. Matt hoped the darkness hid the pain that ravaged his face from the guileless gaze of his son. What a trooper this boy had been. The trips to Grandma and Grandpa Anderson's ranch outside Kanab every week had been a lark to Skyler, but he missed his mom. How could he survive without a mom? How could either of them?

"Well, all right. If you have to," Matt hoped the jest hid the catch in his voice. With Skyler grasped in his arms, he stood and walked to the kitchen. A battle-worn, yellow Tupperware cup sat on the cupboard next to the sink. Matt filled it with cold water and handed it to his son.

"Here you go."

Skyler gulped it down.

"What do you say?" Matt faked a stern look.

"Tank you." Skyler handed the cup back to his dad. "Can I stay up with you?" he asked through a yawn.

Matt smiled. "No way, big guy. You need your beauty sleep." He rubbed noses with his son and tickled his belly as he said this. Skyler giggled.

Matt set the cup on the cupboard and then took Skyler back to his room, deposited him on the bed, and tucked the flannel plaid comforter around him. Stenciled teddy bears danced around the walls, and more bears of all shapes and sizes filled every niche of the room. Melody's obsession.

"When's mommy coming home?" Big green eyes gazed into the pained ones of his father. Matt swallowed hard.

"I don't know, son. You'd better get back to sleep. Remember, Daddy loves you very much." He kissed his forehead, and Skyler's arms flew around his neck and squeezed with childlike fervor.

"Night night, Daddy. I wuv you, too."

Matt lost himself in the circle of chubby arms while moonlight streamed into the room and danced on the hardwood floor. Crickets chirped, and the scent of grass and spring rain drifted through the open window.

Skyler's soft snore tickled Matt's ear. Matt pulled the arms from around his neck and eased the tiny head onto the pillow. Sweat-dampened curls plastered Skyler's forehead, and Matt shooed them away from his eyes with his finger. Thick lashes rested on rosy cheeks. Matt bent down to kiss soft, pink lips. Another little snore escaped the turned-up nose, and Matt smiled through his tears.

Gus, the teddy bear of choice, was lodged between the bed and the wall. Matt rescued him, then studied the matted fur and dangling eyes. Not a real looker, but Skyler sensed he needed a friend, and refused to sleep without him. Or maybe it was because the bear had been his mom's favorite when she was little. Once Mel befriended a teddy bear, it had a home for life.

Another shaft pierced Matt's heart. He touched the hole where a nose used to be and tucked Gus in next to Skyler. Tears flowed down his cheeks. Why? Why wasn't she here to caress the rose-petal softness of their son's face? To tuck the treasured bear into his arms and kiss his forehead?

Why wasn't her hand clutched in his as he tiptoed from the room and eased the door closed? They'd sneak across the hall to their room, and shut and lock the door. Mel would turn to him with eyes the color of a stormy sea, her face framed by silky, golden strands of hair that spilled over her shoulders as she softly kissed his face.

Matt shook his head. He pushed the painful memories away and walked to the door, but turned for one last look before he gently pulled it shut. Kids. Why wasn't he as resilient as Skyler? Without Skyler, he'd never have survived the past six months. Why did it still hurt so much?

His friends advised him to forget Melody and get on with his life. It was over. She was gone. His boss constantly jeered that she'd left him and didn't want to be found, but he refused to believe it. That wasn't like her. She loved him, and she adored Skyler. She'd never leave without a word. Something had happened. But what?

Thoughts of the fight they'd had before she left to go to her parents' tore at his insides and filled him with remorse. The idea that the last words she'd heard from him were spoken in anger ate away at him a little piece at a time. He loved her parents and was glad Melody enjoyed spending time with them. She and her mom liked to get away with "just the girls," but he'd selfishly tried to guilt her into spending the weekend with him instead.

Matt leaned his back against Skyler's door and ran his fingers through already tousled waves of hair. Maybe if her body had been found and he'd been summoned to see it, as gruesome as the thought was, he'd have put the ordeal behind him by now and started to heal. But there was no body. No Jeep. Nothing. She'd simply vanished without hearing how sorry he was and how much he loved her.

"Oh, Mel." His heart twisted as he thought of the anguish in Carol's voice when she'd called to say that her daughter hadn't shown up at the ranch. At first, he hadn't worried, because he knew how she liked to get off on her own and explore little-used roads. She loved the deserts of southern Utah. The places she'd taken that poor Jeep of hers . . .

Matt smiled a melancholy smile and slowly shook his head. The memories sliced at his heart. Why couldn't he just forget? Forget the way she'd teased him when he tried to be stern. Forget the smell of her hair and the way it slid through his fingers. Forget the silky softness of her skin next to his.

He took a deep breath, and a tremor shook his body. Plenty of opportunities for female companionship had presented themselves since she'd been gone. Why wasn't one soft body the same as the next? Why was her touch the only one he craved? Her laugh, her smile, the only sunshine to fill the black void? Time was supposed to heal all wounds. Why was his still a gaping hole?

Mostly, he'd like to forget the highway patrol report that no trace of her or her Jeep had been found, the months of torture since, and the private investigator's dismal reports of failure. Not to mention his own. And, worst of all . . . he'd like to forget the nagging thought that . . . maybe she was dead, and her body was lost forever.

∽∾

The hardwood floor creaked in spots as Matt tiptoed back to the front room and switched off the TV. His room was across the hall from Skyler's, so he had to brave the squeaky floor again.

Skyler's gentle snore brought a smile to Matt's face as he listened outside his door. Mel had teased Matt about snoring. Like father, like son.

Once in his room, he entered the small bathroom attached and splashed cold water on his face. He studied his reflection in the mirror on the medicine cabinet above the sink.

"You look terrible," he told himself as he rubbed the stubble on his chin. The thoughts of work the next day made him groan.

Rick would see his bloodshot eyes, get that smug look on his face, and tell him what an idiot he was for torturing himself over a "broad."

One day, he'd like to wipe the floor with that sneer. But Rick was his boss and Mel's old neighbor, although she never seemed to be too fond of him, so he tolerated it. For now.

Matt scrubbed, groped for a towel, rubbed his face in it, and then chucked it toward the hamper in the corner.

"Yuck." The smell reminded him of the locker room in high school.

He grabbed his toothbrush and scrounged around the medicine cabinet for a crumpled toothpaste tube. Squeezing brought no result, so he sucked the end of the tube until he had enough to brush his teeth, then tossed the tube at the garbage can with a snort of disgust.

"I have got to pull myself together," he mumbled.

He unbuttoned his Levis as he walked to his bed, then peeled them off and kicked them at his closet. Wearing only boxers, he brushed crumbs from the flannel sheets and started to climb into bed, but stopped, and sank to his knees instead.

"Dear God in heaven, thanks for my son. Bless Mel, if she's still alive, and please help us find her. And please . . . if she's . . . if she's gone for good, please help me and my boy . . ."

He shook out the blue comforter covered with pink roses, discarding the book and dirty sock he found underneath, untangled the top sheet, and slid beneath it. On his back, hands clasped behind his head, he watched the ceiling fan make silent circles.

His eyes drifted around the room. The blue in the wallpaper was for him. Blue for boys. It was supposed to offset the fact that the paper was covered with pink flowers. He smirked, remembering the day Melody had brought it home. He'd thrown a fit and told her he wasn't going to have his bedroom covered with flowers. But she'd just smiled and kissed him on the nose and given that ridiculous explanation about blue and boys. Then she'd hung it on the wall anyway. He supposed he was free to redecorate now, but he didn't have the heart.

His eyes locked on the picture of Jesus with children gathered around. That was her favorite. He'd never take that down. He'd learned to love it too.

Melody had taught him to pray. At first he'd thought that kneeling before an unknown being was unmanly, and had mocked her efforts. But she'd persisted, as usual, so he'd humored her. After a while, he no longer prayed to please her, but for himself and the measure of peace it brought to him. Maybe he should go to his knees more often.

Chapter Eight

Matt drove past the neat rows of vans, trucks, and cars, and parked in front of the showroom of Rick's Autoworld. Switching off the engine to his black four-wheel drive Chevy truck, he rested his arms on the steering wheel while he scanned the huge plate-glass windows. *Great. Rick.* He was right inside the door talking to a salesman—not a pleasant sight first thing in the morning. *Maybe I could leave and come back around noon . . . Too late.* Rick spotted him, shooed the salesman away, and waved Matt in.

Matt heaved a sigh and got out of his truck, flicked away an imaginary piece of dust from the door, and shut it. With the push of a button, the doors locked and his truck chirped good-bye. Matt pocketed the keys and, with another sigh, dragged himself up the stairs toward the big, glass doors. Tulips and daffodils had nudged their way through the cedar bark in the flowerbeds on either side of the stairs. Matt made a great show of enjoying their beauty. Mel loved tulips. He found nothing else to delay the inevitable, so he pushed through the doors and came face to neck with Rick. He threw back his head and met Rick's glaring hazel eyes.

"Another sleepless night, eh, Matt?" Rick's lip curled in a sneer beneath his thick, reddish-brown beard.

Here it comes. Matt scowled and tried to push past him without answering, but Rick's fat hand snaked out and grasped Matt's arm.

"Where do you think you're going? I'm talkin' to you."

Matt's eyes narrowed as he looked down at the hand wrinkling the sleeve of his Armani suit, then back at Rick. Rick let go.

"Don't scowl at me," Rick huffed, folding his arms across a massive chest. "I have a business to run, remember? Car sales are going south while you mope around and feel sorry for yourself."

Matt still didn't answer. He gave the fountain in the center of the showroom his full attention, glad no customers were there yet.

"Hey, Matt, you're my sales manager, so manage."

Matt looked at Rick and noticed the color rise up his neck. *He hates it when I ignore him.* Still no answer.

"You have to ride these guys every second or nothing happens. You know that as well as I do. Are you listening to me?" Bright red spread up Rick's face and ears. His breath whistled through his nose. *He's gonna blow,* Matt thought blandly.

Matt noticed a couple of salesmen inch closer and pretend not to listen. He met Rick's surly stare.

"If they don't sell, they starve. They ought to hustle without me constantly cracking the whip," he finally answered.

Rick extended to his full six-feet-four-inches.

"Yeah, and the IRS should send me a big fat check with a letter of apology. Take a reality check, Matt."

Matt's scowl deepened. Three more salesmen had wandered within hearing. Matt glared at them, and they hurried to the cubicles they used for offices.

Rick stuck his hands in the pockets of his slacks and his body seemed to sag. His chest rose and fell with a deep sigh.

"Listen, Matt. I don't want to fight with you. I know how rough this has been. Hey, I loved Mel, too, you know. But face it. It's time to start living again."

Matt was silent. He studied the gray tile floor.

Rick continued, "Why don't you come over to the house tonight and I'll have Kristy barbecue a couple of juicy T-bones?"

"No, thanks." Matt knew it was futile to refuse even as he

mumbled the words. Rick never took "no" for an answer.

"Bring Skyler, of course. Jared loves to play with him." Rick strode off without another word. Matt scoffed as he watched him enter the corner office and ease his bulk into the overstuffed leather chair behind the enormous mahogany desk.

"Henry the VIII reincarnate," Matt muttered as Rick surveyed his kingdom through glass walls. Someone snickered behind him, and Matt turned to see Reggie, the finance and insurance guy, trying to hide behind the contract in his hand. The corner of Matt's mouth twitched, and he nodded at Reggie, then headed toward his own office.

His hands jammed into his pockets and he put his head down as he tried to slip by the secretarial pool unnoticed. No chance.

"Good morning, Matt," Georgette greeted him shyly, holding her hand over the mouthpiece of her phone. Her emerald eyes were wide with anticipation.

"Hello, Georgette." A nervous smile played with the corners of his mouth as he walked by.

"How's Skyler?" she threw at his retreating back. He paused mid-stride, stopped, and turned.

"He's fine."

How he hated this small talk. Georgette fancied herself in love with him, and he didn't like it.

"Any messages?" His tone remained professional.

"They're on your desk." Her smile was hopeful.

"Thanks." His smile barely warmed before he hurried on.

She was pretty, for a redhead, and was put together well. Had a brain, too, but she just wasn't Mel. Nobody was.

Matt dreaded the day when Rick would discover that Georgette was interested in him. The guy was a bloodhound when he smelled a potential love-match. Matt's case would particularly interest Matt. Georgette was shy enough that maybe Matt had another week of peace. Nothing was kept secret for long in the car business.

Georgette's eyes seemed to bore into his back as he entered his office and closed the door. This was his world. Not as ostentatious as Rick's office, but spacious and comfortable. No pink flowers, either. Here, he was at home.

Sight of the family portrait above his walnut desk made him wince. Turquoise eyes smiled at him from beneath a mane of shiny blonde hair. His heart lurched. Maybe he should take it down.

How Skyler had grown in the year since the picture was taken. His green eyes sparkled, and big dimples dented his chubby cheeks. He'd leave the picture up.

Matt studied his own image. What had it been like to be that happy? An unfamiliar smile showed rows of perfect white teeth. His jaw was firm and strong, not drooping in defeat. White surrounded his brown irises instead of a maze of red squiggles. He wasn't bad-looking when he was happy.

Matt made a decision. As much as he hated to admit it, Rick was right. Life must go on. Squaring his shoulders, he marched to his desk and settled into the dark brown leather chair. A pile of papers stared at him, and he stared back. He glanced through the stack of phone messages and filed them in the wastebasket beneath his desk. Punching a button on his phone, he barked into the speaker.

"Georgette, call a sales meeting immediately."

The chair creaked as he leaned back and locked his fingers behind his head, brows lowered in a look of determination. He may not find love again, but he'd throw himself into his work and make a solid future for his son. And maybe, just maybe, he'd forget.

Chapter Nine

"Excuse me. I didn't realize I was asking so much," Esther seethed. Her sleek hair was pulled back in a bun, adding to the severe look of her black silk blouse, buttoned to the neck and fastened with a cameo broach. Her straight, black skirt was cinched at her tiny waist by a wide leather belt with a large gold buckle.

"What a terrible inconvenience for you to date a rich, handsome young man. How rude of me to ask." Sarcasm twisted her lips into an ugly sneer. She clenched the back of a dark green sofa, long, red nails digging into the leather.

Andrea picked the bookmark off the arm of the overstuffed chair and marked her page, then closed the romance she'd been reading and set the book on the end table beside her. Her lips were compressed into a fine line, and her cheek twitched. Folding her hands in her lap, she watched through narrowed eyes as her knuckles turned white. Esther was not going to give up.

"Don't think you can ignore me." Esther's sharp tone stung Andrea. Where had all the tenderness gone?

Andrea's head snapped up, but she bit back her reply and stared out the window instead. Brocade drapes in deep jewel tones stretched from the twenty-foot ceiling to the floor and framed the paneled glass. The sun was sinking, but a golden beam shone through the murkiness of the library and caught the elusive dust particles in their dance.

Why was Esther doing this to her? Andrea had been horrified with David's behavior at her party, and was certain Esther must not know what sort of man she was attempting to thrust on her daughter. But when Andrea told her, Esther had laughed it off like he'd been stealing cookies. "Oh, boys will be boys," she'd said.

Esther was convinced Andrea was simply jealous, and pride prevented her from seeing David again. *Ha. Fat chance.* Nothing Andrea had said dissuaded Esther, though.

"Well?" Esther interrupted her thoughts.

Andrea took a deep breath and exhaled slowly, still looking out the window.

"Andrea!" Esther barked her name.

"What?" Andrea whipped her head around. The afternoon sun through the window backlit Esther and gave her an unearthly glow.

"You know precisely *what*. Are you going to see David this weekend?"

The skin on Esther's face was stretched tight except for large creases at the corners of her eyes. *She needs to loosen her bun.* Andrea pushed up the sleeves of her sweatshirt, then leaned forward and rested her elbows on her knees, covering a hole in her jeans. Her hair fell around her face as she studied her bare toes. She heard Esther's breath whistling through clenched teeth. When Andrea looked up again, her eyes were glistening.

"Please, Mother, don't make me do this."

Esther raised her arms then let them drop to her sides with an exaggerated huff.

"Oh, stop it, Andrea. It's just a date. The world is not coming to an end." She shook her head and began to pace.

Andrea watched her. Was this really her mother? Why was she so insensitive to Andrea's feelings? Why was it so important that she go out with this creep? Where on earth was her real love?

"All right, all right. I'll go. Tell him to call me." Andrea's jaw clamped shut as she stood and gave her mother a searing look before crossing the room to the door. She paused with her hand on the brass knob of the huge paneled door and turned toward Esther.

"Mother, I . . ." she began, but the look of jubilation on Esther's face cut her off. She shook her head as she stomped out of the library and slammed the door. A Ming vase teetered on its stand in the marble hallway.

What had she just done?

"Might as well get it over with," she muttered as she stormed up the stairs. The creases in her forehead threatened to become permanently fixed as she stared at the black jagged lines cutting through white in the sleek marble surface of the stairs on her ascent to her room. Her footsteps resounded throughout the house.

"I'll never get another moment's peace until I go out with the slime. Why can't she just leave me alone with my music?" Her jaw ached from her clenched teeth, and her lips disappeared into a white line.

Thick carpet muffled her approach to her room, but the slamming door rattled the windows and proclaimed her displeasure. *Let them titter,* she thought of the servants. Her and Esther's arguments had become the prevalent subject of their gossip. Diving for the bed, she buried her face in her arms. *I won't cry. It's not worth it. I'll just do my duty and go out with the jerk, and that will be that. How bad can it be?*

She did cry. The impression of large hands gently stroking her hair and tender kisses on her face pressed against the dark shield in her mind. She had known love before. Every element of her being testified to this fact. But who? Where was he now? Had it been David? Was that why her mother pressed so hard for this match? If so, why hadn't she just told her?

No. Surely amnesia didn't have the power to change her nature, and everything inside her rejected the idea of a union with this unsavory human being—if he could be classified in that species.

Questions. So many questions. Why weren't there ever answers?

ᑫᕁ

The antique ivory and brass phone on her nightstand jangled.

"They didn't waste any time, did they?" Andrea let it ring a few more times. *Maybe he'll get mad and hang up.*

It continued to ring.

"Andrea, pick up your phone!" Her mother's furious shout came through the door.

"Oops." Andrea sat up. *Haven't heard that tone before.* What had happened to the sweet, gentle woman from the hospital who sat by her bedside for hours, holding her hand and telling her stories from her past?

"Andrea!"

Gone. Better not push her any further. She picked up the phone.

"Hello." Snails have shown more enthusiasm.

"Hi, doll. I see you finally came to your senses."

Andrea seethed afresh. Her teeth ground, and she squeezed the phone in an effort not to slam it down on the receiver.

"Listen, David, you know this isn't my idea, so let's just get it over with. Do you want to go out or not?"

"Ah, I love it when a girl begs."

"Don't push your luck." This was the most arrogant creature she'd ever encountered.

"Okay, okay. I know you're catching a lot of heat from your ole' lady, but I'm not such a bad guy, really. How does Saturday night sound?"

Like a nightmare. "Fine."

"Great. I'll pick you up at seven. And, uh, wear something sexy."

Her enraged reply was cut short by a click as he hung up. Now she slammed her phone. For about two seconds, she'd thought he was human. No such luck.

ᑫᕁ

Saturday night came far too soon. Andrea slumped in the wing-backed chair in her room and stared into the empty fireplace. A mournful sigh escaped. One date. That's all she had to survive. David must have some redeeming qualities. Something besides looks and money—if those could be considered qualities.

Her dress rustled as she rose and walked to the closet. Where were her white satin pumps? A smile lifted the corner of her mouth. She was going to wear black to signify being in mourning but was afraid David would find it sexy, so she opted for white taffeta with a high neck and long sleeves instead. White for purity. Heat stroke was a more appealing threat than having David think she'd complied with his request.

A car horn blared through her open window. *Typical.* A scowl creased her features. As if she'd run out to greet him.

She took her time slipping into her shoes, then walked to the mirror. Her hair was slicked back and fastened at the nape of her neck. An impish smile lit her face. *I wish I had a pair of glasses.* She'd thought about not wearing makeup, but she did have some pride.

The front door reverberated with urgent pounding.

"Impatient little devil, isn't he?" Andrea was surprised Esther hadn't run to his car and drooled over him.

"Now you're being mean," she told herself. Still, she wondered how she and her mother could be so different. A ghostly figure danced behind a screen in her mind. Andrea closed her eyes. Short, blonde hair, pleasantly plump, round, laughing face . . .

A gentle knock sounded on her door. The ghost fled.

"Andrea, darling, David's here." *No kidding. Back to "darling," are we?*

"Be right there, Mother dear," Andrea called in a sing-song voice. Esther's footsteps retreated.

"Here goes nothing." Her thoughts returned to the night of the ball as she reached for the curved door handle. She'd been filled with such hope as she'd left her room that night. Tonight all she felt was dread.

Chapter Ten

David's red Mercedes convertible purred through the iron gates and around the cobblestone drive, then came to a stop in front of Andrea's house. Palm trees were silhouetted against a full moon. A warm breeze carried the sickeningly sweet smell of roses to Andrea where she sat in the passenger seat of the car. The night air caressed her skin with clammy tentacles.

She felt David's eyes on her as he turned off the engine, but she stared straight ahead.

"I'll see you to the house." He started to get out.

"Don't bother." She pushed open her door and leapt out before he could walk around the front of the car. Her heels clicked a sharp rhythm on the walk. David whisked past her and blocked the path.

"Get out of my way." Her voice was venomous. David moved aside but walked next to her as she strode toward the front door.

"Chill out, Andrea. It's no big deal. I'll pay for your stupid dress."

She yanked the torn edges together and clasped them beneath her chin with a grip far stronger than was necessary for taffeta.

"What's your problem, anyway? Most women can't wait to get me alone." He snickered.

Andrea came to a halt, and David had to backtrack to face her. Her eyes impaled him.

"I'm not 'most women.'" She spat the words.

"I'll say. I'm not even sure you are a woman."

Andrea's hand flew out and she slapped him across the cheek. His head snapped to the side from the impact. She turned and stormed up the walk, but he caught her by the arm and whipped her around. A perfect imprint of her hand was outlined in red on his cheek. His eyes chilled her.

"Listen, you pristine little witch, I had the right to a good time tonight. Wake up and join the real world." His fingers dug into her arm, and his face became the same color as her handprint.

"The right? *The right?*" Her body shook with pure rage. "What gave you that 'right'?" The words seethed between her teeth.

He met her glare, and then his grip on her arm loosened. She jerked her arm away and put one hand on her hips as her eyes continued to sear him.

Straightening to his full six foot three inches, he stuck out his chin.

"I took you out, didn't I? I . . ."

Her finger poked him in the chest, cutting off his words as he took a step backward.

"Do you mean to tell me that for the price of steak and lobster, I'm obligated to sleep with you?" Her voice shrilled to a peak.

"Well . . . yeah," he stuttered, and glanced behind him.

Andrea was incensed.

"If it's a whore you want, I suggest Hollywood Boulevard. And when you find one, don't do her the disservice of making her endure your company for an entire evening. Just give her the money and let her spend it how she wants." Unprepared for the shove that accompanied her final words, David stumbled back another step as Andrea spun around and marched to the front door, fists clenched at her sides.

Once inside, she collapsed against the door and let the tears flow. They came in torrents. What was the world coming to? Was this what all men expected? Maybe there was something wrong with her.

The Mercedes roared to life and squealed down the drive. *Good riddance.* She fingered the rip that went from her neck halfway down her chest. The edges were crinkled where she'd gripped them together in an attempt to cover herself.

The memory of David's hands pawing at her made her shudder. *"Look at the lights,"* my eye. *How stupid am I?* Her purse had come in handy then as she'd pummeled him over the head. The notion that she honestly didn't want him to touch her was beyond his mental capacities.

Her chest heaved. *What I want now is a nice, hot bath and lots and lots of sleep.* She pushed away from the door and sludged toward the stairs.

Her eyes downcast, she almost collided with Esther.

"Oh. What are you still doing up?"

"How did it go?" The fire smoldering in Esther's black eyes revealed that she knew the answer.

"Look, Mother, I'm tired. I just want to go to bed. I went out with him, like you wanted. Can't we leave it at that?"

"'Can't we leave it at that,'" Esther mimicked. Her face contorted.

"Come on, Esther, I . . ."

"Shut up. Now you listen to me. I've given you everything here. A home, a beautiful room, more clothes than you could possibly wear, food . . ."

"But you're my mother . . ." Andrea stared in disbelief.

"I'm not finished yet. All I've ever asked you to do in return is form a simple alliance with David Woodbury."

"An 'alliance.' Is that what you call it?"

"Don't talk back to me. Just shut up and listen for once."

Andrea clamped her jaw shut.

"Niles Woodbury owns the biggest recording studio in the state of California. If we form a partnership with him, we'll be the biggest name in the business." Esther's eyes held a victorious glint as she stared at the ceiling for a moment.

I was right. This is more than simple matchmaking.

"Sorry, Mother, but my body's not for sale."

Esther stopped her premature celebration and grabbed Andrea's arms, shaking her until her hair fell down around her face.

"You're not going to ruin this for me!"

"Stop it!" Andrea threw her arms in the air, breaking Esther's grip. She quickly backed away.

"What has this got to do with David and me, anyway? Can't you merge without my help?" Andrea shouted. *Let the servants hear. I've had enough.*

Esther glared for a moment, then hugged herself, flipped around, and began to pace.

"No. That's just it. That idiot, Niles, doesn't want anything to do with me. He says he's doing fine on his own." Her tone was mocking, and one hand flicked from side to side in the air. "His only weakness is that spoiled rotten son of his." Her words hissed between clenched teeth.

"So you admit it. You don't like David either." Andrea gave her a wicked smile as she folded her arms and lifted her chin.

Esther paused in her pacing to glance at her daughter, then let her arms drop in defeat.

"Yes, I admit it. Nobody likes the obnoxious whelp." Her eyes were pleading now as she faced Andrea, hands clasped in front of her chest.

"But this is so important to me. Andrea, you've got to try and understand."

"Mother, he attacked me." Andrea was incredulous that she persisted.

"You don't have to like someone to sleep with them," Esther sputtered in frustration. "I'd sleep with him myself if he'd have me."

Andrea's jaw dropped, then clamped down tight. Her back straightened.

"I think I'd better go." Her voice was a hoarse whisper. She climbed a couple of stairs.

"Yes, yes, go. Get a good night's sleep. We'll talk more in the morning." Esther waved her away and began her pacing again.

Andrea paused and turned. Tears glistened in her eyes.

"No, I mean I should really go. Move out. Find my own place."

Esther's mouth gaped as she paused mid-stride and stared.

"You can't be serious. Go where? Do what, for Pete's sake?"

"I don't know. I'll manage somehow." Andrea sighed in resignation.

"I won't allow it. How can you think of such a thing?"

"Am I a prisoner here, then?" The words hung in the air like a challenge. Their eyes locked while a grandfather clock crashed away the seconds in the background.

Esther's face metamorphosed into a thoughtful expression as she continued to study Andrea. *What's she up to now?* Andrea backed up a stair. Esther eased toward her and slid her arms around her waist. Andrea stiffened.

"It's all right, Andrea." Spindly fingers stroked her hair.

Humming? Was Esther humming? Confused, Andrea relaxed. Tension flowed from her back and shoulders as her mother's fingertips moved from her hair and continued to stroke. Then the dam broke, and she let herself slump against Esther and weep. Esther's arms clasped her. *So good to be held.*

"There, there, now darling," Esther cooed. "You don't need to go. I'm sorry I've been so intolerable lately. I've been obsessed with business to the point of almost letting it ruin our relationship. Forgive me."

Andrea sniffed and cried harder. How stressful this conflict had been. The release of tears brought this realization riding on their crest: It was so nice to be in her mother's arms rather than fighting with her.

"Forget about David and that awful date. I . . . I have another idea." Esther remained silent while the clock bonged twelve times, and then loud ticks mixed with Andrea's muffled sobs.

"Remember how excited you were about meeting Jason and Nicole, and what they said about your talent in music?"

Of course she remembered. On the heels of that memory was the crushing blow of Esther stomping on her dreams when she'd shared her excitement. "Yes."

"I'm sorry I squelched your enthusiasm that night. I was upset about David. Of course I realize how talented you are. Did you know your father sits outside the door to the music room and listens to you sing and play the piano for hours?"

Andrea was silent. Esther didn't wait for an answer.

"Well, he does. And I have, too. Not as long as him, but enough to know you're exceptionally good."

Silence. Andrea listened to Esther's heartbeat and waited for her next words.

"I've been so caught up in the idea of getting you and David together and didn't want you exposed to the rigors of a career in music, so I haven't given serious thought to your talent before, but . . ."

Andrea held her breath.

"If Starstream Studios had an exclusive contract with a rising new star . . ." Esther's voice was slow, pensive, and her arms slid from holding Andrea.

Andrea raised her face and gasped at the intent look that met her gaze.

"Someone Woodbury couldn't touch. Somebody who'd push us right past him to the top . . ." Esther's fingers gripped Andrea's shoulders, and they stared at one another.

"What are you suggesting, Mother?"

Esther's hands cupped her face. The eagerness in her voice matched the flip-flops in Andrea's stomach.

"I'm not asking you to sell your body this time, Andrea. You've wanted to get involved in the business from the start, only I was afraid. I've seen so many lives wrecked by stardom because the person couldn't handle the money or the fame. But you seem different since the accident. Stronger. I've known you had the talent all along, but I wanted to protect you. Now I need you. Your father needs you. The business needs you. What do you say?"

Words failed Andrea. This is what she'd longed for. Worked for. Hoped for. Yes, she knew her father listened outside the door while she sang. That's why she did it. Well, one reason anyway. She'd even approached him a time or two about this very thing, but he'd always told her she'd have to talk to her mother. And now . . . here was her mother, practically begging her to do exactly what she'd wanted to do for months.

"Andrea, did you hear what I said? Do you know what I'm asking? Will you let me work with you? Make you a star?"

"Yes!" The word burst from her lips and echoed through the enormous entryway.

A servant peered around the kitchen doorway. Andrea laughed. Esther laughed too, and the sound caught Andrea by surprise. It'd been some time since she'd heard that sound. The thought made her sad, but the glitter in Esther's eyes brought the merriment of the occasion back into focus, and Andrea threw her arms around her mother.

"My goodness, child. You'll squeeze the life from me." Esther gently pushed her away and took her hands in her own. Then her voice became serious.

"It's not all fun and games, you know. The music business is tough. A lot of sharks will want to eat you for lunch."

"I know, I know. I'll work hard. There's nothing in the world I love more than music." She felt a pang she didn't understand but brushed it off and beamed at Esther.

"Well, then, my little star, better get some rest, because tomorrow is your baptism by fire."

Chapter Eleven

Andrea pushed on the big wooden door behind Lou's Blue Dolphin Lounge. It didn't budge, so she pounded with her fist, knowing from experience that gentle, or even hard rapping with mere knuckles, produced bruises and splinters, but would bring no response from inside the club.

"Hey, Lou, it's Andrea. Let me in!" Her ear pressed to the door. She wondered if her shout was any better than the dull thud her fist made. Muffled sounds of the blues seeped through the door, but not the sound of footsteps.

Her eyes were searching the alley for a rock to knock with when a small, metal door slid open and a gravelly voice snarled from the five-inch peephole. "Whatdya want?"

"Lou, it's me, Andrea. Open up."

The peephole slammed closed, and Andrea heard locks turn and chains rattle before the door wheezed open.

"You're late. I had to start the moron trio already." Lou turned his semitruck-sized back to Andrea and started down a dark hallway.

"I'm not late, Lou. I'm fifteen minutes early. You always open with Tony and the guys." She shifted the black leather bag on her shoulder, and tugged at the matching miniskirt as she followed him.

A grunt was all the reply he offered.

The saxophone, drums, and guitar could be heard clearly now. Not exactly Andrea's style, but they did a good job.

Andrea ducked into the broom closet, waved her hand around until she found the dangling chain in the middle of the room, and switched on the light. A mirror that hung on the back of the door qualified this as her dressing room. Standing in front of it, she pulled a cotton ball from her bag and swiped at mascara smudges.

"Why do I bother with this stuff when it all ends up under my eyes?" she muttered.

That task accomplished, she set her bag down in a corner and covered it with a pair of greasy overalls. Then she returned to the mirror and tugged at the skirt again. The thing was much too short for her taste. And black in the dead of summer? It was ninety degrees outside and about a hundred and twenty in here. The skirt had been Esther's idea—same with the black hose, spiked heels, and skin tight, lacy top. Sex sells. That's what Esther told her when she complained. Andrea wanted to sell her music, not her body, though she had to admit that her outfit got the attention of the drunk, rowdy crowd that hung out at Lou's, and kept their interest when the soft pop or country music she sang would normally get her lynched. "Baptism by fire" was right.

Only two more weeks of this gig, though, and she was booked at a dinner club in Beverly Hills. It sure helped to have connections. Esther carried some weight in this town. Countless singers came to L.A. looking for fame and fortune. Most would be thrilled to get a start like this, and many who did never made it any further. And here she was, on her way to Beverly Hills after only two months in this dive.

Esther had called Lou the day after Andrea's fiasco with David, and she'd sung here six nights a week since. "A rough place to knock off the rough edges," was how Esther had explained it to her. No problem. As long as she got to sing.

Then last week, at Esther's insistence, Brandon Denny, manager of La Haute Cuisine, had come to watch her perform. He'd liked what he'd seen and heard but told her she'd have to lose the black leather. Thank goodness.

Wiping a bead of sweat from her upper lip, Andrea brushed her hair from her shoulder, opened the door, and started back down the hall toward the stage. Tony's guys, the something or other trio, had just finished, and were busy putting their instruments in their cases. Andrea stood behind a speaker taller than she was, and waited.

Where the heck was Eddie? Andrea preferred to have someone else play the piano when she sang in public, rather than accompany herself. She connected better with the audience that way. Besides, who'd see her nifty miniskirt if she were tucked behind a piano?

A large African American, with a round face and the grin of a Cheshire cat, stepped out from the kitchen area on the other side of the stage. He, too, was dressed in black; he wore jeans and a Rolling Stones T-shirt. Thick gold chains circled his neck, and each pudgy finger sported a ring. In his left ear were no less than seventeen earrings. Andrea knew. She'd counted them.

Her smile was one of genuine affection, and she wiggled her fingers at him in an unobtrusive wave as he made his way to the baby grand piano. He carefully placed a cocktail napkin on the piano and settled a crystal tumbler with amber liquid on it before situating his ample backside on the bench.

Tony and his band finished packing and, with a salute at Andrea, walked off the stage while Eddie played the introduction to "Evergreen." Eyes closed, she took a few deep breaths as the music seeped into her soul and settled the flurry of wings in her stomach. Then she walked out on the stage, took the microphone from the stand, and began to sing.

The audience was silent. All three of them. Well, it was only Thursday. Things picked up on the weekend. This was good practice. If her belly still fluttered with this small audience, what would happen when she walked out in front of hundreds of people? She wasn't sure, but she wanted to find out.

The past two months had been her school, and she was an eager student. Her days were spent at her parents' studio, laying down tracks for songs she'd written. The studio musicians were excellent, and she had two songs almost ready to release and half a dozen others in the works. Esther had wanted them on the air a month ago, but Andrea held her ground on that one. They had to be perfect. Every last note.

She spent her nights honing her performance skills. At each set she'd pick out the least frightening man in the crowd and see if she could bring a tear to his eye. Sometimes her victims were among the hardened women who hung out at Lou's. Her percent ratio wasn't a hundred yet, but it was steadily climbing. She was working up the courage to choose tougher subjects, and by the time she left here, her goal was to get the meanest looking hombre in the crowd to blubber like a baby. Or at least not scowl so severely at her.

Tonight she concentrated on a wiry gentleman with stringy, gray hair and a whole bottle of Jack Daniel's sitting in front of him. His eyes were already watery and red-rimmed, but that wasn't from her singing. Yet. His faded blue jeans were ripped at the knees and frayed at the bottom, which, on a teenager, would be fashionable, but on this grizzled old man, was sad. He looked like he'd seen enough tears. She'd try for a smile.

"Evergreen" ended, and she turned and gave Eddie a thumbs-up signal. He immediately picked up the tempo with "Any Man of Mine." Andrea joined in with the words while she smiled, swayed, and tapped her foot to the beat of the song, then finished with a flourish. Nothing. The man studied his shot glass like it held the secrets of the universe.

No matter. Tough ones rarely responded after one song. A little gospel, maybe. She did a touching rendition of "Amazing Grace." That brought a tear. No good.

How about something downright fun and maybe a little naughty? Andrea sang a song she'd written about a girl from the wrong side of the tracks who landed a rich boyfriend by being less than honest and more than flirtatious. The man finally looked up, but his eyes were still blank.

It sure was hot in here. Andrea excused herself and went to

retrieve the water bottle and towel Lou always stashed behind the monitor for her. If her clothes clung to her before, now they felt permanently attached. An image of the pool in her backyard flashed through her mind and made her knees weak with longing. A cool drink of water and a hasty mop with the towel had to suffice.

She returned to the microphone. What to sing? The man had gone back to studying his glass. The other two customers sat at the bar, heads bent together, quietly conversing.

Peppy hadn't worked. How about sentimental? Worth a try. She looked at Eddie, who watched her expectantly.

"Cassie's Dream," she whispered, and he nodded.

It was another one of her songs, about a woman who died and went to heaven, and then came back as an angel to guide her long-lost love through a heartbreaking divorce and help him find peace with himself and eventual happiness with another woman.

Andrea stared at the man as she sang and poured her heart and soul into the words and melody. After the first verse, he looked up. By the chorus, the glassy look was gone from his eyes. At the divorce, he cried, and by the end of the song, a whimsical smile touched the corners of his mouth.

All was silent as they looked at each other. Andrea mouthed the words "I love you," and his face ignited. Pushing the bottle and glass away from him, the man rose to his feet, bowed deeply, and left the bar.

That's why Andrea wanted to sing.

Chapter Twelve

"Andrea, darling," Esther beamed at her over the *Los Angeles Times* as Andrea walked out on the patio where Esther and Jack were having breakfast. "'Where'd Love Go' is number three on the pop *and* country charts this morning! And listen to this review in the *Times:* 'Surprising new talent, Andrea Kensington, is taking L.A. by storm. Her ability to mesmerize her audience is drawing big crowds in elite clubs all over the city.' They love you. The *Times* usually crucifies new acts. Eat your heart out, Bill Woodbury. I created a star in six short months. Six months! Let's see you beat that. And you can't steal her away."

Andrea grinned as Jack jumped up to pull out a white, wrought iron chair for her. He gently ran his hand over her hair as she settled in her seat, and then he bent to kiss her cheek.

"I'm so proud of you, honey. I knew you had it in you." His cheeks flushed as he sat back down, and Andrea patted his hand.

"Thanks, Father. Mother." She smiled at each in turn. "I'm so happy."

Jack glanced at Esther, then buried his face in the *Wall Street Journal.*

Maria brought a bagel, slathered in cream cheese, and a glass of orange juice, and set them before Andrea.

"Thanks." Andrea watched Maria back away. Everyone

seemed to be grinning this morning.

Esther snorted. "Is that the best you can do? Come on. This is great news. Don't you have any idea what this means?" Andrea had never seen her mother so childlike and excited. She liked it.

"You want me to jump up on the table and do a little jig?" Andrea winked at Jack as she spoke, when he peered at her from behind his paper.

"Always the smart-aleck. Well, fine then. I guess you don't want to hear the rest of my news." Esther sniffed and hid behind the *Times*.

Yup. That pout was definitely childlike. Or should she say childish?

"Okay, Mother. What's the rest of your news?" Andrea took a bite of her bagel to swallow the laughter bubbling up her throat. Her father seemed to be having similar a difficulty, judging by the strange noises coming from behind the *Wall Street Journal*.

"I'm not going to tell you. Just eat your breakfast." Another indignant sniff.

Andrea sighed. The games she had to play with this woman . . .

"Mother, you know I'm thrilled. I'm just overwhelmed, that's all. I can't believe this is happening to me." She took a drink of orange juice and watched the back of the *Times*.

The paper dropped and Esther's eyes shone with an almost maniacal gleam. "Well, believe it, dear, because you're on your way to Las Vegas."

Orange juice spewed across the table. Andrea grabbed a napkin and held it to her mouth as she coughed. Jack put down his paper and patted her back. Maria ran out with a dishcloth, mopped up the mess, and retreated inside. Esther sat back in her chair, arms crossed over her chest, a pleased smirk on her face.

"That's more like it," Esther said.

"More like it?" Andrea croaked. "Choking on orange juice pleases you?"

"More than your smart-mouthed comments. Now. Do you want to hear about Las Vegas, or do you have some bagel you'd like to spit up?"

"Who's the smart-mouth?" Andrea had to hide a smile behind her napkin. She dabbed at the corners of her eyes. Once composed, she looked at Esther's expectant face.

"Please, Mother. I'm most anxious to hear about Las Vegas." Her hands clasped in her lap, afraid to touch the bagel until she'd heard what her mother had to say.

The gleam was back in Esther's eyes. Jack silently sipped his coffee.

"Are you ready for this? You're opening for—Jason Nyberg! He's doing a Christmas special at Caesar's Palace, and you're his opening act. Can you believe it?"

"Wow! That *is* something." Andrea's mind was awhirl. She'd never been to Las Vegas, but she'd heard plenty about it. Stars were born in Vegas. And Jason Nyberg . . . It'd be good to see him and Nicole again.

Andrea bit her lip and began tearing her bagel into pieces. "Do you think I'm ready for that?"

"Andrea. I'm surprised at you. You're not nervous, are you?"

"Well, yeah. Sort of. I mean, Vegas . . . Jason Nyberg . . . That's a far cry from night clubs."

Esther grabbed both her hands and peered into her eyes. "You bet it is. And believe me, you're ready. This is the break we've been waiting for. Jason asked for you personally." She sat back and chuckled. "Actually, with the places where you've been playing and crowds you've been drawing, this should be a piece of cake."

Andrea glanced at her dad. He studied his coffee.

"What do you think, Pop?" His head flew up at the unfamiliar name, and Andrea grinned at him. "Thought that might get a rise. You're being awfully quiet over there. Don't you have an opinion on the subject?"

He opened his mouth to speak, but Esther cut him off. "He's excited, naturally. Who wouldn't be?" Her eyes narrowed as she looked at him. A warning? About what? Andrea watched him.

"Congratulations, dear. It's a great opportunity. Now, if you'll excuse me, I have to go to work." His words were clipped and his back stiff as he rose, did a military turn, and strode into the house.

Andrea watched his retreat, then turned to her mother. "What was that all about?"

"Not a big fan of Vegas. He'll be all right. We've already discussed it." That was all she'd say, so Andrea let the subject drop.

"We have a lot to do to get ready, and less than two months to do it in. The show starts right after Thanksgiving and goes through New Year's. A Christmas show. In Vegas! Do you know any Christmas songs? We'll have to throw in a couple. The place will be packed. You'll need all new costumes. Something in red or green. More dazzling than anything you've worn in clubs around here in the past six weeks. We have to figure out what to do with your hair. I want you to finish the new songs you've been working on . . ."

Andrea's mind drifted as Esther continued to rattle. Her eyes closed, and a fantasy world of sparkling lights came into view. All her dreams were coming true.

A shadow passed over the lights. Nearly all . . .

Chapter Thirteen

Rick unlocked the bottom drawer of his desk and pulled out the *L.A. Times* he'd brought home from his last car-buying trip. He stared at the entertainment section. There she was, more beautiful than ever. Different, somehow, but still Melody. The color in the newspaper made her eyes look blue instead of the shade of turquoise he knew them to be, but it was Mel, sure enough.

A wicked smile crept onto his face. The smile turned to a cackle that rumbled deep in his chest. She'd left Matt. The sap. Melody had abandoned him and that brat kid of theirs to go off and be a singer. Whatdya know? Maybe there was a god.

Rick carefully folded the newspaper and locked it in the bottom drawer of his ten-thousand-dollar mahogany desk. Then he pushed back the huge leather chair, stood, and walked to the plate glass window. He stared at the fountain at the bottom of the steps leading to his office.

A woman holding a little boy by the hand walked up to the fountain and handed the child a coin. The kid's hand cocked behind his ear, and he threw the money into the fountain. Giggling, he jerked his hand away from his mother to clap in delight at the tiny splash. He looked up at the woman expectantly, but she shook her head, took him by the hand again, and led him toward the customer lounge. Rick watched her hips sway beneath a tight skirt.

He sighed. *Melody, Melody, Melody. I'd have given you everything. Skyler should have been our little boy.*

He'd thought she was devoted to Matt and Skyler. Watching her dote on them had been torture. So why did she leave? He'd always known she loved music, but to leave her family to pursue a career? He wouldn't have guessed that. *How delightful.*

Melody could have given him a son. Sure, he had Jared, but he was Kristy's boy. It wasn't the same. Rick's mind turned to the day Kristy told him her tubes had been tied. He was stunned at first, but he'd been too obsessed with her beauty and too devastated by Melody's rejection to think it mattered, so he'd married her anyway. He laughed to himself at that. Rather, he'd made her marry him. Telling him about getting her tubes tied was meant to discourage him, he was sure, but it hadn't worked. He always got his way. Well, almost always.

Then Skyler was born. Rick's guts wrenched as he thought of the look in Matt's eyes whenever his son was around. Rick wanted to gouge those eyes from their sockets. He'd hired Matt when he was a loser used car salesman, taught him everything he knew, and kept him by his side as they went from a two-man used car lot to a multi-million dollar empire. Then Matt had betrayed him. Snuck behind his back and married the woman who should have been his. Matt deserved every miserable, agonizing moment he'd experienced since Melody disappeared.

A couple of salesmen wandered out of the break room, coffee cups in hand, talking and laughing. They froze when they glanced in Rick's direction, then scurried out of sight. Rick scowled. *Spineless bunch of trash.* If Matt weren't so good at keeping them in line, he'd have fired him when Melody disappeared, just to add insult to injury. Nah . . . Matt's marriage stuck in his craw, but he couldn't deny his value as an employee. He'd exact his revenge in other ways . . .

Las Vegas . . . A crooked smile tugged at the corners of Rick's mouth. Matt thought Melody had disappeared in an accident, and that had been tough on him, but what if he knew she'd left his sorry butt to go be a singer? Rick's smile broadened. She was appearing in Las Vegas. Well . . . he'd just have to make sure somebody else "appeared" there too. Somebody with a gorgeous redhead attached to his arm . . .

Rick's steepled fingertips drummed together in rhythm as he stared at the showroom, seeing nothing. His smile faded. Matt and Melody were apart. That's what he wanted. Would it be too risky to have them in the same room? What if she saw Matt and decided she still loved him?

Rick walked back and eased into his chair. Aw, but to see Matt's face when he saw the little missus for the first time in months, not bruised and battered, agonizing over their separation, but surrounded by glitz, blissfully unaware of the pain she'd caused . . . That was worth the risk.

A confident sneer replaced his look of consternation as a menacing laugh gurgled in his throat. Let her see him. Perfect. Matt was a proud man. He may love her, but as soon as he learned she'd left him for her precious music, he'd never want to see her again. His laugh was vicious when it erupted into the air.

Matt would never forgive Melody. And when she saw him with Georgette, she'd know how easy she was to forget. They'd both suffer, and Rick would have a front row seat.

Chapter Fourteen

"Oh, Matt. I'm so excited. Las Vegas! I've never been before. Is it wonderful?"

Matt smiled at Georgette's babblings. His eyes were glued to the road since a winter storm had made it slick and treacherous, but he knew her green eyes shone, the way they had been ever since he'd asked her out three weeks ago. A musky smell of cosmetics wafted through the confines of the cab of his truck, overpowering the pine tree deodorizer hanging from the rear-view mirror.

She was all right. A bit ditzy for his taste, but it helped fill up the lonely hours after dark to have someone to take to movies and out to dinner. Besides, it got Rick off his back. What a jerk. Why did he have to constantly meddle in other people's lives?

Matt slowed as a brown Chevy Impala, a head of silver hair barely showing over the front seat, putted along in front of him, alternately hugging the shoulder, then the centerline. He hated to try and pass. A huge pile of slush had built up between lanes, and he knew his big tires would splatter the poor lady's windshield, making her drive even more difficult. It must be murder to be old. The past fourteen months had significantly sped up that process for him. He sighed, then tried to pay attention when he realized Georgette was speaking again.

"Matt, you never answered my question. Are you in there? I swear, sometimes you seem so far away. Are you all right?"

The smile he flashed was meant to reassure her. Her bottom lip was tucked between her teeth, something he'd noticed she did when she felt insecure. Guilt swept over him as he thought of her desperate efforts to replace Melody in his heart. She obviously wasn't afraid of a challenge.

"I'm fine. Just a little tense. The storm and all." He glanced in her direction, not daring to take his eyes off the road for more than a second. Her spine curled back into the seat as she moved closer to him.

"Want me to rub your shoulders?"

With effort, he suppressed a smile at the eagerness of her tone and watched from the corner of his eye as long, red nails drummed her stockinged thigh. Grateful for her natural timidity that inhibited her touching him without an excuse or an open invitation, he shrugged.

"That's okay. We're almost there." No point getting her hopes up. She was his for the taking, that much was clear, but he wasn't ready yet.

The old woman signaled for about a thousand yards, then made a right turn into a Denny's. Matt hoped someone was there for her. Nobody should have to eat alone. Melody hated to eat alone.

They rode in silence the last mile or so to the restaurant. Matt scanned the parking lot for Rick's navy blue BMW as they pulled in. Rick and Kristy were meeting them here to finalize the details of the Vegas trip. That was Rick's excuse, anyway. He never made plans with anybody. He just told people when and where to show up and expected them to be there. This was his chance to see Matt and Georgette together and gloat over their budding romance.

"Rick's not here yet. Let's go in and wait by the fire." Matt shut off the engine, pushed his door open against the force of the wind, and climbed down. Slush splattered his pant legs as he hit the ground. He slammed the door shut, then broke a trail through a foot of snow as he made his way to Georgette's door. Pulling it open, he held out his hand, then studied the toes of his boots as she grasped his fingers and struggled to get down from the high seat of the pickup in a ladylike manner with her tight skirt. He lifted her the last few inches so her landing wouldn't splatter her legs with gray, gritty slush like his had done.

"Want me to carry you?" he asked, and was surprised when she shook her head.

I'm glad I'm not a woman.

Georgette clung to his arm as she waded through the snow in her high heels, slipping and stumbling. The snow squeaked under Matt's boots as he plodded along beside her. He pulled his sheepskin collar up around his ears to block the icy wind blowing down from the canyon, and wondered if he should pick her up and carry her anyway. Why didn't she wear jeans and boots like any sane person would on a night like this?

They reached the heavy pine plank doors, and Matt pulled on the horseshoe handles. The doors opened wide enough for them to slip inside, and he shut the winter chill behind them. The smell of steak and onions greeted them, and Matt's stomach growled.

Georgette stomped the snow from her shoes and hugged her thin leather jacket tighter around her, shaking her head when Matt offered to hang it up.

"No, thanks. I think I'll hold onto it 'til I can feel my arms again."

He shrugged out of his heavy overcoat and hung it on the rack by the door. Taking Georgette's elbow, he guided her toward the sofa in front of a huge, roaring fire, nodding to the hostess as they passed.

"Evening, Charley. Is there a long wait tonight?"

"No, sir. Not for you, Mr. McCandlass. Will Mr. and Mrs. Thompson be joining you?" Charley's soft brown eyes sparkled as she gave him an impish grin. Pigtails and a gingham dress made her seem younger than her eighteen years. She'd been a cute kid, but as a young woman, she was drop-dead gorgeous.

"Yes'm. Tell Rick and Kristy we'll be by the fire." He gave Charley a wink, and her grin widened. Then he and Georgette hurried to the waiting area.

Now, if Charley were older . . . He'd watched the daughter of the proprietor change from a skinny, freckle-faced tomboy to a raven-haired beauty. Not that she'd have an old codger like him, but Matt enjoyed their easy friendship.

At the fire, he sank into the softness of the couch, while Georgette stood holding her hands out to the welcome blaze. Matt studied the moose head above the massive mantle, then let his gaze slide down to Georgette's slender figure, well accentuated in her tight black skirt. His eyes roamed down her long legs covered in lacy silk stockings. He smiled. This was a different look for her. She was bringing out the heavy artillery.

He'd kept her pretty much at arm's length throughout the past three weeks. His body ached for a woman's closeness, but his heart wasn't ready. It would be unfaithful to Melody. She'd been missing for over a year, but missing wasn't final enough.

Georgette turned, and her cheeks flamed as her eyes met his. Matt ducked his head, embarrassed at what she must have seen smoldering there. Melted snow rolled off his hair and dripped on his clenched hands. A commotion at the entrance interrupted the awkward moment. Rick was here. Nobody made an entrance like Rick.

Matt joined Georgette by the fire. He took a deep breath and noticed the red and white twinkling lights strewn around and the Christmas music softly playing in the background before his boss barreled into the room.

"Hello, Matt. Georgette. It's colder than a nun at a stag party out there." He shook his head like a St. Bernard and sent droplets flying from his hair and beard. Matt and Georgette shielded their faces with their hands to avoid a shower.

Kristy walked up behind him. "Easy there, big fella. Next you'll be wanting a doggy treat." Her smile was genuine as she moved around him to say her hellos.

"Good to see you two. How are you doing?" Kristy's voice chimed.

"Hello, Rick," Matt glanced at his boss. "Kristy, you're

looking lovely tonight." Matt smiled. Poor girl. How did she put up with Rick? He took in her long, brown curls, dusted with snow, her pert nose and wide, smiling mouth. She was a real looker, with the sweetest disposition of anyone he'd ever met. Whatever possessed her to marry an ox like Rick Thompson?

Matt scoffed to himself. She probably didn't have a choice. Rick wasn't easily deterred when he saw something he wanted. It was obvious why he'd want her. His ego demanded a companion of her beauty.

Georgette mumbled hello, her eyes downcast, shifting her weight from one foot to the other. Rick intimidated her, and Matt seethed at the haughty leer on his face as he drank in her appearance. Rick met Matt's glare and flashed him a superior smile.

"Let's eat. I'm starved." Rick didn't wait to see if anyone followed as he spun and tromped into the dining area.

Charley barely had time to grab the menus and fall in step behind him before he reached his favorite table and flopped into the seat. She was setting the menus on the table when the others came up behind her and took their seats.

Matt noticed that Rick's leer had now shifted to Charley. Her face flushed, and she fumbled with the silverware.

"Hey, honey, why don't you plunk down here on ol' Papa Bear's lap and let me tell you a bedtime story?" He patted his beefy thighs with one hand while the other snaked up Charley's arm, clasping her above the elbow.

Matt felt heat rise from his collar. Charley's eyes pled with him before darting nervously to Kristy.

"Let her go, Rick. We came here to eat, not harass the help." Matt kept his tone steady. If Rick knew he cared about Charley, his advances would increase, not abate.

"Ah, I'm just foolin' around. No harm done, right, darlin'?" Rick let go of her arm and swatted her behind. Hopping back, she tried to give him a shaky smile.

"I can't take you anywhere," Kristy reproved, as she elbowed him in the ribs. "Now you behave."

No wonder Melody had disliked Rick. Had he acted this way with her? Not in Matt's presence. The thought made the thermostat on his neck soar. He pictured his fingers closing around that fat neck . . .

Kristy cleared her throat and Matt jumped. Had his thoughts been evident on his face?

"Um . . . Your waitress tonight will be Pam. She'll be right with you." Charley broke the uncomfortable silence with a quavering voice, then bolted from the table.

"Well . . . what's everybody going to have?" Kristy had a unique ability to treat bizarre behavior as perfectly normal and get on with the ordinary. Matt admired that. How else could she live with Rick and survive? Her voice was chipper as she studied the menu. Georgette hid behind hers.

Matt wasn't thinking about food. He calculated how much money he had in investments and how long it would be until he'd be able to open his own car lot. Not long now. He'd have to take lessons from Kristy on how to survive Rick in the meantime. This proposed trip to Vegas was meant to smooth things over between them so he didn't quit before he had enough money saved. That was his reason for going, anyway. He doubted Rick cared. He just wanted to see if Matt and Georgette would sleep together.

The waitress came with water glasses and asked if anyone wanted to order a cocktail. Everyone refused but Rick, who, with a defiant look at Kristy, ordered a Bloody Mary. She ignored him and tried to engage Georgette in conversation.

"So, Georgette, are you excited about the trip?"

Georgette came alive. "Oh, yes. I've never been to Vegas. Have you?"

Kristy laughed. "More times than I'd care to remember." She cast Rick a sidelong glance. He sat up straighter and stretched his arms across the back of the booth, studying Georgette.

"You and Matt going to finally take the tumble while we're there?"

Matt shot Rick a searing glare. "Keep your filthy trap shut, Rick."

Georgette slumped in her seat and looked like she'd like to keep going right under the table.

"Ah, there is life in the ole' boy after all," Rick taunted.

Why did he rise to the bait? He knew what Rick was like. But he couldn't sit there and let him insult Georgette. Rick's other employees might laugh at his crude jokes and demeaning ways, but Matt's blood boiled every time he made disparaging remarks about women.

Everything he was he owed to Melody, and although Rick would never admit it, he was nothing without Kristy, either. Women gave men the incentive to try. No, not just try, but excel. What else was there? Money and all the nice things it bought were hollow rewards without someone you loved to share them with.

Kristy came to the rescue. "Now, now, you two. We came out tonight to have a good time, and I fully intend to, so stop squabbling before you spoil my appetite." She looked at Georgette. "Don't pay him no mind, honey. He's just a big, dumb kid who never learned any manners." Her elbow jabbed Rick again.

Matt and Georgette's laughter was strained, and Rick maintained a smug sneer.

Pam showed up, pencil and pad in hand. She was either unaware of or chose to ignore the tension at the table.

"Hi, there. So, what's everyone going to have? The usual?"

Rick ordered two filet mignons and Alaskan king crab. Kristy ordered a small-cut of prime rib, but Rick changed hers to a large-cut and added lobster to her order. Matt and Georgette each ordered small filets.

Pam left, and Matt took a deep breath, determined to ease the tension and make it a pleasant evening for the women.

"So, what's the plan, boss?"

Rick's face relaxed and almost took on a pleasant expression. He folded his pudgy fingers and rested large forearms on the table as he leaned toward Matt.

"Well, I thought we could leave right after work next Friday, drive straight through, and be to Vegas by four AM their time. I've already got suites booked at Caesar's Palace, so it won't matter what time we get there. That town never sleeps anyway. Those who want to can catch some shut-eye. We'll have all day Saturday to play, and I have tickets for the dinner-show that night with Jason Nyberg."

Georgette's eyes sparkled like emeralds when she looked at Matt. He smiled.

"Sounds like fun." There was real warmth in the look he returned, and Georgette's face turned as crimson as her hair. Rick had a self-satisfied expression when Matt turned his attention back to him, but he refrained from commenting.

"I can't believe you're taking a Saturday off, boss. And me with you." Matt slid his arm behind Georgette and let himself slump against the back of the seat.

"I wouldn't if it was any month but December. Things are as dead as Friday night in Salt Lake City around there. It will do us both good to get away for a weekend." Rick leered at Kristy as he sat up and put his arm around her.

Pam arrived with their salads. "Whew, it's good to see some smiles at this table. I was beginning to think someone had died." She, too, wore a short, red and white checked gingham dress with full petticoats underneath that made the skirt stick out and showed off a length of shapely legs. Her brown hair was pulled back in a ponytail that bobbed up and down as she set their plates in front of them.

"Fresh ground pepper, anyone?"

Everyone declined but Matt, who watched the black specks dust his salad. "That's enough," he said after several turns of the grinder.

"Enjoy," Pam chirped with a dimpled smile, and bounced away.

"Who's tending Skyler when you go, Matt?" Kristy asked.

"Well, he hasn't seen his Grandma and Grandpa Anderson since the weather turned bad, so I thought we could drop him off at their place. I know it's out of the way, but then I'd be with him for most of the trip. But if we don't get there until the middle of the night, I don't know." He gave Georgette a quick glance. Her head was bowed as she attacked her salad.

"We can leave earlier, can't we, Rick?" Kristy gave him a hard glare, then turned back to Matt.

"The ranch is, what, about five hours from here? So, if we leave at six in the evening, that'd put us there around eleven. That's not too bad, is it? And we could still be to Vegas by two or three in the morning."

"No, no. My in-laws will be thrilled. Skyler's their only grandchild, and all they have left of Mel." Again, he glanced at Georgette. Her head came up, and she gave him a brave smile.

"I think it will be wonderful to have him along," Georgette said.

Matt smiled at her, gratefully, then looked at Rick. "How about it, boss? You said yourself that things are pretty dead. What's three or four more hours? Bob can handle things at the lot."

Rick's cheeks puffed out as he exhaled, and his brows met above his nose when he looked at Georgette, but she was intent on her salad again, so finally, he consented.

"Sure, why not? It'll give me a couple more hours at the tables. Just so long as you don't stay and chit chat with the ex in-laws for too long." He put special emphasis on the "ex," and gave Matt a look that threatened to shatter their truce, but Matt gritted his teeth, took a couple of deep breaths, and managed to smile.

"Thanks. It'll mean a lot to them, and to Skyler. My only problem will be getting him back from them." Matt meant it as a joke, but a dark and gooey lump settled in his stomach like he'd eaten tar instead of salad as his words brought back a memory of something Melody's mother had said about a month after her disappearance. Would Skyler be better off with two stable adults who stayed home with him, instead of a distraught, single man who worked long hours? The lump moved up and lodged in his throat. He'd die without Skyler. He was like an invisible golden thread that kept Matt from floating into a black void.

Pam arrived with their dinners. Everyone was silent as they ate. Facing Mel's parents was becoming increasingly difficult.

He felt like he'd failed them. And himself. All those months of searching and not one shred of evidence. He'd been certain he'd turn up something. How does someone disappear without a trace?

A familiar ache began to close his throat, making his steak taste like wood. Time had yet to heal his wounds. He sure wished it'd get started.

Chapter Fifteen

The stage was dark. Andrea clenched the microphone in her sweaty palms and stared at the toes of her shoes peeking out from beneath her green sequined dress. The curtain in front of her moved slightly, and a shaft of light caught her shoes and made them sparkle.

The show had been open for a week, and she still felt like a baby chick amidst a pack of coyotes. What was she doing here? Who was she trying to kid? *I want to go home.* The tinkle of crystal and silverware on china and the din of conversation roared in her ears. Behind her, violins whined and clarinets screeched as the orchestra tuned their instruments. Andrea's stomach twisted.

"Good evening, ladies and gentlemen. Welcome to the fabulous Caesar's Palace."

Oh no. Here we go again. Would she ever get used to it? She was here . . . in Las Vegas . . . about to sing . . .

"Please welcome the lovely and talented Andrea Kensington."

The curtains parted like the opening of the cage doors that held the lions at bay. Andrea stood exposed with only the protection of darkness. Then the spotlight focused on her and slowly brightened as the strains from the orchestra behind her played a death march.

No, no. That was no death march. She knew this song. She

could do this. Her head raised, and she gazed out toward the audience but saw only a black, gaping hole.

Sing, Andrea. Sing with your whole soul.

Faces materialized out of the blackness along the front rows, and she focused her attention on a bald, middle-aged man in a black tuxedo who was fingering the stem of a wineglass.

Andrea opened her mouth, and to her relief, notes and words came out. Not her best, but good enough to boost her confidence. The man sat straighter and uncrossed his legs. Good. I've got his attention. *I must not sound too bad.*

"Walk toward the light," she sang. Her fingers shook, so she clasped the microphone tighter with both hands. The smell of charred meat and tobacco made her stomach roil.

"And reach for the stars . . ." She prayed her knees wouldn't buckle.

The bald man smiled and tapped his foot to the music. Andrea looked at the woman beside him. She smiled, too. *This is good.* Light seemed to glow through the darkness. Her insides unkinked a bit.

The orchestra crescendoed in unison with Andrea. Her eyes closed as she felt the song permeate her soul. Other faces appeared in the crowd as she opened her eyes. All smiling. Attention focused on her.

Her head came up, and she released the death grip on the microphone. They liked her. She could feel it. Her right hand held the mike while her left arm emphasized the words of the song. She was one with the audience and the music.

"Life will give you what you ask, so why not ask for the moon?" The joy in Andrea's heart was reflected in the faces around her. She was going to get the name and address of every person there. They were definitely all on her Christmas card list.

"Dare to want it, dare believe and you'll arrive there soon . . ." Background singers echoed her words.

The song was ending too soon. *Big finish, Andrea.* The universe emptied as she sang the final words, face uplifted, arms outstretched.

The last note lingered in the air as she bowed her head and let her arms drop to her sides. Silence. *They hate me.* She didn't dare look up. The wavy grain of the hardwood floor danced before her eyes and she wished the boards would part and suck her down . . . down . . .

Then the audience burst into applause. Andrea raised her head. Whistles and catcalls mingled with the clapping. The smiling faces blurred and swam behind a film of tears.

"Thank you," she whispered, then cleared her throat. "Thank you so much." *I love these people.* The room glowed and sparkled with a thousand twinkling lights. *I love this town.*

The orchestra began another introduction. Andrea walked from center stage onto the ramp.

"I'll be holdin' my baby in my arms tonight . . ." her next song began.

From this vantage point, she felt more a part of the audience. Tables surrounded the ramp, while large, high-backed purple booths with scrolled tops nestled four to six people a little farther back. In one of these booths, two women had their heads together, one red, the other brown, and seemed to be whispering intently while staring at Andrea. A burly guy with a full beard sat back in the same booth with a satisfied grin on his face. Something about the group disturbed Andrea, but she shook it off and turned her attention elsewhere.

Most eyes were on her, but some people were engaged in quiet conversation, while others picked at the food on their plates. Lights danced off clear liquid in crystal glasses on the tables. A shapely girl in a tiny toga, her hair piled in an auburn mass on top of her head, stopped at the booths and tables to snap a picture with the large camera slung around her neck. The air was thick with smoke.

"When he's gone I hurt all over . . ." Andrea moved down the steps at the end of the ramp and made her way between tables, stopping at the bald man to tickle him under the chin.

"Like a part of me ain't there . . ."

A skinny, pimple-faced kid with glasses and a bow tie turned crimson as Andrea sat on his lap and ran her fingers through his sandy colored hair. A girl with brown curls, wearing a pink satin dress and a corsage on her wrist, slugged him on the arm and hooted with laughter. Her laugh ended in a snort, and another young couple at their table joined in with embarrassed giggles.

"Ooh, baby, it's you who drives me crazy," Andrea pinched the boy's red cheek and moved on. "Oh, baby, I'm lost when you are gone . . ."

The words died on her lips as an electric current shot through her body. Storming down the aisle toward her was a man with dark, curly hair, eyes fixed on her face with emotion so intense she stumbled back a step. His face was chiseled from granite and colored the same hue.

The orchestra played on, but Andrea had lost all the air from her lungs. Her fingers tingled, and her legs felt numb. What was going on?

"Melody!" the man shouted. Wasn't she singing the melody? How absurd. Who was this guy?

Two large security guards hurried down the aisle and grabbed the man from behind. He kicked and struggled while he continued to shout "Melody!" over and over as they dragged him through the auditorium toward the back doors.

The black curtain in her mind bulged as if a giant monster on the other side fought to break through. She felt drawn to the man, but her body had turned to stone, her eyes fixed on the struggling figure. Who was he? How had his mere presence rendered her helpless?

The music repeated the same line like a scratch on a record. Where had she heard that song before?

The big guy with the beard she'd noticed earlier was seated on the same aisle. He jumped up and headed after the man and the guards, leaving the redhead and brown-haired lady glaring at Andrea before sliding from their seats and hurrying after the odd procession.

A lighting man with a sense of humor took the spotlight off Andrea and shone it on the curly-haired man and the security guards. Andrea caught a glimpse of his face before he was hauled through the double doors. The anguish she saw there was so intense that Andrea's breath caught in her throat. A tear in the curtain of her memory emitted a shaft of light and the room began to spin. The music was confused, out of sync . . . then something crashed into her face . . .

๛

Matt slumped forward in the hard chair in the small security office, his elbows on his knees, holding a bag of ice to a spot on the back of his head where one of the guards who'd dragged him from the auditorium had whacked him with a billy club as soon as they were outside the doors. Matt didn't remember anything after that until he woke up a few minutes ago on the floor of this cubicle.

The guard had been seated at a small desk, talking on the phone. Or listening, rather. The conversation had been pretty one-sided with the guard interjecting an occasional "Yes ma'am." He'd ended the conversation when he heard Matt stir and had gotten up from the desk to come help Matt to his feet, then had set him on the hard chair and left the office, locking the door behind him, only to come back a few minutes later with the ice. Now he was outside the office having what appeared to be, at last glance, a heated discussion with Rick.

Matt raised his head again, wincing at the pain, and watched them through a double-plated window that had some kind of mesh wire throughout. The office must be soundproof, because he couldn't hear what they were saying, but he recognized Rick's belligerent stance as he stood toe to toe with the guard. The other guard who'd helped drag Matt away from Melody must have gone back to his post at the auditorium.

Melody. Matt's heart lurched. He'd seen her. She was alive. He'd been within a few feet of her, yet she'd just stood there, staring at him. With what? Confusion? Shock? Why hadn't she run to him and thrown herself in his arms? Why had she watched, frozen, as the guards had dragged him away like a common criminal?

Over a year. He hadn't seen her for over a year, and when he finally did, she acted like she'd never seen him in her life.

Matt replayed the events in his mind, trying to make sense of them even as his emotions started to overwhelm the pain in his head and make his whole body shake. Carol had called Matt's cell phone just as the show was about to start and said Skyler was afraid to go to sleep. Something about monsters under his bed. He wanted his daddy, so Matt had stepped out of the auditorium to sing Skyler his favorite lullaby. He'd finally calmed down, so Matt had told him he loved him and said goodnight.

Matt had to slip the usher twenty bucks to get back in since the show had already started, and when he stepped into the darkness of the auditorium, his heart stopped. That voice. That face. So familiar. So dear.

His legs had frozen as his mind whirled through a thousand scenarios. How? When? Why? What was she doing here? How did she get this far? Why did she leave without telling him? When had she made this decision?

That song. Matt had heard her sing it a thousand times. He'd fallen in love with her singing that song. She'd looked so happy walking around singing, flirting with the audience. Something had snapped. That was his song. Their song. His legs had started toward her of their own volition. He'd been so close . . .

Something had died inside Matt when his eyes collided with turquoise and she'd merely stared at him. The months of agony crashed back like a flash flood upon his senses, ripping, slashing . . .

Had Melody really abandoned him and Skyler to be a singer in Vegas? The jokes. Her telling him he'd better behave or she'd run off to be a rock star. Their fight. They'd had worse ones. It hadn't been that serious. Had it? Was it possible she hadn't been joking afterall? No way. That was so not her. Yet, there she was, in front of God and everybody, prancing around without a care, like she didn't have a husband and son at home agonizing over her disappearance, mourning her loss every single day. Her stunned look as their eyes met. She knew he hated Vegas, but did she honestly think he'd never find her here? It wasn't even that far away. How had his PI missed this? He'd often suspected he'd hired a moron. Working with a small budget had severely limited his options.

Matt knew she loved music. It had been as much a part of her as the ocean mist in her eyes. But she'd always seemed content to share her talents with only those closest to her. Why hadn't she said she wanted more? Or had she? Had he just not listened? He'd always assumed she was joking when she'd brought it up. He'd laughed it off. Trivialized her dream. And now it had cost him.

Matt sucked in his breath and sat up, chucking the bag of ice onto the desk. He would have supported her. He'd have tracked down agents and producers with voracious intensity if he'd known it was so important to her that she'd abandon her family. He'd have called God and had the moon made into a pendant if he'd thought that's what it would take to make her happy. But somehow, he'd assumed he and Skyler were enough. How could he have been so wrong? She'd gone for a ride in her Jeep and rode right out of their lives.

Rick had taken a step back from the guard, his lips a thin line as he fished in his pocket and brought out a wad of bills. He peeled off several of them and handed them to the guard, who then selected a key from the bunch hanging at his hip and opened the door of the office.

"You there," he said, pointing at Matt. "Get on out of here."

Matt slowly stood and walked to where the guard blocked the doorway. When he was within reach, the guard grabbed the front of Matt's suit and pulled him close, his garlic breath menacing as he said, nodding toward Rick, "Your pal here has bought you a break. You're lucky you're not in jail. Or worse . . ." He let the last words hang in the air between them for a moment before letting go of Matt and stepping aside to let him through the door.

"Get out of town, now," the guard said to Matt's back. Matt turned to look at him, fists clenched at his sides. Rick grabbed his arm.

The guard continued, "And if you get within a hundred

yards of Miss Kensington or this hotel again, you'll get no second chance."

Rick started leading Matt away before he could say anything. Kristy and Georgette fell in step beside them, half running, half walking to keep up with Rick as he led them to the elevator.

Nobody said a word as they made their way to their rooms. Georgette produced a key for her room, and they all went inside. Matt felt everyone's eyes on him as he slumped onto the edge of the bed. Georgette pulled her suitcase out, set it on the bed, and began hurriedly throwing things in it.

"She's here," Matt said, his voice forlorn. "She's right here in this hotel."

Rick and Kristy exchanged glances, and then turned to face Matt as he spoke.

"How can I just leave when I'm so close after all this time?" His eyes burned as he looked into the faces of the three people who had paused to stare at him.

Kristy moved to sit beside him on the bed and take his hand in hers. He looked into her big brown eyes.

"Matt, honey," she said, squeezing his hand, "This is the hardest thing I've ever had to say to anyone." She took a deep breath.

"You know I loved Melody, er, love Melody," she corrected when she saw the hurt in Matt's eyes. "But, we were watching her up there, and she was loving every minute of it. Then she looked right at us and just went on singing like she couldn't care less." Kristy watched the emotions play across Matt's face.

"I hate to say it, honey," she gripped Matt's hand even tighter, "But I think she's made her choice. I never would have believed it, but it seems she left on purpose and is now doing what she loves."

A heavy silence fell over the room. Matt wanted to leap to his feet and shout a denial, but Kristy had simply put into words the fear that had already lodged in his chest.

"Besides, dude," Rick broke the silence, "these guys are serious. According to the guard, Melody's manager is a tough old broad who'd like nothing better than to crush anyone who tries to interfere with Melody's career. You try to go near her, and you'll be buried in the desert somewhere. Then what'll happen to Skyler?" Rick let these last words sink in.

Matt looked at Georgette, who'd been studying the contents of her suitcase. She must have felt his eyes on her because she turned toward him, her eyes filled with tears.

"Please Matt," she pleaded. "Can we just go? I don't want to see anything happen to you."

Matt's shoulders sagged in defeat. That was it then. Months of searching had come to this bitter end. Melody wanted to be a singer so badly that she'd walked out of their lives without so much as a backward glance. Hurt and betrayal threatened to rip him in two. What was he going to tell their son? A shudder passed the entire length of him as he released Kristy's hands and got to his feet.

"Let's go, then," he said with grim resignation, coldness seeping into his veins. But to where? Not a spot in the universe was far enough away from the woman who'd taken him to the mountaintops just to dash him on the jagged rocks below.

Chapter Sixteen

Andrea blinked, trying to clear the fog from her brain. Where was she? Seemed like she was always trying to figure that out. The last things she recalled were sparkling lights and tinkling glass. Then darkness. Like now.

Reaching up, she pulled a damp washcloth from her forehead. The universal cure-all. Slowly, she raised her head, pushed herself onto her elbows, and swung her feet off the edge of the bed. Her hotel room. At Caesar's Palace. At least she remembered that much.

Heavy curtains were drawn over the window across the room, but they didn't quite overlap all the way, so a trace of light stole into the room and silhouetted pieces of furniture.

Andrea switched on the lamp by her bed. The illumination didn't improve the looks of the room. Obviously, the management's goal wasn't to entice people to spend long hours cooped up here; there was no money to be made that way. *Next time, I get Jason's room.*

"Oh my gosh!" Jason. The show. What happened? Where was everybody?

"Did I sleep through it?" she wondered aloud. Glancing down, she saw her glittering gown and knew she hadn't worn that to bed.

An image flashed through her mind. That man. Who was

that man? The one with steel flint where his eyes should have been. Why had he looked at her like that? Like ice on fire. His face had been a mask of betrayal, yet she'd never seen him before. Had she? Her mother told her she'd had no serious relationships, so why had this man looked at her with such hurt?

She had to know. Her feet hit the floor, and she made a beeline for the door. Yanking it open, she startled a big man who snorted, mid-snore, as the front legs of his chair crashed to the ground. Beefy arms, which had been crossed over his massive chest, came stiffly to his sides as he stood to face her.

"Miss Kensington, ma'am. Uh, pardon me. I was just . . ." he stammered.

"You were just what? Who are you?" Andrea was puzzled and a little frightened.

"Name's Greg," he thrust out an enormous hand to her. She took it without thinking, and he gave it two curt shakes before dropping it and coming to attention.

"Okay, Greg, but who exactly are you and what are you doing outside my room in the middle of the night?" Andrea took a step backward, wrapping her arms around herself.

"Oh, right. Sorry, miss. Uh, your mother, Mrs. Kensington, she hired me to be your bodyguard."

"Bodyguard? Why on earth do I need a bodyguard?" Andrea's hands came to her hips.

"Well, after what happened during the show, with that crazy man and all, she figured it would be a good idea to have someone keep an eye on you. You know, make sure nothin' bad happens."

Andrea's fingers drummed against her arm while she thought about this. "I really don't think that man wanted to hurt me." The man's stormy look flashed in her mind and she wondered if that were the truth. Andrea's fingers paused their drumming, and she took a deep breath. Greg loomed like a mountain in her path.

"Okay, okay. So you're my bodyguard." Andrea looked him up and down. He certainly seemed capable of keeping people away from her. He looked strong—yet sweet.

"Now I need a favor, Greg. I need to go downstairs for a

while, but I don't want to attract any attention, so could you please stay here and pretend I'm still in my room?" She hoped her smile was fetching, her eyes pleading as she leaned in closer to him.

"Oh, no miss. No siree. Your Mother—"

"Is sound asleep and won't budge for hours. What time is it anyway?"

He glanced at his watch. "Two o'clock AM." His face was grave, brows furrowed in consternation.

"There. You see? I'll be back in half an hour. No chance anybody will even come looking for me in that time." She felt slightly ashamed for batting her eyelashes.

"But I can't let you go down there alone. I'm not 'sposed to let you out of my sight."

"What do you mean? I've been out of your sight all night. I've been in there, you out here. We'll just pretend nothing's changed." This logic seemed to baffle him, but he crossed his arms and planted his feet wider apart.

Andrea decided to change tactics. "Nothing's going to happen. Nobody will even notice me. I just want to have a quick look around. Fifteen minutes, tops."

He looked like a stone statue with a permanent frown. Except for his eyes, which had a thunderstorm brewing in their depths.

His face cracked and he spoke. "People will definitely notice you, miss. Especially in that gown." Andrea had forgotten what she was wearing. "And I am going with you."

"Okay. You're right. Thanks. I'm going to go change. I won't be but a minute." She flashed him a grin darted back in the room, shutting the door behind her.

In the bathroom, she looked in the mirror. *Good grief.* Thank goodness he hadn't let her go downstairs like this. Black smudges made half moons under her eyes, and her hair was a matted mess. She laughed to herself—she'd thought she was being sexy for him.

After scrubbing her face, she brushed her teeth and used a pick to get the snarls out of her hair. With her face bare, except for moisturizer, she went to find something else to wear.

She removed her dress, hung it in the closet, then opened her dresser drawers and grabbed a pair of jeans, a sweatshirt, and some socks. More comfortably clad, she retrieved her tennis shoes from under the bed and put them on.

Standing in front of the mirror hanging over the dresser, she surveyed her image. Her hair shimmered as it cascaded over her shoulders. That might attract attention. She wanted to be like wallpaper as she looked for the man who'd knocked her world off its axis. Greg would have to be furniture.

I wonder where they took him. She hoped they'd just evicted him from the show and he was now downstairs somewhere, gambling. Maybe if she found him and watched him unseen, she could put her thoughts in order and make some sense of the images tumbling around her brain.

From the top shelf of the closet, she got a baseball cap, then walked back to the mirror, where she stuffed her hair under the hat and pulled it down to her eyebrows. Much better. How about sunglasses? Nah, she was trying to actually be unobtrusive, not look like someone trying to be unobtrusive. That would be more difficult with Greg tagging along, but oh well. She'd tried. Besides, she might need him to carry her back to her room if she fainted again.

"Okay, mystery man, ready or not, here I come."

∽∾∾

Andrea stepped off the elevator into a lobby filled with cigarette smoke, her hulking shadow right behind her. The purple carpet with gold paisleys, the massive columns, and statues of people in togas with wreaths on their heads all made her feel like Brutus and Cassias might walk by at any second. That illusion disappeared the moment she stepped into the casino. Flashing lights and clinking coins compelled her into the twentieth century.

It was the middle of the night, but she might have just walked into the New York Stock Exchange at midday for all the noise and activity. Little old ladies who should have been clothed in long, flannel nightgowns, rubbed down with Ben Gay and tucked into bed, were, instead, guarding three or four slot machines at a time like pitbulls, furiously pumping quarters and pulling the handles like the machines would explode if not fed every few seconds.

Andrea had learned the hard way what happens to a person who tries to cut in on a gambler's territory. As she and Esther and their entourage had walked through the casino on their way to their rooms when they'd first arrived a week ago, Andrea had innocently stopped and plunked a quarter into one of these machines, smiling sweetly at the elderly woman seated on a stool nearby as she'd done so. The woman grew fangs and claws right before Andrea's eyes, handed her a quarter, and ordered her to leave. Andrea felt she'd barely escaped with her life. That was her one and only attempt at gambling.

She'd seen the volcano at The Mirage, the ship fight at Treasure Island, and the water fountain show at the Bellagio, as well as things seen from her car as they'd driven by, but most of her time was spent practicing her music.

But now she was on a mission: find the man who'd probably ended her career. What Esther had to say about her passing out in the middle of a performance was something she didn't even want to think about. Sympathy was not the anticipated response. Otherwise, she'd have woken up in a hospital, not abandoned in her room, still fully clothed. Her mom. *Good thing I didn't have a heart attack instead of just passing out.* A wet washcloth on her forehead had been the only ministration. And that had probably been placed there by her dad. He was usually good for a sympathetic pat and a hug, if not an abundance of words.

Andrea walked past the slot machines to the Blackjack tables, Greg on her heels. What was she hoping to find? What would she say to the guy if she did see him? What made her think he'd still be around? And what of the three people who'd hustled after him? One of the women must have been his date. Girlfriend? Wife? She assumed it was the redhead, since the other one had been seated next to the burly guy with the beard. Would she still be with him? Would she find them squinting through this smoke at some smooth dealer who graced them with a slick smile every time he scraped their chips to his side of the table?

This was hopeless. At least nobody paid her any mind as she weaved in and out of the gaming tables. Greg was forced to walk around.

Surely she'd recognize the guy again. One doesn't forget being run over by a truck. *Ha.* That was a laugh. A freight train might have plowed over her for all she knew of her past. Her face had certainly looked like it when she'd first seen a mirror after the accident.

Something had happened when she saw that man. Healthy young women don't just pass out because someone looks at them wrong. What was it?

Shifting directions, she headed to the auditorium, back to the exact spot she'd passed out. Maybe if she reconstructed the event, she'd remember something. That was it. It was about remembering. Images pushing against the black curtain in her mind. Then a tear and a blinding light . . .

Andrea stopped and squeezed her eyes shut, and Greg almost toppled over her. *What? Who are you? How do you know me? Or do you know me?* If he knew her, why had he kept shouting "Melody"?

Tears of frustration seeped from the corners of her eyes. She wanted to reach into her head and claw at the curtain, ripping it away until there was no more blackness. This man was a clue. Of that she was sure. But she didn't know how. And now she didn't know where to find him. He might be registered at this hotel, but without knowing his name . . .

"Excuse me, ma'am."

Someone jostled Andrea, and she opened her eyes to see the retreating figure of a security guard. Maybe they'd gotten some information about the guy before releasing him. Yeah. In fact, they'd probably checked him out thoroughly to make sure he wasn't some kind of nut and of any danger.

Andrea started walking after the guard. She'd have to keep

her intentions hidden from Esther. Mad probably didn't begin to describe how she felt about the night's performance. This would only be viewed as a distraction. Andrea had promised to work hard if Esther helped her get her start, but she had to find this man. Even if he didn't want to be found.

Chapter Seventeen

Matt looked around the sparse A-frame cabin. The floors were covered with linoleum wanna-be squares, puke green in color. The fake wood paneling on the walls was the color of dried mustard.

Evidence of his month-long stay stood in mounds on the kitchen table and cupboards: paper cups and plates, pop cans, candy wrappers, and chip bags. A straggly Christmas tree stood forlornly in one corner by the window of what served as his living room. Most of the needles were on the floor, and the popcorn strands and construction paper ring garland drooped on the almost bare branches like the pathetic leftovers they were.

Melody always had beautiful Christmas trees. Masses of white lights twinkled amidst stuffed bears, wooden bears, ceramic bears, whatever-else bears: the result of years of collecting, ever since she was a kid. She claimed she'd give it up when Skyler was older and do a Victorian tree, or something more elegant, but Matt never believed her. A knife twisted in his gut. He had to stop thinking about her. About the way it had been. It was over.

Shaking his head to clear the memories, he wandered over to stare out the dirt-coated window. With the sleeve of his thermal shirt, he wiped a circle on the pane, but most of the dirt was outside, so it didn't help much. Not that the view was worth seeing. Skunks had ripped open the big, black garbage bags he'd set outside, scattering wrapping paper, boxes, disposable dishes, and food containers amidst the piñion trees. Blue-winged camp robbers perched here and there on the trash, pecking and scratching like there was gold to be found amidst the heaps. Matt had considered cleaning up the mess, but watching the mischievous birds was his only form of entertainment these days.

Except when Skyler came. He was still staying with his grandparents at the ranch, about ten miles away. Matt rode over there on his four-wheeler—or rather Burt and Carol's four-wheeler—every few days to see him and take him for a ride. He'd spent Christmas Eve and Day with him at the cabin, but Matt was in no shape to take care of him full-time and didn't want his son to see his current state of wreckage.

After the hideous night in Vegas, no one had spoken the entire way to the ranch. Georgette had reached for his hand when they first got in the car, but he'd jerked away, turning to stare out the window, and she'd slid to the other side and softly cried the rest of the way. Matt had felt a twinge of guilt every time she sniffled, but he was an emotional wreck and in no condition to comfort anyone else.

When they'd finally pulled up at the ranch, Matt had hopped out of the car, grabbed his bag, and told Rick he wouldn't be to work for a while. He hadn't even watched them drive away.

Once inside the Andersons' house, he'd paused long enough to envelop his son in a crushing hug, fighting to keep his emotions in check. When he'd faced Burt and Carol, he'd searched their faces for some sign that they'd been a party to their daughter's treachery. All he saw was confusion, love, and . . . pity? He decided they were as clueless as he'd been, but how could he tell them what he'd learned? How could he destroy the image of their perfect daughter and send them plummeting to the depths he now experienced?

The thought occurred to him that they wouldn't view it like he had. They'd probably just be thrilled to learn she was still alive. If that were the case, he was in no mood to hear anyone try to defend her, so like a coward, he kept silent, except to ask for the keys to the four-wheeler. Then he'd kissed his son, told him he'd be back to get him for Christmas, and driven to this cabin. It was Burt's deer hunting cabin, and they kept it maintained, but it made Matt feel more cut off from the world to imagine he'd found it and was the only one who knew it was here.

Skyler knew, too. True to his promise, Matt had picked him up and brought him here for Christmas. Good thing Grandma and Grandpa had bought him gifts. Even though Skyler thought it a great adventure to be in the wilderness all alone with his dad, he'd have been terribly disappointed if Santa Claus hadn't found their whereabouts. Matt had picked up a couple of little things in Kanab, but Grandma and Grandpa really came through.

The wind rattled the window and jostled Matt out of his reverie. The sky was thick with heavy gray clouds that looked like snow was coming. Maybe he'd get snowed in and die. What was starvation like?

A shudder went through him. Enough of that kind of thought. He looked around the room again and snorted in disgust. In fact, enough of this hibernation. He didn't want to die, although he'd felt many times this past month like he already had. So Melody ran off. It happens. *What do you want to do, Matt; stay here 'til you're buried in garbage and suffocate?* No. He had a life. He had a son. He had a beautiful girl who was in love with him, if he hadn't blown it with her. That relationship had potential.

So what now? Matt gulped. Divorce. He'd divorce her. He had to. She had a new life, and it was time he got on with his. He was free to do that now. At least there wasn't the constant agony of wondering what happened to her. Rejection was easier to deal with than that. Wasn't it? Sure. People get rejected all the time. All kinds of people. Why not him? *Because we had the kind of true love that only comes around once in a lifetime.* He stuffed that thought way down deep in his soul.

It was time to get this place cleaned up and go home. The stench alone should have driven him out weeks ago. He'd collect Skyler, decide whether to destroy Burt and Carol by informing them their daughter was alive and performing in Vegas, then start a new life. Perhaps he'd sell the house and . . . yes . . . maybe ask Georgette to marry him. He'd been alone long enough.

Chapter Eighteen

The sound of the giant doorknocker reverberated through the marble hall of the Kensington mansion. Martin, the butler, slinked to the door, and slowly pulled it open. A short, balding man in a blue suit, his tie askew, stood on the stoop.

"May I help you?" Martin's tone indicated the only thing he wanted to help the man do was fly backward off the step onto his rear.

"Um, I have some papers here for an Andrea Kensington, alias Melody McCandlass." The man squirmed like he was uncomfortable in his skin.

"I'm sure I don't know who you mean." Martin's English accent was the result of years of practice. He was born in Brooklyn.

The man rifled through the papers. "Yes, yes. Andrea Kensington. I believe she's a singer? Could you please tell her I'm here?" The man fiddled with his tie and it ended up even more crooked.

"I most certainly will not. Would you please leave before I have to call security?" Martin felt the heat on the back of his neck start to rise. He didn't like to get angry, because that was the only time his accent slipped.

"Is there a problem, Martin?" Esther appeared at the top of the stairs.

"No, madam. This gentleman was just leaving." Martin turned to look at his employer, as the man shifted from one foot to the other.

"Ye . . . yes," he stammered. "There does seem to be a problem. I have papers to deliver and your butler here doesn't want to cooperate." Martin turned to glare at the man, and he ducked his head to avoid his look.

Esther descended the stairs and came to stand beside Martin.

"What seems to be the trouble?" She cut in.

"I have divorce papers here—"

"Divorce papers?" Esther's voice cracked.

Martin gave the man a last withering stare, then leaned down until his lips were right by her ear. "For Miss Kensington, mum."

Esther's eyes widened. "Andrea? But . . ." A mask dropped over her face, and she looked up at Martin. "Would you please excuse us? I'll handle this."

Martin's brow furrowed, but after a moment, he squared his shoulders, and his back became ramrod stiff. "Very well, madam. If that is what you wish."

"That's what I wish."

The man raised his head as Martin walked away, fists clenched at his sides. Esther watched until he entered the library and closed the door behind him. Then she faced the man on her doorstep.

"Now, would you mind telling me what this is all about?" Esther silently thanked her lucky stars that Andrea was at the studio.

"As I was saying, I've got divorce papers for an Andrea Kensington, alias Melody McCandlass, at this address."

Esther's heart beat faster. What should she do? How was she going to handle this? This could ruin everything.

"I'll take those." Esther said coldly, but her hand shook as she made a grab for the papers. She wasn't quick enough. The man snatched them away and took a step backward.

"Um, excuse me, but I have instructions to deliver them to Mrs. McCandlass myself." His eyes darted from Esther's face to his hands. Esther smelled cheap cologne mixed with persperation. She stared at the shiny bald spot on top of his head and her lip curled.

"Listen to me, you weasel. I'm only going to say this once before I have you thrown off my property by the seat of your pants. *Miss Kensington* is out of the country, and will be for the next two months. So if you want any shot of serving those papers, you'd better give them to me, because if you think for one second that I'll tolerate your weak excuse of a person to camp out on my doorstep for all that time, you have some serious reconsidering to do." She poked him in the chest and the man stumbled back a step.

His eyes hesitated to meet hers. "Um, well, okay. I guess under the circumstances . . ." He held the papers out to her with shaky hands and Esther snatched them away.

"But could you please make sure Mrs. McCandlass knows she's only got three months to contest this before it becomes final?" he said as he backed down the porch steps. Not waiting for an answer, he turned and half ran to his waiting car.

Esther slammed the door behind him, then had to steady herself so she didn't collapse. *I must think.* Her legs trembled as she made her way to her private study to go over the papers and decide what course of action to take. When she reached the study, she locked the door behind her, then sank into the burgundy leather chair behind her desk, letting the divorce papers slip from her hand onto the floor as the memories began to flow.

She'd known Andrea was married when they first found her lying on the edge of the ravine. Jack had spotted her and had instantly landed their plane and gone to her rescue. Esther went over to help and picked up the girl's hand to check for a pulse while Jack saw to her head wound. The wedding ring was there, caked with mud. Esther had looked at the girl's face and on impulse slipped the ring from her hand and into her own pocket. Then the girl had woken up, muttering something about not knowing who she was, and a plan had hatched in Esther's brain. The hard part had been convincing Jack, but he could never say no to her for long.

Something about the young woman's face had brought back a flood of memories of her little Andrea and the horror of losing her. It wasn't fair. Why had her baby been taken? Her only child. They'd tried and tried but were never able to have another. Esther was too heartsick to consider adoption, but she'd channeled her ache for her child into ambition, moved from the East Coast to the West, and built an empire. Esther's chest swelled, proud of her accomplishment. She hadn't turned into a simpering idiot and let her life waste away. Except for that one year . . . Esther didn't let her mind go there. Ever. But when this girl, who looked just like she imagined Andrea would if she'd lived to this age, was dropped at their feet, Esther saw it as her just reward.

Now this. Who was this man, and how had he found her? Not much of a husband if he was willing to give her up without a fight. That was good. That worked to her advantage. Three months until the divorce was final . . . Andrea would never need to know.

Jack mustn't know, either. He'd never have gone for her plan if he'd known the girl was married. It was partly his guilt over never being able to give Esther another child that had made him agree in the first place, but even he had his limits of what he'd allow Esther to get away with.

Bending over the arm of her chair, she gathered the scattered papers from the floor and put them in order on top of her desk. Then she began to read. *Matthew Daniel McCandlass. Sounds like a loser.* A twinge of conscience pricked her as she wondered if they had children. No. She couldn't think about that.

Vs. Melody Anderson McCandlass, she continued. Melody. Of course. With a name like that, she was destined to be a singer. Esther glanced at the address: Ogden, Utah. Just as she thought. The girl was from Utah. What had she been doing in the desert by Kanab alone? They must have been having marital trouble. And if she'd stayed in Utah, she'd never have a singing career.

Esther had done this girl a monumental favor. Given destiny a little helping hand.

Secure in her sainthood, Esther picked up the papers and walked over to her wall safe behind the picture of nymphs playing in a pool under a waterfall in an enchanted forest. This was her own, private safe. Not even Jack knew the combination. In fact, he didn't even know of the safe.

She opened it and slipped the papers inside. Then, she reached in the very back and pulled out a wad of tissue. Carefully unwrapping the tissue, she studied the solitary diamond, which sparkled in its gold setting. Only one-third of a carat, she guessed, on a simple gold band, with a plain band soldered to it. Cheapskate. With Esther, Andrea would have a cluster of diamonds. Yes, she was definitely better off where she was. And Esther planned to keep it that way.

Chapter Nineteen

Rick looked up from the auction report he'd been studying. What were those jerks doing? His crew was huddled in front of the first sales booth. Rick pushed back from his desk and went to stand by his window. It seemed they were all staring at the entrance to the dealership while trying not to look like they were. Their heads were bent together, their mouths moving, but to a person, their eyes were glued to the front doors.

Rick followed their gaze, then froze while hot and cold battled for supremacy in his veins. Maybe his eyes were playing tricks on him. The pounding of his heart told him they weren't.

Melody. She was here!

Think. Where is Matt? Oh yeah, at the auction. Thank goodness. What about Georgette? At her desk. He had to keep her there. And get to those bozos before one of them opened his fat mouth. Then he had to get Melody out of here. He snapped into action and scurried out his door as quickly as his two-hundred-and-ninety-pound frame allowed.

Melody seemed frozen in the doorway. Only her head moved from side to side, up and down. Rick didn't want to snap her out of her daze, so he approached the salesmen silently. They jumped like they'd been slapped when Rick hissed at them to get to their booths and stay there.

Melody hadn't moved, so he crept over and peeked around

the corner to Georgette's desk.

"I'm gonna be gone for a couple of hours. Hold down the fort." His tone was quiet but urgent. Georgette's eyes widened, but she only nodded.

Where to? What was he going to do? Thoughts flooded his mind and his heart pounded even harder as he walked toward the woman he'd been obsessed with for years.

What was she doing here? He thought he'd seen the last of her after that fiasco in Vegas. Matt had finally popped the question to Georgette, and he'd only recently become a worthwhile employee again. Rick wasn't about to let Melody mess things up.

Inches before he stopped in front of her, he remembered the stage name she'd taken for herself, and decided to use that instead of Melody. If she wanted a new identity, he was all for it.

"Andrea Kensington. How nice to see you again." His voice was smooth as cream. Her face was a complete blank when she looked at him, and his mind whirled.

"I'm sorry. Have we met?"

It was his turn to look blank. Was she kidding? What did this mean? Suddenly it dawned on him, and a huge smile crept across his face. She hadn't sought a new identity, she'd lost her memory and one had found her somehow. How wonderful. Things couldn't have worked out better if he'd planned them. But what was she doing back here? That's what he intended to find out—but not where there was a chance of some loud-mouth spilling the beans. Taking her by the elbow, he guided her back out the door.

"Would you mind coming with me for a little while, please?" If he'd ever convinced anyone of anything in his life, he had to convince her to leave with him now. Matt was due back any time.

She stopped and pulled her arm out of his grasp, and his heart leapt to his throat.

"Excuse me, but I don't even know you."

Rick had to think fast. A test drive, maybe? He switched gears. Backing up a few steps, he put his hands in the air.

"You're absolutely right. I'm so sorry. How presumptuous of me. You see, I saw you in Vegas, and was so enamored I feel like I've known you all my life and I guess I just forgot that you don't know me from Adam. I'm Rick Thompson. Humble owner of Rick's Autoworld." He gave her his most charming smile, then bowed his head.

"Well, I uh . . . thank you. I guess."

He took advantage of her hesitation and grasped her arm again, guiding her down the steps and toward his demo, a shiny, red Porsche 911.

"You're going places, lady, and you need a car that can take you there, don't you think?" He opened the driver's door, then stepped out of the way while he put his hand on her back and gave her a gentle push forward so she was right next to the car.

"But I didn't come here to buy a car." She tried to turn around, but he had one hand on the door and the other on the car, forming an effective corral.

"Now, why do you suppose folks always say that when they walk on a car lot? This ain't no Tupperware party, lady. Come on. You owe it to yourself to at least take a look, right?" He held his breath until she bent over to look, then he slowly exhaled. When she tried to stand up, she bumped her head on the doorjamb.

"Ow."

"Oh dear, I'm so sorry. Here, you'd better sit down." With one hand rubbing her head, he placed the other on her shoulder and forced her into the driver's seat. She left her leg outside the car, so he gave that some help in, too, then slammed the door and hurried around to the other side, retrieving the keys from his pocket as he went. He climbed in beside her and shoved the keys in the ignition. Beads of sweat formed on his forehead when he glanced at his watch. He prayed Matt was sitting in a long line of traffic on I-15.

"But I . . ." Melody seemed confused, so he made her decisions for her.

"Let's just go for a little drive. There's no harm in that. You're driving. What could happen?" He'd guide her up the canyon and hope she didn't remember the way back.

A tense moment passed when neither of them moved as their eyes locked. Then she shrugged and started the car. Rick sank into his seat and took a deep breath. They turned right out of the parking lot, and Rick nearly fainted with relief when he glanced in the rearview mirror and saw Matt's truck sitting at a red light at the intersection before the dealership.

That was too close for comfort. Somehow, he had to arrange that they never came that near each other again. Vegas had had just the effect he wanted on Matt, but who knows what another encounter would bring?

No doubt his blabby salesmen would blurt out the news as soon as Matt walked in the door, but they were always playing practical jokes, and not particularly known for their honesty, so it wouldn't be hard to convince Matt they were lying. And a few bills would change their story. Good thing they could be bought.

ಌಌ

What on earth had just happened? One minute Andrea was standing in the doorway of an automobile dealership, images flashing through her brain like a disjointed movie on fast forward, and the next, she was driving a Porsche up a winding canyon, a complete stranger sitting next to her. Or was he not a stranger after all? Andrea couldn't tell. The pictures in her mind were as elusive as dreams.

When Frank, the private investigator she'd hired, called with the location of where the man she'd seen at Caesar's Palace worked, she'd been elated. Then terrified. Her life suddenly felt like she was in a downward spiral, as if she were in a huge funnel, and she didn't know, once sucked through the hole and spewed out the other side, whether she would land in a desolate wasteland or a beautiful garden. She only knew the sands were shifting beneath her feet and she felt compelled to follow where they led.

A glance at the man beside her confirmed that his mouth

was still moving, though she hadn't heard a word he'd said in fifteen miles. Where exactly was he directing her? Wasn't this an unusually long test drive? She had no intention of buying a vehicle, but that didn't seem to make the slightest difference. Were all car salesmen this pushy? Was the dark haired man she came looking for? Matthew. The security guard had told her his name, but that had been all she'd been able to get out of him. Matthew McCandlass. The name was musical to her ears and the notes somehow familiar. Is this what he did for a living? What else was there to do at a car dealership? What did she expect to happen when she saw him again? It was time to get some answers.

"Uh, you said you saw me in Vegas?" She interrupted the man mid-sentence.

"Uh huh." He shifted in his seat. His back toward the door. Andrea glanced at him. His eyes had narrowed.

"Were you, by any chance, with a dark haired man?"

The man's chest puffed out, then his cheeks. He exhaled heavily before he answered.

"What are you suggesting, lady?"

"No, no, that's not what I meant." Andrea sensed that he knew that. "I think he was with a redheaded lady, but I remember seeing you, too, and another woman with brown hair."

The man faced forward again, and then turned his head away from her to look out the window.

"Yeah, yeah. That was me. I told you I'd seen you."

"And the other man . . ." Andrea's breath caught in her throat. The smell of new leather filled her lungs as she breathed deeply before continuing. "Who was he?"

Andrea wanted to study his face for clues, but the road they were on was narrow and winding, so she could only afford brief glimpses and still keep the car on the road. He turned slowly toward her, then stared until she shifted in her seat and started tapping her index finger on the steering wheel. Was that such a tough question?

Finally, his face relaxed and he shrugged, turning to look out the windshield. Branches of huge trees hung over the road on one side, while a solid wall of jagged gray rock towered a mere foot or two beyond the white line on the other.

"Nobody. Just a guy who works for me."

That's it? That's all the answer I get after being forced into this car when I was so close to my objective? I don't think so.

"And this nobody. Does he have a name?" It was the same guy. She was sure this was the burly man she'd seen hurrying up the aisle after the dark haired one. Frustration of having been deterred from her mission now seeped into her voice.

Rick's head flipped around to meet her look. "Yeah, sure. He's got a name." The sarcasm in his tone matched her own, and she didn't like the way his eyes darkened like an ominous cloud. It occurred to her that this might be a really bad idea. As she studied the scenery on both sides of the road, she realized she had no earthly idea where she was. She was totally dependent on this guy to get her back to her rented car and at least partially familiar surroundings.

The sun was setting in the opposite direction of where they were headed, and the branches of the trees began to look like fingers reaching down to snatch her away. Maybe she should stop the car right now, get out, and call a cab. Rats. Her cell phone was in her car. What were the chances a taxi would wander up this canyon? Zilch.

Rick began to whistle a mournful tune, and she turned to look at him again. He was studying her with a bemused smirk on his face, as if he'd been able to read her thoughts. She took a deep breath and let it out slowly. What was she getting so worked up about? He was the owner of a huge car dealership. Surely people there had seen them leave. Imagine what it would do to his customer ratio if people went on test drives and never returned.

A smile spread across her face, and her grip on the wheel relaxed. They came out of the twisty canyon by a dam and a deep blue body of water in a beautiful valley. The last rays of the sun shimmered on the surface of the reservoir while bathing the distant hills in gold. Andrea gasped as more ghostly films flitted across the blank screen of her memories.

She pulled over by the side of the lake and stared across the valley, trying to pin down one of the flighty scenes. It was like trying to capture Peter Pan's shadow.

Darkness settled over the valley. And her mind.

ᗜᗝᘓ

Something was wrong. Where was everybody? Several customers wandered around the lot, but there wasn't a salesman in sight. Matt saw Rick's car pull out while he waited for the light, but where was everybody else? Rick always scheduled at least six salesmen to work on auction days.

Matt's truck slid into his parking stall, and he shut off the ignition. Should he talk to one of these customers or go see if a mass murderer had wreaked havoc throughout the dealership? If he talked to one, the others might lose interest and wander off. He'd better go chase some salesmen out here.

Jumping from his truck, he gave a quick wave and "howdy" to a young couple nearby studying a Honda Civic, then scooted up the stairs and into the building. Not an employee in sight. *While the cats away, the mice will play.* Matt felt heat rise up the back of his collar.

An older couple and a middle-aged man with a teenage girl were in the showroom, but still there were no salesmen. He nodded and smiled at the people.

"Someone will be right with you." He hoped. They'd dang well better be.

Heading for the break room, Matt found them all there, huddled in a mass, nursing their coffee cups and chatting amongst themselves like this was a cocktail party instead of a business. Even the secretaries. His temper exploded.

"What in the Sam Hill is going on in here? We have customers all over the place and you guys are hiding out in your own little moron convention. You're all fined fifty bucks each. Now get the heck out there!"

They all just stared at him.

"Move!"

Coffee cups flew in all directions as they scrambled over each other, knocking chairs over in the process, and beat a hasty retreat from the room. Georgette stayed. Matt glared at her, then ducked his head and ran his hand through his hair when tears welled up in her emerald eyes. He was still too angry to speak.

What had gotten in to everybody? He'd never known them to leave the place completely deserted like that before. Sure, they were a rag tag, rowdy group, ready to party at a moment's notice, but they'd been decent employees. He'd at least been able to trust them to do their jobs.

Georgette stepped forward and took his hands in hers. His eyes studied the floor. Even she'd been a party to this. Rick's explosion would make Matt's look like a hiccup if he found out what happened the minute his back was turned. Matt better make sure they sold five or six cars before he got back.

Where had he gone, anyway? This was usually their busiest time of the day, and Rick knew Matt was at the auction. It wasn't like him to take off and leave money unmade. And who was he with? Matt thought he'd seen two heads instead of one. Nobody but himself or Kristy ever rode in the Porsche with Rick, and Matt hadn't seen Kristy's car out there.

"Matt, honey . . ." Georgette's voice was shaky, and when he looked up, her bottom lip quivered. With a deep breath, he tried to calm his roiling emotions.

"What was going on here, Georgette?" His tone was more accusatory than he intended. She was so fragile he had to constantly guard his voice to keep her waterworks at bay. Looking at the corner of the room, she blinked, and tears rolled down her cheeks while she chewed her bottom lip.

"I'm sorry. I don't mean to take it out on you," Matt consoled.

Her attention turned to him and she took a breath like she wanted to say something, but changed her mind and studied the corner again.

"I gotta get back to work, sweetie. No telling what those guys are doing out there without me. K?" His puppy dog look finally enticed her to smile and nod. His hands squeezed hers, and he placed a quick peck on her cheek, then turned and strode from the room. Whatever the powwow had been about, he wasn't going to learn from her, and right now they needed to sell cars, so he'd have to corner a salesman later.

As he hustled to the showroom, he was satisfied to see every salesperson with a customer, but each of them stopped and stared at him as he walked by. Had his little speech made that big of an impact? They'd heard him blow up before. He thought he'd been extremely controlled under the circumstances. Rick would have cussed the air blue around them and had heads flying off shoulders.

No, it was something else. Something he couldn't put his finger on. But he meant to get to the bottom of it before this night was over.

Chapter Twenty

Andrea let the water spill over her face and mingle with the tears of frustration. *That beast. That complete jerk.* She'd never felt so helpless and manipulated in all her life.

Her head bowed, she clasped the showerhead with both hands, letting her hair stream down her face. It was ten o'clock, and Rick had barely dropped her off at her hotel. He'd insisted on driving back from the lake, and then he had taken her to a restaurant with the slowest service she'd ever seen. As hungry as she was, she'd been too angry to eat and had only picked at the huge amount of food he'd ordered for her. So he'd finished hers, too, then taken another hour to get to her hotel. He refused to take her back to the dealership to get her rental car. "I'll have one of my salesmen drop it off a little later," he'd told her, and no amount of arguing had made the slightest dent in his resolve. In fact, he'd acted like he was doing her a huge favor. Yeah, favor. Now she was trapped in this dump, unless she wanted to pour money into cabs.

Her stomach rumbled, and she slammed her fist against the tile and made a choking sound, but it didn't make her feel any better. When she'd walked through the doors of Rick's Autoworld, she'd felt so close to answers. Like ghosts coming in and out of focus, she'd felt almost able to reach out and grab one and finally pin it down. Then Rick had barged into her reverie and whisked her away, with no intention of letting her return. What was he trying to hide?

He'd been elusive when she'd questioned him about Matt. Did he have a reason to keep them apart? Was Matt the shadowy figure of her romantic fantasies? Were they connected somehow? If so, what possible reason did Rick have for keeping them apart?

A groan escaped her lips, and she stood up straight, flipping the hair out of her face. Fumbling for the washcloth, she wiped the water from her eyes. Steam filled the tiny bathroom, and her skin was red from the hot water.

What about the redhead who'd hurried after Matt in Vegas? Were they an item? Maybe he wasn't her knight in shining armor after all. So what was the connection? From the look he'd given her that night, she was his mortal enemy. Why, then, was she so intent on seeing him again?

Good or bad, she had to know. Rick be hanged! She'd return to the car dealership tomorrow if she had to crawl on her hands and knees. Grabbing the mini shampoo bottle provided by the hotel, she poured a generous amount in her hand and vigorously scrubbed her hair. It smelled like a cross between soap and cheap perfume. On tour, she stayed in much better hotels, but this was her dime and she had to use cash. She didn't want Esther to be able to track her down and didn't figure she'd think to look in a dive if she found out where she'd gone. She had two weeks off before her next gig, and she'd told Esther she was going to hike the Grand Canyon. That way she wouldn't keep trying to call her. Sometimes Andrea felt like she lived in a box of Esther's creation. She'd even gotten away without Greg, her bodyguard. No way was he going to hike anywhere. His exercise was limited to weight lifting.

No conditioner for her hair had been provided, and she had forgotten to bring her own, so she shaved her legs, rinsed her hair, and then turned the water off and reached for a towel. The more she thought about Rick, the harder she dried her hair. How was she going to avoid him tomorrow and get to Matt? What would Matt do when he saw her? Would she have to endure that icy glare again? She shivered despite the clouds of steam in the enclosed space.

Wrapping her hair in the towel, she reached for another and dried her feet before stepping out on the white towel used for a bath mat. She flipped on the fan and opened the door of the bathroom to unfog the mirror. Someone was pounding on the outer door. A glance around the room revealed no terrycloth robe, so she wrapped the towel around her and went to look through the peephole on the door. A strange man with straight, dishwater blond hair and freckles across his nose stood poised to start his barrage against the door again.

"Who is it?" Andrea yelled through the door.

"Name's Chuck," came the reply. "I brung you your car."

Andrea glanced at the clock. Ten-thirty. At least Rick was prompt about returning her car, but she wasn't comfortable opening her door to a stranger at this time of night. Especially being unclad as she was.

"Just a minute, please," she called to the man, then hurried to find a pair of jeans and a T-shirt to slip into.

Once dressed, she returned to the door and peered through the peephole again before taking off the chain. The man turned when he heard the chain rattle on the door. Andrea didn't like his eyes. They were beady and too close together. Like a rat's. And way too pale. She couldn't even tell if they had a color. Nobody had eyes like that.

Despite the uneasy feeling in the pit of her stomach, she opened the door, thinking, too late, that she should have left the chain on. The man barged into the room like he owned it, making Andrea's heart thump in her chest.

"Just give me the keys and leave, please. I'm tired and would like to go to bed." Andrea wanted to bite her tongue on that last word when she saw the glint that came into those unearthly eyes.

"Well sure, little lady. Whatever you say." He moved to within inches of her. His breath smelled putrid. She wanted to gag and step back from him, but didn't want to show fear, so she straightened her shoulders and held out her hand, glaring into his pale eyes.

"My keys."

He cackled and took a step back, reaching for his back pocket. "You're still as uppity as ever."

Instead of keys, however, he placed in her hand the envelope. "Maybe these will bring you down to size." Then, laughing in a manner that was devoid of mirth and sent chills up and down Andrea's spine, he sauntered to the door, tossing the keys on the bed before giving her a mock salute and slamming the door. She heard him laugh all the way down the hall.

Andrea stood frozen until she heard the ding of the elevator and the doors open and close. Then she ran to the door and put the chain and dead bolt in place. Stumbling to the bed, she sat down and opened the envelope with shaking fingers. What had he meant, "still as uppity" and "these will bring you down to size"? Had they met before? Surely she'd remember someone as creepy as that.

Reaching inside the envelope, Andrea pulled out three snapshots. Hope crumbled as she stared at the radiant redhead, displaying a huge diamond on the third finger of her left hand, Matt's arm draped around her shoulder as they sat in a booth of a western-style restaurant. His smile was almost . . . forlorn? Must be her imagination, for in the next picture, they were engaged in a passionate kiss, dangerously close to upsetting their water glasses.

The third picture stopped her heart. They were no longer in the restaurant, but sitting on a pink sofa in someone's living room. Matt still had his arm around the redhead, but his eyes sparkled and his smile was genuine as he looked at the curly-haired boy perched on his lap. A spitting image—except for the eyes. They were green. Just like the redhead's.

Chapter Twenty-one

Georgette sat on the sofa in Matt's house, staring at the television without seeing it. Her knees were pushed together tightly as her hands clasped and unclasped in her lap. Every little noise made her jump and stare at the front door, where she expected to see Matt any second. What was she going to tell him? She hadn't seen Melody; she'd only heard the talk about her. In fact, nobody had seen her up close except Rick, who had left with her before anyone else got near. What was that all about, anyway? What exactly was he up to? Another five minutes and Matt could have seen her. Not that Georgette minded Rick hustling Melody out of the dealership. She was actually relieved. She lived in the shadow of Melody's memory. It hurt, but she'd loved Matt from the moment she'd laid eyes on him five years ago when she came to work for Rick. A hopeless love. Matt was obviously head-over-heels for his wife. Always had been. Always would be.

Then Melody had disappeared. Georgette had cried herself to sleep at night over the anguish Matt went through, all the while secretly hoping she'd never reappear. It was a paradox, but she couldn't seem to help herself. Matt was everything she'd ever dreamed of—kind, gentle, loving, caring, not to mention devastatingly handsome. And the way he was with Skyler—that was the clincher. The sun rose and set on that little boy as far as his papa was concerned.

Georgette looked at the back of Skyler's curly head as he sat on the floor watching the Disney movie she'd rented for him. Every now and then he'd giggle and clap his hands, looking back at her with a twinkle in his eye. What a doll. Georgette loved him almost as much as his father. How could she not? He was a miniature version of Matt. Except for those eyes. Melody's eyes.

Every night when she got off work, she'd pick Skyler up from the babysitter and bring him home and fix dinner for the three of them, then give him his bath and get him ready for bed. Then they'd watch TV or read stories while they waited for Matt to come home. Usually they waited with eager anticipation, but not tonight. Tonight was different. Matt was going to want answers, and she didn't have any. Well, she had one, but she didn't want to tell him.

Matt had been devastated all over again the last time he'd seen Melody. He'd disappeared for over a month. Georgette didn't think she'd ever see him again. When he'd finally come home, there was a new resolve about him. Not that he'd actually gotten over her, but he at last seemed determined to put it all behind him. He and Georgette had started dating with a seriousness that hadn't been there before, and then, one magical night, he'd finally asked her to marry him. Georgette had never been so happy in her life.

Then Melody had walked into the dealership. What would he do when he found out? Would he run away again? Would he try to find her? Her betrayal had cost him dearly, and Georgette didn't think he'd forgive her and run into her arms, but the trouble was, she didn't know what he would do, and that's what had her insides tied in knots.

A noise at the front door made her jump. Dread filled her as she stared at the door, but it never opened. Probably one of the neighbor kids horsing around. Her nerves were a jangle of frayed wires. She was no closer to knowing what she was going to say to him than she'd been when he'd confronted her in the break room at work.

A glance at her watch told her it was almost nine o'clock.

Unless he had a late deal, he'd be home anytime. The smell of the lasagna she'd made for dinner wafted through the house. Her stomach churned. What if it was the last dinner she ever fixed for him? That was silly. Those thoughts had to stop.

A whimper from Skyler brought her attention back to him. Tears filled his eyes as he turned to look at her. Pointing to the TV, he whimpered pathetically again. Georgette glanced at the television then back at him.

"What is it, sweetheart?" she asked.

"The bad men. They got Tarzan's momma in a cage." His gaze was fixed back on the movie and he let out a little sob.

"Oh, honey." Georgette slid to the floor and gathered him into her arms and pressed his head to her chest while she rocked back and forth.

"It's okay. You wait and see. Tarzan's gonna save his momma; then he'll be with her always." Something in her words almost choked her before she got them out. She looked at Skyler to see how he'd react. He'd stopped crying and sat quietly in her arms, his brow furrowed slightly, his attention no longer on the movie. Then he looked at her with his big green eyes and Georgette thought she'd drown in the depths of the sorrow she saw there.

"Can I save my momma so I can be with her always?"

Georgette's quick intake of breath almost stopped her heart, and she stifled the sob that threatened to tear from her throat. Skyler looked at her expectantly, hope shining in his eyes. What could she say? What should she say? With childish faith, he expected her to have all the answers. She didn't have any answers. Why did he have to do this now? Those eyes were tearing her apart. He'd seemed so buoyant, so accepting through the engagement. And all these months she'd spent with him, she really thought she'd replaced Melody in his heart.

How foolish. She'd never replace Melody in either of their hearts. Deep inside, she'd known that all along, but her blinding love had made her ignore the facts. Now they were staring her in the face, and her heart suddenly shattered. She knew what she had to do. How could she keep this child from his mother if there was a chance of getting her back? Sure, Melody had run out. She didn't deserve him. But he needed her, and that's what mattered. Georgette had to find out why Melody left. As much as she loved Matt and Skyler, she couldn't contribute to the break-up of their family. She'd find Melody and talk to her. Then, and only then, if she wouldn't come back, Matt and Skyler belonged to her. Forever.

And if Melody did come back? Well, Georgette was a fighter. She'd survive. Besides, she deserved better than to play second fiddle to a ghost her whole life.

She knew now what to tell Matt. And Skyler.

"Yes, baby. If anyone can save her, it's you. Then you can be together always."

Chapter Twenty-two

Matt stormed into Rick's office the next morning, slamming the door behind him, rattling the plate-glass windows.

"What the heck went on here yesterday, Rick? Why was Melody here and where did you take off to with her?"

Rick slowly raised his head, hazel eyes blazing like molten lava. "How dare you burst into my office and yell at me like some pre-menstrual housewife? Who the crap do you think you are?"

Matt's fists balled and his teeth ground together. Just like Rick to avoid blame by throwing it back at Matt. Still, he knew he'd get nowhere until he calmed down and played the game. His chest heaved as he took several deep breaths and then lowered himself into the chair opposite his boss.

"Okay, I'm sorry. It was just a little disconcerting to find out my wife, who's been missing for a year and a half, first shows up in Vegas as some nightclub singer, then waltzes into my work and takes off with my boss. Please explain."

Rick's eyes bored into him, but Matt stared right back, unflinching.

"You're losin' it, pal. Who told you Melody was here?" Rick finally asked.

"Georgette."

Rick's cheek twitched and his lips thinned. He looked down at the paper he'd been writing on when Matt came in.

"Well?" Matt prodded. "Do you mind telling me what's going on? What did she say? Where did you guys go? I saw you pull out while I was at the light. Why didn't you wait for me?"

Rick's pencil dug into the paper in front of him. He stared at it, not speaking. Matt waited, curious as to what went through Rick's mind—something he'd never been able to figure out.

Finally, Rick sat back slowly and crossed his arms over his chest.

"What made Georgette think Melody was here?" he asked.

Was he kidding? Matt's mouth gaped open slightly as he stared at him.

"What are you talking about? Everybody saw her. The whole dang crew was sequestered in the break room when I came in, babbling about it."

Rick studied him a moment then asked, "Did you hear them talking?"

"Well . . . no. I didn't actually hear what they were saying. They all shut up the minute I walked in. But Georgette—"

"Did Georgette see Melody?"

"No," Matt stammered. What was Rick trying to do?

"So, let me see if I got this straight." Rick leaned back in his chair and locked his hands behind his head. "Georgette listens to some idle gossip from a bunch of lying salesmen, passes it on to you, and you come barging in here accusing me of . . . Exactly what are you accusing me of?"

"I'm not accusing you of anything. I just want some answers." Matt cursed himself for raising his voice again. Nobody could push his buttons like this big oaf. He took more deep breaths.

"What are you saying, Rick? Are you trying to tell me that Melody wasn't here yesterday?"

"That's exactly what I'm telling you." Rick leaned forward and rested his massive forearms on the desk, hands clasped, and stared at Matt.

Matt had been on the edge of his seat, hands gripping the arms like he was ready to pounce on Rick, but now he sat back and crossed his ankle over his knee, leaning on his elbow as his thumb and forefinger played with his mustache. The smell of Rick's aftershave overpowered the office. Matt heard people in the showroom, but his eyes never left Rick's face.

"Well, what was all the hubbub about then? There wasn't a salesman in sight when I came on the lot last night. That's not like them to completely abandon customers."

"How the heck should I know what goes on in their pea-brains? I'll tell you what, though: they're each getting a bracket voucher for a buck and a half for that."

"I already fined 'em fifty," Matt told him.

"For leaving the lot unwatched? That's not nearly enough. They get both fines. Two hundred dollars will make 'em think twice before ditching their posts to make up wild stories."

Matt didn't say anything as he studied Rick. This was a first-class salesman. He'd managed to turn this whole thing around in a matter of minutes. Had Melody been here? Matt didn't think Georgette had lied. Heck, if she was going to lie about anything it would be to tell him Melody hadn't been here even if she was. But she was gullible, and if, for whatever reason, those jokesters had decided to cook this whole thing up, she'd buy the whole package.

"So, where did you go yesterday?" Matt asked.

"None of your stinkin' business. I own this place, remember? I don't answer to you or anybody else. I'll take off whenever I feel like it."

Matt sighed. It was obvious he wasn't going to get any answers out of Rick. Something out of the ordinary had happened here yesterday, and Matt thought he'd found out what when he came home last night and a sobbing Georgette had rushed into his arms, then sat him down on the couch, after he'd put Skyler to bed, and told him what the salesmen had said about seeing Melody standing in the doorway of the dealership.

That had been like a knife to his heart. Seemed like every time he resolved to get on with his life, Melody popped up and sent him headlong into the abyss again.

Georgette. What a gal. He loved her all the more for having

the courage to tell him. What a risk she'd taken and a price she'd paid to let him know Melody was close by, even if it wasn't true. Last time he'd seen Melody, he'd disappeared for a month.

That was then. This was now. Melody would always be a part of him. Even after what she'd done. He'd never understand why she left him and Skyler when they'd been so happy together. All the glitter the world had to offer couldn't replace a real home and a family's love. She'd taught him that. Then she'd left. But he still believed it. That's why he was working on a new life, and if she wanted back in, she'd have to do more than just show up. She'd have to come begging.

Chapter Twenty-three

Andrea watched the raindrops gather in pools on the window, then break away and race to the bottom in a crooked path. Beyond the race, blurred by the downpour, stood the brown and orange plane that waited to take her away from this dismal Salt Lake airport back to sunny Los Angeles. Her hands fanned out, palms against the pane. She leaned forward and rested her forehead against the cool glass. Her eyes closed and teardrops joined in the race, meandering down her cheeks to her chin before dripping to the floor. Confusion scrambled her brain. What was she doing? What should she do?

The green-eyed boy from the picture haunted her. Every time his image flashed into her mind her heart did flip-flops and she broke out in a cold sweat. He was obviously Matt's son, and she assumed the redhead's. But the boy looked to be about three or four years old, so why were his mom and dad just getting engaged? Nowadays, she supposed he was lucky they were getting married at all. Anything goes. Yet something about the whole situation didn't sit right.

Maybe it was the memory of the redhead's look when Matt had shouted "melody," staring only at Andrea. Or the look on his face in the picture from the restaurant. They didn't feel like a couple.

What was she thinking? She'd never met them. Why was it any of her business? Her hands clenched into fists and she pounded the window. Why, why, why . . . anything?

A voice came over the intercom, announcing the pre-boarding of her flight. She pushed away from the window and fished a tissue from her pocket, wiped her nose, then got another one and dried her eyes and the rest of her face. Then she reached into her other back pocket and retrieved the plastic boarding pass with a large number three printed in bold black. She'd been anxious to leave when she woke up this morning. In fact, she'd have left last night if there'd been a flight available and she hadn't been so exhausted, mentally and physically.

When she picked up her bag and turned around, people were crowding toward the gate, even though they were still preboarding. Little good her number three was going to do. No matter.

The smell of cinnamon rolls drifted through the terminal and Andrea's stomach growled, a reminder she hadn't eaten yet this morning. She'd been too upset and in too big a hurry. She'd just wanted to go home and delve into her singing, forget about trying to find her past, and learn to enjoy what she had. The past was too painful, and she didn't even know why. She was tired of being confused. What did the past matter anyway? Whoever Matt was, or had been, his life was obviously in order. What made her think she was a missing element? Where could she possibly fit in?

Then she remembered the family she'd seen by the security gates. A whole mob of them. Young, old, short, tall, fat, skinny. But all with the same glow on their faces and the same beaming smile as they'd held up their balloons and big sign that read, "Welcome home, Elder Bingham!"

Andrea hadn't been able to resist watching them to see who they were meeting. Who was so beloved as to warrant such a greeting? She'd expected to see a white-haired gentleman, but instead, it had been a young man in a dark suit with a white shirt and tie. Two of them, in fact. No, more, now that she thought about it. But she'd been too engrossed in the mobbing of "Elder Bingham" to notice what happened to the others. He must have been gone for a very long time and been everybody's favorite brother to receive such a welcome. Or maybe this was a strange Mormon ritual that happened any time one of them went on a trip. She was in Utah, after all.

That had started Andrea's tears, and they hadn't stopped until a moment ago. They still bubbled near the surface. Why couldn't she have a family like that? Sure, she had Esther and Jack, but the fact that she called them Esther and Jack spoke volumes.

"Now boarding rows one through thirty. Passengers holding boarding cards with numbers one through thirty only, please step forward," echoed the announcer.

Andrea glanced at her pass, then at the crowd. People waved their cards in the air as they tried to inch through the throng without much success. This was going to take a while. Andrea hung back. She should have been one of the first on the plane, but her feet seemed planted to the floor.

Turning her head, she looked out the window. The rain had stopped and sunlight streamed through holes in the bank of clouds. The raindrops on the window had stopped their mad race and now stood soaking up the sunshine, sparkling like mini prisms. Everything seemed washed and fresh, and Andrea felt her spirits being inexplicably buoyed up.

A fresh start. A new beginning. That's what she needed. How could she go back to her life without knowing who she was?

Rick was trouble. That much she'd learned. So she'd avoid the dealership. Find out where Matt lived. Maybe talk to the redhead. And the little boy. If they were a happy family, so be it. But she had to know why Matt seemed to hate her, and why the little boy set every nerve on fire.

Chapter Twenty-four

"Martin, Martin. Come here at once. Where are you, Martin?" Esther's shriek reverberated through the marble hallway as she flitted about.

"Here I am, Madam. Please calm yourself." Martin stepped out of the library, wiping whipped cream from his mustache with one of her best linen napkins. Why didn't she fire this impertinent fop? Who did he think he was fooling with that phony British accent, anyway?

"Martin, I need you to find Andrea and get her back here immediately. We have a shot at a European tour, but she needs to leave in two weeks, which doesn't give us near enough time to get ready, so I need her back here yesterday." Usually, she wouldn't bother explaining her commands, but she knew Martin would try to argue with her and she didn't have time.

"But, Madam, isn't she in the Grand Canyon?" He argued anyway.

"Yes, you moron, I know that's where she is. That's why I need you to find out how to get in touch with her and get her back here." Her fingers itched to wrap around his long, wrinkled neck below his huge Adam's apple and squeeze until his eyes bulged.

"Very good, Madam." His words complied, but the roll of his eyes before he turned his back let her know what he thought the chances were.

Esther didn't dwell on the ineptitude of servants, however. She had too much to do and no time to force the servants to do their jobs correctly. Not a servant in her employ was worth a bag of rock salt. Did competent people exist? Certainly not in the area of domestic engineering.

Esther's heels clicked down the hall to her office. Two months until Andrea's divorce was final. It had taken Esther every second of the past four weeks to arrange this European gig, which lasted six weeks. By the time Andrea got back, she'd be legally free from her past and officially Esther's forever. Not likely anyone would come looking for her after that. Shoot, nobody had come now. Her bum of a husband had hired some loser to serve the divorce papers. He didn't even have the guts to face her, which suited Esther's purposes just fine. She didn't need some deadbeat husband distracting Andrea.

Of course, she may someday wish to marry, but Esther would oversee that whole process. Hand pick the type of person who would improve Andrea's position in the world. And hers. David was perfect. Unfortunately, Andrea didn't see it that way, but she may still come around. If not, Esther knew other eligible bachelors she'd win to her side, one way or the other.

Esther pushed into her office and stopped dead, her eyes surveying the scene. The nymph picture was pushed aside, and her private wall safe gaped open. Jack stood in the center of the room, his back to her. When he turned to face her, she felt the blood drain from her face and her knees became Jell-O. His features were an odd mixture of pain, confusion, and anger, his skin a pasty green. His arm slowly extended, his hand turning over and his fingers uncurled to reveal a diamond ring.

Their eyes met. Esther saw the question and deep hurt in his.

"Wha . . ." he stopped and cleared his throat. His Adam's apple bobbed. "What is this?"

Esther had questions of her own.

"What are you doing in here? This is my private office. How did you find my safe? Where did you get the combination?"

"Esther." The one word was a barked command that stopped her stream of questions cold. He'd never used that tone before, and Esther knew she was in trouble. Martin was shark food. He'd been spying on her again, that spineless snoop.

"Where did you get this ring?" Each word was clipped and precise. His eyes bored into hers, color blossoming on his cheeks.

"I, uh, it . . . she . . ." How was she going to get out of this one?

"Esther." The warning was unmistakable.

Esther studied his face for a moment, then heaved a sigh. "You'd better sit down." Taking him by the elbow, she led him to one of the burgundy leather chairs facing her desk, then moved around behind and took her own seat. More control this way. At the moment, she needed every advantage.

How to begin? Jack sat ramrod stiff on the edge of his chair, the ring clenched in his. *Better give it to him straight.*

"It's mine."

"Esther." Her name grated when he said it like that. Two more months. All she needed were two more lousy months. She lifted a steel ball from her desktop pendulum and dropped it into the others, causing the end one on the other side to swing up and down, repeating the process. After only three clicks of the steel balls, Jack loudly cleared his throat.

"Okay, okay," Esther said. "What do you want to know?"

Jack rolled his eyes and Esther sighed again and then looked straight at him. Her mouth opened, but her mind froze at Jack's next words.

"Andrea's married," Jack stated. Accusation dripped from every syllable.

Esther knew her world was held intact by a wall which had been built brick by carefully laid brick over the years. The mortar softened at Jack's look. His face hardened to stone before her eyes. The balls clicked for what seemed an eternity.

Finally, he eased back in his chair. Esther smelled the lemon furniture polish the maid had used on her desk that morning. A pleasant smell, usually, mixed with the rich smell of leather. Now it sickened her.

Jack opened his fist and stared at the ring. "When did you get this?" he croaked.

No use for anymore lies. The truth was out. "At the accident. When we first found her. It . . .it was a whim. I slipped it from her finger. She looked so much like our Andrea, I . . ."

Jack held up the palm of his hand like a policeman directing traffic and she stopped. Steel tapped against steel. He slowly raised his head to look at her, and her heart caught in her throat. He'd been frustrated with her at times over the years, and tolerant, but never before had she seen loathing. It shook her to her depths.

To the outside observer, she dominated Jack, even bullied him. People's opinions didn't matter to her, though. Nobody knew of Jack's inner strength. He was her rock. Her core. She often pretended she didn't care, but he never did, so to see this look of utter disgust on his face directed at her was the most bone-rattling experience since losing her daughter.

"Jack, honey . . ."

"Don't "honey" me, Esther. How could you do such a thing? You lied to me. Tricked me. And worst of all, you used that poor girl. Took her away from her husband, her family. What if she has children? Did you think of that? Or do you already know that, too?"

Esther felt her reserve slip under the barrage of searing questions from the man who rarely raised his voice at her. Black spots danced in front of her eyes and her temples throbbed. She put her elbows on the desk and pressed the heels of her hands to the sides of her head. Jack was still speaking. Still yelling, but she no longer knew what he was saying. His voice mixed with the jumble of other voices from her past.

"Why can't you ever do anything right? Why can't you be like your sister? Don't be such a crybaby. You're such a loser. You'll never amount to anything." The voices spun round and round, and the room soon joined their crazy dance, until a loud thud and sharp pain on her forehead plunged them into silence and her world into darkness.

Chapter Twenty-five

Andrea stared out the window of the airplane. Ironic. Yesterday she'd been right up to the gate and had decided not to board, unable to leave until she'd figured out how these people who filled her head related to her past. But she'd made the mistake of calling home this morning to let Esther know she'd be gone longer than planned, only to learn that Esther was in the hospital. Martin was mum about why or how serious the situation was, and Jack was at the hospital with Esther, so Andrea had called the airlines again, and made the now familiar trip to the Salt Lake airport, and this time, had boarded the plane.

Her emotions were torn as the plane cut through the clouds. In some ways she was relieved to be going back, and that made her feel like a coward. On the other hand, she felt like a giant rubber band was wrapped around her chest and anchored somewhere along the Wasatch Front. The farther away she flew, the tighter the pain in her heart.

Guilt wound its way through the turmoil. Esther had to be okay. Nothing serious could happen to her. She was invincible. Still, a gnawing in Andrea's stomach warred with the annoyance at having her plans interrupted. This was probably a ploy of Esther's to get her home sooner. Andrea felt ashamed for thinking such a thing, but it was certainly Esther's way.

Her mind turned to singing. That part had been great,

but how important was it to her really? Music itself was vitally important. Like air. But did she need all the glitz? The fancy clothes, fancy parties, and fancy people? Now it seemed so trivial. Did she really want all the crowds, fans, bright lights, and cameras? Esther's constant pushing, wardrobe fittings, all-night sessions in the recording studio—sometimes she dreamed of being alone and taking a deep breath of fresh, clean air. Or curling up in her sweats on a soft bed with a good book and an entire afternoon with nothing to think about but whether or not the boy gets the girl.

A scene flashed through her consciousness like the clip of a long forgotten movie. She was lying on a blanket under a huge tree whose branches spread and twisted above her. Sunbeams played hide and seek among the leaves and left the ground mottled with lemon drops. Andrea closed her eyes as she sat on the plane and imagined she could still smell lilacs being carried on a gentle breeze that cooled her cheeks and danced with the hem of her yellow dress where it lay against her long, brown legs.

A man lay next to her on the blanket. His eyes were closed, but his hair was dark and curly. A child laughed somewhere behind her. Sweet, tinkling laughter like wind chimes. Andrea smiled and tried to bring the child into focus, but the image was fading, though the laughter continued. Then Andrea heard a smack and the giggles turned to wails. Her eyes jerked open, and she craned her head around to peer toward the rear of the plane. The child was hidden from view behind the seats, but she heard its cries and wanted to offer comfort. The other passengers were either oblivious to or ignoring the situation. A flight attendant stopped beside a seat several rows back and held out her hand. Andrea couldn't tell what was in it, but the contents were snatched from her grasp and the crying ceased. Andrea turned back around, content the situation was under control.

Long bus rides and endless hotel rooms loomed large in her mind. What kind of a life was that? Sure, the money was great if you made it, but where did a home and family fit in? Besides, Esther handled the money, and what portion Andrea received didn't make it worth giving up her life for. Not that she cared. What did she need money for? Esther and Jack provided everything. What Andrea got was pocket change. Some day she'd move out and be on her own, and then she'd need more, but it didn't make sense to leave a nice mansion for a dingy apartment all by herself.

Andrea's thoughts turned to Esther in the hospital. Her mind's eye saw the same room they'd spent so much time together in when Andrea had been hurt. Whatever Esther's condition, a heart attack or stroke would be imminent if she knew the line Andrea's thoughts were taking. Andrea had been convinced that a singing career was the most important thing in the world to her, and had made Esther believe it, too. Then came Vegas. The shock of seeing Matt. The hurt in his eyes. Now, she just wasn't sure anymore. Not sure of anything. And so tired of being confused.

The flight attendant came by with the drink cart and handed Andrea her apple juice and peanuts. The man in the aisle seat, who wore a rumpled suit and smelled of Brut and body odor, slept on. Andrea smiled and thanked the young woman, the same one who'd gone to the child's rescue. She put the treats on the tray in front of her and went back to staring out the window. Nothing but clouds. Big, white, fluffy ones. It looked as though she could jump out and land on them and bounce up and down forever.

Forever. What a sad, long, lonely word. Standing on a stage—forever. Being on a plane—forever. Sitting in a sound studio—forever. None of them sounded very appealing.

Beams of light shone through the clouds. New images of forever began to form in her mind. Walking hand in hand with a man she loved, adoration shining in his eyes, a child in her arms. This thought brought her inexpressible joy. No comparison. That's what she wanted. A home and a family.

The longer she held the vision in her mind, the more the man's features took on Matt's, and the child in her arms, the dark, curly-haired boy from the picture. The redhead was nowhere in sight. It was Andrea that Matt looked at with love, not hate. And the boy? The more she thought about it, his eyes weren't emerald like the redhead's. They were much closer to turquoise.

Chapter Twenty-six

"Mom . . . Mom, can you hear me?" Andrea looked at Jack, seated on the other side of Esther, when she got no response. "So what happened? What's wrong with her? How long has she been like this?" Andrea held Esther's cool, delicate hand.

Jack's eyes were red-rimmed. His white shirt, usually crisp and pristine, was crumpled and stained. Esther's other hand was grasped in his large ones, and Andrea feared he'd crush it. "Dad, please, answer me. How long has she been unconscious?" Andrea wondered if she needed to slap him across the face to snap him from his daze. He'd yet to speak to her, and she'd been here ten minutes. What was wrong with him? Was Esther's condition so serious he didn't dare tell her? He hadn't even looked up when she'd entered the room.

Finally, he turned absent eyes from his wife to his daughter. Nothing registered there but pain. The depth seemed endless, but the reason unclear. This pain came from a dark, hidden place that Andrea had never touched before. Torment etched his every feature, carving, slicing, contorting until Andrea barely recognized him as her father. Where was the quiet, calm reserve? The warm twinkle that made her feel loved and special, despite the lack of physical contact? Now she was scared. Her anchor appeared to have abandoned ship and lie rusting in the sand.

She squirmed under his gaze, even though it seemed to go through her, rather than focusing on her. A steady beep from the heart monitor began to sound like the pounding of a drum. What had he done to be so tortured? This was more than concern for his wife. Had he beaten her? Is that why she lay here in a hospital room unconscious? Andrea quickly dismissed the thought, chiding herself for allowing it to enter her mind. A gentler man didn't exist. If the roles were reversed, if Jack was lying there with Esther at his side, Andrea might consider such a scenario, but not Jack. His hand raised in anger or violence? Unimaginable.

So what was it then? Something seemed to have eaten away his essence, leaving an empty shell of raw, tangled nerve endings. Andrea didn't know how to reach him, to help ease the anguish and assure him that life was good, that things would work out.

Jack opened his mouth. "I can't . . . you're not . . ." he buried his face in the hospital sheet that covered his wife and wept. Andrea was stunned. On a scale of one to ten, Jack's emotions had never ranged far from five on either side, so this display unnerved her. She stared at his shaking shoulders for a moment, and then turned her attention to Esther once again, whose countenance was unchanged.

Guilt washed over her—a familiar emotion in Esther's presence. Even unconscious, she had that effect. Andrea had no idea what was wrong with her mother, yet her attention and sympathies had been diverted to her father, whose sobbing had subsided, and he stared out the window, his death grip on Esther's hand intact.

It was time for some answers. Andrea located the nurse call button on the arm of Esther's bed and pressed it. She'd been in too big a hurry to get to Esther's room to stop and talk to anybody on her way in, and Martin, playing the stoic butler, still wouldn't tell her what was going on when she'd dropped her bags off at home. Andrea wondered if he actually knew anything. He always pretended to know everything, but wouldn't tell anybody. Andrea suspected he was clueless.

Several moments passed before a large, African-American woman in a nurse's uniform entered the room, and a jolt of recognition jarred Andrea.

"I's here, honey chil'," she said as she shuffled across the room. "Better late than never, I always say. Being horizontally challenged, I don't move so fast. Now, what can ole Buhla do for y'all?" She stopped at the end of the bed and crossed beefy arms across a massive bosom.

"Hey, I know you." Andrea studied the nurse while memories of her hospital stay crowded her mind.

Buhla stared back, then recognition dawned on her face. "Well, I'll be horn-swaggled. If it ain't the little miss who lost her memory. I must say, you look bushels better than you did when you was here your own self." Large lips parted in a dazzling, white smile as Buhla waddled over and patted Andrea on the back.

"How are you feelin' these days? Did you ever get your memory back?" Buhla's smile faded as Andrea's face sank.

"No, no, I never did." Andrea's voice was barely above a whisper, and her chin dropped to her chest.

"I'm sorry, chil'. I didn't mean to upset you." Buhla cleared her throat. "Was there something you wanted from me?" Pillowy fingers continued to pat Andrea's back.

"Oh, yes. I'm sorry." Andrea shook her head to clear her thoughts and looked at the nurse. "I . . . What's going on? I mean with my mother. Nobody's told me what's wrong with her, or how long she's been like this, or when she'll come out of it." Andrea turned her gaze to Esther and petted her hand.

"Well," nurse Buhla walked over and picked up the chart at the end of the bed. "Looks like your mama suffered some sort of severe trauma." Dark eyes sought Jack, who seemed unaware that anyone had entered the room. "Didn't your papa tell ya what happened?"

"No, no. He hasn't told me anything. In fact, he's hardly spoken since I got here. Frankly, I'm worried about him, too." Andrea glanced at Jack, then back at the nurse, who was silent for a moment, as she seemed to mull this over in her mind.

"Yeah, right," she finally said. "I can see why." Buhla dropped the chart, folded her arms across her ample chest, and leaned against the bed directly in front of the chair on which Andrea was seated.

"You been outta town or somethin', or you just not livin' at home anymore?"

Andrea was surprised by the personal nature of the question, but she needed answers, and here was someone willing to talk to her, so she chose not to get defensive. "I was out of town. I don't know what happened. I just called home and they said she was in the hospital. Nobody would tell me why."

Nurse Buhla studied her. "Okay. Here's all I know. Yesterday, your papa come staggerin' up to the doors of the emergency room, carryin' your mama. She was out like a firefly in a rainstorm, and she ain't come to since."

Andrea waited for her to continue. When it was clear her story was done, Andrea said, "Wait a minute. That's it? That's all you know?"

"That's it."

"But there has to be more. Some medical explanation. What does her chart say?"

"Just vital signs, medications given, stuff like that. No explanation."

"Well, who's her doctor? When can I talk to him?"

"He'll be back to check on her at nine o'clock tomorrow mornin', but I don't think he's a gonna have all the answers you's a seekin'."

Andrea chewed her bottom lip as she stared at a spot on the wall. What was going on here? What had happened that was so traumatic her mother was unconscious, her father in a daze, and none of the servants would talk about it? Exhaustion crept in. She'd been holding it at bay with adrenaline, but discouragement and anxiety sucked the life from her cells.

Buhla cleared her throat again. "You might as well go on home, honey. There's nothin' you can do here."

Andrea looked at Jack. "What about him?"

"Far as I know, he ain't budged from that chair since his

woman was put in this here room. If'n you can't get him to talk, you ain't 'bout to get him to move. Jus' go on home. I'll keep an eye on both of 'em and give you a call if there's any change. Promise."

Andrea became aware of an unwelcome pattern in her life. Again, she'd sought answers and only had more questions.

Chapter Twenty-seven

Andrea's eyes opened to the familiar surroundings of her bedroom. She breathed in a happy sigh; then reality hit. A glance at the clock on her nightstand told her it was way past time to get back to the hospital.

Rubbing her eyes, she threw the covers back, swung her legs over the edge of the bed, and started to stand up, but went to her knees instead. Her prayers had been infrequent since her accident, but she felt at home kneeling beside her bed.

"Dear Lord, I need your help. I'm confused. My mother's lying sick in the hospital. My dad . . . well, I don't know what's wrong with my dad, but he sure needs your help. I don't know who I am or where I belong. I feel a strong tie to Utah, but I don't know what I should do about it. Please, please, help me. Amen."

She knelt there a while longer, not saying anything, just . . . listening. No flash of light or stream of inspiration filled her mind. Just the ticking of the old fashioned alarm clock by her bed, so she rose slowly, gathered some clean clothes from her drawers, and went into her bathroom to shower.

Two hours later, she was again seated beside Esther, gently holding her hand. Her father, more crumpled and pale than ever, still sat on the other side. But today when he looked at her, there was more than a void behind his eyes; there was a look of determination. Maybe he'd fight after all.

"I have to talk to you," Jack said.

Andrea was so relieved he'd finally spoken to her that the gravity of his tone failed to make an impact.

"Oh, Dad," she said as she rounded the bed and bent down to throw her arms around his neck.

Jack's iron grip clamped around her biceps and pulled her back so he could look her in the face.

"I said I have to talk to you."

"I know, I know. We have so much to talk about. What happened? Is Mom okay? Are you okay? What's going on? I've been so worried."

Jack stood and put his hand over her mouth to shut her up. The intensity of his gaze was not lost on her this time. He removed his hand.

"Not here. Let's go get something to eat," he said.

"Right. You must be starving." Her inhalation of breath was meant to be followed by another barrage of questions, but his look stopped her, and she straightened and took a step back instead. "I'll get my purse," she said, feebly pointing toward the chair where she'd sat.

As she bent to retrieve her purse, she thought she noticed Esther's finger twitch.

"Dad, I think Mother just moved her hand." Her excited voice brought a flash of hope to his tired blue eyes. Andrea sat back in her chair as Jack snatched Esther's other hand in his and brought it to his chest.

"Esther . . . Esther, dear, can you hear me? Blink your eyes if you can."

Andrea held her breath, and a quick glance at Jack showed he was doing the same.

No response from Esther, so Jack tried again.

"Sweetie, it's me, Jack. Please come back to us. Can you hear what I'm saying?"

Still nothing, so Andrea decided to try.

"Mom, it's me, Andrea. I'm right here, Mom. Please, move your finger again. Can you do that?" Andrea stared at the hand she'd held so delicately the day before. There. Did it just move again? Her eyes flew to Jack's face.

"Did you see that? It moved, didn't it?"

A tear squeezed from his eyes as he crunched them shut and slowly nodded his head. Bringing Esther's hand to his lips, he held it there while tears continued to roll down his cheeks.

"Oh, Mother." Andrea laid her head on Esther's chest and put her arms around her as best as she could. "Welcome back. I knew you could do it."

Chapter Twenty-eight

Esther sat up in bed and slurped at the Jell-O Andrea spooned to her. In the past twenty-four hours they had seen miracles in her recovery. Jack still occupied the chair across from Andrea, but he'd taken the time to go home and get some sleep, shower and change, and get a good meal in him, Andrea hoped. The life was coming back to his eyes, but they were still tinged with guilt and oddly troubled, like a winter storm brewed beneath the pale blue surface.

Esther's awakening had precluded their talk, so Andrea still didn't know what he'd deemed so important. Her curiosity had taken a back seat to Esther's care.

"That's enough, darling." Esther put her hand up to block the spoonful of red gel. "There's something so unsettling about food that slips into your mouth and swishes between your teeth. Jack, can't you be a dear and order me a Steak Oscar with new potatoes and fresh green beans?"

Did she just bat her eyes? Andrea shook her head. She must have imagined it. That honeyed tone was real, though. She'd heard it a thousand times before. It never failed to get Esther what she wanted. Not that Andrea had seen, anyway. Jack surprised her.

"No, sweetheart. You know what the doctor said. No solid food until tomorrow." He patted her arm. Esther jerked away from him.

"What does that peabrain know? I heard he's being sued for killing a small child." Her arms folded across her chest.

"Esther. You behave. That's no way to talk about the man who's trying to help you." If that was an attempt to put her in her place, it was a feeble one. More affection than reprimand was evident in his voice.

Andrea sighed. "What about some ice cream, Mother? Would you like that?"

The eyes Esther turned to Andrea were adoring. "You're such an angel. Anything would be better than this red goo." Her smile seemed calculating. What was she up to?

"Fine. I'll go see what I can scare up. Be back in a jiffy."

ാ

Silence engulfed the room when the door clicked shut behind Andrea. Jack leaned forward and rested his elbows on his knees, studying his hands. After several pregnant moments, he looked up.

"Esther, I need to know what you're planning. What are you going to do about Andrea? When are you going to tell her?"

"Tell her? Why should I tell her anything?" Esther refused to look at him.

"But, sweetheart, she's married. What about her poor husband? These past couple of days thinking I might lose you . . . well, it's unthinkable."

Her head flipped around to meet his imploring gaze. "For your information, her husband knows exactly where she is. He filed for a divorce. He wants nothing more to do with her." Jack caught the triumphant gleam in her eye when she played this trump card. His emotions were mixed. He supposed he should be happy, but something didn't sit right.

"What are you talking about? How do you know he wants a divorce? Who is he? What do you know about him?" Jack watched the gleam dim somewhat, replaced with uncertainty.

"I don't know who he is," Esther snapped. "All I know is he sent some whimpy loser to serve divorce papers. He didn't even try to talk to Andrea in person first. What does that tell you?"

It was Jack's turn to be uncertain. Why would a man serve divorce papers to his wife who'd been missing for who knew how long, without even trying to see or talk to her first? And how had he found out where she lived? Andrea was such a sweet, beautiful girl. Why would her husband be anxious to be rid of her?

"What whimpy loser? When did this happen?"

"I dunno. A month or so ago, I guess."

"A month? What did he say? Why didn't you tell me about it?"

"What for? It didn't change things." Esther avoided his eyes.

"Didn't change things? You knew Andrea was married and that her husband wants a divorce but it didn't change things?" Jack tried to keep his voice under control. Esther had just returned to him and he didn't want to send her back to wherever she'd gone, but sometimes she tried his patience to the breaking point.

"No, it didn't change a thing. If they're divorced, then it's like they were never married, so why confuse the issue?" The defiant lift of her chin dared him to contradict her.

Jack stared at her a moment, his jaw slack. Then he shook his head and placed his face in his hands, rubbing his eyes. What was he going to do with this woman of his? He loved her so much. All he wanted was for her to be happy. That's why he'd managed to turn a blind eye to Andrea's past when they'd found her and Esther had been so adamant about keeping her, like a kid with a stray puppy. Esther's wacky sense of logic always managed to confuse him just enough to give in to her. But how far should his loyalties go? Did he have the right to deprive Andrea of the knowledge of her husband, even though that husband didn't want her anymore? Maybe it was kinder not to tell her. Save her the agony of divorce and rejection. The whole, "what she doesn't know won't hurt her," philosophy.

He looked at Esther. Her defiance had turned to an anxious chewing of her bottom lip. She was so delicate. For all her brusqueness, she was like a thin crust over a bubbling volcano that could break through at any moment and the demons of her past would consume her. Jack had been deathly afraid that he'd pushed her over the edge with his anger and accusations, but when Martin told him about the secret safe and he'd discovered the wedding ring, he'd somehow known it was Andrea's, and guilt and fury had enveloped him.

A breeze from the open window tickled the back of his neck and sent a shiver down his spine and the smell of exhaust to his nostrils. What should he do? Ignore Andrea's past and go on like nothing had happened, like Esther wanted him to do? Or tell Andrea what he knew and let her make up her own mind about her past? Would it make any difference now? Was that just opening her up to all the pain and ugliness of divorce? Would her husband take her back? Would she want him to? Jack didn't know. He didn't know anything about the husband, so how could he make a rational decision? He'd made up his mind to tell Andrea everything he knew. Then Esther had awakened, and everything had changed. It was like she could sense what he was about to do and had woken up to put a stop to it. Ridiculous, he knew, but there it was.

He sighed. "Who is he, Esther? What's her husband's name?"

Esther fiddled with the sheet covering her skimpy hospital gown. "Mark or Mike something or other. I don't know."

"Where are the divorce papers? You have them, right? His name would be on them."

"Of course his name is on them. Don't be stupid. I just don't remember what it is."

"Well, where are they?" *The safe. They must be in her safe.* He'd been so shocked at seeing the ring, he hadn't noticed what else was in there.

"They're home in my *private* safe. I'm surprised you didn't find them, too, while you were ransacking my personal belongings." Her arms folded across her chest while she glared at him.

Jack was always amazed that she could be so caustic when she was completely in the wrong. Well, maybe she wasn't completely wrong. A person should be entitled to some privacy. Not when it was someone else's life they were hiding, however.

The door opened and Andrea entered, carrying something on a stick with a white plastic wrapper in each hand.

"This is the closest I could find to ice cream." She held both arms out toward Esther. "I have a fudgesicle." Andrea lifted her right hand. "And a creamsickle." She wiggled the one on the left. "Take your pick. Or take them both."

Esther smiled as she reached for the creamsickle. "You're such a dream. What would I ever do without you?" Esther cast a meaningful look at Jack, and his shoulders drooped in defeat.

If Jack told Andrea the truth, she'd most likely leave. Whether or not she got back together with her husband, she would never stay knowing they'd lied to her. And if Andrea left, Esther would, too. If not physically, then mentally, and Jack couldn't bear the thoughts of going through that again. Losing one daughter had nearly cost him his wife. He doubted he'd dodge that bullet again.

Chapter Twenty-nine

Georgette walked through the automatic doors onto the curb, her only bag slung across her left shoulder. She hailed a cab with her other arm, and then climbed into the back seat, keeping her bag with her, glad she hadn't had to fight baggage claim, and not wishing to be separated from it now.

"6927 Rosewood Lane," she read from the piece of paper she'd pulled from her pocket. The driver was a shriveled little man with dark hair and dark skin. He reminded her of those dancing raisins on TV, only he didn't look so happy. *I hope he speaks English.* The last thing she wanted was to find herself in a bad part of town. She'd heard horror stories of L.A. and didn't want to end up a statistic on a police report. That's all Matt needed. Another woman to disappear from his life.

Georgette felt guilty about lying, but what was she supposed to tell him? That she was going to confront his soon to be ex-wife and ask why she'd abandoned him and his son? Besides, after Rick had gotten through with him, he didn't believe Melody had shown up at the dealership. He about had Georgette convinced it had been a lie concocted by the sales crews until she'd overheard Chuck bragging to one of his sleezeball buddies about how he'd broken up Melody's marriage for good. Georgette had cornered him later and confided she'd overheard, and acted excited at the news and begged for details. He'd been only too happy to fill her in, including the name of the motel where Melody was staying, supposing Georgette, of all people, to be firmly on his side. Unfortunately, by the time she got up her courage and went to the motel, Melody was gone.

Having gone that far, however, Georgette decided to see it through. It had taken a couple of paychecks to save the money for airfare. And she'd changed her mind half a dozen times, but her promise to Skyler that he'd see his momma again was like a lead weight chained to her heart. So she'd gotten Melody's address off the divorce papers from Matt's file at work, told Matt she was going to visit her parents in Florida, and here she was. He was taking Skyler to Melody's parent's this weekend, anyway.

Georgette stared out the window at the smog and traffic and wondered why anyone wanted to live in this mess. Salt Lake in the summer with all the road construction was bad enough. What was she doing here? Did Melody remember her? Why would she confide in her? Because she had to. For Skyler's sake. Georgette wasn't leaving until she could give that little boy a good reason why his momma ran out on him. What was she thinking? No good reason existed. A reason, then.

The taxi pulled off the freeway and after a few turns, pulled onto a tree-lined road that wound up a big hill. The farther they climbed, the bigger the houses became. Georgette stared in awe at the massive wrought-iron gates, and the glimpses of mansions tucked behind. No wonder Melody ran away. If Georgette knew she'd wind up here, she'd be tempted herself.

They slowed and stopped in front of a brick guardhouse at the entrance of one of the gates. A sandy-haired man with huge dimples and dreamy blue eyes leaned out of the window of the hut onto tanned, muscled forearms showing beneath the rolled-up sleeves of his uniform, his hat tipped back on his head, a grin displaying rows of straight, white teeth.

"How are y'all doin' today?" His drawl made Georgette's heart beat a little faster as she rolled down her window and poked her head out to talk to him.

"Is this 6927 Rosewood Lane?" Georgette asked.

"Of course it is, lady. What? You think I bring you to wrong address?" The driver answered before the guard said anything.

"No, no, I was just—" Georgette tore her eyes from the guard to look at the fidgety little man.

"That nineteen dollar. You get out now." The driver cut her off before she finished her thought.

"Well, wait a minute. I don't even know if I can get in," she protested as she pointed at the formidable gate looming a few feet in front of them.

"Not my problem, lady. Me on lunch break. You get out now." He leaned over the seat to open her door from the inside.

"Hey, you can't just kick me out like this. I need a ride to my hotel when my business is finished here."

"I do what I want. My cab. You pay, then leave."

Georgette looked to the guard for help, but his grin had broadened and his shoulders were shaking. He was enjoying the exchange. Fine. Digging in her purse, she pulled out a twenty, wadded it up and chucked it at the driver, then slung the purse on her shoulder, grabbed her bag, and climbed out. The door barely shut behind her when the driver peeled the car around and pulled back out the direction they'd come, spraying her with fine gravel and waving jauntily out the window as he headed down the road. Georgette squealed and jumped back, stepping on a bigger rock as she did, twisting her ankle. Before she crumpled to the ground, two strong arms grabbed her from behind.

"Whoa there, little lady, ya better take it easy." The guard set her back on her feet, but her right ankle refused to support her weight, and she had to turn and clutch the sill of the window the guard was hanging out of to keep from falling again. Embarrassed, she looked up at his face. The grin had disappeared.

"Hey, you're hurt, ain't ya?"

Georgette didn't know whether to laugh or cry at the genuine concern in his eyes and voice. She chose to cry. Her situation suddenly seemed hopeless and ridiculous, so she set her bag down, plunked on top of it, set her purse down beside her, buried her face in her hands, and sobbed. What was she doing here? This was crazy.

A hand patted the top of Georgette's head. The guard must have left his hut. She felt even more ridiculous, so she dried her eyes and stared at her bare legs, poking from beneath her sundress. She was too humiliated to meet the gaze of the cute guard.

Her ankle had swollen until it practically buried the thin strap of her sandal, and her creamy white legs now looked like she had the measles from where the pebbles had sprayed her. She bent over to undo the sandal strap, but the guard beat her to it.

"Here, let me do that." His large hands were surprisingly gentle as he undid the buckle and slipped the high-heeled shoe from her foot, resting her ankle on his lap as he crouched in front of her. "Goodness, girl, no wonder you tipped over, wearing them things." He dangled the shoe on his finger before tossing it onto the grass nearby. "You're lucky you just twisted your ankle and didn't break your neck."

His grin was infectious, and the corners of Georgette's mouth twitched. She smiled and finally broke into a laugh. *Careful,* she warned herself. *A girl could drown in those blue eyes.* Her laugh trickled off and died, and they stared at each other in silence until he thrust his hand out.

"Nate Spears, originally from Houston, Texas. And who might you be?"

Georgette's hand was swallowed in his as she shook, not knowing what else to do. "Georgette. Georgette, uh . . ." For the life of her, she couldn't remember her last name. Nate laughed. A good, hearty, down-home laugh. Georgette felt her heartstrings popping and wasn't sure what that meant. Matt's image leapt into her mind, then faded into a deep blue sea. The throbbing in her ankle brought her back to reality.

"You don't have any ibuprofen in that shack of yours, do you, Mr. Spears?"

His grin was immediately replaced with concern.

"Oh sure. We have a whole first aid kit. I'll have you fixed up in no time, but ya gotta call me Nate. None of this Mr. Spears stuff. That's my old man." Before she realized what was happening, he scooped her into his arms and had carried her to the grassy spot under a huge tree. He gently set her down next to her shoe, and then hurried into the hut. Within seconds, he was back with a first aid kit and a bottle of water.

His hands deftly administered to her needs. He'd done this before—many times, by the looks of things.

"So, what are you—a doctor on the side or something?" Georgette asked after swallowing a couple of Advil.

Her question was rewarded by another toothy grin that made his blue eyes flash. "Naw. Lifeguard. Down on Newport Beach."

"That explains the tan. You don't get that dark hanging out in security guardhouses."

"Sure don't. But lifeguarding don't pay much, so I do this at night to help support my addiction."

Georgette felt the color rise in her face as he laughed at her wide-eyed expression.

"Surfing. I'm nuts about it. Moved out here from Texas and put up with all these California freaks just so I can surf every day."

The wave of relief that flooded over Georgette shocked her as much as his addiction pronouncement had. What did she care what this guy did?

Silence stretched on as the two stared at each other in a trance-like state. Shadows stretched along the drive, and a slight breeze rustled the leaves of the tree overhead. A dog barked in the distance, and Georgette finally shook her head to clear the fog that seemed to have rolled into her brain.

"I . . . oh good gracious, you almost made me forget why I'm here. I need to see Mrs. McCandlass," she stammered.

"Who?" Nate rocked back on the heels of his cowboy boots and sat on the grass, forearms resting on his knees, his right hand holding his left wrist. His brow was furrowed in a look of complete puzzlement.

"Melody McCandlass. I was . . . told she lived here." It was just a little lie.

Nate shook his head. "Nobody by that name here."

Now Georgette was puzzled. "Are you sure?"

"Yup. This here is the Kensington mansion. Big music producers. They own Starstream Recording Studios. Their daughter's a singer." Nate suddenly looked contrite, and Georgette wondered if he regretted sharing that information with her. She didn't imagine security guards were usually so free with personal information about the inhabitants of houses they guarded.

They were both silent as Georgette digested this latest development while Nate studied the toes of his boots. Then she brightened.

"Kensington! That's right. Andrea Kensington. That's the name she used in Las Vegas." The name had been on the divorce papers as an alias, too, but Georgette didn't say that part out loud.

Nate looked up, relief evident on his features. "You know Miss Kensington?"

Georgette stifled a giggle. "Yes, I know her." *And no, you darling man, you didn't share pertinent information with a dangerous criminal.* "She's the one I need to see. Sorry about the mix-up. My mistake. Must have been the fall." She hoped her smile was sweet and placating. It seemed to do the trick for a moment. Nate had the look of a teenaged boy who'd been asked to dance by the homecoming queen. In the next instant his face drooped.

"Uh oh. I hope you haven't come too far." He glanced at her bag still sitting in the driveway in front of the guard shack. The concern he showed as he turned back to her would have been comical if his words hadn't set off alarms in Georgette's head.

"Why? What do you mean?"

"Well, Miss Kensington is out of the country. On tour in Germany, or somewhere like that."

Georgette felt her lip start to quiver.

"Oh no, miss. Don't cry." Nate grabbed for her hand.

Georgette took a breath and tried to calm herself. "Are you sure?" Something told her this man never said anything he wasn't sure of.

He nodded and wiped a tear from the corner of her eye with his thumb.

"How . . ." Georgette stopped to clear her throat. "How long will she be gone?" She looked at him through a shimmering film. It had taken all her nerve, not to mention her money, to come this far. Now to be thwarted so near her goal . . .

"Oh, she'll be gone a long time, miss. Three or four months, I reckon. I'm sorry. I can see it meant a lot for you to see her. Are y'all good friends?" The curiosity that registered in his voice went a tinge beyond casual conversation. This piqued Georgette's interest.

"Why do you ask?"

"Oh, I dunno. You seem so disappointed she's not here, but . . ."

"But what?" Georgette urged.

Nate looked into her eyes while a war of emotions waged across his face. He must have found what he was looking for in hers, because his expression calmed, and he went on.

"Well, it just never seemed like Miss Kensington had any friends."

Her look implored him to continue, so he did.

"There was that snooty, rich fella who called on her a time or two, but she never 'peared to care for him much, from my reckoning."

"Go on," Georgette begged when he hesitated.

"Heck, I dunno. It was just so strange how she showed up here all sudden like, all growed up, and no recollection of her past."

Georgette's heart skipped a beat. She scrambled to her knees, ignoring the pain in her ankle and took both of Nate's hands in hers as she looked intently into his face.

"Nate. This is important. You have to tell me everything."

He studied her for what seemed an eternity, then finally shrugged.

"I dunno that much. It's not like I spy or eavesdrop or anything. Heck, I'm just a security guard, but I'm buddies with Hank, the chauffeur, and the guy likes to talk . . ."

"So tell me. What do you know?" Georgette tried to keep the

hysteria out of her voice but wasn't sure she'd succeeded.

Nate watched her, a wicked gleam coming into his eyes. "I'll tell ya what I know, but it'll cost ya."

Georgette dropped his hands and sat back. "What do you mean?" She looked at him through narrowed eyes.

He started to laugh. "Now don't go gettin' your lariat in knots. I'm only talkin' 'bout dinner."

Georgette relaxed and smiled. Dinner would be nice. She was starving.

"There's a catch, though," he said. She became wary again and he chuckled.

"I don't get off here 'til midnight, so I hope you don't mind a late supper."

Georgette couldn't help the groan that escaped her lips, followed by a rumble in her stomach.

Nate stood and brushed off the seat of his pants while he continued to chuckle. Then he reached down to help Georgette to her feet. "I always bring a little somethin' to tide me over, though," he told her. He put his arm around her waist and hers around his shoulders to support her bad ankle as he steered her toward the guard hut.

"Come on in to my humble abode and we'll see if we can't put a stop to all that racket in your belly."

Georgette felt her face get hot, but she didn't say anything as she hobbled to the shack. Actually, *shack* was not the best word to describe the charming gray stone outbuilding with the Swiss chalet eaves. She'd seen much worse houses in Mexico, when she'd gone with her family as a teenager.

Inside was just enough room for two chairs, and Nate helped settle her into one, then went to retrieve her purse, shoe, and overnight bag. After stowing them under her chair, he reached under the front counter and retrieved a large brown paper bag, from which he extracted a couple of sandwiches and soft drinks. Handing one of each to Georgette, he took the others and sat in the chair across from her.

"This is a pretty easy job," he said around a mouthful of

sandwich. "Not much goes on, usually. I just have to watch and make sure nobody gets in that gate the Kensingtons don't want to see." He gestured with his head toward the big wrought iron gate Georgette remembered seeing when she pulled up in the taxi.

Georgette nodded and said, "Umm," not wanting to speak with her mouth full.

Nate continued, pointing to an electrical gadget attached to one wall. "When someone pulls up, I get their name, then radio in on that there intercom to the house. If I get the okay, I push that big red button, and the gate swings open. Tough job, but somebody's gotta do it." He grinned. His sandwich was gone now, and he brushed his hands off on his trousers, then downed his soda in three or four chugs. Georgette watched his Adam's apple bob up and down as he did so, fascinated by the muscles in his neck. She didn't know necks had muscles.

Her eyes drifted to the V where the collar of his shirt opened. Golden, curly hairs gleamed against the dark bronze of his skin. Her pulse quickened, and she had to force the bite of sandwich in her mouth down her throat. When she looked up, she was embarrassed to see him watching her, a somber look on his face, the chattiness gone. Little beads of sweat had popped out on his forehead.

Georgette grabbed her own soda and took a huge swig, then almost choked. Her coughing brought him to his feet beside her before she hardly blinked. For a big man, he was fast. One hand was on her shoulder while the other alternately rubbed then patted her back.

"You okay?"

Her eyes watered as she continued to cough, but she nodded her head. It seemed she was destined to humiliate herself around this man.

The coughing subsided, but he remained crouched at her side, gently rubbing her back. His other hand had moved down to encircle her forearm.

Georgette fished in her pocket for a tissue and daubed her eyes. "What a mess I am," she mumbled. "One disaster after another." She didn't dare look at him.

"I don't think you're a mess." His voice was soft, soothing. He cupped her chin in his hand and turned her face to him.

Her breath caught and her heart pounded at the way his eyes smoldered. It was like someone had set fire to a lake. He leaned toward her, and she closed her eyes and parted her lips. Then another pair of eyes came into view. Brown ones.

Georgette leapt to her feet, forgetting about her ankle, and quickly collapsed in the chair again with a yelp of pain, but not before sending Nate sprawling backward to hit his head on the shelf under the counter. Again the dilemma: laugh or cry. This time, she chose laugh.

"I'm so sorry. Are you okay?" she managed between bouts.

Nate groaned and rubbed his head. "I changed my mind. You are a walking disaster. Or at least a sitting one."

She continued to giggle hysterically, and he slowly sat up and let a smile steal onto his face.

"Geez, girl, you better settle down or you're gonna do yourself another injury."

Georgette was out of control. Tears streamed down her cheeks, but the laughter continued unchecked. Maybe she was crazy. What was she doing here? Why had she made that promise to Skyler? Who was she to set the world straight? Why did she want to? She loved Matt and Skyler. Why risk what had taken her years to achieve by trying to contact Melody? Laughter turned to sobs. Great heaving ones. She was so confused.

Nate was beside her again, arms wrapped around her, so strong, so sure. He pushed her head to his shoulder.

"I'm sorry. I'm so sorry. I shouldn't have done that. I had no right. Please forgive me. It'll be all right."

He was pleading for her forgiveness for trying to kiss her. Imagine. He wanted to kiss her. Wanted to. Really wanted to. Not . . . obligated.

She burrowed into his chest and drank of the warmth and smell of him as she pictured his eyes just before she'd shut hers. She'd have given all she owned to see that look in Matt's eyes.

Even once. They were engaged, but she still felt that every touch, every kiss was initiated by her, and his response was out of duty. He was a good man. As good as they come. But he was in love with someone else. He denied it. Even tried to fight it. But he would never fully belong to her, and she knew it. She had always known it. But it had seemed worth it.

Until now.

Chapter Thirty

"We have to find her and tell her. She doesn't know." Georgette was on Nate's back deck, seated on a beige patio chair with plastic straps. The expanse of sand that separated them from the ocean grew smaller as foamy green fingers licked the shore then retreated, only to advance again. Her bad ankle was propped on a similar chair, but she was anything but laid back. Her forearms rested on the glass table top in front of her, while her hands were clasped together, her eyes boring into Nate's, who sat across from her. One of his hands caressed her leg that was propped up next to him, and the other was wrapped around a glass of orange juice. He hunched forward, giving Georgette his full attention.

A seagull flew over and landed on the porch railing, bobbed its head in every direction, then hopped onto the deck next to Georgette and began to peck at the crumbs from her bagel. Her eyes followed its actions, then turned back to Nate.

"Don't you see? It all makes perfect sense now. She didn't walk out on Matt and Skyler. She doesn't remember they exist."

Shouts caught her attention at the same time the seagull flew off the porch. A group of teenagers, surfboards under their arms or over their heads, ran toward the ocean, where the rays from the early morning sun glinted off the waves like nuggets of gold.

"I understand what you're saying, I just don't see any way to track her down."

Georgette looked at Nate. It seemed his gaze never left her face. Not even to gaze longingly at the surfers, although she knew this was the time of day he usually reserved for the sport he loved enough to leave his home and family to pursue. Her heart did a little dance at the thought.

After their late supper, Nate had offered to let her spend the night at his place, and she'd been too tired to refuse. Then he'd begun to talk about Andrea on the way home, and any thoughts of sleep had dissipated. Their discussion had continued after they arrived at his little townhouse on the beach, and had extended through the night.

Amnesia. Melody had amnesia. That's why she hadn't come home. Not because she didn't love Matt anymore or that she wanted to be a singer instead of a mother. But exactly how she ended up with the Kensingtons and why they claimed she was their daughter was still a mystery. One she'd have to investigate further before she went back to Utah—if she went back.

Of course she'd go back. No way would she disappear like Melody had done. Even though Georgette knew now she couldn't marry Matt, he'd meant too much to her for too long to skip out without a word. She still loved and respected him, although that love had taken on a warm, gentle glow like her affection for a favorite uncle, in light of the sparks that had kindled into a raging fire ever since she'd laid eyes on Nate. She'd never considered herself fickle, but she couldn't deny how she felt. Being able to explain the mystery of Melody's disappearance to Matt would go a long way toward assuaging the guilt she felt over leaving him.

"What about her mother? This Esther person you told me about? Surely she knows where Melody is. She must have some sort of itinerary." Georgette had filled Nate in on the other side of the story, and in so doing had elicited a firm ally—especially when she mentioned her engagement to Matt. Nate reared back in his chair and his eyes widened at the mention of Esther, however.

"No way, man. She's the enemy. I'm sure she's the reason Melody ended up here. I just don't know how or exactly why. I mean, Mrs. Kensington must make good money off Melody's singing and all, but there has to be more to it than that."

Nate slid his orange juice to one side and leaned forward, his forearms resting on the table. Georgette leaned toward him like he was about to share a great secret.

His voice was lowered as he said, "Rumor has it that Jack, her husband, you know?" When Georgette nodded, he continued. "Well, they say up at the house that Jack found something in Esther's private study one day that had him mad as a hobbled stallion in a herd of mares."

Georgette's eyebrows raised, but she didn't comment.

"I mean, this is a guy who's never so much as raised his voice to his wife, and he was hollerin' at her so the whole house could hear."

Georgette's curiosity burst out of her. "What? What did he find?"

Nate sat back in his chair and steepled his fingers, drumming them together. "I don't know."

Georgette let out an exasperated cry. Nate leaned forward again and took her hands in his, and began to twist her engagement ring around her finger. Georgette felt a pang at not having taken it off, but she didn't want to seem too presumptuous. She'd only met this guy last night.

"All I know is Mrs. Kensington ended up in the hospital right after that. Some say she faked a seizure or something to take the heat off." He looked at Georgette, and she knew the shock of his statement must have registered on her face.

"Anyway, whatever it was, it worked. Jack came home three days later, docile as a whipped pup. Next thing anyone knew, Miss Kensington . . . Melody, packed up and headed to Europe, and Esther was struttin' around like the Queen of Sheba again."

Georgette was at a loss for words. What was going on here?

"Somethin' else I just remembered," Nate continued, "A while back this feller showed up saying he had urgent business with Miss Kensington, only he called her Mrs. McCandlass. I didn't know who or what he was talking about then, and tried to send him packing, but he showed me these divorce papers for her, and when I radioed up to the house, the butler told me to let him in, so I did. He wasn't gone long, but he left me with some choice names for the "lady of the house" before he drove off. I knew Miss . . . Melody was gone, so he had to have been talking about Esther. Not that anyone would talk that way about Melody, anyway."

"What did he say?" Georgette asked, her curiosity piqued, but not sure she wanted to know.

"Oh, nothing I can repeat, but it seems to be the sentiment of most people Esther meets who she's not trying to impress for one reason or another."

A shudder passed through Georgette. What had Melody gotten herself into? This glamorous new life had taken on a grayish hue. Georgette listened to her thoughts, mingled with the roar of the ocean and squawk of gulls. The early morning haze was about burned off. It was going to be a beautiful day. More people had congregated on the beach. Dogs barked and chased Frisbees while little kids chased the gulls.

A realization crept into Georgette's consciousness. "You don't think . . ." she wasn't sure how to put the thought into words. Nate looked at her expectantly.

"You say that Melody wasn't home when that guy brought the divorce papers?"

"No," Nate answered.

"And the guy spoke with Esther?"

"That's the impression I got."

"Do you think . . . I'll bet . . . Melody doesn't know about the divorce, does she?"

She saw the same realization dawn on Nate's features.

"You know, I'll bet she doesn't. I mean, how could she if she doesn't even know who she is?" he said.

"Yeah, but Esther does, doesn't she? I mean, how could she not if someone delivered divorce papers right to her?"

"True, true." Nate sat back and rubbed his chin with his hand, cradling the other one under his elbow.

"Matt told me the divorce had been uncontested so far, but

if Melody doesn't even know about it . . ." What did it all mean? Who was this Esther person? Was she holding Melody hostage or something?

"I have to call Matt. He has to stop the divorce." Georgette glanced around, trying to remember where she'd left her purse and cell phone.

Nate made an odd noise deep in his throat, and Georgette's attention was immediately brought back to him. He studied his orange juice as he twisted the glass between his fingers. His face had taken on a crimson hue beneath his tan. Georgette waited.

"I . . ." he cleared his throat and finally brought his head up. Their eyes locked.

He started again. "I know we just met last night, and I hate to sound like an old movie, but I've never felt like this about anyone before. I feel like I've known you all my life." He slid the orange juice aside and reached across the table to take her hands in his before he continued.

"I don't know this Matt feller, but it sounds like he's been through a lot, and I figure he'd be darn lucky to have you."

Georgette started to say something, but he squeezed her hands and his gaze intensified, so she kept quiet.

"I don't wanna seem too forward, and I hate to add to the poor guy's suffering, but I can't stand the thought of you being with anyone but me." His head ducked, his eyes hidden by a wavy lock of blond hair.

Georgette didn't answer for a moment. Her voice was unable to squeeze past the lump in her throat. The squawk of gulls and salty smell of seaweed seemed to be replaced by the song of nightingales and the scent of roses. At last she knew what it felt like to be cherished.

The silence pressed on until Nate looked up, panic in his eyes. Georgette laughed and leaned forward to throw her arms around his neck. The table pressed into her stomach, so she sat back and took his hands in hers again.

"You don't know what it means to me to hear you say that," she told him. "I've had those same feelings practically since the moment I laid eyes on you, but I didn't want to assume too much."

Nate's eyes glowed like someone lit a bonfire behind them. Then his brow furrowed.

"What are you going to tell Matt?"

Georgette loved him all the more for being concerned about the feelings of the other man in her life.

"Don't worry about him. When he finds out the truth about Melody, he'll be happy I've found someone else."

Nate cocked an eyebrow, so Georgette continued.

"He tries to pretend he doesn't care about her anymore, and he really did give our relationship a good try, but the fact is, he never stopped loving her. And he never will."

Chapter Thirty-one

Matt stared at the phone in his hand. It had been ten minutes since he'd said good-bye to Georgette, yet he gripped the black receiver like it was a lamp with a magic genie inside. Melody had amnesia? He felt like he'd been hit with a stun gun. His limbs were concrete blocks, but his mind was a kaleidoscope of activity. Barely perceptible flutters began in his chest where his heart used to be, and he recognized them as the first signs of life he'd felt in a year and a half. Did he dare hope?

Georgette had met someone else. Wasn't anger the appropriate response when an engagement was broken? All he felt was relief. He had planned to marry her. He'd have done his best to make her happy, too, but she deserved more than he was capable of giving. His heart had been entombed in stone, but the tiniest chinks now began to appear.

His thoughts turned to his son. For a moment, he wished Skyler was here with him instead of at the ranch, but then he thought better of it. Best not to get his hopes up yet. Children expected immediate results, and Matt had no idea what was in store for them in the near future. He had big hopes for eternity, but he suspected turbulence before they reached that shore.

What if Melody's amnesia was permanent? A mental image of their reunion filled his mind. She'd rush into his arms, full of love and apologies for what she'd put him through. A smile spread across his face as he savored the picture. A cloud drifted over. That hadn't happened the last time he'd seen her. In fact, their chance meeting in Vegas had nearly sent him careening into a dark abyss from which there was no escape. She'd looked right at him and frozen like a statue. What did that mean?

Matt set the phone down on the end table next to the couch. He glanced at the TV where the movie he'd been watching prior to Georgette's call still played. The actors mouthed words while a red "mute" sign flashed in the corner of the screen.

In Vegas, he hadn't known what he knew now. He'd thought she'd been kidnapped or swept away by a flood. He'd never dreamed she was alive and well, and living a different life somewhere. So when he saw her on that stage, blissfully happy, oblivious to his shredded heart and the lonely nightmares of her motherless son, his blood had turned to ice and his heart had broken into a thousand pieces.

Now he knew. She hadn't disappeared by choice to pursue her career. Well, he'd won her love once, and he'd do it again. Memory or no memory. She was all he'd ever wanted.

His hands clasped in front of him as he rested his forearms on his knees. He had to go to California and confront this Esther person and find out the whole truth. What made her think Melody was her daughter? Did she think relatives were up for grabs? Someone had forgotten to have a certain talk with her as a child.

And how had Melody ended up on that stage in Vegas? Something very strange was going on. Now Georgette said Melody was in Europe. That didn't matter, though. Nothing did, beyond the fact that Melody hadn't walked out on him. He'd fly to the ends of the earth to get her back. What a fool he'd been to ever doubt her. He'd been so wrapped up in self-pity he hadn't stopped to consider what she'd been through.

Matt reached for the phone again. First thing, he had to get hold of Rick and get some time off work. What would his reaction be to the news of Melody's amnesia? He'd have to take back all his taunts and sneers.

Matt's finger froze, poised above the speed dial button. What if Melody had been to the dealership that day? What if Rick had seen her and knew, and had lied to Matt about it? What if she'd come to see Matt and Rick had somehow prevented it?

Naw. Rick was a jerk, but he wasn't that low. Nobody was. Not after he'd seen what Matt had been through. The guy had some strange notions about friendship, but he wasn't complete slime. Still, he set the phone down.

Matt looked around the room as if seeing it for the first time in over a year. The wallpaper was streaked and torn in places and covered in black, greasy smudges. The carpet, which used to be light beige, now had a definite gray hue and was spotted with juice and food stains. He could probably plant a garden in the layer of dust that covered everything from the TV to the baby grand piano in the corner. That was just the front room. Matt shuddered when he thought about the kitchen and bathrooms. He'd have to get busy. Melody would scurry right back to her other life if she came home to this dump. Georgette had helped out whenever she came over, but her occasional attempts at cleaning were no match for the wreckage Matt and Skyler left in their wake. Especially in the state of mind Matt had been in. If he could walk from room to room without too much difficulty, the house was okay to him.

He wished his parents were still alive. Strange, he hadn't thought that in years. A wave of vulnerability swept over him, and he suddenly wanted someone to confide in. Someone to give him advice without judging. Someone who loved him unconditionally. Mel had been that for him ever since they'd met in college. He was in love the moment he'd laid eyes on her, but she'd taken some convincing that she felt the same way about him, although they'd been the best of friends right from the start.

Their religious differences had been the biggest deterrent. Melody was a staunch Mormon, and he'd been a "fundamentalist," meaning, whatever was fun, that's what he'd been into. He didn't remember his parents being any religion. They'd been killed in a car crash when he was in high school. He had no brothers or sisters and no other family to speak of, so he'd fended for himself, working at hamburger joints, then going to work selling cars for Rick when he was only a senior. He was a natural, but he couldn't imagine doing that for the rest of his life, so he'd saved up enough money and gone to college and met Mel.

She became his main focus after that. He'd thought of nothing but her, so after a year of intense courtship on his part while playing the role of her best buddy, he'd convinced her she couldn't live without him either, and they'd been married. As much as her parents liked Matt, they'd been bitterly disappointed that Melody hadn't been married in one of their Mormon temples.

Without an education and with a wife to support, he'd gone back to work for Rick, and that's where he'd been ever since. Funny thing was, Melody had known Rick before she met Matt. She'd never talked much about it. Just said that she knew him. And she hadn't been pleased that Matt went back to work for him, but she'd supported him. Her manner had always been cool but cordial in Rick's presence.

Matt had asked Rick about it once, but all he'd said was they'd lived in the same neighborhood once, then clammed up like Matt had asked him for the combination to his safe, so Matt had left it at that.

Matt glanced at the dusty clock hanging on the wall. He knew he had to call Rick, but now that he thought about it, it was still too early, anyway. Rick never got up before noon on Sundays, and he made anyone who tried to infringe on that sorry they were born.

Excitement crept into Matt's every fiber. He was going to get his wife back. All the months of hopelessness were about to end. A light had appeared at the end of very long, dark tunnel.

Matt was glad he'd taken Skyler to Mel's parents, because the temptation to tell him about his momma would be too great if he were here. Gathering toys and clothes from off the floor, Matt headed to the bedroom where his laptop perched on a pile of unopened mail atop a small desk. He needed to check flights to California leaving this morning, or this afternoon at the latest. Georgette had given him the address of the house where Melody, who called herself Andrea Kensington, lived with Esther and Jack Kensington, who claimed to be her parents. Something was seriously screwy with that.

After dumping the armload of toys and clothes he'd gathered on his bed, he plugged in his computer, sat down, and drummed a pencil on the desk until the computer booted up, then began pecking at the keys. Eleven o'clock. Perfect. He'd just have time to shower and pack. He'd have to call Rick from California. He booked the flight online, shut his computer down, then hurried to the bathroom. From his new perspective, it was even more disgusting than he remembered, but he didn't have time to do anything about it now. He was a man with a mission. Adrenaline mixed with endorphins and raced through his veins. Melody hadn't left him. The words rang through his mind and became a song. Who could think about soap scum at a time like this? He'd hire someone to clean the place while he was gone.

He hummed and scrubbed himself as he dodged the green and black growth here and there in the shower. The more he thought about Melody, the more excited he became. She was coming home. Her music would soon fill the house again. Her laughter. Her smiles. He thought about Skyler and how thrilled he'd be to have his momma home again. Life was good. The nightmare was practically at an end.

The phone was ringing when he turned off the water, so he hurriedly grabbed a towel to wrap around himself, and walked, dripping, to the phone on the nightstand by the bed.

"Hello," he said into the receiver.

"Matt?" said a voice.

"Speaking," he was trying to place the muffled voice. It sounded like someone trying to keep her emotions in check.

"Matt, honey, it's Carol," said a woman's voice.

"Oh, hi, Mom. How ya doin'?" Should he tell her the good news? Seeing the concern in Carol and Burt's faces for him when he'd come down from the mountain after his month-long stay in their cabin, he'd been unable to add to their burden by telling them their daughter had left them and their church to pursue a music career. Now he wouldn't have to.

"Not so good, I'm afraid. I have some bad news," Carol's pained voice interrupted his thoughts.

Matt's blood ran cold. "It's not Skyler? Where is he? What happened?"

Carol's sniffles and muffled sobs were her only answer for several moments. Finally, she found her voice again.

"I don't mean to worry you, dear . . ."

"It's too late for that, Carol, just tell me," Matt felt bad for being sharp with her. He liked his mother-in-law, and it was obvious she was having a hard time, but the bloodied, mangled images of his son running through his head were too much to bear.

"It's just that . . . well . . ."

"What? What?" Veins popped out on Matt's arms as he gripped the phone in one hand and his towel with the other.

"We . . . we can't find Skyler," Carol dissolved in sobs.

Matt's knees buckled and he sank to the bed. The blood must have drained from his face because his head suddenly felt light and the room began to spin.

"What do you mean you can't find him?" His voice cracked and rasped out of his suddenly dry throat.

"He was out doing chores with his grandpa, just taggin' along like a trooper, feedin' the chickens 'n such, and then next thing Burt knew, he turned around and Skyler was gone. We've searched high and low, and called him 'til our voices are hoarse, but it's no use. I can't imagine how he would have got that far, but we can't find hide nor hair of him." Carol broke down again.

Matt was speechless. His mouth moved up and down, but no words came. This was not happening again. Not just as he was about to have his family back together. Not Skyler.

"Listen, Carol, don't give up. You keep lookin'. Get all the hands out lookin' . . ."

"They are. Have been since early this mornin'."

"Early this . . . ? And you're just now calling me?" His voice shook with anger. Carol only sobbed harder.

"Never mind. Call the sheriff. Do whatever it takes. I'm not goin' to lose my boy. I'm on my way." Matt hung up without another word. His mind tumbled with thoughts and images, none of them good, so he shook them off and jumped up to get dressed. He wished he could fly to the ranch. He'd always wanted to get his pilot's license, and right now, he was kicking himself for not having done so. No time to worry about that. He scrambled for his clothes, threw some on, and shoved others in an overnight bag. He had no idea how long he'd be gone.

In the bathroom, he scooped up his toothbrush and razor and threw them in the bag, running his fingers through his wet hair. The elation of a few moments before had been replaced with sick dread. Melody had to wait. He must find his son. Failure was not an option. This time, he'd only quit if he dropped over dead. Death sounded blissfully peaceful compared to the cold, steely fist that had entered his chest and clutched his heart, threatening to rip it out between his ribs. *Not again.* It wasn't humanly possible to endure the disappearance of someone he loved a second time. He'd never survive. How many times could the human heart be pulverized and keep on ticking? Matt felt sure he'd reached his limit.

He was about to head out the door, but dropped to his knees by the side of his bed instead.

"Dear God in heaven. Melody says there is a God, and that you're Him. She says we're all your children and that you love us all equally. She also says that you can help us when we ask. Well, I'm askin'. I know I didn't ask like I should've when Mel came up missing. I guess I was too proud. Figured I should be able to find her on my own. Well, I didn't do so good, and I don't wanna take any chances with my boy. Won't you please . . . please help us find him? And make him be all right when we do. I don't think I could bear to have anything happen to him. I know you're busy and all, but this is real important. Uh . . . thanks a lot. Amen."

Matt wiped a tear from his eye as he stood up. He glanced at the picture of Jesus on the wall. Little children crowded around Him. Such love radiated from His face. He knew how He felt. Skyler had become everything to Matt in the past year and a half. If anything happened to him, Matt didn't think he could face the future. Not even with Melody.

Chapter Thirty-two

Andrea stared at yet another wall in yet another dingy hotel room. Her tolerance level was at its peak. What had she been thinking when she agreed to this tour? The hour or two of exhilaration she felt on the stage each evening as she performed was not enough to counter the deep loneliness that overwhelmed her each night. Esther might get on her nerves, but she was still family. And as quiet and unassuming as Jack was, he provided a solid anchor in her life, someone she looked up to and could occasionally talk to. Here she had no one but Greg, the band—who stayed in a separate hotel because Esther didn't want to be responsible for the damage they caused with their raucous parties—and the roadies who set up the equipment every night but who kept to themselves. Oh, and the tour manager, Kevin, a snotty little man who Andrea tried to avoid as much as possible.

This was like a nightmare that never ended. One city after another, with no time to even take in the sights. It seemed that all she'd seen of Europe in the three and a half weeks she'd been here were airports, bus depots, and hotels with old plumbing and strange food. This was not the life she envisioned for herself. Real life never turned out like her dreams.

She wanted to go home. She missed America. Maybe she'd come back someday for a vacation when she could actually see the things people were always raving about. But even if there were time to sightsee, there was no one to go with, and things were never as fun or exciting when you had to experience them by yourself. Greg was not exactly a companion. He just lurked in the background, never saying much. Even when Andrea tried to engage him in conversation, she only got grunts for replies.

And there was still the unsolved mystery of her past. With this whirlwind tour she'd been on, she didn't have a whole lot of time or energy to spend speculating about her experiences in Utah, or this Matt person she'd tried to find, but he was always in her dreams when she closed her eyes at night. Always laughing and smiling, brown eyes twinkling, not stone cold and hard like they'd been in Vegas. And with him was often the shadow of a much smaller person. Andrea could never distinguish the features in her dreams, but awake, she pictured the small boy in the picture that horrible man had shown her at the motel in Utah.

What was the boy to her? Why did his image evoke such strong emotions within her? And who was the redheaded lady in the picture? Andrea was getting antsy to find out answers to these questions. She'd agreed on this tour because she feared for Esther's health if she refused. Esther had ended up in the hospital once for no apparent reason, and Andrea didn't want to cause her any more stress. Esther had acted like this tour was life or death to their business, so Andrea had felt trapped.

Punching buttons on the TV remote, she switched channels several times, but everything was in Italian, so she turned it off. She'd finished the two novels she'd brought on the trip a week ago, and couldn't find anything that interested her from the limited English selections in the small bookshops at the various bus depots, so she was stuck staring at the ceiling at nights until she fell into an exhausted sleep.

Two months to go. Andrea didn't know if she'd make it. She was ready to scream with boredom and loneliness. She'd heard they had swingin' nightclubs in the area, but she was too tired after her concerts or traveling to go anywhere like that. Besides, that wasn't her scene, and there was the whole going-by-herself issue to deal with. Sometimes she and Greg ate in restaurants, but she mostly took her meals in her room. Some life. The band members bragged about the great times they had at parties, but their bloodshot eyes and haggard looks told Andrea a different story. She wanted no part of that.

So here she sat. *Might as well get ready for bed.*

The phone on the nightstand jangled, and Andrea snatched it up like a canteen found in the middle of the desert.

"Hello," she said anxiously.

"Hello, darling," came Esther's reply. "Is anything wrong?"

"Oh, no, no. Just glad to hear from you." *Glad to hear from anybody.*

"How sweet, dear. How are the concerts going?"

"Fine, fine. Everything's just fine." Andrea couldn't keep the gloom from creeping into her voice.

"There is something wrong, darling. What is it? You can tell mummy."

Mummy, huh? How continental Esther sounded. Andrea thought she was the one in Europe.

"No, really. Everything's fine." Andrea knew she'd get a lecture rather than sympathy from her mother if she told her the truth about how miserable she was. Besides, she didn't want to risk causing Esther undue stress.

"Well, that's wonderful. I knew you'd have a good time, and the ticket sales are phenomenal, so keep up the good work, darling."

"Okay, I will." *Say something, you idiot. Tell her you want to come home.*

"Well, I've gotta run, dear. Your father sends his love. Good-bye." Esther hung up before Andrea said good-bye, so she whispered it to the buzz in the receiver before hanging up.

Maybe she should run away. She'd heard of people backpacking through Europe. Why not her? Why not take off on her own and see the sights? Work at odd jobs here and there if she ran out of money until she'd seen everything she wanted to and had enough to get back to the States.

No. She realized she was already doing the thing she was best qualified for. The thing that she loved. Maybe it was time to stop feeling sorry for herself and enjoy the rest of the tour. Get out and learn the language, meet the people. Make time to see the sights. Yeah, that's what she'd do. How many young women got the chance to sing all over Europe? Why walk away from money and opportunity to sleep in the streets? Did she think that would be less lonely?

No, she'd been going about this whole thing wrong. From now on, she was in charge. She had been the whole time, but she'd let Esther's stage manager push her around, call the shots. Well, no more. She'd enjoy the concerts more, and subsequently do a better job if she enjoyed herself during the day.

Anything to keep her thoughts away from Utah.

Chapter Thirty-three

Matt wiped the sweat from his forehead with the bottom of his T-shirt and looked around at the desolate countryside. He hated Kanab. Hated every spiny shrub, creepy lizard, and blood red rock.

Two days. For two days now he'd traipsed up and down every gully, wash, and ravine within a five-mile radius of the ranch. Skyler was only four. Surely he couldn't have gotten any farther than that on his own. Where was he? For the zillionth time, the question tore at Matt's brain, just like it had a year and a half ago when he'd searched for Skyler's mother.

This country had claimed two people Matt loved. Melody had disappeared here and shown up as a different person, and now Skyler was gone as well. Matt was mad. Mad at the buzzards that circled overhead like pirouetting omens of death, mad at the longhorn cattle that grazed lazily here and there, contradictions to the turmoil that threatened to churn his insides to unidentifiable globs. He was even mad at the fine, red silt that clung to his sweat and coated him with grit.

Enough was enough. Matt looked up at the glaring sun in the endless blue sky and a single word tore from his parched throat: "Why?!"

The only answer was the squawk of a buzzard and an inquisitive moo from one of the cows that looked up briefly, then went back to munching the sparse salt grass.

Matt sank to his knees and buried his face in his arms. Tears flowed as sobs wracked his body. *Not again. Dear God, please not again.*

What was it with this place? Was it some sort of bedeviled, southern Utah version of the Bermuda triangle, bent on claiming everyone near and dear to him? What had he done to deserve this? He'd tried to live a good life. He gave to charities, when he had the money, and he was always good for a buck or two to the bums on the street with their hands out. Why had God taken the only two people on the face of this miserable planet he really cared about?

The hum of an approaching four-wheeler entered his consciousness. The noise stopped, and Matt looked up. His father-in-law sat a discreet distance away. Matt wiped at his eyes and nose with his hands, trying to collect himself, then slowly stood and made his way to where Burt waited on his dirt-caked ATV. Branches of sagebrush stuck out of the wheel wells, evidence of Burt's part in the search.

"Any luck?" Matt knew by Burt's dejected expression that the question was useless even before he asked it, but he had to hang onto a glimmer of hope.

Burt shook his head as his chin dropped to his chest. Matt swore Burt had aged twenty years in the past two days. His thick head of graying hair had turned stark white. Matt knew Burt blamed himself for Skyler's disappearance, and while part of Matt wanted to comfort the grieving old man, another part wanted to take him by the throat and shake him.

"Uh, the rest of us are headin' back to the ranch for a lunch break. You wanna join us?" Burt asked in a hesitating manner, raising his head to look at Matt, but not quite able to meet his eyes.

Matt shook his head. "You know I can't do that."

Burt nodded. "I figured." He turned and opened a saddlebag slung behind him on the seat of the four-wheeler and pulled out a large, brown paper bag. Turning back to Matt, he handed the sack to him. "Carol fixed a little something for you in case you wouldn't come back. There's an extra bottle of water in there, too. Can't be too careful in this heat."

Matt took the bag and nodded his appreciation. With pursed lips, Matt stepped away from the four-wheeler. Burt started the machine. With a final nod at Matt, lips clenched, Burt circled Matt and headed back the way he'd come.

Matt stood still and listened to the engine drone away into silence. Then he took a deep breath and looked at the sky. The smell of junipers tickled his nose. The sun was starting its downhill slide. How many more hours could he keep this up? How many days? How many weeks? A shudder passed through him. What must be going through Skyler's mind? How does a little tyke like that cope with being lost and alone? Matt's vision started to blur at the threat of more tears, so he squeezed his eyes shut, causing rivulets to run down his cheeks, then shook his head. That wasn't going to do Skyler any good. Him neither. This situation required action. No matter how long and arduous. And action required strength, so Matt found a flat rock, then sat down and opened the bag.

His stomach growled at the sight of the two roast beef sandwiches on thick-sliced, homemade bread. Breakfast had been a long time ago. He removed the sandwiches and found an apple, banana, and a huge piece of chocolate cake. The promised bottle of water was also there, and Matt realized how thirsty he was.

He devoured the food but used the water sparingly. It was still several hours before sunset. Flies buzzed around and tried to share his picnic, and in an amazingly short amount of time, a column of ants had been organized to carry away any crumbs he dropped. The buzzards must have sensed a delay to their dinner plans, because they were no longer in sight.

Matt sat still for several moments after he finished his meal, arms resting on his knees, right hand clasping his left wrist. He needed a better plan. This endless walking was getting him nowhere. Burt had offered to let him take a four-wheeler, or even a horse, but Matt had been afraid he'd miss something that way. Even the tiniest clue as to where his son had gone was too important to risk passing by, so he'd walked, and walked, and walked.

Fatigue and hopelessness settled on him. There had to be a better way. Someone, somewhere must know where Skyler was.

The only one Matt could think of was God, so he raised his voice and prayed aloud. "Dear Lord above. You are the God of all creation. My wife said You number even the sparrows and the very hairs of our heads. Surely You must know where my son is. I can't do this on my own. I've looked everywhere I can think of, as has half the county. Lord, we need Your help. I need Your help. And it's sure as shootin' that Skyler needs Your help. Comfort him, Lord. Let him know his papa's on his way. Then show me where the he . . . where the heck that way is, 'cause I sure ain't findin' it on my own. Amen."

When he finished, Matt stuffed the empty sack under the rock he'd been sitting on, grabbed the water bottle off the rock next to him, and started walking. He didn't know where he was going, but his footsteps felt more sure. "I'm coming, Skyler!" he shouted.

A flash of red caught his eye. A cardinal was perched on a sagebrush a few yards ahead of him. Maybe it was a sign. Maybe God had heard him.

The cardinal sat motionless, watching Matt's approach. When Matt was close enough to reach out and touch it, it flew twenty yards away and alighted on a fallen cedar tree, then turned to watch him again. A shiver passed through Matt. He'd been half joking about the sign thing, but now he wasn't so sure. Was God really trying to tell him something? Well, whether He was or not, Matt had no better plan, so he might as well follow the dumb bird.

Matt scratched his head, then swiped his forehead with his arm and took a sip of water from the bottle he carried. Replacing the lid on his precious store, he stepped over a cactus and walked in the direction of the cardinal. Again, it sat perfectly still until Matt was within arm's length, then took flight, but didn't go far. This was eerie.

Matt repeated the ritual of following the cardinal until the sun sat low in the sky. He stopped and studied the landscape in the direction it led. The brush seemed to get thicker for a ways, then disappeared altogether. Must be another ravine.

This area didn't look familiar. Matt thought he'd covered every square inch of territory, if not during this search, then certainly when he'd looked for Melody. But glancing around now, he knew he was somewhere he hadn't been before. Big boulders were strewn about and he had to pick his way carefully to keep from twisting an ankle as he started toward the bright red bird.

Twice more the cardinal landed, then flew away and disappeared as Matt found himself on the edge of a deep, rugged ravine with steep, sharp sides. Tangled brush, trees, and debris were piled high at the bottom where the gully took a sharp turn, but the sides were wiped clean of anything but new growth for as far as Matt could see. A flash flood had been through here, but it had been some time ago.

Matt glanced at his watch. He only had a couple hours of daylight at best, and he wasn't exactly sure where he was. Why had that darn bird led him here? Or maybe it had just been his imagination that it was leading him anywhere. What a fool he was, caught up in some childhood fantasy about signs from God. Now he'd be hard-pressed to get back to the ranch before dark.

No way had Skyler wandered clear out here, over all these rocks, cactus, and sagebrush. And he sure couldn't have gotten past this ravine. Matt turned away in disgust. Then a thought froze him mid-stride and turned his blood to frost. No, Skyler couldn't have made it *past* the ravine.

Matt spun back and studied the sides and bottom of the ravine more carefully. Nothing. The red dirt that clung to the rocks of the steep slope hadn't been disturbed by anything bigger than a lizard for a long time.

Matt walked along the edge of the gulf, studying the slope as he went. Not watching where he was going, he stumbled on a rock and nearly slipped off the edge. He sat down hard and the water bottle flew from his hand. He caught it on the way down.

"Whoa. I'm gonna have to be more careful," he mumbled to himself, shaken as he watched the cavalcade of dirt and rocks careen down the gully and land in the pile of debris.

One large rock landed with a metallic thud. Matt's breath caught in his throat. The whine of mosquitoes in his ears was suddenly silenced. The air was still as Matt contemplated what this meant. A hunk of dirt broke away from where the rock had landed, and Matt saw a patch of red that was deeper and brighter than the mud surrounding it. He willed himself to breathe. It could be anything. Someone's old tractor.

Before he thought about what he was doing, Matt propelled himself to the bottom of the ravine, sliding on the seat of his pants, bringing another onslaught of rocks and dirt. His hands and arms were gouged and scraped as he fought to keep from tumbling headlong, the water bottle forgotten. His lungs and nostrils filled with red dirt, as did his eyes and mouth.

A cry of pain escaped his gritty throat as he tore through stickery tumbleweeds and collided with the metal object. Dirt and rocks continued to pour down on top of him, pelting his back and filling his pants while he bent forward and shielded his head with his arms.

At last, all was still, and Matt lowered his arms and shook his head, causing another cloud of dust. He coughed and spit, trying to clear his throat and mouth. His eyes felt like sand. And that was just his head. He was folded up like a Chinese fan, but at least his feet had hit first, so his legs had cushioned the blow.

What a stupid thing to do. What if he'd seriously injured himself out here in the middle of nowhere? He didn't know where he was, so it was a sure bet no one else did, either. Another victim of the "Kanab Triangle." What good was he to Skyler then?

Pushing with his feet, he tried to straighten his legs. A stab of pain shot through his left knee, reminding him of an old football injury from high school. *What an idiot.*

He rolled to his side and had to stick his hand in the thorny bushes to help himself to his feet. His hands were already thrashed, so what were a few more stickers? The dirt down his pants was the most annoying thing. He tried unzipping them and shaking what he could out, but most of it went down his legs, into his boots.

He looked around for a sticker-free place to sit down again so he could take his boots off, but stopped when his eyes rested on the object of his foolhardy plunge. It was no tractor. More dirt had been knocked off by his collision, and Matt now tore at the remaining debris and caked-on mud, heaving it to the side in a frantic dig that made his fingernails match the palms of his hands.

When he finished, he stood back, panting. Cold chills washed over his body as he stared at the remains of a Jeep. A red Jeep.

Chapter Thirty-four

Andrea wandered around the small tables in the dimly lit room, microphone in her left hand, leaving the fingers of her right hand free to run through the hair of various males seated throughout the club. Playing to smaller crowds was more her style. It gave her a chance to mingle with the audience, look into their eyes, and see what they thought of her. The faces turned toward her tonight might have belonged to any from the good ole' USA, but they didn't. Berlin was a long way from home. Her German was limited to asking for bottled water and directions to the bathroom, so she didn't understand the comments directed at her, but judging from the wolfish expressions and gleams in the eyes that gazed on her hungrily, she decided that was a good thing. The women's eyes she avoided, as most of them were filled with venom.

Andrea wasn't sure why she was playing this game, flirting with the men, exuding sexuality she hadn't known she possessed. Loneliness maybe. Or perhaps she was tired of grasping at shadows, hanging her hopes on the wisp of a man who had no more substance than the smoke that filled the air, burning her eyes, making her take shallow breaths to avoid choking out the words to the songs.

Esther had extended the tour four more months, and somewhere between Italy and Germany, Andrea had entered a trance-like state, performing each night like a trained dog. Her determination to enjoy herself and see the sights had ended the day after she'd made that decision. While walking down a quaint, cobblestone street, she'd been mugged. A gang of street thugs had slithered out of an alley, grabbed her purse, and tossed it to a dirty little kid, no more than nine or ten years old, who'd disappeared back into the alley. Then five older teenagers with tousled dark hair, glaring dark eyes, and even darker looks on their smudged faces had shoved her back and forth between them like a pin ball, making comments in Italian which she hadn't understood. She'd recognized the leers and mirthless laughter, however, and when one of them grabbed the front of her shirt and tried to rip it open, she'd kneed him hard in the groin. That one doubled over in pain, but the others had pounced, slugged her in the face, knocked her to the ground, and then pummeled her with kicks. Fear had constricted her chest and clenched her guts as she'd curled into a tiny, helpless ball and tried to protect her head and face with her arms.

She'd silently prayed over and over that Greg would find her. Remorse for ditching him and the thoughts of how proud she'd been that she'd managed to do so had caused the knot in her stomach to pitch and roll. All she'd wanted was to soak up the atmosphere of the small Italian town without the hulking presence of her bodyguard, which made the locals eye her suspiciously, or avoid her altogether, clearing a wide swath as she walked down the street.

How she wished she'd avoided those street rats. Good thing Greg hadn't given up looking for her. One look at him bearing down on them and the thieves had bolted. Thank goodness he'd shown up when he did, or who knows what would have happened? Thick makeup at her next few concerts had covered the cuts and bruises on her face, but she'd had a difficult time masking the stiffness of her movements from the aches and pains all over her body. Those shows had been performed strictly from the stage.

Andrea sighed as the song came to an end. Her hand still

rested on the blond head of a man in his mid-twenties, seated at a bistro table with two buddies. Empty beer bottles covered the small table. All three wore business suits, but their ties were loosened and their white collars gaped open.

The blue eyes of the one she stood next to gazed at her in adoration, then took on a mischievous glint as his hand left his lap to slide up the satiny smoothness of her black evening gown and clasp the firm roundness of her rear-end. Andrea gasped and jumped back, wagging her finger at the young man. All three men roared with laughter. Bottles clinked and wobbled precariously as they reared back in their chairs, kicking the table in the process.

Andrea made her way back to the safety of the stage as the intro to the last song began. *Dumb, dumb, dumb.* What did she expect? You play with fire . . .

Her mouth moved, and words to the song came out as she glanced back at the table she'd just left. The men had stopped laughing but still wore huge grins on their faces. Andrea felt her face heat up, but her thoughts shocked her. Not that she wanted to be groped at in nightclubs, but the physical contact had awakened something in her. That's what she craved, alone in her hotel night after night. That's why she played these games, tempting fate.

She had to get out of here. Somewhere in her gut, she knew this wasn't the kind of place to meet the man of her dreams. Offers of sex were plentiful, but that wasn't what she was about.

Images of dark, curly hair and brown eyes swam to the front of her thoughts once again, blocking out the blond-haired, blue-eyed leer. No matter where she went, or how many men's faces she stared into, this one always surfaced to the forefront.

The song crescendoed, and Andrea sang it with a passion and verve she hadn't felt in some time. Anger, actually. At her mother. Andrea had been on a quest to find her past, and felt like she'd been getting close, before Esther had reeled her back in like a kite on a string.

The clank of glass and usual hubbub of conversation had ceased. Even the waitresses in their skimpy tops and short skirts had paused momentarily in their scurrying about, trays poised in the air as Andrea finished her song. The applause was louder and more prolonged, and without the usual catcalls.

Andrea bowed, then stared out into the smoky dimness. Her eyes burned. Her lungs burned. And something else had started a slow burn deep inside her.

"Thank you, and good night." She blew kisses at the crowd and heard the normal noises resume as she nodded at the band, walked off the back of the stage, passed Greg without a glance, and headed to her dressing room.

Was Esther hiding something from her? What did she really know? The illness, the hospital, had that been a ruse? Some sort of elaborate trick to get Andrea back within her clutches?

A stab of guilt shot through Andrea at these thoughts. This was her mother. The giver of life, the maker of her career. The keeper of her prison?

Why didn't she feel more for this woman? Ever since Esther had sat by her bedside in the hospital after the accident and told Andrea about her life, Andrea had delved deep, trying to come up with the immense love she imagined a daughter should feel toward her mother. Regardless of the fact she'd lost her memory, wouldn't she still love her mother? Didn't feelings and emotions supercede memory? Try as she might, most often all she felt was annoyance and resentment. These emotions were always followed by guilt. What kind of a sick woman was she that she was incapable of loving her own mother?

Andrea pushed through the door of her dressing room and slammed it shut behind her, then leaned her back against it and closed her eyes, taking deep breaths of the slightly cleaner air.

Her eyes opened and she stared at the tiny room. Her jeans were draped over the only chair, which sat in front of a small vanity that was cluttered with her makeup, hairbrush, and curling iron. Her whole life seemed to consist of tiny packages. Tiny dressing rooms, tiny hotel rooms, tiny bars with tiny people living out their tiny lives. There had to be more. The only thing that wasn't tiny was Esther's ambition and the grip she had on

Andrea's life. Her whole existence was clenched in Esther's fist.

Something had to give. Andrea pushed away from the door and walked over to stand in front of the little vanity mirror. A turquoise-eyed beauty with honey-blonde hair looked back at her. Not a shriveled little woman with black hair and dark, beady eyes.

"Sorry, Mother, but you're just going to have to live your own life." Determination shone from the turquoise depths.

Andrea recovered her purse from beneath the vanity and fished out her cell phone. She punched in the number of Kevin's hotel room. He was the tour manager, yet he never bothered to come to the concerts. He preferred to remain in his hotel rooms, and he was not often alone. Where had Esther dug him up?

The phone rang and rang, as Andrea knew it would, but she wasn't about to give up. She had to get this over with before she lost her nerve.

Finally, an angry voice answered, "Hello."

"Kevin, this is Andrea. Cancel the rest of the tour."

"What?" That got his attention.

"You heard me. I'm going home. I don't care what you have to do." Andrea's words were full of bravado, but she cringed and held the phone away from her ear as she awaited his reply. She needn't have bothered, because his words were deathly quiet.

"Does your mother know?" came the snakish lisp from the other end of the line.

"What?" She knew what he'd said, but she stalled for time.

"I said, does your mother know?" An even more deadly tone.

Andrea paused, still not sure how to answer. Then she caught a glimpse of her reflection again, and her spine straightened.

"No." What did she have to fear from this slimy little man? *He* was Esther's lackey, not her.

"I see," he hissed. Andrea pictured a forked tongue slipping in and out between thin lips.

"Anyway, I'm leaving tonight, so call the airport and arrange for the next flight out of here, then send a car by my hotel. I can be ready in half an hour." Andrea had barely spoken to Kevin on this entire tour, and never to give orders. What would he say?

Nothing, for what seemed a day, but was only a few seconds.

"I'm afraid I can't do that. Not without clearing it with Esther." The sound came through clenched teeth, and she imagined the muscles working along his narrow jaw. "This is her baby, and I can't very well just drop this bomb on her without losing my job, and possibly my life." His attempt at a snicker after this came out as a snort.

Andrea was silent as she thought about how to reply. Unzipping her dress, she climbed out of her gown and set the phone down while she changed into her jeans and a T-shirt. Let him wait. He wouldn't dare hang up on her.

No doubt what Esther's response would be. Cutting the tour short was not a consideration. She'd only recently extended it, despite Andrea's vehement arguments, begging, and pleading to the contrary. "It'll be good for you, darling. You'll love it. Look at all the exposure you'll get, not to mention the publicity for Starstream. You know how much we need you." Guilt was always her tool of choice to get Andrea's cooperation.

Andrea picked the phone up again as she brushed her hair.

"Call Esther if you want, Kevin. But one way or the other, I'm leaving. Tonight. Now, are you going to call the airlines or do I have to?" Kevin always made the travel arrangements, but Andrea was sure she'd manage. The cogs clicked in Kevin's mind, she was sure, as he considered his options. The interruption to whatever it was he that was doing was probably his biggest source of annoyance. Andrea felt he couldn't care less about her or the tour. But Esther . . . she was his bread and butter. He'd want to please her at all costs.

"Just give me ten minutes while I find out what Esther has to say. I'll ring you right back on your cell phone."

"Fine," Andrea said, and hung up before Kevin said anything else. Now what? She knew she'd stirred up trouble. Would Kevin try to stop her from leaving? Well, there was little doubt of that, but what methods would he employ? How low would he stoop? Maybe she should have waited to call him from the States. Naw, she was booked solid for the next four months. He'd need to cancel right away to allow people time to find replacement acts. Andrea felt bad about that, but not bad enough to stick it out. Alternative entertainment always lurked in the wings. Trouble was, Kevin would probably waste his time buttering up to Esther and not bother to call and cancel. Too bad. That was his funeral. He was the tour manager. Andrea had done her part in notifying him. She was beyond caring about what damage it did to her career.

But, how to get out of there? Andrea needed an ally. Striding to her dressing room door, she swung it open to find Greg outside, as always.

"Could you come in here for a moment, please?" Andrea stepped back from the door and held it open expectantly. Greg's face registered open shock, but he stepped into the confines of the small room.

Andrea turned her back to him as she gathered her things and stuffed them into a bag. "I'm leaving," she told him. "Tonight." She straightened and looked at him to gauge his reaction to this news. Concern washed over his face.

"Is there a problem, Miss Kensington?" His eyes darted from her face to a spot just above her head. His fists clenched and unclenched by his sides as he stood practically at attention.

"No, no, I'm fine. Just tired. I want to go home. Will you help me?"

Greg allowed his eyes to rest on her face. She saw the warmth in his tawny eyes, but worry also flickered there. "Yes, ma'am," was all he said, although his mouth opened and shut like he wanted to say more.

"Good." Andrea didn't press him. "I called Kevin to arrange a flight, but he wanted to talk to my mother first." She peered at him intently. "Are you afraid of my mother, Greg?"

He shifted his weight from one foot to the other and stared at some spot above her. "N . . . no, ma'am," he stuttered, then looked at her again. "But . . . if I help you do something she doesn't like, I will lose my job." His eyes pleaded with her.

"Well," she began, wondering how best to phrase this. She couldn't afford to lose him to Esther, too. "Your job is to guard me, right?"

"Yes, ma'am." His tone was wary.

"So, that means you should stay with me at all times, right?"

"Yes, ma'am." His eyes darted between her face and the spot above her head.

"So, if I leave, and you stay with me, aren't you still doing your job?" She smiled sweetly and resorted to eye-batting again.

A smile crept onto his face and a twinkle appeared in his eyes as he looked directly at her. "Yes, ma'am."

Andrea had her ally. Now she needed a plan.

Chapter Thirty-five

Andrea's heels clicked on the tile of the airport terminal as she hurried to catch her flight. Greg lumbered behind her like a mama bear guarding her cub. A woman's voice came over the loudspeaker frequently, announcing different flights, repeating the information in several languages. Andrea listened only long enough to determine if her flight was being mentioned. Other people were mere objects that Andrea passed without seeing. Her attention was focused on one thing—catching her plane home. Once they'd cleared security, she was like a racehorse headed for the stable.

Andrea's escape from the club had been relatively uneventful. The band had been leaving their dressing room as she'd exited hers, so she'd informed them of her plans and apologized for cutting the tour short. A few growls and scowls had been directed at her by the drummer, Scott, who was single and had no other life, but the others seemed relieved to be able to return home.

Kevin had caught up with her at her hotel room and laid the guilt on thick in an effort to make her stay. Andrea had ignored his remarks, so he'd resorted to nasty references about her character, which had earned him Greg's beefy hand around his throat as he'd shoved him against a wall. In the end, Kevin had slunk away, muttering under his breath and rubbing his neck.

Now Andrea was fifteen minutes from boarding a plane

for home. The only seats available had been first class and had cost a fortune, but her credit card had covered the fare. She'd half expected Esther to have cancelled her credit cards already. Paranoia was setting in. She'd seen too many late night movies, alone in hotel rooms.

Andrea and Greg reached their gate. Boarding hadn't started yet, so after they checked in at the desk, Andrea collapsed in a chair next to an old lady whose hands rested on a cane in front of her while her head sagged to her chest. Her deep, rattled breathing and occasional snorts indicated that she'd found a way to pass the time while waiting for the flight. As late as it was, however, Andrea was too wired to sleep. Greg stood behind her. Andrea glanced at him over her shoulder. His hands were clasped in front, and his eyes darted around like he expected someone to sneak up and snatch her. While she found it amusing, she was comforted by his presence. She hadn't been gung-ho to venture out on her own since her experience in Italy. A chill passed over her whenever she thought about it. Now, with this bold gesture, she felt like she'd escaped prison. Her nerves were stretched to the breaking point.

Her cell phone jangled and she jumped. She'd put it in the pocket of her jacket to keep it handy, but now that it rang, she didn't want to answer it. Only two people had her number: Kevin and her mother. She didn't wish to speak to either of them now. Or ever, in Kevin's case. She'd have to deal with her mother eventually.

The phone continued to ring while Andrea debated with herself. It stopped for a moment, her voice mail picked up, and then it started again. Must be her mother. Kevin didn't care enough to persist. He'd make up some lame excuse to Esther why he'd been unable to reach Andrea before she left. Esther, however, was no doubt furious at Andrea's escape. Andrea was amazed it took her this long to call. Then she remembered she'd turned her phone off until they'd passed security. What had possessed her to turn it back on? Some sick, innate sense of responsibility. If only she could tell Esther to go away and not care how that made her feel. But Andrea knew that she'd eventually have to smooth it over, get Esther to understand her point of view, and make amends.

The loudspeaker blatted over the sound of Andrea's ringing phone. They'd started to board first class. That was it, then. No time to get into a big argument now. Andrea pulled her phone out of her pocket and switched it off. Esther was an ocean away. Andrea hoped that was enough time to figure out what to say.

Chapter Thirty-six

Matt glanced at the pinkening sky and then at his torn-up hands and filthy clothes. How was he going to get out of this mess? The last thing he needed was to add his name to the list of missing persons in the Kanab Triangle. Maybe that was the fate of his family. Maybe there was a rabbit hole somewhere that they all fell into and emerged from in another life. Melody sure seemed to have. Now Skyler. He only hoped Skyler was as well and happy as Melody seemed to be when he'd seen her in Vegas. He had to get to her somehow and remind her of her past and her love for him. But not until he'd found her son. Remembering her past would be like a knife wound to the chest if her son was gone.

Matt was running out of options. And now he was stuck in the bottom of a ravine in the middle of the desert with night coming on. As warm as the day had been, he knew the night would be chilly. He had no jacket, no water, no shelter. What must Skyler be feeling if Matt was worried and he was a grown man? Matt only hoped Skyler could still feel at all. As much as it tore at his heart to think of him wandering lost, scared, and alone, the image of him lying still and lifeless was far worse. He had to get to him. He had to know. But what next?

Matt thought of the stupid bird he'd followed all afternoon, only to land in the bottom of a ravine. Sure, he'd found Melody's Jeep. But that was just one of the many puzzle pieces he'd have to deal with later. He already knew she was alive and well, even though she couldn't remember him. What he needed now was to find Skyler. And fast. If he didn't, Matt didn't think he wanted to survive.

Matt glanced around to see if, by some miracle, his water bottle had landed anywhere in the vicinity. No sight of it, but what he did see made his blood run cold, while sending a flash of hope at the same time. A small piece of cloth was stuck to a sticker bush behind the Jeep. Matt had landed on the hood when he'd plummeted down the side of the ravine, and had cleared away the debris enough to identify it as Melody's Jeep. Now he made his way slowly to the back, picking his way over rocks, brush, and debris.

Matt tried to imagine how the Jeep had ended up there. Had Melody been in it when it went over the edge? If so, how did she survive the fall? And how did she escape? Another chilling thought caused a deep crease in his brow. Maybe she'd pushed it over the edge on purpose. Maybe she'd wanted to disappear. Was her life as his wife and Skyler's mother so stifling that she'd thought that was her only way out? Was she that desperate to pursue a singing career?

Matt shook his head to clear these thoughts. He'd been down this road, and it only led to anger and heartache. Georgette had told him Melody had lost her memory and was living in California with an old man and woman who claimed to be her parents. How that had come about was something he couldn't begin to fathom. Had Melody duped them somehow into taking her in? No, that couldn't be right. That just wasn't her. So what had happened?

Matt was shaken from his thoughts by a rattling sound that made him freeze instantly, his right foot poised in the air to step over a log. He knew that sound too well from his experiences in the Utah deserts. He peered over the edge of the tree trunk he'd been about to cross and saw an enormous rattlesnake, its tail shaking furiously. Matt would have stepped on it if the diamondback hadn't awakened from its nap in time to issue a warning.

Beads of sweat formed on Matt's face, despite the coolness of the evening air. His leg began to ache from holding it aloft, but he didn't dare move. What was he going to do? The rocks in his left boot dug into his foot. In his frenzy to uncover the Jeep, he'd forgotten about emptying the rocks and dirt from his boots. Now he was paying for it, as he performed a deadly balancing act. He gritted his teeth against the pain.

The snake showed no signs of moving, but the angry rattle continued. Slowly, he moved his right leg back, praying his balance would hold and he wouldn't tumble sideways, causing the snake to strike. Sweat meandered down the dust on his face. A mosquito whined in his ear. Dust clogged his nose, making him take shallow, imperceptible breaths through his arid mouth. His tongue was like a thick piece of felt.

His foot had almost reached the ground behind him when a shot rang out. Matt jumped like he'd been jabbed with a branding iron and fell backward. He heard more shots as he scrambled away from the log and behind a big rock as fast as his numb legs and scratched hands would let him.

The firing ceased. Matt patted himself down to make sure there were no extra holes, then peaked out from behind the rock toward the snake. It resembled a pile of stew meat. Matt looked up at the edge of the ravine. Three of Burt's ranch hands sat atop horses, waving their rifles and grinning at him like they'd won first prize at the County Fair.

Despite the pain in Matt's hands and legs, and the pounding of his heart, which had slowed to a mere gallop after taking off like a runaway racehorse when the shooting began, he grinned and waved back. The cavalry had arrived.

Chapter Thirty-seven

Matt's heart stuck in his throat when the cowboys plunged their horses over the edge of the ravine. After clearing the first few feet of sheer drop, the horses half slid on their haunches and hopped on their front legs down the remainder of the slope. Matt was reminded of the old movie *Man From Snowy River* as the three hands flattened themselves backward on their mustangs to make the harrowing descent in a cloud of dust and rocks.

They made it to the bottom intact, and Matt let out the breath he'd been holding. His legs still shook and his heart pounded as he pulled off each boot and emptied a shower of debris. Donning his boots quickly, he pushed himself off the sticker bush he'd been seated on and stood up. *Much better without the rocks. No time to do the pants, though. Have to get to that piece of cloth.* He hurried to the back of the Jeep where he'd spotted the cloth snagged on a bush. *Skyler. Burt said he was wearing a shirt of this stuff when he disappeared.*

Matt studied the Jeep, amazed it was right-side-up after what had to have been a mad careen down the wash in the wake of a flood. A strange thought hit him, and he moved closer to the Jeep, clearing away dirt and debris as he went. His heart started thumping hard and he wasn't sure why. As he got close enough to peer into the back seat, his heart stopped altogether. Skyler was curled up on the thick layer of dried mud in a pathetic heap.

An involuntary cry escaped Matt's throat as he vaulted over the back of the Jeep and landed next to his son. Matt couldn't tell if Skyler was breathing as he reached for the mass of curls caked with dirt and dried sweat and gently brushed them away from his face. Skyler's eyes were closed, his face the color of gauze except for angry red scratches on his cheeks and forehead, but he was warm to the touch.

The thought flashed through Matt's mind that he shouldn't move him. Wasn't that what was taught about an injured person? But he quickly dismissed it. Skyler hadn't been in the Jeep when it crashed; he'd somehow found it and climbed in himself. Besides, Matt's arms ached to hold his son, and the relief at finding him was so great that his chest felt ready to explode.

Matt maneuvered his own bulk in the cramped confines of the Jeep until he slid one arm under Skyler's neck and the other under his knees and gently lifted him. He put his ear to Skyler's chest and heard the faint thump of his heart. Matt's spirits soared. He buried his face in Skyler's neck and hugged him tightly as he rocked back and forth, thanking God he'd found his son alive.

The sound of a horse snorting made him open his eyes and lift his head. The three ranch-hands sat atop their mounts surrounding the Jeep, tears watering their cheeks.

"Is he . . ." the big, burly one named Ethan couldn't finish the sentence as he peered at Matt, anguish etching deeper lines in his already weather-beaten face.

"He's alive!" Matt managed to choke out.

All three men let out a war whoop that echoed down the ravine. Ethan grabbed his pistol from its holster and fired three shots in the air. Matt remembered that was the signal for finding a missing person in the wilds. Lon, the wiry one, jumped off his horse and tossed the reins to Jimmy, the youngest of the group. He untied his canteen and scrambled over a pile of rocks to offer his assistance.

Skyler didn't stir, and Matt was smacked with the urgency of their situation. They were miles from the ranch, and another sixty miles from the nearest hospital, in Kanab. Skyler was alive, but for how long? The horrors of what he must have gone through the past two days ricocheted through Matt's mind, but he pushed the thoughts away and concentrated on the here and now and what had to be done to save his son.

Matt laid Skyler on his lap while he gave him a cursory examination. He felt up and down his arms and legs. No broken bones. He lifted his torn, dirty shirt. Some scratches and bruises, but nothing serious to the naked eye. Skyler's lips were cracked and dry. Matt put his cheek next to Skyler's mouth and felt his faint, warm breath. He looked at Lon, who immediately handed him the canteen.

"How about a handkerchief?" Matt asked him, and Lon quickly untied the one around his neck and handed it over, also.

Matt unscrewed the lid on the canteen and wet a corner of the handkerchief then gently touched it to Skyler's lips, squeezing a few drops into his mouth. His tongue made a sucking motion like when he was a baby and sucked phantom bottles in his sleep, but he didn't wake up. Matt filled the canteen lid with water and trickled it into Skyler's mouth slowly so he wouldn't choke, then wet the handkerchief again and dabbed at the scratches on Skyler's face. They were superficial. After another drink of water, which Skyler sucked down, Matt washed his face with the handkerchief, then handed it back to Lon. He took a long swig from the canteen himself before handing that back.

"We need to get going," he told the guys as he scooped Skyler into his arms and pressed him to his chest. Skyler's head was snug against Matt's shoulder, supported by his right hand. Matt had a difficult time struggling to his feet and negotiating the debris as he jumped off the side of the Jeep, but he refused offers of help from the cowhands. He wasn't letting go of Skyler now that he finally had him back in his arms.

Lon offered to ride on back of Jimmy's horse and gave Matt his to ride. Mounting would have been considerably easier if he'd let Lon hold Skyler, but instead, Lon gave him a push from behind and Matt managed to get in the saddle with the use of one arm. He grimaced. Gravity had taken care of some of the dirt and rocks in his pants, but enough still remained to make him realize his rear end was going to resemble his hands by the end of the ride. But daylight was slipping, and his boy needed help. He'd just have to "cowboy up," as the guys liked to say.

Besides, studying the sides of the ravine, Matt knew he had another problem. No way was he going up the way they'd come. It was a physical impossibility. Especially with Skyler in his arms. Ethan rode up beside him and followed his gaze.

"Don't worry, boss. Me and the boys saw another place up yonder where we can climb out." Ethan gestured up the wash with his arm as he said this. Relief washed over Matt.

"Good," he nodded. "Let's go then."

Ethan smiled and reined his horse in the direction he'd indicated. Matt followed, and the others fell in behind. Ethan turned in his saddle.

"Those shots should have brung some help. I'm guessin' we won't have to ride too far before someone shows up with a truck." Another wave of relief flooded Matt.

"By the way, guys, I never thanked you for saving my skin back there with the rattlesnake." Matt spoke loudly so they could all hear.

Ethan grinned at him. "Our pleasure, boss," he said.

Matt wasn't Ethan's boss, but he'd noticed Ethan called everyone that. Matt suspected it was so Ethan wouldn't have to remember names, but people would still feel like he knew who they were.

"And guys," Matt paused to swallow the lump in his throat, his eyes moist. "Thanks for being here. I don't know how we'd have made it without you."

Nobody spoke or moved other than to sway back and forth with the movement of the horses.

Ethan cleared his throat, and Matt noticed there was a catch in his voice when he spoke.

"Jimmy, you boys come on up and take the point. I'm gonna ride on ahead and see if I can't hurry that truck up." He nodded at Matt, blinking back tears, then spurred his horse to a trot as

Jimmy and Lon passed Matt to take the lead. They smiled as they passed, but they were blinking back tears, too. Some tough guys.

The first stars appeared in the wide, maroon brushstrokes on the horizon that could be glimpsed in the gash made by the ravine. Crickets chirped and mosquitoes buzzed. The horses kicked up puffs of dust that tickled Matt's nose, and their shod hooves clicked on the rocks in a steady rhythm. He'd have liked to be galloping headlong in a flight for Skyler's life, but a broken leg on one of the horses could prove disastrous.

Matt looked at Skyler, cradled in his arm. Maybe it was the pink glow of the sky, but he imagined he saw a little more color in his son's cheeks. Glancing ahead, Lon and Jimmy were becoming a black outline in the gathering darkness. Matt's heart filled with gratitude for these tender-hearted, sunbaked, weather-roughened cowboys. Lon and Ethan had been with Burt and Carol as long as Matt could remember, and Jimmy almost that long. Three more loyal employees didn't exist. They'd come to Matt's rescue when he needed them most.

A warm feeling washed over Matt, and some of the anxiousness he felt for Skyler ebbed. Surely the Lord wouldn't have allowed him to find Skyler only to take him away now. A flutter of movement to his right caught Matt's eye, and he turned to see a bird perched on a sagebrush at the edge of the ravine. The cardinal. The sign. God had known where Skyler was. Matt'd just had to ask.

Chapter Thirty-eight

Matt sat next to Skyler's hospital bed and clutched the tiny hand that wasn't hooked up to an IV. His bowed head rested on the thumbs of his clasped hands. He hadn't slept for three days as he kept a constant vigil on his boy.

The horseback ride from the ravine had been harrowing, but luckily short-lived as Ethan met a truck from the ranch and led it back to them shortly after they'd climbed out of the wash. Matt had happily given Lon's horse back to him and climbed in the truck with Skyler. Burt had been the driver. Tears streamed down his face when he saw Skyler clutched in Matt's arms. He hadn't been able to choke out a word. Matt had assured him Skyler was alive, but they needed to hurry. He'd wondered at the wisdom of that statement as Burt peeled off into the darkness, spraying rocks and dirt as he'd crashed over sagebrush, narrowly missed jackrabbits, and eventually pulled onto a set of tire tracks that roughly passed for a road. Matt had clutched Skyler to him and bounced up and down on the seat, hitting his head on the ceiling a few times, but he hadn't complained, even when he'd felt rocks grinding further into his backside than they had on the horseback ride.

Again, he mumbled thanks to God that Ethan, Lon, and Jimmy had shown up when they had. Matt figured he'd have either died of snakebite or thirst, or wandered in the desert and watched his son's life ebb away if they hadn't found him. He certainly wouldn't have gotten Skyler back to civilization in time to get the medical help he needed. As it was, they'd lifeflighted him to Primary Children's Medical Center in Salt Lake City.

And that's where Matt had set up camp. The nurses had taken one look at him and put a cot next to Skyler's bed. They'd barely been able to keep him back far enough in the emergency room to get the team of doctors around Skyler to work their magic.

Skyler was badly dehydrated, and Dr. Olsen, the physician assigned to him, told Matt that he wouldn't have lasted more than a few hours longer. Other than that, everything seemed to be intact, but he still hadn't awakened, and that fact had everyone concerned. Matt had dozed in the chair next to Skyler's bed a couple of times, but the cot remained unused. Every little noise brought him bolt upright in the chair, eyes riveted on Skyler's face, but the fan of dark lashes always remained in place, resting softly on Skyler's cheeks. Matt was glad to see the color back in Skyler's face, but he wished more than anything to again gaze into the bright green of Skyler's eyes.

The door opened, and a perky little nurse walked in. "Time to check his vitals," she told Matt when he looked up.

"It's always something, isn't it?" he replied.

Her laugh tinkled through the heavy air. "Yes, sir." Her eyes lingered on Matt longer than necessary. He shifted in his seat and cleared his throat as he tenderly laid Skyler's hand back on the bed.

"Well, then," her voice trembled a bit, and she fumbled with the chart on the end of Skyler's bed. She finally managed to get it off the hook and walked over to read the numbers on the machines that constantly beeped and whirred on the other side of Skyler's bed. A blood pressure cuff encircled his arm and puffed up every now and again, squeezing his arm, then deflating. His temperature was monitored by a clip on one of his fingers. The nurse made notes of his vital statistics.

"My name's Camie," the petite blonde informed Matt as she replaced the chart at the end of the bed. "I'll be on duty all night." The tremor was gone from her voice, and it now sounded more like a purr. Matt stared at the floor. He didn't have the strength for this.

Matt heard Camie move again and glanced up to see her checking Skyler's IV. She changed the bag and adjusted the lever on the hose. She looked at Matt again, and his eyes shot back to the floor.

"Can I get you anything?" Was that annoyance or desperation Matt detected now? He shook his head but didn't look up. The beeping machines blared in the silence that followed. Matt held his breath for a moment or two before he finally heard retreating footsteps and the door open and close. When he looked up, he was alone with Skyler again.

What had been with her? Matt must be ten years older and look like he'd been in a desert sandstorm. Were the women around here that hard-up, or was abject anxiety appealing?

A movement from the bed jerked Matt from his musings. Skyler's hand twitched, and Matt's heart did a back flip. He leapt from his chair, snatched Skyler's pudgy fist, and cradled it in his rough mitts.

"Skyler . . . Skyler, can you hear me, son? Daddy's here, sport. Come on, champ, open your eyes. Open your eyes and look at Daddy. Let me see you, big guy . . ." He let the words trail off and held his breath as he studied Skyler's face. Skyler's eyelids moved. Then, like great pearly gates opening to heaven, they slowly lifted. Matt let out a cry of joy and bent down to envelop Skyler in his arms as his tears washed his cheeks.

"Oh, son. I love you so much," he whispered in his ear. "Daddy's been so worried about you." He raised his head to drink in the glow of the shining green orbs now looking at him with pure innocence.

"I'm hungry." Skyler's voice was cracked, but it was the sweetest sound Matt had ever heard. He laughed out loud.

"Okay, big guy. I'll see if I can rustle you up some grub." Matt wiped his face with the back of his hand as he reached for the nurse's buzzer and pushed it, his eyes never leaving Skyler's face.

"Why are you crying, Daddy?" Skyler asked in a scratchy tone. Matt reached for a water cup on the side table by the bed and held it to Skyler's lips as he lifted his head with the other hand.

"Just a sip, now, sport. You can't have too much yet. You've been very sick."

Camie burst through the door. "What's the matter?" Rushing to the side of the bed, she snatched the cup from Matt. "What are you doing? You can't give him that."

"I was just going to wet his throat so he could talk, not drown the kid." Matt resented the inference that he'd do anything to harm his child.

"Talk?" Camie looked at Skyler, realization dawned. "He's awake." Her statement of the obvious brought a smile to Matt's lips.

"Yes, yes he is. And . . ." Matt paused for dramatic effect. "He's hungry." He stood next to the bed, still holding Skyler's hand in one of his, a smug grin splitting his face.

"Well," Camie glanced at Matt then back at Skyler. "That's very good news, young man, but I'm afraid we're going to have to start you off slowly. How does some juice sound?" Skyler looked disappointed, but he nodded.

"Maybe tomorrow you can have some ice cream." That brought a more enthusiastic nod. "I'll be right back." Camie patted Skyler's hand then smiled at Matt. "Congratulations, Dad." She turned and fled the room before Matt responded.

Her retreating footsteps sounded in Matt's ears as he sat on the bed next to Skyler and traced his cheeks with the back of his fingers. "Welcome back, young man. You scared the dickens out of your old dad."

"I'm sorry, Daddy."

"It's okay, son. I'm just glad I found you." Matt decided to wait until Skyler was stronger to try to find out what happened. For now, all that mattered was that he was going to be all right.

Chapter Thirty-nine

Matt watched Skyler sleep, but this time without the panicky feeling deep in his gut. He'd even managed to grab a couple of hours sleep himself but was now back at his post.

Skyler was okay. The words sang in Matt's heart. His boy was back. He'd never leave him again. Well, that might be a bit drastic, but he sure wasn't going anywhere for quite some time. An image of Melody popped into his mind as he thought this, and he felt a pang. His concern for Skyler had pushed her to the recesses of his mind for a few days. Now he remembered where he'd been headed when he'd received the news of Skyler's disappearance. His family had been about to be reunited. The pang stirred a deep longing. How he wanted his family together again. What he wouldn't give to bring Skyler's mom back to him.

Skyler's eyelids flickered and slowly opened. "Hi, Daddy," he said as a smile spread up his chubby cheeks.

"Good morning, son," Matt returned the smile. "Have a nice night?"

Skyler yawned and tried to stretch but was reeled back in by all his attachments. He frowned as he looked around and seemed to notice them for the first time. "Why am I tied up, Daddy?"

Matt chuckled. "Oh, you're just so cute the doctor was afraid the nurses would try to steal you away." He tickled Skyler's belly as he said this and Skyler giggled.

"You wouldn't let them, though, would you, Daddy." Skyler's face became serious as he said this, and Matt quit smiling as he looked intently at his son.

"No, big guy, I sure wouldn't. I'll never let anything happen to you again." He gently cradled Skyler's tiny hands in his and bent down to kiss his forehead.

"Good." Skyler perked up again. "Can I have some ice cream now?"

"Ice cream for breakfast?" Matt teased.

"The lady said I could have ice cream tomorrow. It's tomorrow, isn't it, Daddy?"

Matt laughed. Kids had amazing memories when it came to ice cream. "Yes, son, it's tomorrow. I'll see what I can do." Matt picked up the nurse's button and started to press it, but then held it out to Skyler instead. "Do you want to push it?"

"Yeah," Skyler said eagerly as he grabbed the button and pressed it repeatedly. "Does this get me ice cream?"

"If the nurses are on the ball it will," Matt answered.

They didn't have to wait long. A rather large nurse burst into the room, "What can I do ya for?" She grinned at them.

Matt beamed and pointed to Skyler. "He wants some ice cream."

"Well, whatdya know about that?" The nurse continued to grin. "If it's ice cream he wants, ice cream he shall have. Feeling better today, huh, little man?" She checked his IV and monitor and then scribbled something on his chart. "I think ice cream would make a perfect breakfast." The edges of her smile were lost under the mounds of her cheeks as she patted Skyler's foot. Then she turned and waddled from the room.

"I'll bet you do," Matt muttered under his breath, then was immediately ashamed of himself. At least this nurse didn't try to flirt with him.

Skyler was watching him when he turned his gaze back from the nurse's retreating bulk. Matt watched him in silence for a moment, then could resist the urge no longer to try to find out what happened.

"Skyler . . ."

"Yes, Daddy?"

His blood pressure cuff inflated, then made a small whoosing noise as the air went back out. Red digital figures appeared on the monitor as it beeped. Skyler watched it. "Cool," he said.

Matt took a breath that smelled of antiseptic and began again as he caressed Skyler's tiny fingers. "Where did you go that day you were with Grandpa and got lost? What happened?"

Skyler looked at him with huge, green eyes as he seemed to contemplate this. Dark, tousled curls covered his head and framed his face. "I went to find Momma."

The statement was so matter-of-fact it shook Matt to his core. His breath caught in his throat, and he flopped back in his chair. He didn't know what he'd expected, but it hadn't been that. He'd honestly begun to believe that Skyler had accepted his mom's disappearance and had adapted to life without her, as kids tend to do. How was he supposed to reply?

"Wow. Uh . . ." Matt ran his hand through his own curls. Skyler just watched, his face somber. "Where? . . . How . . . ?" *Think, Matt, think.*

The door opened, and the nurse came in with a dish of ice cream. Matt was grateful for the reprieve. He needed time to collect his thoughts and decide how to respond.

"Here you go, young man," she said, but she handed the ice cream to Matt. "Just give him little spoonfuls at a time. By lunchtime we can get him something a little more solid." She smiled and patted Skyler's hand and then moved to change his IV.

"My name's Becky, by the way." She finished the IV and stood at the foot of the bed, writing on the chart. "If you need anything else, just buzz me." Her smile was jolly as she turned to go.

Matt was spooning ice cream to Skyler, so they hardly noticed as the door clicked behind her. Birds chirped outside the window, the promise of a beautiful day. Skyler was in a private room, and Matt was grateful for the solitude as he joyfully watched his son slurp down the ice cream.

"Yummy." Skyler laid back on his pillow with a satisfied smile.

Matt set the bowl on the end table by the bed and took hold of Skyler's hands again.

"Skyler, why did you go off by yourself to find Mommy? Didn't you know how dangerous that was?"

"Sorry, Daddy."

"Remember how we've talked about staying close to Grandma or Grandpa when you're at the ranch?" Matt decided to stick to the safety angle.

"Yes."

"Then why did you wander off alone?"

"I told you already."

Matt had to duck his head to hide his smile at the furrowed brow and protruding bottom lip of his son.

"I know, big guy." His face was serious again as he raised his head. "But don't you remember how Daddy looked and looked for Mommy for so long? And the nice policemen and everyone who helped? All those people for so long . . ."

"But you didn't find her," Skyler stated. Kids called it like they saw it.

"And you thought you could?" Matt asked this as gently as possible. He wanted to get to the bottom of this without crushing his ego.

"Yes. Tarzan found his mommy and saved her." Skyler was sitting up now, his gaze steady.

Matt recalled the Disney movie Skyler always made him rent. Now he knew why.

"But how, sport? How were you going to find her when all those grown-ups couldn't?"

"The birdie."

Matt froze. Tingles like tiny electric shocks went through his body.

"What birdie? What do you mean?" he asked carefully, thinking he already knew the answer.

"The red one. I followed it to Mommy's Jeep." His face

puckered. "But she wasn't there." Tears pooled in his eyes.

Matt pulled him close, tucked his head against his shoulder and patted his back, angry at himself for upsetting him.

"I know, big guy, I know. It's okay. It was very brave of you to try." Should he tell him? Should he let him know that his Mom was alive and in California? How would he explain that? How could he tell his son that his Mom was living with a different family under a different name? This four-year-old had risked his life, wandered off alone in the wilderness to look for her, and she was living a different life somewhere. A surge of anger quelled inside Matt, and he had to remind himself that Melody had lost her memory. Maybe she didn't know she had a son who loved and missed her enough to wander for days without food or water.

Skyler made a squeaking noise, and Matt realized he was holding him too tightly. "Sorry, buddy." He loosened his grip but didn't let him go. His emotions were warring inside him like two huge storms confronting each other. Love and concern for his son fought with anger at the boy's mother for putting him in danger, while confusion at her disappearance and how she'd ended up in California battled with his own love and longing for her. What a mess. For his own sanity he had to resolve this. He had to go to California. But how could he leave Skyler? As close as he'd come to losing him, he never wanted to let him out of his sight again. But how could he take him with him? The possible emotional devastation if his mom didn't remember him was far too great to risk.

Where was the red bird to guide him now?

Chapter Forty

The plane landed at LAX. Andrea looked at the jagged stubs that had once been her fingernails. As exhausted as she'd been from the show and the stress of escaping Germany, sleep had eluded her the entire flight. She still hadn't figured what to say to Esther, and the moment of confrontation was drawing near.

The blacktop flowed beneath the wheels of the jet as they taxied to their gate. Andrea stared at it, then glanced at Greg, who sat next to her. Sleep hadn't been a problem for him. Apparently he considered Andrea safe, sandwiched between him and the window of the plane, and had relaxed his vigil. He'd only awakened when she'd had to crawl over him to use the restroom and when they'd changed planes in New York.

A snort escaped his mouth as his head jerked upright. His cheeks reddened as he looked at Andrea, then out the window.

"We there?"

The answer was obvious, but what else was he going to say?

"Yeah." Andrea thought of the jokes she'd heard from one of the comedians on the "Blue Collar Comedy Tour" but resisted the urge to say, "Naw, we pulled into a rest stop. Here's your sign." The big guy was shy enough. A joke like that would humiliate him.

Silence rested on the pair of them like a blanket and lasted through the whole process of deboarding, retrieving their luggage, and hailing a taxi. Andrea was sure Esther would have sent a car to pick them up, but she wasn't ready to face her yet. She'd probably have come herself and tried to get Andrea to turn around and get back on a plane.

Andrea gave directions to the cab driver, and they eased into traffic and began the agonizing ride home. Why did she come here? Why hadn't she gone straight to Utah? Again, the old sense of responsibility. Better to face the music and get it over with than slink off and try to hide.

Yeah, that's exactly what she was going to do. Tell Esther right to her face that she was through trying to be a rock star. She'd thank her for her efforts and the opportunity but explain that it just wasn't the life for her. Then she'd try to tell her about the dark-haired man who haunted her thoughts, and then go to Utah. And Esther would know. She was through slinking around. It was time to take control of her own life. She appreciated everything Esther had done for her, but she needed to live for herself. She'd thought having a music career was what she wanted to do with her life but these deep longings and the misery she'd experienced on the road had convinced her otherwise. Music would always be an important part of her, and maybe once the mysteries that constantly plagued her mind were solved, she'd want to think of a way to share it that didn't consume all her time, but the thrill of performing hadn't equaled happiness or contentment. Something was missing. Something huge. And until Andrea found out what that was, nobody was going to goad her into another life.

Silence filled the cab almost as much as Greg's bulk beside her. The driver rattled off what she assumed were curses in Spanish every now and again as they inched through the traffic, but no attempts at conversation were made. Andrea wondered if Greg was as worried as she was about facing Esther.

Everything looked gray as she stared out the window. The sky, the buildings, the never-ending stream of cars. L.A. wasn't for her. Even if this Matt guy didn't want anything to do with her, she was through with L.A. Maybe she'd find a cabin in the mountains and live in solitude, where it didn't matter if she didn't know anybody and nobody knew her. Most of what she'd earned performing the past several months was tucked in a bank account she'd opened herself that Esther knew nothing about. Regardless of what happened, she'd known she didn't want to be dependant on Jack and Esther. Her tastes were much simpler, and she had enough to get by on her own until she found her life.

Andrea's street came into view, and the butterflies started afresh. The cab smelled of stale cigarette smoke and vomit, and she felt like she might add to that smell.

Nate was at his post at the guardhouse when they pulled up. Andrea had always thought he was cute and had kind of flirted with him from time to time, but he'd maintained professional courtesy and never became too personable. Now, when he saw her through the open window of the cab, his jaw dropped and the color drained from his tanned face.

"Melo . . . er, Miss Kensington!," he exclaimed in surprise.

Andrea's brow furrowed and her eyes narrowed as she looked at him. This was a new greeting.

"Hello, Nate. Is my mother at home?" *Please say no.* Andrea silently chided herself for the thought. *Chicken.*

Nate seemed at a loss for words, then finally stammered, "Ye . . . Yes, miss. She's been home all day. Didn't go to work today or nuthin'."

Nate's face twisted as expressions warred with themselves. Andrea watched in fascination. *What was with him?*

"Well, could you open the gate, please?" Again, Andrea half wished he'd say no. Her bags were already packed. All she had to do was tell the driver to turn around right now and she could be on a plane to Utah within the hour. The temptation was great, but she'd already decided against the coward's way out.

Nate's mouth opened and shut, but no words came out as he hesitated. Then reached for a button, and the huge iron gates slowly swung open.

"Thank you." Andrea still watched him, shaking her head as the cab eased forward. She rolled up her window and then turned and looked out the back. Nate was hanging halfway out of the guardhouse, staring at her retreating cab. Andrea shook her head again as she sat back in her seat. Why was he acting so strange? Sure, she was home early from the tour, but it was more than that. He was acting like she'd returned from the dead instead of from Europe.

Puzzling over Nate managed to occupy her mind, holding the upcoming storm at bay, until the cab pulled onto the large, circular, cobblestone driveway and stopped at the front door. Andrea stared at the house, in no hurry to exit the taxi. The driver sat silently waiting. Andrea suspected he didn't speak English, or he might have asked to her leave. Greg remained stone-faced and still.

Andrea felt attached to the seat, her limbs like lead. She may have stayed that way if the big, wooden doors hadn't flown open and Esther's imperious presence filled the entry. *Time to face the music.* Andrea took a deep breath and caught a scent of the roses surrounding the driveway. They smelled sickly sweet. Andrea swallowed the bile in her throat and then reached for the door handle.

"Allow me," Greg said. He climbed out his own door, and hurried around to open hers.

Andrea fumbled in her purse for money to pay the driver as she waited for Greg to open her door.

"Thank you," she mumbled as she handed him the bills. Her door swung open and she exited the cab. Her mother remained rooted to her spot in the doorway as Greg unloaded the luggage and Andrea made the death march up the walkway.

"Andrea, darling, how wonderful to see you again." The words were pleasant, but the tone dripped venom as sparks flew from Esther's eyes. This was going to be every bit as fun as Andrea had anticipated.

Chapter Forty-one

"I don't care." Andrea felt like a dishrag that had been used to scrub bricks for the past hour. Her eyes burned and her head pounded.

"Of course you don't. That much is obvious. Why should you care about the months and months of time, effort, and money I've poured into your career?" Esther repeated the same guilt trip she'd been grinding into Andrea for the past hour. Andrea sat curled up in one of the chairs in front of Esther's desk in her private office while Esther paced behind her, stopping long enough to breathe hot flames down her neck every few seconds.

Andrea was beat. She'd had it. No more. She hadn't slept in nearly thirty-six hours. Jack was nowhere to be seen, or he might have offered some reprieve. None of Andrea's reasoning and pleading had had the least effect on Esther. If ugly was what it was going to take, that's what Esther was going to get.

Andrea mustered her energy and stood to face Esther. Placing her hands on her shoulders, she looked her squarely in the eyes.

"Mother, I do appreciate what you've done. I thought it was what I wanted, and you gave me that opportunity. And for that, I will be forever grateful." Esther sneered and started to interrupt, but Andrea gave her shoulders a shake.

"I'm not through." Her voice was firm, and Esther stopped, her mouth gaping.

"I'm leaving. I'm going to Utah, and nothing you can say or do is going to stop me. Do you understand?"

Esther was silent. Deathly so. Her mouth closed to a hard line, and an almost evil glint came to her eyes. Her shoulders shrugged Andrea's hands off and she took a step backward.

"So, you want to know about this mystery man in Utah, do you? You're willing to throw away everything to go running to his arms?"

Andrea was leery. The tone of Esther's voice sent warning signals up and down her nerve endings. Esther turned her back and walked toward a large painting of nymphs and water. Andrea stood silently watching and waiting. What was she up to now?

The picture swung back to reveal a safe. Esther glanced over her shoulder at Andrea as she stood, blocking the dial while she spun it a few times, then clutched the handle and pulled the safe open. Andrea inched forward and tried to peer past Esther at the contents of the safe, but Esther's head snapped around, her face a storm cloud, and Andrea stepped back.

When Esther turned, closing the safe so the contents were hidden but it didn't click shut, she was holding what appeared to be a wad of tissue. Curiosity consumed Andrea, chasing away fatigue and anger.

"What is that?" Her eyes never left Esther's hands as she walked toward her. Andrea was rooted to her spot. Trepidation turned the warning signals to alarm bells in her head.

Esther cupped the tissue in her hands. "I've tried to protect you, Andrea."

Her tone took Andrea by surprise. Glancing at Esther's face, she was shocked to see her softened features and the intense pleading in her eyes.

"Before your accident, something terrible happened. That's the real reason you were off alone."

Andrea's eyes narrowed but she remained silent, not sure she wanted to hear what Esther had to say.

"I think you'd better sit down, dear."

Good things rarely followed when Esther called her dear.

Andrea eased into the chair, her eyes never leaving Esther. Esther sat in the chair next to her and turned to directly face Andrea, her hands again cradling whatever secret lurked within the tissue.

"Like I said, I've been protecting you from something. Something terrible. When you woke up in the hospital and had lost your memory, I saw it as an opportunity for a fresh start. Without the pain of your past." Esther paused, but Andrea had no response. Her gaze was fixed, her mouth a tight line.

"You see, dear . . ." there it was again. Esther began to unwrap the tissue. Andrea held her breath.

"You were married." Esther held up a diamond ring.

Tremors took over Andrea's body like the aftershocks of a huge earthquake. Her voice shook as she asked, "Wha . . . what do you mean?" That was all she could squeak out as she stared at the ring, making no move to take it from Esther.

"I mean just what I said." Esther set the ring back in her lap. "You were married to a man named Matt McCandlass and you lived in Utah. But he was a drunken louse who beat you unmercifully, and you finally escaped and were headed back home when you had your accident."

Andrea sat in stunned silence. Her mouth moved, but no words came out. Esther set the ring on the desk and leaned forward to cover Andrea's hands with her own.

"I'm sorry I lied to you, sweetheart, but I honestly thought it was for the best. Your father and I were so happy to have you away from that awful man that we didn't see the point in dredging up the past and burdening you with such unhappiness when you'd already forgotten it."

Andrea still didn't speak. A tear crept out the corner of her eye and slipped down her cheek.

Esther continued. "Most people take years of therapy to achieve the peace and happiness your memory loss afforded you after suffering for so long. You have to understand why we wanted to let it lie." One gnarled finger with a long, red nail reached up to wipe a tear from Andrea's cheek.

"H . . . how long was I married?" Andrea had to swallow

a lump in her throat to choke out the words. Tears blurred her vision as she looked into the dark eyes of her mother.

"A year. A long, dreadful year. The beatings began after only a month or so. Your father and I begged you to leave him, but at first you thought he'd change, and then you feared for your life if you tried to escape."

"Well, he must know I'm here. Why hasn't he come?" Andrea thought of the hatred she'd seen in Matt's eyes in Vegas and a chill ran down her spine.

"Oh, he has, trust me. Why do think I wanted you in Europe for so long? I know you've thought me cold-hearted, but I've had more than your career in mind."

"I saw him once. In Vegas . . ."

"Yeah, I know. We all did. How could we have missed him? That's why I hired Greg. That weasel, Tom, who booked you, was furious and threatened to find a new opening act for the rest of the engagement. Jason stepped in and said he'd quit if that happened. His only concern was for you. I had to talk hard and fast to get him to go on that night instead of taking you to the hospital."

Andrea remembered waking up alone with nothing but a wet washcloth for comfort after a harrowing experience. Her mother's only concern had been the show. Tiredness seeped back into her consciousness, right down to her bones.

The tremors had ceased, but a shudder passed over Andrea when she thought how close she'd come to putting herself back in Matt's clutches when she'd gone to Utah. Had that horrible man at the car dealership—what was his name?—Rick, been trying to protect her? What about the redhead and the little boy from the picture? Matt had obviously found someone else. Did he beat her, too? And the boy? Another shudder.

Sorrow greater than anything Andrea had ever experienced engulfed her like a suffocating sand storm. Emotions swirled and beat against her heart and her mind. Esther was forgotten as she gave in to the deep, bone-rattling sobs that tore through her chest.

Why? Why had she felt so driven to find this man when he

only meant to harm her? Was she one of those stupid women she'd read about who continue to return to abusive relationships despite the danger to them and their children?

Children. The thought brought her back to some awareness of her surroundings. Esther was still there, sitting quietly with her hands in her lap. Andrea puzzled over her expression. Not happy, certainly, but not grief-stricken as Andrea was. In fact, she looked almost satisfied.

Esther caught Andrea's eyes and a frown immediately creased her forehead as she reached to take her hands in her own. "Are you okay, dear? See, this is exactly why I kept it hidden from you."

An "I told you so"? Her mother was giving her an "I told you so" in the middle of the most devastating moment of Andrea's life? Andrea slowly withdrew her hands and sat up straighter. Fishing a tissue from her jeans pocket she wiped her face and blew her nose.

"What about children?" she asked.

"What about them?"

Andrea sighed. Games. Always games with this woman.

"Did I have any? Me and Matt, did we have any children?"

"Oh, no, no. Thank goodness."

Andrea chewed on this for moment.

"Are you sure I don't have a little boy?" she asked again.

"What? Don't be ridiculous. Of course I'm sure. You think I'd forget my own grandson?" Esther stood abruptly, walked behind her desk, and sat in her throne, steepling her fingers while her elbows rested on the desk.

"You look exhausted, dear. I'll have Rosa unpack your things. Go get some sleep."

The ordeal was over. No more questions would be asked or answered tonight. Andrea slowly rose from the chair.

"Goodnight, Mother," she mumbled and walked to the door.

"Goodnight, dear. And welcome home."

Home. That used to have such an inviting ring to it. Did

Andrea really have a home? All she wanted right now was to crawl in a hole somewhere and never come out. Hope had been drained. She felt cold, hard and empty. No true love awaited. No loving arms. Just Esther. And Jack. And a music career she no longer wanted.

Chapter Forty-two

"I need a few days off." Matt stood in Rick's office and confronted him as he lounged back in his huge, overstuffed chair behind his desk.

"What do you mean? You just got back? Do you still work here, or what?" Rick's sneer was unsympathetic, considering what Matt had just been through with his son.

"Yeah, I know. And I'm sorry, but this is important." Matt stepped around one of the chairs facing the desk and sat down. Leaning forward, he placed his forearms on Rick's desk.

"I know where Melody is living." Matt let the words sink in as he watched Rick's face. One side of his mouth twitched as the sneer disappeared and an expressionless mask dropped into place. Rick gripped a pencil between two fingers and drummed it on the desk.

"What are you talking about?" Rick's voice was gruff. His eyes darted around the room.

"Georgette found her. She's in California."

"What's Melody doin' there? I thought she was in Vegas." Rick put the pencil down and rifled through some papers in front of him.

"Apparently, she lost her memory and somehow ended up living with an older couple in California who call themselves her parents. She was just doing a show in Vegas."

"Hmm," was Rick's only reaction, his gaze fixed on the papers.

"Did you hear what I said?" Matt stood and leaned on his fists on the desk. "Melody didn't leave me. She doesn't even know who she is." His voice raised several decibels.

"Of course I heard you. I'm sitting right here. You don't have to shout." Rick glanced at Matt, then leaned back in his chair, his hands clasped in front of him with his index fingers resting on his chin. He stared at the ceiling for a moment then looked at Matt.

"Sit down," he commanded.

Matt hesitated, then obliged and held his tongue.

Rick was silent a moment longer. "Look Matt," he finally began, "I wasn't going to tell you this, but Melody was here that day."

Matt flew out of his chair, "What?" He'd have had Rick by the collar if he could have reached him across the desk. Instead he had to settle for leaning over and glaring at him.

"Sit down, sit down. Don't get your shorts in a bundle."

Matt had to take several deep breaths to calm himself before he complied. Seated on the edge of his chair, he clasped both armrests, ready to pounce.

Rick stood and pushed his chair under the desk and then paced behind it, his hands clasped behind his broad backside.

"Yeah, she came in here looking for you."

Matt raised from his seat, but a glare from Rick eased him back into his chair.

Rick stopped pacing, placed his hands on the back of his seat, and looked intently at Matt.

"She told me she'd suffered a concussion from the accident and had lost her memory, but this old couple found her and wanted to give her a singing career, so she'd gone with them."

Matt started to protest, but Rick held up a hand. "Just let me finish." The pacing began again.

"That night she saw you in Vegas, her memory returned." Rick shot Matt a quick peek, but his jaw had dropped and his eyes were open wide, so he continued.

"She remembered all about you and Skyler, but she loved her new life and didn't want to give up her career. That's what she came here to tell you that day." Rick faced Matt and looked him right in the eyes.

"I don't believe it!" Matt exploded off his chair, knocking it backward.

Rick ran a hand over his face and pulled his seat out and plopped into it. "I know, buddy, it's terrible." His face was buried in his hands.

Matt now paced, in quick, furious steps. "She would never do that. She loves us. And Skyler? No mother would just abandon her child that way."

Rick gave Matt an incredulous look from between his hands when he stopped to look at him.

"Well, okay, so lots of mothers would." The pacing began again. "But no decent ones. And Melody was more than a decent mother; she was a great mother." Matt stopped and his shoulders slumped. What he didn't want to face was the fact that if Melody had chosen to leave for good, it must be because of him. Life with him had been so forgettable that she'd even sacrificed her son. A tumult of emotions rolled over him and he collapsed in the chair.

"See?" Rick was saying through the fog in Matt's mind. "That's why I kept her away from you. I lost you for over a month when you saw her in Vegas. I knew this would push you over the edge."

Matt slowly raised his head to glare at Rick. "You're scum, you know that?"

Rick's hands fell to his desk with a loud thud, his eyes wide.

Matt continued. "What makes you think you have the right to toy with my life like that? Melody's my wife. For better or worse. What happens between us is up to her and me, not you."

A familiar smirk took over Rick's face. "Was your wife, you mean. You filed for divorce, remember, buddy?"

Matt was numb as he sat in silence. He didn't know what to

think anymore. Rick was a liar, that much was certain, but he peppered his lies with enough half truths that Matt never knew what to believe. Enough was enough.

"I quit." Matt rose from his seat and plodded to the door.

"Quit? What do you mean you quit? You can't quit, you mealymouthed simpleton."

Matt shook his head and opened the door. *That'll bring me back.* A nonchalant crowd of salesmen had gathered at the fountain.

Rick's footsteps stormed up behind him and he grabbed Matt's arm. Matt spun around, his face tight.

"Get your hand off me," he spat. Rick's hand dropped.

"Listen, Matt, if you're sore 'cause I lied to you about Melody being here, I'm sorry. I did it for your own good. I mean, look at you. You'd finally gotten yourself back together, and now what are you going to do? Slink off to a cabin in the hills and leave Skyler alone again while you lick your wounds? Come on."

Matt stood rooted to the spot. What was he going to do? He'd promised Skyler he'd never leave him again, and he meant that. Especially now. But if he took him to California with him and confronted Melody and she rejected them, what would that do to Skyler? Besides, hadn't Georgette said Melody was in Europe on tour?

Even if Rick were full of crap, Matt had filed for divorce. What if Melody felt rejected and abandoned by him? What if her memory hadn't returned and never would, and she was content in her new life without the complications of a husband and child?

He had to tell Melody's parents what was going on. With all the trauma of Skyler's disappearance, he hadn't told them she was alive. Now he would. He'd do them that courtesy, then maybe he and Skyler would pack up and go somewhere memories didn't haunt him at every turn. He had enough saved to open his own car dealership, if that's what he wanted to do, although the thoughts of dealing with people like Rick the rest of his life made his skin crawl. He'd find something to do. Somewhere where nobody knew anything about him or his past.

He had to think of his son. Skyler had been hurt enough. After risking his life to find his mom, if she didn't even remember him, and didn't want to try because she was so busy with a successful career . . . well, Matt just didn't think he could take that. Matt was a grown man, and the memories of Melody looking at him with that blank stare he'd seen in Vegas still made him shiver. What would it do to Skyler?

A brand new start. That's what they needed.

"Good-bye, Rick. Give my regards to Kristy." With one final glare, Matt turned and walked out the door, ignoring the stares from the salesmen and the curses from Rick that filled the air behind him.

Heading for his office, he acknowledged his new secretary with a brief nod and then burst through his door and looked around. His eyes locked on the family portrait hanging on the wall behind his desk. He walked around the desk and took the portrait down. Nothing else held any significance for him anymore. Putting the picture under his arm, he turned and walked away without a backward glance.

The salesmen had scattered from the fountain when he came back to the main showroom and Matt was sure Rick had laid into them like a fox in a henhouse. A few of them nodded at him as he made his way to the front door. Rick was back on his throne, not one to beg. *Good riddance.*

Matt stopped at the entrance and turned to take one last look. Georgette had been the only one he'd gotten close to here, and she'd only come back from California long enough to gather her things and move back there to be close to Nate. Matt was happy for her.

She'd stopped by the hospital to see him and Skyler on her way out of town, and Matt had a long talk with her. She'd made several unsuccessful attempts to see the woman who called herself Melody's mother to try to find out what was going on, but had never made it past the front door. And with Melody in Europe, there hadn't been much else she could do. Matt appreciated her efforts. Georgette was a good person. Let her hold on to her fantasy that Matt and Skyler would hook up with Melody and they'd live happily ever after. That way she could get on with her life with Nate without being riddled with guilt.

Facing the doors, Matt pushed through and took a deep breath of the spring air and one last look at the tulips and daffodils blooming in the flowerbeds by the entrance. Then he strode to his truck, climbed in, and drove off to find a new life for him and his son.

Chapter Forty-three

Matt drove south on I-15. It had taken him over a month to sell his house and practically everything in it. He'd taken a hit, but he'd just wanted to be rid of it and away from there. He'd even sold Melody's piano, guitar, and all her clothes—what he didn't give to Deseret Industries, anyway. All he had in the back of his truck were his and Skyler's clothes and personal items, Skyler's toys, and various household items he figured he'd need to get by someplace new.

Skyler sat in his booster seat, on the passenger side. Not the safest thing, but Matt didn't know how else he was supposed to have him ride. At least the airbag was disabled.

Skyler's cheeks were flushed, and a soft snore escaped his rosy lips as his head lolled to one side of his booster seat. That had always been the best way to get him to sleep: stick him in the truck and go for a ride. This time, they'd made it almost two hundred miles before he'd stopped asking questions about where they were going and everything he saw out the window. His battered bear, Gus, was tucked under his arm, where it always was when Skyler slept. A sharp pain shot through Matt every time he looked at it, but no amount of coaxing had convinced Skyler to add it to the pile of junk they'd cleaned from the house. Matt wanted to forget about Melody, but Skyler needed this little piece of his mother.

Country music played softly on the radio as Matt enjoyed the sunshine pouring in through the windows. Tired of winters, he'd decided on Arizona for their new life. It was not the optimum time of year to be headed down there, he realized, but he wanted to find a place and be settled before Skyler started school this fall.

Another pain wrenched his guts. Skyler's mom ought to be there for his first day of school. Matt stopped the "why?" that reared up in his mind. He could do this on his own. He had to.

They'd celebrated Skyler's fifth birthday on the fifth of May. A twinge of guilt pricked Matt. He probably should have made a bigger to-do, but he hadn't had the heart. He'd taken Skyler to McDonalds's and bought him a hamburger, which Skyler had ignored as he'd opted to play in funland. Matt had picked at his own Big Mac and polished off his and Skyler's fries as he'd watched him. Only the promise of ice cream and a trip to Toys 'R Us had lured Skyler away from the play area, where he'd managed to make fast friends with two other youngsters.

Matt glanced at his sleeping boy and smiled. It was so good to see his cheeks rosy again. The nightmare of nearly losing him was never far from his mind. Matt cherished very moment they were together.

A song about divorce came on the radio, and Matt was reminded of the papers stashed in a box somewhere in the back of his truck, finalizing his divorce. He was a free man. The thought brought no pleasure.

Switching channels brought only static. Country music was all he could tune in to—and only one station at that as he sped down the highway through the sparsely populated expanse of southern Utah. He'd passed Beaver and would have to turn off the freeway soon to catch the strip of road that wound through the hills to Highway 89. No radio stations would be available then, and he'd be stuck listening to his old CDs he'd heard over and over. Next time he stopped for gas, he'd see if they had any new music he liked.

Skyler stirred and his head flopped to the other side of

his booster seat, but he didn't wake up. His mouth made little sucking noises then stilled, and he was soon softly snoring again. *Just like his old man.* Matt had received many pokes in the ribs from Melody over the years for his snores. Skyler was in trouble when he got older.

Matt's stomach growled. Breakfast had been a few hours ago. His drive-thru sausage biscuit from McDonald's had worn off. Melody had always packed food for their trips so he'd had something to munch on to keep him awake. *Darn.* Everything reminded him of her. Would the torment ever end?

Soft notes played a haunting tune on the radio. A singer joined the instruments and Matt's heart stopped. It was her. A voice as familiar as sunshine in June filled the cab of his truck. Matt glanced at Skyler, but he slept on, unaware.

Matt's mind told his hands to shut it off, but they remained frozen to the steering wheel. Despite his best efforts to remain detached, he absorbed the sound of her voice and let it permeate his soul. Tears pooled in his eyes and blurred his vision as he listened to the words.

"Why must I wander this world all alone?
Haunted by thoughts of a love I'd once known.
He was my reason for breathing the air.
Now that he's gone, I just don't care"

Tears spilled down his cheeks as Matt maintained his death grip on the wheel. Melody had written the song. He was sure of it. The cadence was typical of many of hers he'd heard a million times during the five years they'd been married.

"Where'd love go? I ask again.
Where is my lover, my soul mate, my friend?
His shadow lurks behind a veil in my mind.
Why won't he break through and be mine for all time?"

A car honked as it whizzed past him and Matt jumped. He glanced at the speedometer. Fifty miles per hour. His foot pressed down on the gas. Then he noticed a sign for Cedar City and realized he'd missed the turnoff for Highway 20. *Dang it.* No matter, he'd go over Cedar Breaks. The drive was longer, but much prettier, anyhow. He was in no hurry. Besides, he needed a decent meal, and chances were much better to find a good place to eat in Cedar City than Panguitch.

The song ended, but the words lingered in Matt's mind and in his heart. He repeated them again and again. She'd sounded as tortured as he'd felt over the past year and a half. Maybe she wasn't wrapped up in her career. Maybe she did want to remember him.

"Where is my lover, my soul mate, my friend?" The words echoed in his mind. *I'm right here,* he thought.

A tinny song about someone doing someone else wrong grated in the background, and Matt switched the radio off. Skyler's gentle snores and the sounds of the wheels on the road made the backdrop for his thoughts. The dotted white line ticked past his eyes.

Had he been too rash? Too quick to give up on Mel?

The haunting lyrics of Melody's song drifted through his mind again. Her songs had always been performed with a depth of feeling that left him breathless, but this time . . . Melody was in agony. Memory or no memory, she needed him as much as he needed her. He knew it in the depths of his soul.

Exit signs for Cedar City appeared on the side of the road. Matt kept going. Skyler would be hungry when he woke up, but Matt would grab them a snack at a gas station in St. George. Now he was in a hurry. Not to get to Arizona, but to California. He had to see Melody face-to-face. Fear shot through him. The risk was tremendous. All the emotional bandages he'd been able to patch on his heart over the past month as he'd convinced himself to start a new life would be ripped to shreds and he'd have to start again—not to mention what it would do to Skyler if he was rejected outright by his own mother.

Matt took a deep breath and held it for a couple of seconds before slowly exhaling. He'd passed Cedar City, and the desert now surrounded him on both sides again.

Georgette was in California. He'd look her up and leave Skyler with her before going to see Melody. Besides, he needed her to tell him where Melody lived.

A pang of guilt hit him as he thought of Burt and Carol. He still hadn't told them anything about Melody. He was going to stop on his way to Arizona and let them see Skyler one last time and explain everything then. They'd waited this long; they'd have to hold on a little longer. They didn't know the difference anyway. As far as they were concerned, Melody was missing, presumed dead. Why upset them with these new complications until he had all the facts?

Skyler's head came upright, and he yawned and stretched one chubby arm as the other clung to Gus. Wide green eyes turned to Matt.

"Are we there yet?" The typical kid question.

"Not yet, buddy," Matt replied, smiling at his son. "Did you have a good sleep?"

"Yup. How far to Arizona?" Skyler yawned again.

"A long ways, big guy." Matt reached over to tousle Skyler's hair.

"Say, how'd you like to go to Disneyland?" Matt glanced at Skyler to see his reaction.

"Yeah, Disneyland. Yay!" Skyler's eyes were even wider as he nodded vigorously.

Matt decided not to mention Georgette yet. Skyler had been upset when she'd come to say good-bye at the hospital and Matt had to tell him she wasn't coming back. How do you explain to a child why the women in his life keep disappearing? Especially when you don't understand yourself.

Chapter Forty-four

Andrea stretched and yawned. A glance at her bedside clock told her it was only five AM. Of course, she'd been asleep since seven PM. And that was following an afternoon nap. And not getting up until eleven that morning. This had pretty much been her schedule the month or so since Esther had told her about her husband. Time held no meaning. Life overwhelmed her. Esther left her alone to wallow in her grief, which suited Andrea fine. Her room served as good of a hole as any. If Esther had pestered her, she'd have felt compelled to find somewhere else to seclude herself, and she didn't have the energy for that.

Her stomach growled and she decided to slip down to the kitchen for a snack. Hazy, pre-dawn light filtered into her room as she slid out of bed, felt around with her toes for her slippers, and stuck her feet in them. Next, she fumbled for her robe, which she'd dropped on a chair in the corner of her room. A glance at the full-length mirror as she stumbled past shocked her. Her hair looked like wadded-up straw. Dark circles underscored her eyes, and her sunken cheeks were the color of onion skins. A shudder rippled through her, and she pulled the robe shut over the flannel PJs she'd worn night and day—she didn't remember for how long—and made to leave the room. A pile of clothes and a pair of shoes in the middle of the floor almost sent her headfirst into the door, but she managed to get her feet under her in time to grab for the doorknob.

The house was quiet except for the ticking of the grandfather clock in the entryway as she shuffled to the kitchen. Andrea had seen little of the servants or anyone else in the past few weeks, and she wanted to keep it that way. Let them draw whatever conclusions they wanted.

The door to the kitchen swung open, and Andrea was surprised to see Jack sitting at the counter sipping a cup of coffee and reading the paper.

"Oh, sorry," she mumbled and started to turn to go.

"Wait," Jack said. "Come on in here. You don't have to leave on my account."

"That's okay," she answered. "I was just going to get a little something to eat, but I don't want to disturb you."

"You're not disturbing me. Come sit down."

Holding the door open, Andrea glanced behind her, and her stomach growled again while she debated if she wanted to tolerate another human presence for a few minutes in order to eat a bowl of cereal. With a weak smile at Jack, she let the door swing shut and went into the room.

A search of the cupboards netted her a box of Grape-Nuts. She poured herself a bowl and then added a couple of teaspoons of brown sugar and sliced a banana on top. At the sight of the food, her belly rumbled louder. How long had it been since she'd eaten?

Only skim milk was in the fridge. Not Andrea's preference, but she poured some on the concoction in her bowl and sat next to her father after retrieving a spoon from the silverware drawer.

The rattle of the newspaper and munch of Grape-Nuts were the only sounds as Andrea contemplated each spoonful. A pink glow filled the room, and a beam of sunlight streamed in through the French doors that led to the patio. Jack's coffee cup clinked on the saucer as he set it down and then folded the paper. Swiveling his stool to face Andrea, he cleared his throat. Andrea peeked at him from under the mass of snarls on her head.

Impeccable, as always, in crisp white pants and a turquoise golf shirt, Jack sat with his hands folded in his lap, watching her. Her munching slowed and she raised a hand to her hair, remembering the image in the mirror. Heat rose up her cheeks. The Grape-Nuts turned to sawdust in her mouth, and she quit chewing and took a big swallow.

"Andrea, I have to talk to you."

Andrea studied the brown mass in her bowl. "Okay," she choked out.

"Not here. Not now."

Andrea looked at Jack. His eyes darted around the room, rested on the door for a moment, then came back to her. She ducked her head, unable to meet his gaze in her present state, but her ears were keenly tuned to his furtive tone.

"Meet me at Julio's for lunch."

Her head jerked up despite herself. This was a first. Jack had never asked her to meet him anywhere. In fact, he'd always been uncomfortable being alone with her in the same room.

"O . . . okay," she managed to stammer. She'd barely left her room in over a month, much less the house, but curiosity overwhelmed her. The last time Jack had wanted to talk to her had been when Esther was in the hospital, and it had never happened. Besides, it was about time Andrea cleaned herself up. Some fresh air sounded good. Sunshine now streamed in the room. It looked to be a beautiful day.

A black cloud rolled across Andrea's mind, but she pushed it away. Jack stood and nodded at her, giving her half a smile. Then he walked swiftly across the room and pushed through the swinging doors.

Andrea heard movement. The household was awakening. Not wanting to be seen by anyone else, she took her bowl to the sink and dumped its contents down the garbage disposal. She rinsed the bowl out, and left it in the sink. Then she scuttled across the kitchen, pushed through the doors, and half ran through the house and up the stairs to her room. Leaning against the door, she caught her breath for a moment and looked at her bed. Her body moved toward it, intending to crawl back in, but she caught herself. She had several hours before lunch, but another look in the mirror convinced her she might need every bit of that time to pull herself together. Besides, she'd slept enough in the past month to make up for a lifetime.

Chapter Forty-five

Andrea fingered her straw as she sipped her soda and peered at Jack across the table. His eyes flitted around the room, anxious for anywhere to land but on her. His silverware clinked against his empty plate as he fiddled with it. *What's he so darn edgy about?*

Andrea set her drink down and helped herself to more chips and salsa. The basket was nearly empty, and Jack hadn't even touched the chips. Her stomach was almost full, leaving no room for the chicken chimichanga on the way, but her hands seemed to have a will of their own as they reached for the chips and stuffed them in her mouth.

"What is it, Dad? What's eating you?" she asked around a mouthful of chips.

His eyes lit on her briefly before darting away again, but he set the silverware down and rested his hands in his lap. His chest rose and fell as he took several deep breaths. When he did look at her, Andrea wished his eyes would continue their dance. The intensity in their blue depths put a halt to her chip stuffing. Her hands also went to her lap as she sat up straight and studied him. Conversations of the lunchtime crowd roared around them, punctuated by the clank of dishes. Spicy smells of salsa and grilled meat filled the air.

Jack looked at her for several moments. Andrea waited. Inhaling deeply, he opened his mouth, but closed it again when the waiter showed up at their table with a tray full of food.

"Chicken chimichanga?" He held up a plate and Andrea nodded and lifted her index finger.

"Be careful, the plate is very hot," he said as he set it in front of her.

"Thank you," Andrea replied.

Lifting the other plate, he set it in front of Jack. "And beef fajitas for the gentleman."

Jack nodded and grunted.

Straightening, the young man flashed them a gorgeous smile, showing rows of perfect teeth. "Can I get you anything else?"

"No, thank you," Andrea answered for both of them, returning the smile.

"Very well, enjoy your meal." A dark curl flopped on his forehead as he bowed briefly before he turned to go, and Andrea's heart lurched.

Dark curls. They seemed familiar. If Matt had been so abusive, why did her heart do acrobatics whenever she thought of him?

"Let's eat, and then we'll talk," Jack's voice interrupted her reverie.

Andrea looked at him and nodded, then looked at her plate. Her chimichanga was enormous. Why had she filled up on chips? A glob of guacamole sat atop the chimichanga, and Andrea spread it over the whole thing with her fork before plunging it in the end and removing a bite. She chewed in silence, concentrating on her plate, and managed to eat about half of it before her stomach threatened to burst. Taking a big drink of water, she pushed her plate away and sat back in her seat, letting her eyes rest on Jack. His plate was practically full, and he was staring at it, pushing chunks of marinated beef around with his fork.

"Don't play with your food," Andrea teased, trying to lighten the mood.

Jack looked up and gave her a pained smile and then dropped his fork and sat back, also. Their waiter stopped at the table again.

"How is everything?" A frown creased his brow when he saw Jack's plate.

"Fine, fine," Jack mumbled.

"Would you like refills on your drinks?" he asked, as he filled their water glasses.

"Yes, please," Jack said and handed the waiter his empty iced tea glass.

"And you, miss?" That smile again. Andrea shook her head, glad she'd combed her hair and covered the dark circles with makeup.

"Very well. I'll check back with you in a few minutes." He turned and disappeared around a corner.

The booth they were in offered a semblance of privacy from prying eyes if not a barrier for the noise, which had died down as many of the yuppies returned to their high-powered lives. The varied tunes of different cell phones went off every few minutes. People no longer seemed content to converse with present company. Andrea was amused to see two women at a nearby table speaking in animated tones, but not to each other. They both had cell phones pressed to their ears.

Jack cleared his throat, and Andrea turned her attention back to him.

"Maybe this wasn't the best place to come," he began, starting to fiddle with his silverware again.

"No, no. This is fine." Andrea reached across the table and covered his right hand with her left one. "What is it you wanted to talk to me about?"

When he lifted his head to meet her gaze, Andrea gasped at the pain she saw in his eyes. Her right hand jumped to cover his left.

"You can tell me, please." Andrea pled for the release of whatever demons he had cooped up that were tearing at his insides.

"Andrea," he choked out her name then cleared his throat again and swallowed hard. "You have a husband."

Andrea let out the breath she'd been holding. That was it? That was the painful secret that had practically consumed him? Didn't he and Esther ever communicate? She squeezed his hands.

"Dad, I know. Mom already told me." Instead of the relief

she'd expected at this pronouncement, tears filled his eyes and he ducked his head again.

"No, no. It's not like that." He tried to remove his hands from under hers, but she held on.

"Not like what?" she pressed.

He squeezed his eyes shut and tears ran down his cheeks, then he lifted his head again.

"Esther lied to you. He never beat you. Or at least, we don't know whether he did or not."

"What are you talking about?" Andrea slowly dragged her hands back.

"Oh, Andrea," a sob escaped his throat. Andrea looked around to see if anyone took notice of their little drama. No one had. She turned her attention back to Jack.

"What do you mean she lied? Lied about what?"

"About everything!" This pronouncement burst out of him like the gush of a mighty river breaking through an obstruction. His eyes were pleading now, and he held his hands up to her. Andrea waited, unflinching. She made no move to take his hands and they plopped heavily to the table, rattling the silverware and sloshing their drinks.

"The fact is . . ." Jack paused and his chin dropped to his chest, "You're not even our daughter." The words were a hoarse whisper that reverberated through Andrea's soul.

"What did you say?" Every word was enunciated precisely. A roaring in her head blocked any ambient noise. Andrea felt alone with Jack in an unearthly world.

Jack slowly raised his head and met her glare. "I said, you're not our daughter. Mine and Esther's."

"Do you mean I was adopted?"

Jack shook his head. "No." Again he paused as he seemed to be looking for the right words. Andrea waited.

"I mean, we found you."

Like that explained anything.

"I don't understand. Like a baby in a basket left on your doorstep?"

"No." Jack took a deep breath and sat back, resting his hands in his lap again.

"About a year and a half ago, Esther and I were in my plane, flying over southern Utah. It was early fall, and we'd been over Zion to see the leaves, and circled over Cedar Breaks and Bryce Canyon . . ." These names meant nothing to Andrea, and her face must have registered that fact. Jack's head shook and he waved one hand.

"Anyway, we were somewhere over the desert outside Kanab when I spotted something on the edge of a ravine that didn't go with the red dirt and sagebrush. I circled back a little lower and realized it was a person, lying in the mud." Jack hesitated as he studied her. A shiver washed over her. She knew about lying in the mud.

Jack continued. "A pretty good storm had moved through that area the day before, so I really didn't want to try to land the plane, but a nagging feeling wouldn't let me fly off and leave whomever it was down there."

Andrea's scalp began to tingle.

"So anyway," Jack was speaking again, "I saw a dirt road not far from the ravine that had a straight enough stretch that I could land the plane, so I did." He took a big gulp of water and then set the glass down and drew circles on the rim with his index finger.

"Esther yelled at me the whole time, saying I was crazy, that there was nothing down there, and I was going to get us both killed. She refused to get out of the plane at first when we landed, but when I came back for the first aid kit and told her I'd found a young woman who was unconscious and needed help, I guess her curiosity got the better of her, and she came back with me to where you were lying."

His last words sent a jolt through Andrea. "Me."

Jack's eyes were serious as they bore through her. He leaned forward and rested his forearms on the table.

"Yes, Andrea, you."

Their staring contest was interrupted once more by their

waiter as he set a glass of iced tea in front of Jack.

"Did you folks save room for dessert?" He reached for his pencil and pad as he looked at their uneaten food.

"No," Andrea and Jack snapped in unison.

Andrea felt bad when his smile disappeared and he took a step back, pocketing his pad and tucking the pencil behind his ear.

"Very well," he said, producing a leather folder with the bill in it and setting it on the table. "I can take care of that whenever you'd like. Can I get some of these dishes out of the way for you?"

Andrea and Jack both nodded, and Jack moved his arms out of the way as the young man reached for his plate then stacked Andrea's on top. He left without another word.

Now Andrea leaned forward. "But Mom told me you guys went looking for me in your plane when I didn't show up on my way home from Utah after leaving Matt." Doubt seeped into Andrea's mind. First it was New York, then Utah . . .

"Yeah, and we just happened to fly over the exact spot you were lying in a remote desert in Utah." Jack's words dripped with sarcasm. Andrea was shocked. She'd never heard him use that tone before.

"No, no, she said I'd telephoned her and described where I was going to explore some Indian ruins . . ." Andrea desperately tried to hold on to what she knew, or thought she knew, but her voice trailed off at the expression on Jack's face.

"Lies!" he practically shouted, his fists pounded the table as his face twisted with anguish and frustration. "Don't you see? She made it all up so she could keep you."

"No, I don't see." Andrea's voice quivered. "Why would she do that?"

Jack's shoulders sagged and his head dropped. When he looked up again, his face was smooth, but his mouth was a grim line and his eyes still tortured. He exhaled deeply.

"We did have a daughter. She'd have been about your age if she'd lived, but she died of pneumonia when she was four."

The picture of the little girl that Esther had shown her in the hospital flashed through Andrea's mind. The one she'd said was her.

"When she died, Esther . . ."

Andrea sat frozen and waited for him to continue. When he did, his voice shook with emotion.

"Well, she had a nervous breakdown. She had to be institutionalized for a year. They had to feed her through a tube because she wouldn't eat. She wouldn't drink. She wouldn't do anything but stare out the window. Her beautiful black hair became stringy and streaked with gray, her eyes lifeless." Jack choked on a sob and wiped his eyes with the back of his hand.

"I'm sorry," he said, reaching in his back pocket for a handkerchief and blowing his nose. Andrea said nothing while he got his emotions in check. She felt numb.

"When she saw you, lying there caked with dirt and blood, I think something snapped inside her. Your age, the blonde hair . . . Andrea's never been far from her mind in all these years." Jack wiped his eyes and nose again, then pocketed the handkerchief. His glance fell on the leather folder, and he reached in his other pocket and pulled out his wallet. He removed a Visa card and placed it in the folder. Then he pocketed his wallet.

Andrea took a sip of water and waited. Her heart felt like a lump of clay in her chest and her skin tingled from her scalp to her toes. Her hand shook when she tried to raise the glass to her lips again, so she set it down and clasped her hands together under the table.

Jack leaned toward her and continued, his voice calm now. "When we loaded you in the plane, you kind of woke up, mumbling something about not knowing who you were, and it got Esther thinking. I wanted to radio local authorities and get you to the nearest hospital as quickly as possible, but Esther wouldn't hear of it. She was like a crazy woman, possessed, saying that you were Andrea, sent back to us for a second chance." Jack sat back and ran a hand through his thick, silver hair. His cheeks puffed, and he expelled a breath through pursed lips while he stared at the ceiling.

"I'll tell you, it scared me." His eyes met hers. "I thought I was going to lose her again."

Their gazes remained locked while the waiter quietly retrieved the bill and slipped away.

"I know it's no excuse. I had no right to take you away from your life, whether you had any memory of it or not, and quite frankly, I only intended to humor Esther for a short time until she came to her senses. I decided it'd make no difference if you recovered from your injuries here or in Utah, so I brought you here."

"But my family, my friends . . ." Andrea's voice was a tortured whisper.

"I know, I know. Believe me, I agonized over that. But Esther was so . . ." Jack's eyes fell, and when he lifted his head again, they were filled with tears. "I just couldn't go through that again. I'm so sorry." His chin dropped to his chest and his shoulders shook as he silently wept.

Coldness clamped around Andrea's heart and seeped through every fiber like a pervading frost. A year and a half. The life she had, the only life she knew was nothing but a lie. All her memories, lies. No past. No present. Not even her name was hers.

"So who am I? How do you know I'm married?" Her voice quavered.

The waiter returned with the leather folder and set it on the table. "Thank you, folks. Please come again." His somber expression matched the heaviness of the air around them. He disappeared for the last time. Andrea hoped Jack would leave a generous tip as he reached for the folder and extracted the receipt and his credit card. After wiping his eyes on his napkin, he scribbled on the receipt then put one copy back in the folder and the other in his wallet, along with his card.

"Well?" Andrea pressed.

Jack settled in his seat and looked at her. Quiet resolve replaced some of the agony in his expression.

"Your name is Melody McCandlass. And, as you know, your husband's name is Matthew. Er . . . was, anyway."

"Was? What do you mean was?" Andrea leaned forward, peering intently into his face.

Jack faltered under her gaze. His hands clasped on the table in front of him and he stared down at them.

"You're divorced."

Andrea sat back. "You mean I wasn't already? Esther said my marriage only lasted a year . . ." She trailed off at his quelling look.

"More lies." Andrea's words were tinged with anger. "So what are you talking about?" Enough was enough. First her family wasn't her family, now her husband wasn't her husband. How much rejection could one person handle in a day?

"Start at the beginning and tell me everything. Don't leave anything out this time." Andrea folded her arms across her chest and glared at Jack.

He cleared his throat and sighed, then met her glare and began to speak.

Chapter Forty-Six

"Matt!" Georgette's squeal echoed down the empty halls of her apartment complex as she threw her arms around Matt and the sleeping Skyler, who lay on his shoulder. Skyler stirred.

"Ssh." Matt patted Skyler's back and he quit squirming. "I'm glad to see you, too, Georgette, but let's try not to wake him or he'll start bugging me to go to Disneyland again. I've heard nothing else for the past eight hours," Matt whispered.

"Oh, right," Georgette giggled. "Come in, come in." The door swung wide behind her, and Matt stepped into her apartment. A ceramic lamp, the only illumination, sat on a wooden end table next to a beige couch with thin stripes. The smell of curry lingered in the air, and Matt was reminded of the shrimp and curry stir-fry Georgette had made for him and Skyler on occasion. Not Skyler's favorite.

"Did you have any trouble finding the place?" Georgette asked, following them into the apartment, her voice subdued.

Matt turned to face her. "Naw. I bought a map at a gas station in Bakersfield, and your instructions once we hit town were right on." He smiled, and she smiled back.

"I'm glad." She paused. "It's good to see you, Matt." Warmth emanated from her emerald eyes.

"You too. Thanks for letting us crash on you like this." His smile was full of genuine affection.

"Hey, anytime. It's absolutely my pleasure." Their gazes locked.

A cat rubbed against Matt's leg and he jumped, looking down. "Whoa, where'd that come from?"

Georgette laughed and scooped the cat into her arms. "She's mine, aren't you, baby." Her nose rubbed against the pink one of the ball of white fluff as she held the cat in front of her.

"Her name's Felicity, huh, baby." Her tone sounded like she was speaking to a small child.

Matt shook his head as he watched the display. "I don't mean to interrupt, but is there someplace I can lay him down?" He glanced at Skyler. "He's not as light as he used to be."

"Oh, of course, I'm sorry." Georgette set the cat on the floor and turned to walk down a hallway. Felicity began sinuous figure eights between Matt's legs and he had to nudge her out of the way with his foot to follow.

Georgette went through a darkened doorway. Matt stopped and waited for her to walk across the room and flip on a light. The tiffany lamp on an oak nightstand cast a glow on the white eyelet bedspread on a full-size oak bed piled with lace and floral pillows.

Matt started to cross to the bed but noticed the closet on the way, which was full of women's clothes and shoes. He stopped.

"Georgette." He shot a stern look in her direction. "This is your room, isn't it?"

She shrugged and tossed pillows on the ground. "Yeah, so what?" Her chin tilted upward when she stood to face him, hands on her hips.

"We are not putting you out of your room." Matt glowered and then spun around the way he'd come.

Georgette grabbed his arm and he stopped to look at her. "Oh, come on. What's the big deal?"

"Why didn't you tell us you didn't have room? We'd have grabbed a hotel." Matt's cheeks burned, and embarrassment caused his voice to come out harsher than he'd intended. His regret was immediate when he saw Georgette's face fall and her bottom lip poke out. He'd forgotten how tender-hearted she was.

"I'm sorry. I don't know what I was thinking. I never should have called." *Way wrong thing to say.* Georgette dissolved into tears and ran from the room.

"Shoot." Matt pulled down the covers on the bed and laid Skyler on the pink sheets, took off his shoes, then covered him up. Switching off the lamp, he slipped from the room and quietly closed the door behind him. He nearly tripped over the stupid cat on his way back down the hall to find Georgette.

Her arms were wrapped around her legs, hugging her knees to her chest, crushing a yellow throw pillow to herself as she sat on the end of the couch. Her eyes shimmered with tears as they met his.

Matt sat on the other end of the sofa and rested his forearms on his knees.

"I'm sorry, Georgette. I didn't mean to hurt your feelings. You know what a jerk I can be." He sent a crooked smile her way and received a half one in return.

"Truth is, I had to call you. I had no where else to turn." The half smile disappeared. *Darn.* He'd done it again.

"I mean, I wanted to call you, you know, to see how you are and all . . ." Matt twiddled his thumbs while he fumbled on his words.

"Aw, heck with it." He sat back and propped one leg on the couch while resting his left arm along the back of the sofa. The cat jumped in his lap and he stroked it with his right hand.

"So, Georgette, how are ya?" He flashed what he hoped was his most charming boyish grin and a laugh escaped her pouty lips.

"I'm fine, Matt. How are you?" She sniffed and used the back of her index finger to stem the flow of mascara under her eyes. Matt set the cat on the floor and fished in his jeans pocket for the extra tissue he'd gotten in the habit of carrying for Skyler and handed it to her.

"Thank you," she said, and gave her nose a delicate blow.

"No problem. It's the least I can do."

She wiped her eyes, leaving black smudges on the tissue.

Matt glanced around the small living room and attached kitchenette. A small TV sat on a wooden table similar to the end table on the opposite wall. A boom box was next to it, and CDs and DVDs were stacked beneath the table. A wok still stood on the counter of the kitchen.

"Nice place." He didn't know what else to say.

"No it's not," she laughed. "But it's just temporary until Nate and I get married.

"So that's still on, eh?" Matt favored her with another crooked smile.

She beamed. "Yes." A dreamy look veiled her eyes. "It's still on."

Matt recognized that look and his heart filled with happiness for Georgette then twisted in pain for himself. What if his mission here failed?

"Did you talk to Nate about me? I mean, what I want to do?"

Georgette put her feet on the floor and set the pillow down beside her. Felicity leapt into her lap.

"Oh yes. In fact, he left just before you got here. He had the night off, so we've been talking about it ever since you called." The cat purred as Georgette petted it.

Matt raised one eyebrow. "What does he think about me staying here?"

"Well, I didn't tell him that part." A sheepish grin danced across her face. "I'd have never gotten him to leave otherwise, and then we would have been crowded."

Matt laughed, and Georgette joined in.

Matt's face grew serious. "I don't want to cause any trouble for you, Georgette. I'm really happy for you and Nate."

Moisture jumped into the corners of Georgette's eyes and she ducked her head. "Thanks, Matt. I appreciate that more than you know." Her head raised and she looked at him. "And I'm sorry about the way I acted earlier. I guess . . ."

Matt waited while she toyed with the tassel on the yellow pillow with one hand and stroked the cat with the other.

"I feel guilty about abandoning you and Skyler." Her eyes were large, round emeralds as she chewed her bottom lip.

"Oh, hey, forget about it." Matt's tone was flippant as he waved a hand at her, but his gaze was intent.

"I hope you know how much I cared . . . care about you, it's just . . ." Matt's head dropped and he had to swallow hard.

Georgette set the cat down, scooted toward him, and took his hands in hers. "I know, Matt. You don't have to apologize for a thing. I care about you, too. But now, I've finally found what you and Melody had."

Matt's head snapped up.

"Have, have. You're going to get her back." Georgette said. "Nate's working tomorrow evening, so we can all go to Disneyland in the morning. Then I'll stay here with Skyler while Nate takes you to see Melody."

Butterflies danced in Matt's stomach at those words. See Melody. Tomorrow. After a year and a half of agony, searching, wondering . . . This was going to be the longest night of his life. He glanced at his watch. Almost midnight. *Too late to go bang on her door. Better to get a good night's sleep.* He knew he couldn't put Skyler off anymore. Mentioning Disneyland so early in their trip had proved to be a huge mistake. The kid had talked nonstop about nothing else and hadn't dropped off to sleep again until they were almost to Georgette's.

Tomorrow evening it was, then. Once again, he'd be face to face with the woman he loved. The woman he would always love. Then he'd know if he had to endure as an empty shell and raise Skyler on his own, or if his family would be reunited. And this time the decision would stand forever.

Chapter Forty-seven

Melody studied the map of Utah while she munched a Hostess cherry pie. She'd been on the road since a little after seven, and the pie and carton of chocolate milk she'd bought were the first things she'd eaten since her lunch with Jack.

Jack had given her directions out of L.A. He'd even offered to fly her himself, but she'd opted to drive. She needed time to think. Melody McCandlass. It seemed right, somehow, but after a year and a half of being Andrea Kensington, it hadn't quite gelled.

Her thoughts drifted to her run-in with Esther after she and Jack had returned home from lunch. Esther had been at the studio all day, which is the reason Melody had been able to slip away from the house in the first place. Melody and Jack beat Esther home, which gave Melody time to collect her thoughts, and her things, before facing her. Melody shuddered.

A great calm had settled over her when she'd glimpsed Esther's car pull in the driveway, even though she'd shaken with fury the entire time it had taken her to gather her clothes, shoes, makeup, and other personal items, and shove them into the suitcases she'd had Rosa retrieve for her. Some of the clothes brought back memories of Esther's and her shopping trips after the accident and all the stories Esther had told her. No wonder nothing had been familiar or stirred the slightest sentiments in her. None of it had been real.

Esther had metamorphosed into a banshee when Melody told her she was leaving for good. Jack had stood by Melody's side and confessed he'd told Melody everything. When her shrieks brought no acquiescence, Esther had tried fainting, but Jack had simply carried her into the library and dumped her in a chair before going to make sure Melody's car was ready.

Jack and Esther owned several vehicles, and he'd let Melody take the little red Mercedes convertible she'd always been fond of. The trunk and back seat were now stuffed with Melody's belongings. Perhaps she'd have been better off with the Tahoe, but this was her favorite, and she felt no compunction at taking it. A car was a small enough trade for stealing a year and a half of her life.

Melody felt a twitch of conscience, which she suppressed with a swig of chocolate milk. Technically Esther and Jack had stolen that time, but Melody hadn't exactly been locked away in a dungeon. They'd lavished her with whatever she'd needed and even provided the means to pursue her music, which she knew had always been a part of her. In fact, it was the only real thing about her life. When Jack had seen how happy she'd been at first with her music, he'd delayed telling her the truth.

Melody wedged the carton next to the emergency brake on the center console, then folded the map and put it in the glove box. Exiting the car, she brushed pie crumbs off her jeans and T-shirt and threw the wrapper in a trashcan by the doors of the convenience store. She'd filled the car with gas before using the restroom and buying her map and "dinner," so she took one last stretch while looking at the stars and filling her lungs with the juniper-scented air. The evening had become chilly with the going down of the sun, so she fished a sweatshirt from the back seat and put it on rather than put the top up on her car. Then she climbed in, started it, and pulled onto the highway. She was only about a hundred and fifty miles from Las Vegas. I-15 would take her all the way to Ogden.

Vegas. That was the last place she'd seen Matt. His cold, steely eyes still gave her a chill when she thought of that experience.

What must he have been thinking? Melody tried to piece the puzzle together in her mind. Her accident had been over a year before her Vegas show, so she'd been missing all that time. Then, wham, there she was on a stage in Vegas. How must that have appeared? No wonder he'd stormed down the aisle, calling her name.

Jack had told her the divorce papers were served before she went to Europe, so she'd still been married when she went to Vegas. Melody tried to imagine how she'd feel if her husband disappeared for a year and then showed up on a stage somewhere, singing like he hadn't a care in the world. She cringed. He probably thought she'd abandoned him to go after a singing career. Melody's heart ached, for him and for herself.

But what about the redhead? She'd been with him in Vegas, then again in the picture, wearing a ring. A tingle of fear crept up Melody's neck. Was she too late? Was Matt remarried? A year and a half was a long time. Was she chasing moonbeams?

Maybe she'd find him and get her memory back only to wish she'd forget again. Was not knowing really worse than realizing what she'd had and lost?

Melody switched the radio on and cranked up the volume. Her thoughts were becoming the enemy. She was going to Utah. That was that. The temptation was already great to disappear.

The music was largely drowned out by the rushing wind, but Melody took deep breaths of the desert air and tried to calm the pounding in her chest and ignore thoughts of the risk of unbelievable heartache that lurked in her mind.

Chapter Forty-eight

Matt was exhausted, yet pulsing with nervous energy. A whole day of standing in line while trying to contain a five-year-old at Disneyland had worn him out. But now he was on his way to see Melody. A hot shower had revived him somewhat, and anticipation was slowly dissipating the remaining tiredness.

A glance in his rearview mirror prompted him to say a quick prayer of thanks that his belongings were still intact, which he considered a miracle for L.A. Georgette did have underground parking at her apartment complex, and he'd bought a tarp and covered everything securely before going to bed last night, but he hadn't slept much, worrying about it. And thinking about his pending reunion with the love of his life. They'd gone in Nate's car to Disneyland to avoid leaving Matt's stuff exposed in the parking lot all day. He'd generously tipped the parking garage security guard at the apartments to keep an extra watch on his truck while they were gone.

A scrap of paper with Melody's address and instructions to her house was clutched in his right hand as he held the steering wheel so he could peek at it frequently. After all this time, all the agonizing searching, her whereabouts were scribbled on this piece of white, lined paper torn from an ordinary notebook. Matt wasn't sure why that amazed him so—after all, the address had been on the divorce papers all along—but he held onto the paper like it was a map to King Solomon's treasure.

"Rosewood Lane," he read on a street sign, then glanced at the address. This was it. He flicked on his left blinker and drummed the steering wheel with his fingers while he waited for a line of cars, then peeled onto Melody's street. His heart pounded in his chest and beads of sweat popped out on his forehead.

Huge trees lined the street that wound up a hill. Matt caught peeks of mansions behind massive iron gates.

"Wow," he said under his breath. *Is this what I have to compete with?* How was he going to drag her away from this life?

A trickle of sweat rolled down the side of his face. He looked at the crisp sleeve of his freshly ironed cotton shirt and decided against using it to wipe away the perspiration. Skyler's sweatshirt lay on the seat of the truck, and he grabbed that instead. Switching the address paper to his other hand, he wiped his forehead with the sweatshirt, then tossed it back on the seat.

Number 6927, he read from the paper. An ornate metal 5935 was woven into a gate on his right. He was close. A glance at his watch showed a little after seven. Nate should be there already. He'd dropped Matt, Georgette, and Skyler off at Georgette's and then hurried home to shower and change after Disneyland so he could be to work by six. Matt had made sure Skyler was fed and bathed, then had gotten ready himself. He'd been too nervous to eat the tuna sandwiches Georgette had made for them.

A guardhouse came into view, and Matt recognized Nate's grinning face as he hung out the window and waved at him. Matt pulled up next to it.

"Hey, buddy. You ready for this?" Nate thought the whole thing a great adventure. All day at Disneyland Matt had had to continually give him dirty looks and nod at Skyler to keep him from bursting out with questions or comments about Melody, which had added to Matt's exhaustion. Mental exhaustion was often much worse than physical.

Matt's smile was less sure. "I hope so." He sucked in a breath.

Nate's grin disappeared. "Seriously, Matt, good luck in there."

"Thank you. I have a feeling I'm going to need it."

Nate pushed a button and the gates slowly opened. Matt stared straight ahead, watching them and wondering. Were they the gates to heaven or hell?

Chapter Forty-nine

Matt's truck crept along the driveway. Now that he was here, so close to Melody, fear clamped manacles on his heart and brain. What if her memory had returned and she'd chosen this life instead of returning to him and Skyler? What if she didn't remember him and didn't care to? What if all the hurt and anger he'd experienced when he saw her in Vegas returned and he was unable to function and care for his son? He was alone now. Georgette was a good friend, but he couldn't expect her to help, given her situation. And he'd never be able to return to Melody's parents.

These thoughts were getting him nowhere. *Remember the song.* Matt's foot pressed on the gas, and he pulled onto a circular drive surrounded by rose bushes. He stopped in front of a beautiful Tudor style mansion with balconied windows. A whistle escaped his lips. *Not bad.*

Pushing his fears aside, he opened the door of his truck and climbed down, slamming it behind him. A momentary pause allowed him to take a couple of deep breaths, then he walked to the front door, grasped the brass knocker, and pounded firmly.

A spindly man in a tux answered the door. *Is this a restaurant or a house?* Matt wondered.

"May I help you?"

Matt suppressed a smile at the phony British accent. He cleared his throat before he spoke.

"Yes, I'm looking for Mel . . ." *Wait, what did they say she called herself?* "For Andrea," Matt finished, as his stomach did flip-flops.

The skinny man looked him up and down. Skin drooped from the guy's jowls despite his almost emaciated appearance. Beady eyes peered over a hooked nose, and his expression suggested he was inspecting a pile of garbage. Matt wanted to punch his scrawny face. "I'm afraid Miss Kensington isn't in." The "Miss" was emphasized until he sounded like a hissing snake.

Matt's nerves were already taut, and he was losing patience with this pretentious jerk, but he sensed he'd get nowhere by losing his cool.

"Well, could you please tell me when you expect her to return?" His voice was tight, but controlled.

"Never." An even more smug look stole across the man's face, if that were possible.

"What do you mean, never?" The muscles in Matt's jaw flexed as he gritted his teeth.

"Who are you?" The disdainful scrutiny continued as Matt's question was ignored. Two could play that game.

"Is the lady of the house in?" *Esther? Yeah, that's the one who called herself Melody's mother.*

"Whom should I say is calling?" Same question, different wording.

"Tell her *Andrea's* husband is here." Matt put special emphasis on "Andrea." This guy was obviously a servant. Matt wasn't about to let him call the shots.

"Wait here, please."

The door closed in Matt's face before a response came to his lips. Several uncomplimentary descriptions of the servant popped into his mind. Fiddling with the keys in his pocket, Matt looked around, hoping the man had actually gone to get Esther and had not just left him hanging. A fly buzzed around Matt's head and he swatted it away. Bees hummed and the scent of roses drifted on the air. His hand reached for the knocker again just as the door swung open to reveal a shriveled little woman wearing a hot pink skirt suit, her jet-black hair streaked with gray and pulled back into a bun.

"Mr. McCandlass, I presume?" Her voice was honey sweet, underscored by a bitter tension that was reflected in her bloodshot eyes and the lines around her bright pink lips.

Matt was surprised at the array of emotions that flew through his system at meeting this woman. Was she responsible for Melody's disappearance, or was she just a player in this bizarre scenario? How could she claim to be Melody's mother? Would she try to keep him from seeing her? There was only one way to find out.

Matt hesitated, then extended his hand. "Matt McCandlass. I'm here to see my wife." His tone remained as neutral as manageable under the circumstances.

Esther ignored the proffered hand and laced her fingers, with their hot pink nails, together in front of her, and lifted her chin. "I'm afraid you're too late, Mr. McCandlass. Andrea doesn't live here anymore." Bitterness crept into her voice, replacing any semblance of sweet. Her eyes were cold and hard as they glared at Matt. "Now if you'll excuse me . . ." She reached for the door and attempted to close it, but Matt blocked it with his foot and shoved it open.

"Hold on now, lady. You're not gettin' off that easy." His emotions boiled. "I want some answers and I want them now." Matt was all done being civil. He towered over the woman, meeting her glare, but she didn't back down.

"What do you care? You're not even married to her anymore." Esther spat the words and Matt stepped back like he'd been slapped, but quickly recovered.

"And who the heck are you? Where do you get off claiming to be her mother?" His shouts brought curious looks from inside the house as various white-capped heads poked from doorways.

Esther's chest heaved and she glanced over her shoulder. "Perhaps we should discuss this in the library," she acquiesced in a clipped tone as she took a step back and to the side, holding her arm toward the interior of the house.

"Yes, perhaps we should."

Chapter Fifty

Melody sat in her car in front of the address Jack had gotten for her from the divorce papers. She'd driven right to the place, even though the sun was barely peaking over the mountains and she was a little loopy having driven all night. Her head buzzed from the Mountain Dews she'd downed in an effort to stay awake. Perhaps it would have been smarter to pull over and get a hotel somewhere, but Melody knew she wouldn't have been able to sleep much anyway, so here she was.

Her skin tingled as she studied the red brick of the house and the cement steps with an iron railing leading to the front door. White shutters framed a large plate-glass window on the front and another smaller one over the stairs. The place seemed familiar, yet she couldn't quite remember it.

A moving van sat in the driveway, which made her stomach lurch. Melody glanced at her watch. Six o'clock was too early to knock on anyone's door. Particularly when the owner, in all likelihood, was extremely angry with her already.

A rumble emanated from her mid-section. Breakfast wasn't a bad idea. Maybe he'd be up by the time she came back. A glance in the rearview mirror assured her she didn't want to greet him in her present state, anyway. In Cedar City she'd succumbed to the cold and put the top up on her convertible, but the many miles before that had blown her hair to an unruly mess, despite the ponytail she'd worn to keep it under control.

Fear pinned her to the spot. Was he moving? Where was he going? What if he planned to get an early start, and was gone by the time she returned? A small bike with training wheels lay in the driveway by the truck, and toys were scattered throughout the yard. The tingling continued across her scalp as she considered the meaning of this. The boy from the picture must live here. Whether he belonged to Matt, or to the redhead . . .

Melody's stomach growled again. The house was dark and still. A rooster crowed somewhere. Surely she had time to grab a quick bite and fix her hair and makeup. Maybe even change her clothes. At the very least, the toys had to be picked up before the truck left.

A car passed and Melody pulled out behind it, her mind a jumble of thoughts. Was the mystery about to end? Would Matt jar her memory loose once and for all? Were her days of heartache and loneliness coming to a close—or just beginning?

Chapter Fifty-one

The moving truck was still in the driveway and the toys in the yard. Melody heaved a sigh of relief. She'd only been gone an hour, so it was unlikely the truck would have left already, but in her present state of nervousness, she wasn't thinking rationally.

Lights were on, and she could see movement inside the house through the front window, so she checked her reflection in the rearview mirror again. She'd splashed cold water on her face in the restroom at the Denny's where she'd had breakfast, then reapplied her makeup. The snarls in her hair had taken some effort to work out, but her hair now shimmered around her face and fell to her shoulders. A liberal application of deodorant and a fresh T-shirt, followed by a spritz of perfume, had finished her grooming. Now she was ready. Well, as ready as she was likely to get.

With a deep breath to quell the antics in her stomach, she reached for the handle and pushed open the car door. Then, squaring her shoulders, she marched up the driveway, stepped over the bike, climbed the steps, and rang the doorbell. She held her breath while she waited.

A blond-haired, freckled-faced boy of about four or five wearing Spiderman pajamas answered the door and Melody's heart jumped. Close on the boy's heels was an attractive young woman, about Melody's age, she guessed, holding a baby on her hip. Gray sweats with a big, blue BYU across the shirt front hung on her slender figure.

"May I help you?" the woman asked, tucking a wisp of blonde hair behind her ear as she met Melody's stare.

"Um." Melody was stunned, not sure what to say. The woman hefted the baby girl higher on her hip while the little boy turned and ran back into the house.

"I, uh . . ." Who was this person? Where was Matt? "I'm looking for Matt McCandlass," she finally managed to say.

"Oh, he moved. We bought the house from him, and as you can see, we are just moving in." The woman gave a self-conscious chuckle as she glanced behind her, and Melody noticed the boxes stacked everywhere.

Tears bubbled near the surface as Melody tried to contemplate what this meant. She'd been so geared up for this moment that the disappointment now pressed upon her like a concrete slab.

"Do you . . ." Melody cleared her throat and struggled to maintain her composure. "Do you happen to know where he went?" Hope was slipping away.

The woman seemed to sense Melody's distress. Her face showed concern, and she pushed open the screen door that separated them.

"I'm sorry, but I don't." A frown creased the woman's forehead, and compassion radiated from her blue eyes. "Would you like to come in?" Her efforts to hold open the screen were being thwarted by the youngster on her hip, who began to squirm and whimper. Melody looked at the beautiful child with the mass of blonde curls and huge blue eyes. Her chubby cheeks were smeared with some kind of white goo, and Melody suspected she'd interrupted her breakfast.

"Oh, no, no. That's okay." Melody took a step back. "I can see you have your hands full." Tears forced their way to her eyes. What was she going to do now? How would she ever find Matt? A shudder shook her frame when she thought of the car dealership where he worked. Melody had sworn she'd never go near that place, or that man, Rick, again, but she was out of options. This address had been her only other clue to Matt's whereabouts.

As she turned to walk down the stairs, the woman spoke again. "Wait, please." Her plea caused Melody to stop and face her.

"Let me ask my husband if he knows anything. He talked to Mr. McCandlass more than I did. Please, come in." Her smile radiated warmth and Melody melted. No friendly faces existed in her life. She had no one. Fatigue and despair washed over her and she felt like slumping to the ground where she stood, but instead, she took a step toward the woman.

"Are you sure? I don't want to be a bother." She bit her lip to keep it from quivering.

"Of course I'm sure." The woman's smile broadened and a twinkle came in her eye. "You'd better watch out, though, because I might put you to work."

Those were the magic words. Melody didn't know why, but she felt an instant bond to this woman. A smile tugged at the corners of her mouth.

"You're on," she said with a timid chuckle, taking hold of the screen door. "By the way, my name is Melody." She paused, realizing the name had rolled off her tongue without a moment's hesitation.

"I'm Karen. And this is Jessica." Karen rubbed noses with the baby. "Welcome to our mess."

Chapter Fifty-two

Matt sat in a leather wingback chair across from Esther in an ornate library with more books than he'd ever seen in a private residence. His elbows rested on his knees as he leaned forward and stared at Esther, unable to believe what he was hearing.

"But Nate said she returned from Europe over a month ago." The scowl he'd been sporting ever since beginning this conversation deepened.

"And who, might I ask, is Nate?" Esther sat upright in a matching chair, legs crossed, fingers steepled.

"Huh? Oh, he's your guard out front." Matt immediately wished he could suck back the words when he saw a dark look cloud Esther's face. *Dang. I hope I didn't get him fired.*

"I see." Her fingers drummed together and Matt could picture her standing over Nate, laughing while he lay prone, tied to railroad tracks.

"Well, it might surprise you to learn, Mr. McCandlass, that I don't confide all the happenings in this house to the guards out front." Her snippish, sarcastic tone was meant to intimidate him, but Matt was used to dealing with Rick. This woman was minor league.

"Whatever, lady. The fact remains that you still haven't explained what she was doing here in the first place or where you get off calling yourself her mother. I'm about two inches from calling the police and reporting you for kidnapping."

The finger drumming stopped, and fear flitted across Esther's face before a cold mask dropped into place.

"I did not kidnap her," she hissed. "I told you, we found her half dead, with no idea who she was, and I merely cared for her and gave her a life." Her chin jutted into the air.

"But why, in the name everything holy, did you tell her you were her mother? And why didn't you contact the authorities in Utah? Didn't you think that maybe somebody was looking for her?" Anger seethed through Matt's words as memories of his search pressed upon his heart.

Instead of backing down, she took the offense.

"Oh, like you were so concerned. It's been over a year and a half, and this is the first we've seen your mug. You sent some flunky to serve divorce papers without so much as a hello." She folded her arms across her chest, a satisfied, evil grin lurking on her features at Matt's crestfallen look.

Her words hit him like a slug to the gut. He'd been so quick to assume the worst when he'd seen her in Vegas. His life had been sent down a wind tunnel, and when he'd come through the other side, he'd thought a fresh start his only option.

His head dropped and he stared at his hands while he collected his thoughts. That was between him and Melody. This woman had no say in either of their lives and he certainly didn't owe her an explanation. He glared at her.

"That's none of your business. Now where the heck is she?" He sat straight in his chair and grasped the arms like he was ready to lunge at her.

This lady was obviously not easily intimidated. She flicked a piece of lint off her suit jacket and answered him in a flippant tone. "I told you, she's on tour in Europe. And quite successful, you know. If you go storming back into her life, you're only going to ruin her career, which is what she wants more than anything. She knows all about the divorce." Her eyes were hooded as she shot him a quick look.

Matt felt a knife twist in his heart. Maybe Esther was on a par with Rick. This conversation was going nowhere. Frustration mounted and his head dropped again, his hands folded in his lap.

"We have a son, you know." The words were barely above a whisper.

Except for the ticking of a clock somewhere, silence engulfed the room. Matt raised his eyes and caught the barest hint of human emotion on the lined, sculpted face before the stone hardened again, but Esther said nothing. Her mouth opened, but closed into a hard line and she clasped her hands in her lap.

Matt waited and watched. The musty smell of the room was not quite masked by lemon-scented furniture polish. Darkness crept up the windows, adding to the dimness of the room. The only light came from the lamp on a table next to Esther.

A knock on the door interrupted the silence. The jerk in the penguin suit stuck his head in the door without waiting for an invitation.

"Would madam care for some tea?" he asked, in his Hollywood British accent.

"No, madam would not," Esther snapped.

"And the gentleman?" He stepped into the room, seemingly unaffected by Esther's dismissive tone, and stared at Matt.

"No," Esther practically shouted before Matt could answer. "Now leave us, Martin, and don't interrupt again."

"Very well, madam." His eyes never left Matt, and he stood still and tall with his hands folded in front of him.

"Mr. Kensington apologizes for being late and wanted you to know he's on his way home." Martin's eyes bore into Matt. Matt looked from him to Esther. What was going on here? Panic cracked Esther's mask and she held up her hands like claws toward Martin.

"I told you to leave." This time she did shout.

Martin slowly backed out of the door, his eyes never leaving Matt. Was he trying to tell him something? The door closed behind him and Matt watched in fascination as the imperious statue in a hot pink suit dissolved to jelly.

"You have to leave too." Her snide, superior voice had turned to a shrill squeak and she wrung her hands as her eyes flitted back and forth.

Matt was dumbfounded. What had happened? Was she terrified of her husband? Did he beat her? She hardly seemed the type to put up with that. But seeing her in her present state, Matt didn't know what to think. He sat frozen to his chair, his mouth sagging open.

"Go, go!" Esther was on her feet now, closing the gap between them.

Matt stood to meet her and towered over her.

"I think I'll wait and speak to Mr. Kensington."

"No!" Esther grabbed his arm and tried to drag him to the door. He didn't budge. No chance he was leaving now. He shook her off and took a step back.

"What is wrong with you? Calm down." The coldness in her eyes had been replaced by a wild look that made Matt think of the time he'd visited the mental hospital in Provo with his psychology class. Realization dawned.

Of course. She was mentally unbalanced. Why else would she claim a stranger as her own daughter? This is what Melody had put up with for a year and a half. Was she being held prisoner? How did Mr. Kensington fit into the picture, and why was Esther so afraid of him?

Matt put his hands on Esther's shoulders and backed her gently to her chair. He knelt beside her and took her hand in both of his.

"It's okay," he soothed, patting her hand.

She snatched it away and glared at him. The bitterness was back.

"Get away from me," she hissed.

Matt about toppled over at the sudden change. This lady was looney tunes for sure. Poor Mel. He had to find her and get her away from this craziness.

Matt thought of Carol, Melody's real mother, with her sweet disposition and helpful attitude. Two minutes was the longest anyone sat at her place without her rustling up a plate of food for them and trying to cover them with a blanket. What a contrast to this nasty little person.

Matt stood and walked back to the other seat and sat down. They stared at each other in silence until headlights shone through the window and a car pulled into the drive. Esther's shoulders sagged, and a look of defeat crossed her face.

Matt felt sorry for her. He didn't care what she'd done; no woman deserved to be abused. Matt would face this guy, man to man, and get to the bottom of this whole mess once and for all.

Chapter Fifty-three

Words tumbled from Melody's mouth. Mechanically, she unpacked boxes of dishes and put them in cupboards while Karen finished feeding Jessica. Karen smiled and nodded, or frowned and shook her head and said, "Uh huh," or "Wow" as the occasion dictated, but she mostly just listened.

Melody couldn't stop talking. Nobody had really listened to her for over a year and a half, and now that the floodgates were open, her emotions gushed forth. She started from when she woke up in the ravine and went through every memory she had. When she reached the part about her singing career, Karen stopped, the spoon halfway to Jessica's mouth, and stared.

"You're *the* Andrea Kensington?"

"Uh huh," Melody answered, sticking a stack of plastic cups in the cupboard like she'd done it a hundred times before. Catching Karen's dumbfounded expression, she paused.

"You mean you've actually heard of me?"

Jessica squawked and grabbed for the spoon suspended in front of her, sending white goo flying everywhere. Karen let out a disgusted grunt and wiped a big glob from her face.

"Okay, okay," she cooed at the baby, and resumed her feeding.

"Mom, can I have some Cheerios?" A small voice called through a doorway leading down a narrow flight of stairs.

"Sure, honey," Karen yelled back. "My son, Steven," she explained at Melody's raised eyebrows.

Melody remembered the boy in the Spiderman pajamas, and her heart did another jig.

"You'll have to come up here to eat them, though," she called over her shoulder as she scooped the last bites of goo from the bowl and fed them to Jessica.

"Let's see if he can pry himself away from his video games," Karen said with a wink at Melody. "I hate to admit it, but the TV was the first thing off the truck. I knew I'd never get a thing done with him under my feet complaining about being bored and having no one to play with." She headed for the sink with the bowl and spoon.

"Have you seen a washcloth around here anywhere?" Karen asked, rinsing the dishes in her hand and putting them in the sink.

"Top drawer by the sink," Melody answered without thinking.

"Thanks." Karen gave her an odd look, retrieved a cloth, wet it, and went to wash Jessica's face and hands before untying her bib and releasing her from the chair. Jessica crawled into the front room, making happy, gurgling sounds as she went. There was no sign of Steven, yet.

Karen tossed the rag at the sink and grabbed Melody by the arm as she was about to reach for another box.

"Oh no you don't, missy. You've earned a break." Karen pulled her toward the kitchen table and set her down in a chair next to it, then took one herself. "And don't think for a minute I've forgotten what we were talking about."

Melody laughed. "You mean me. I've been jabbering my fool head off."

"And I've enjoyed every minute of it. I was so afraid I wouldn't have anyone to talk to when we moved. I can't tell you what a treat this is. And what a story! Seriously, Andrea Kensington?"

Melody shrugged. "In the flesh. I can't believe you've heard of me."

"Are you kidding? 'Where'd Love Go?' is my favorite song. Anytime I get in the mood for a good cry I just lock myself in my room and listen to your CD." Her expression became serious.

"And now I know where all that sadness comes from." She reached for Melody's hands and clasped them in her own. "You wrote that, didn't you?"

Melody nodded and ducked her head.

"This is so bizarre. You were married and didn't know it, and now you're divorced, but have just learned about your marriage . . . Sounds like a movie." Karen was shaking her head and staring off into the corner when Melody looked at her.

"Or a really bad soap opera." Melody choked out a laugh to suppress the lump rising in her throat.

"Are there any other kind?" Karen looked at her and they both laughed.

Jessica continued her baby chatter in the other room and Melody glanced through the doorway to see her sitting amidst a pile of toys, happily banging them together.

She turned back to Karen. "Did you say your husband might know where Matt is?"

"Yeah, I did. Sorry I've been hogging you to myself. I dragged you in here on the pretense of talking to him and then put you to work." Karen grinned at her. "He's still asleep. He was up until the wee hours of the morning unloading the truck, so I thought I'd let him sleep in a bit. I'll get him up in a few minutes."

"What about you?" Melody asked. "Something tells me you didn't get to bed none too early yourself."

Karen stifled a yawn. "True, true, but the kids never let me sleep in too late. Wes is good about getting up with them sometimes, but he was dead to the world this morning."

A blond head poked around the corner of the door to the basement.

"Mooomm. I said I wanted some Cheerios."

"Yes, I heard you. And I said you'd have to come up here to eat them. Now here you are." Karen walked over, picked Steven up, and gave him a big hug.

"Come meet my new friend." Karen carried him to stand in front of Melody, who also stood up.

"Stevie, this is Melody. Melody, Steven."

"Nice to meet you, Steven." Melody held out her hand to him, but he buried his face on Karen's neck. Karen laughed and patted his back.

"I'm afraid he's a bit shy, aren't you, big guy?" Karen said.

Melody's arms ached to take the boy from Karen and squeeze him to her heart. Such overwhelming feelings of love and loss rolled through her that her legs gave out and she plunked back to her chair. Karen's face showed concern.

"Are you all right?" She sat next to Melody, still holding Steven against her.

Melody felt deflated.

"I'm fine," she lied. Her sleepless night caught up to her in a wave. Something about this little boy threatened to pull her heart from her chest.

"When was the last time you had any sleep?" Karen asked, her brows drawn together.

Melody yawned. "A while," she admitted and managed a crooked smile. "I suppose I ought to go find a hotel. I can come back in a couple of hours to talk to your husband and help you unload." She stood on shaky legs and pushed the chair back under the table.

"Nonsense," Karen stated in a firm voice. "You sit right back down there while I go get Stevie's bed ready for you." Standing, she set Steven on her chair. He whimpered and tried to cling to her, but she pried him off. "It's okay, honey. I'm going to get your Cheerios." She headed for the cupboard.

Melody knew she should protest but didn't want to. The thought of wandering around in search of a hotel was overwhelming. The one she'd stayed at last time she was here flashed through her mind, but she didn't remember exactly where it was and was too tired to think about it, so she pulled her chair out and plopped onto it.

Steven looked at her with wide, blue eyes, his index finger in his mouth. What was it about him that made her feel like she was missing an appendage? Her eyes were glued to his face, and as she stared, his features seemed to shift. His hair darkened and his eyes turned to green. Melody wanted to cry out but instead bit her lip and choked back a sob. Memories danced in the recesses of her mind like dreams she'd had where important events were taking place, but she couldn't pry her eyes open to see clearly. Oh, how she wanted to see.

Chapter Fifty-four

Melody was gone. Back to Utah, no less. Matt had driven all this way . . . Now how was he going to find her?

He weaved through late night traffic as he made his way back to Georgette's. Jack had offered to let him stay at the mansion, but there was no way Matt would let himself get trapped in that nuthouse.

What were all these people doing out so late? He cursed under his breath. Was there ever a time this confounded place wasn't overrun by cars? His foot slammed on the brakes as a BMW pulled out in front of him, narrowly missing his bumper.

What was he going to tell Skyler now? His fingers drummed on the steering wheel while he waited for a red light.

Grandma and Grandpa. That was it. He'd say they forgot to tell them good-bye and they'd go to Burt and Carol's. He owed them that, anyway. And it was time to involve them in the search. Melody wouldn't go there because she didn't know they existed, but perhaps they'd have some idea where else she might go.

Guilt washed over Matt for leaving them out of the loop for so long. They'd suffered terribly thinking she was dead. But, oddly, their religion offered peace in that regard. They believed Melody was alive in the next life and much better off, and that they'd be together again forever. Matt was going to give that a serious look when his family was back together. He never wanted to feel this hopeless, gut-wrenching sense of loss again. "'Til death do us part" wasn't nearly long enough.

Matt entered the freeway, and the traffic wasn't quite so thick. Good thing, since his mind was preoccupied.

Jack had given Melody Matt's address, but since he no longer lived there, where would she go? What would she do? He had to find her before she disappeared. Again.

A glance in the rearview mirror served as a reminder that Matt was homeless. Precious little remained of their lives. His Adam's apple moved up and down as he thought of all Melody's things he'd gotten rid of. Maybe it was a good thing she'd lost her memory. But could he make her remember him? And if not, could he win her back? Their courtship had been no picnic. Matt had worked long and hard to convince her to marry outside her religion. If given another chance, he'd do things her way.

His long talk with Jack had been enlightening. Unlike Esther, who was a few cars short of a fleet, Jack deeply regretted taking Melody away from him. And when he'd heard about Skyler, Jack had collapsed in grief. Matt wished he hadn't told him. He'd never seen a man suffer such deep remorse. Jack was a good man. And Melody hadn't suffered. They'd given her a good life, however misdirected their intentions had been. Esther's, anyway. Jack had simply gone along.

A song came on the radio and Matt recognized Melody's voice. It wasn't the same song he'd heard on the way here, and he was able to listen without his insides being torn apart. At least she'd had a chance to give her music a shot. They'd have been content to live out their lives as a happy family, the sole beneficiaries of her wonderful talent. For the first time since she disappeared, Matt felt a semblance of peace.

Melody had always told him that everything happens for a reason. That God has a plan, and good can come of any situation. Even if it's a lesson learned, or strength received from overcoming an obstacle. But the good had to be looked for and recognized.

Matt flipped on his turn signal and exited the freeway, deep in thought. If strength came from trials, he was a fortress. He'd tapped into wells he hadn't known he'd possessed to pull him through the past year and a half.

Drawing a deep breath, Matt squared his shoulders. He'd use that strength to find his wife and put their lives back together. He just hoped he had enough.

Chapter Fifty-five

Melody wandered into the chaos of the kitchen. Jessica sat in her highchair, pounding the tray with a spoon. Cracker crumbs were smashed all over the tray and scattered on the floor around her. Karen stood at the stove, stirring a pot that threatened to boil over, while Steven clung to her leg, crying, still sporting Spiderman PJs.

Melody stretched and yawned. "Boy, I can't leave you alone for a minute, can I?" she said, smiling broadly.

Karen looked up from the stove, her hair dangling in wisps around her face, the scrunchy barely maintaining a tenuous grip to her long tresses.

"Help!" She gave Melody a lop-sided grin.

Melody hustled over and took the spoon from her. "Here, let me do that, and you see to Steven." Turning the heat down, she stirred the macaroni while Karen picked Steven up and carried him to the table.

"Did you have a good sleep?" Karen asked Melody as she soothed Steven for a moment, then sat him on a chair.

"I did, thank you," Melody replied, stifling another yawn as she stirred the macaroni. "Now it's your turn. Do these guys take naps?" She nodded toward Jessica and Steven.

"Yes, thank goodness. I'll put them down as soon as they've had lunch." Steven whimpered and Karen handed him a cracker.

"Your macaroni will be done in just a sec, hon." Walking back and rummaging through a cupboard, she came up with a bottle of mashed carrots and then seated herself in front of Jessica.

"Do you have a colander?" Melody asked. She didn't remember unpacking one.

"Somewhere." Karen shrugged and smiled at her, twisting the lid off the baby food jar.

"How about a lid for this pan, then?"

"In the drawer under the stove."

Melody turned the heat off the burner and dug in the drawer for the lid, then poured the water off the macaroni, using the lid to keep from dumping the noodles. Steven started to cry again, so Melody set the pan down and handed him another cracker.

"Almost done with the mac and cheese, buddy," she told him, patting him on the head. Then she opened the fridge to retrieve some milk and butter. "I hope you don't mind me helping myself." Melody smiled at Karen.

"Oh, please. Make yourself at home." Karen wrested the spoon from Jessica, producing a loud squawk, which she silenced with a mouthful of carrots.

Melody felt an odd twang at Karen's words. She felt completely at home. She sliced a chunk of butter into the macaroni, then dumped the yellow powder from an envelope into the pan. She stirred until both were melted, then poured in a splash of milk and finished stirring. Other than the occasional bowl of cereal, she didn't recall fixing herself, or anyone else, anything to eat for the past year and a half, yet standing in this kitchen, making macaroni and cheese, felt as natural to her as breathing.

Grabbing a bowl from the cupboard, she dished up some of the macaroni and then blew on it while she fished a spoon from the drawer. She continued to stir and blow until the macaroni and cheese had cooled slightly, and then set the bowl in front of Steven.

"What do you say, sweetheart?" Karen asked him.

"Thank you," came the shy reply as he took the spoon and began to eat.

"Do you want some?" Melody asked Karen.

"In a minute, maybe." She scraped an orange glob off Jessica's chin and spooned it back into her mouth. "Mac and cheese isn't my favorite. I can fix us a sandwich when I'm through here, if you'd like."

"I can do it," Melody volunteered.

Karen gave her a sheepish yet grateful smile. "You're a life saver. I feel guilty making you work. You got a lot more than you bargained for when you knocked on my door."

Melody's insides reeled, and her emotions threatened to overcome her as thoughts of Matt flashed through her mind. She grabbed for the back of Steven's chair.

"Are you okay? Did I say something wrong?" Karen hesitated in the feeding process, but this time held the spoon out of Jessica's reach.

"I'm fine. Just a little woozy." Her fingers dug into the back of the chair.

"I can fix the sandwiches; you sit down," Karen ordered. "Besides, Wes will be hungry, too."

As if on cue, the front door opened and a large box with jeaned legs and tanned, bulging arms entered. The man underneath deposited the box on a pile in the living room, and then joined them in the kitchen.

"Hi, I'm Wes." He wiped his hands on the front of his shirt, leaving black smears, then stuck one out to Melody.

"I'm Melody. Nice to meet you." Her hand slipped into his as she swallowed hard. Wes was gorgeous. Melody estimated him to be about six feet two. A white T-shirt stretched across his muscled chest. Light brown hair framed a tanned face with amber eyes that twinkled when he flashed snow-white, straight teeth.

"Nice to meet you, too." He shook her hand vigorously while favoring her with a smile that made her heart skip a beat.

Dropping Melody's hand, he turned to Karen. "Got anything to eat?"

"Yeah, I was just going to fix us some sandwiches." Jessica blew a raspberry, spewing orange baby food everywhere. "Oh yuck. I guess that's my cue," Karen said, setting the jar and spoon on the cupboard and wiping her cheek with the back of her hand.

"I can make us sandwiches. Hon, you . . ." Wes looked at Jessica and grinned. "You do whatever it is you have to do."

He ruffled Steven's hair on his way to the sink. "How ya doin', sport?"

"Good," was the muffled reply as Steven continued to eat.

Wes washed his hands and then tossed Karen a wet rag.

"Need some help?" Melody looked from Karen to Wes, embarrassed at her reaction to her new friend's husband.

"I'm fine," Karen sighed, struggling to wipe Jessica's face with the rag while the baby turned her head from side to side and screamed.

Melody laughed. "Looks like it." She turned to Wes. "How about you?"

"Sure. Wanna slice some tomatoes?" He was lining up pieces of bread on the cupboard.

"You got it." Melody went to the fridge and rummaged through the crisper to find a tomato.

"Cutting board?" She looked at Karen who just smiled and shrugged, so Melody took a knife from the drawer and began slicing the tomato on the countertop across from Wes.

"Karen tells me you're looking for Matt McCandlass," Wes commented as he walked to the fridge and rummaged for sandwich makings.

The knife slipped and Melody almost sliced her finger. "Uh, yeah," she stammered. Why did mention of that name turn her legs to jelly? "She says you might know where he went."

Wes returned with his hands full of Miracle Whip, mustard, turkey, and cheese. He set the food on the counter. "I think he said something about Arizona," Wes replied as he untwisted the jar on the Miracle Whip.

Melody's heart dropped to her toes like a stone in a pond. Arizona? How would she ever find him in Arizona? "Did he say where exactly in Arizona?" She supposed it would be too good to hope for an address.

"Naw. He didn't even know. He and his kid were going to make a fresh start or something."

Melody's eyes blurred. Her hands shook, so she set the knife down and wiped them on a paper towel, then reached for a chair and slowly lowered herself into it.

"What'd I say?" Wes held a butter knife covered with Miracle Whip poised in the air while his glance shifted between Karen and Melody.

Melody had begun to shake all over as tears coursed down her cheeks. Karen quickly removed Jessica from the high chair and set her on the floor, then came and knelt beside Melody and put her arm around her.

"It's okay, honey, you'll find him. And we're going to help." Karen looked at Wes, who stared at the women, his mouth agape.

"You said . . ." Melody swallowed hard and tried again, peering at Wes through a watery film. "You said Matt and his kid?"

"Yeah," Wes hesitated and looked at Karen. She merely shrugged, so he continued. "He has a little boy about Steven's age." Wes clamped his jaw shut and watched warily.

Melody buried her face in her hands as tears flowed. Karen patted and stroked her back.

"It's okay, Melody. Please don't cry. We're here for you, honey."

Mental, physical, and emotional exhaustion hit all at once and Melody gave in and let the great cleansing sobs roll through her. Karen continued to stroke her back.

"All done, Mommy," she heard Steven say in a shaky voice.

"Okay, sweetheart," Karen whispered back. The stroking stopped and Karen stood.

"What's wrong with the lady?" Steven asked in a timid whisper.

"Nothing, honey. She's okay." Karen reassured him.

Melody's sobs slowed to a trickle. Feeling self-conscious, she wondered how to get out of this gracefully. Something soft tickled her hands and she slid them apart enough to see a wad of tissues being held in front of her face. Gratefully, she took them and began mopping up.

"I'm sorry," she croaked, not daring to look at anyone.

"Don't be ridiculous. You don't need to apologize." Karen's words were sincere, but when Melody finally looked at her, she saw confusion mixed with concern.

Wes had gone back to making sandwiches. His head was bowed, intent on his task when Melody glanced at him. She felt like an idiot. Talk about bad first impressions.

Steven was gone, presumably back downstairs to the TV, and Melody heard Jessica gurgling and clanging toys in the front room.

Karen sat in a chair facing Melody. Melody took both her hands in hers.

"I didn't mean to lose it like that."

Karen started to protest, but Melody shushed her. "I appreciate your kindness more than you can imagine. This was a horrible time to crash in on you like this."

Karen would no longer be shushed. "Melody, it's our pleasure, really. You've been a great help, not a burden."

Melody turned to Wes. "I'm sorry, Wes. I hope I didn't make you feel bad. It's not your fault."

He grunted and walked over to join them, carrying a plate full of sandwiches. When he was settled next to Karen, Melody peered at both of them.

"It's just that . . ."

They watched her, their faces questioning.

Melody took a deep breath and continued. "I didn't know I had a son."

Chapter Fifty-six

Matt sat in his truck and stared at the ranch house. Evening sun turned the pine logs to burnished gold and sunlight reflected off the windows, giving him a headache. What was he going to tell Burt and Carol? Where did he begin?

"Let's go, Daddy. I want Grandma." Skyler pushed the button to release his seat belt and wiggled out of the straps over his shoulders.

"Hold on there, big guy. I'll get you." Skyler was out of his booster seat by the time Matt opened the door and climbed out. His arms extended and Skyler dove into them.

"Oooh, I love you Daddy." Skyler said, giving him a big squeeze.

"I love you, too, Son." Matt returned the hug. Moments like this made life worth living.

Matt shut the truck door and crunched across the gravel to the front of the house. Carol threw open the door before Matt had a chance to knock.

"My darlings. Oh, where have you been? We thought we'd missed you. Come in, come in." Skyler went willingly into her waiting arms and she hugged him tightly.

"Good to see you, Matt." She patted his arm before turning and walking into the house, still clutching Skyler to her.

Matt paused, breathing in the familiar smell of fresh

baked bread and chili as he took in his surroundings. He felt sure nothing had changed about this house in twenty years. Sandstone slabs tiled the entryway, and reddish brown carpet covered the floor in the front room and down the hall to the kitchen. A well-worn brown leather sofa and loveseat framed a wagon wheel coffee table, across from the TV, which sat in front of the window. The wood paneling and low ceilings of the long, rambler home made Matt feel a bit claustrophobic, but decorative pillows, oil paintings Melody had done as a teenager, and the numerous family photos that decorated the place gave it the feel of home—as, of course, did the heavenly smells that emanated from the kitchen.

Matt followed his nose, and was soon salivating at the sight of large loaves of homemade bread sitting under a dishtowel on the cupboard. In three strides he crossed the yellow linoleum to the wooden cabinets that Burt had made out of rough-hewn pine. Burt jumped up from the kitchen table and met him, his hand extended.

"Matt, good to see you, my boy." He slapped Matt on the back with his left hand while his right one grasped Matt's in an iron grip and shook vigorously.

"Good to see you, too." Matt grimaced. The old man didn't know his own strength.

Skyler sat on a stool at the counter and Carol was already slicing bread. Butter melted on a steamy piece as she slathered it on and set it in front of Skyler.

"There you go, sweety."

"Thanks, Grandma." Skyler carefully picked up the huge slice in both hands and opened his mouth wide to take a bite.

Matt chuckled. "That piece is as big as you are, sport."

Skyler grinned as he chewed, his cheeks puffed up like a chipmunk.

"I'm assuming you want some, too, the way you barreled in here like a horse goin' for oats," Carol smiled at Matt as she sliced.

"You better believe it." Matt smiled back. "Best stuff in the whole state. And with all these Mormon women around, that's sayin' somethin'." He winked, and Burt joined in her laughter as she handed Matt a thick slice.

"Flattery will get you everywhere, young man." She slid a saucer with a cube of butter on it and a knife toward him. "You can butter it yourself, though. I have to go feed the chickens before supper. Wanna come, Skyler?" His head bounced up and down, his mouth still full.

Carol walked around the counter and lifted him off the stool, careful not to upset the bread he still clutched in his hands. "Watch out for that ole' tom turkey in the yard, or he'll steal that right away from you."

Skyler's eyes widened, and he covered the slice with both hands as he held it against the front of his shirt and walked through the screen door Carol held open for him. Matt groaned. "What's a few more grease spots? They'll go with the ketchup from lunch." Burt chuckled as Matt grinned at him.

An uncomfortable silence settled over the two men as Matt bit into his bread. He fiddled with the butter knife as he chewed. Acid bubbled up from his stomach and diminished the enjoyment he usually relished while eating Carol's bread. A knot in his throat made it difficult to swallow. With Skyler out of the room, it was a good time to bring up the subject he could no longer avoid, even though he needed Carol there, too, when he launched into the whole story.

Matt swallowed the bite he'd been chewing and looked at Burt, who was staring at the ceiling, arms folded across his chest. Matt liked Burt but had never been comfortable alone with him. Carol was the social one. Burt didn't say much, unless he felt he had something profound to add to a conversation. The tension had increased ever since Skyler's disappearance, and Matt suspected Burt still dealt with feelings of guilt despite Matt's efforts to assuage them.

Matt cleared his throat. "Um, Burt, there's something I need to talk to you and Carol about." Carol had asked him to call them Mom and Dad, but he only did occasionally.

"Oh?" was all Burt said, facing Matt.

"Yeah." A heavy silence filled the room as the olive green cat clock that hung on the kitchen wall ticked loudly, its tail swinging back and forth as its eyes moved from side to side. "It's about Melody."

Burt's eyebrows lifted, but he made no comment.

The screen door rattled and pounded, then Skyler's voice shouted from the other side, "Daddy, Daddy! Look what I got!"

Matt dropped his bread on the counter and strode to the door. Skyler gave the door a solid kick just as Matt arrived. His hands were cupped together in front of him, his head bowed, concentrating on whatever he held there. Matt opened the door a crack, and Skyler stepped back to let him out.

"What ya got there, little man?" Matt stooped beside him and Skyler carefully lifted his top hand a crack to reveal a yellow ball of fluff. The chick began to cheep loudly, and Skyler quickly shut his hand and looked at his dad and giggled.

"It's a baby chick. Grandma let me hold him." His green eyes sparkled as a huge grin lit his face.

"That's cool. Does it have a name?"

Skyler's eyebrows drew together and his lips puckered. Carol walked up behind him.

"That's for you to decide, sweetypie." She tousled Skyler's hair. The grin returned.

"I wanna call him Stevie."

Matt and Carol both laughed.

"Stevie? What made you choose that name, son?" Matt refrained from pointing out that Stevie was a strange name for a chicken.

"Stevie's my friend from pre-school." Skyler stared at his hands.

Matt was stunned. He'd forgotten Georgette had enrolled Skyler in pre-school for a short time.

"I miss him." Skyler's quiet declaration made Matt's throat constrict. His eyes burned as his arms gently encircled Skyler and pulled him closer. Desperate to distance himself from memories of Melody, he hadn't considered the disruption to Skyler's life.

Matt swallowed hard. "Stevie's the perfect name."

Chapter Fifty-seven

"Wait a minute," Wes said. "If you were married to Matt and this was your house, wouldn't the neighbors know you?"

Melody, Karen, and Wes sat around the small kitchen table. Crumbs were all that remained on the plate where the sandwiches had been.

Melody smacked her forehead with the heel of her hand at Wes's comment. "Of course. Why didn't I think of that?" An image of Esther flitted across her mind. Melody hoped she hadn't been anything like her. She had no idea who her neighbors were in California and was sure Esther didn't either. Any socializing Esther did was strictly business.

"There's only one way to find out." Karen took Melody's hand as she peered at her.

Melody inhaled deeply. "Right." Her heart pounded as she slowly let out her breath. What sort of person had she been? Did her neighbors like her? Would they know her? What was she likely to find out about her life?

"Will you come with me?" Her eyes pleaded with Karen. "I'm sorry to ask. I know you have so much to do here . . ." Her words trailed off and she glanced at Wes.

"Go," he said to Karen. "I'll put the kids down for a nap and clean up in here."

Karen threw her arms around his neck. "You are such a dear.

What would I ever do without you?" She kissed him hard on the mouth, and Melody thought her heart would rip in two. She had to find Matt. Fast.

Melody stood and wiped the moisture from her palms on the front of her jeans. "Let's go." Her voice wavered, but she started for the door, glancing over her shoulder as she went.

Karen released Wes and gave him a peck on the cheek before rising and following Melody. She stopped to give Jessica a hug. "Mommy will be back in a minute, okay, sweetheart?" Jessica started to fuss and clung to Karen's neck, so Wes came to the rescue. Taking her from Karen, he rocked her back and forth and patted her back. Karen slipped to the door where Melody waited.

Once out the door and down the stairs, Melody stopped in the driveway and glanced at the houses on either side of them. "Where should we start?"

Karen pointed to the left. "Mrs. Brown lives there. She's really nice. She brought over brownies the first day we got here."

"Works for me," Melody replied.

Karen linked her arm through Melody's and they headed for Mrs. Brown's. Sunshine warmed their shoulders, and a cool breeze tickled their faces. Children's laughter floated from the schoolyard across the street. Trees bursting with pink blossoms lined the narrow strip of grass between the sidewalk and the curb in the neighbor's yard. The house was white with blue trim. The scalloped eaves and window boxes filled with flowers reminded Melody of a Swiss chalet. The smell of freshly mowed grass filled the air as they walked up the sidewalk to the front door.

An older lady answered their knock. Her pure white hair was pulled up in a bun. She was short and round and wore a cotton housedress with a floral print and an apron. Her smile lit her round face as she looked at them through the screen door.

"May I help you?"

Melody's stomach sank. The woman didn't recognize her.

Karen glanced at Melody, her expression sympathetic. Then she took the lead.

"Uh, Mrs. Brown? My name is Karen Helstrom. I just moved in next door. We met a couple of days ago."

"Oh, yes, yes, certainly." Mrs. Brown pushed open the screen and then froze as the color drained from her face. "Oh my. Oh dear, oh my." She stumbled backward, and Melody and Karen reached simultaneously to grab each of her arms and help her into an overstuffed chair in the front room.

"Thank you, my dears." The old woman put a hand on her chest while she fanned her face with the other one. Looking at Melody, she repeated, "Oh my, oh my."

Melody let her catch her breath for a moment, then knelt beside her and ventured a timid, "Mrs. Brown? Do you know who I am?" The answer seemed obvious, but it was a place to start.

Mrs. Brown didn't seem to hear the question as she reached for Melody's hand and held it tightly. "Oh, Melody, my dear, I thought you were dead." Tears welled up in her eyes, and she fished a handkerchief from her apron pocket, never releasing Melody's hand.

A golf ball-sized lump rose in Melody's throat. Finally, she had a connection to her past. This was the first person she'd met since the accident who knew her. Swallowing hard, she wondered where to start. She had so many questions.

"Where have you been, dear? Your husband was beside himself with grief. He finally moved away, you know." Her milky gray eyes peered through thick glasses at Melody.

Melody glanced at Karen, who stood on the other side of Mrs. Brown's chair, her hands folded in front of her, then looked back at her old neighbor. How much should she tell her? Where should she begin?

Melody took a deep breath. "I had an accident and lost my memory. An older couple rescued me and I've been living with them in California."

"Oh my," Mrs. Brown said again. "You poor dear. Poor Matthew and Skyler."

Pinpricks of light danced in front of Melody's eyes at the

mention of Skyler's name. Skyler. Her son. Attaching a name to the phantom wisps in her mind brought the reality of a son crashing into her brain. Sagging back on her heels, her hand slipped from Mrs. Brown's and dropped into her lap. She didn't collapse into tears like she had at Karen's, but numbly stared at the wall behind Mrs. Brown's chair.

"Are you okay, dear?" Concern laced Mrs. Brown's voice.

Melody didn't answer. The boy from the picture with Matt and the redhead loomed in her mind, amd snatches of other images flitted through her brain. Her little boy. Her baby. A year and a half. If he was the same age as Steven, he'd only been about three when she'd disappeared. Would he remember her? Would he want anything to do with her? Would he forgive her?

"She just learned she has a son about an hour ago," Melody heard Karen murmur to Mrs. Brown.

"Oh my goodness," was Mrs. Brown's reply. "You mean, she still doesn't remember?"

"No," came Karen's hushed answer.

Melody sighed heavily. "I have to find them."

"Well, have you checked with your mother?" Mrs. Brown asked.

Melody's head flew up. "You know my mother?"

"Oh gracious, of course you haven't. You don't remember her, do you, dear?"

"No, no. Who is she? Where is she?" Melody knelt upright, her heart pounding.

"Well, I've only met her a couple of times at church myself when she came to visit, but Matthew and Skyler spent a great deal of time at their ranch down by Kanab after you disappeared."

"Their?"

"Yes. She and her husband's."

"Her husband? My father?"

"Yes, of course, dear."

"What are their names?"

Mrs. Brown's face crunched in concentration. "Oh dear, you do put an old lady on the spot. Let me think for a second . . ."

Melody's heart attempted to burst its bounds and leap from her chest as she waited, unable to breathe.

"Anderson. Yes, that's it. Carol and uh . . . Burt. Yes, Burt. Burt and Carol Anderson."

Chapter Fifty-eight

"Melody's alive." Matt watched Burt and Carol's faces change from curiosity to confusion at his revelation. They sat on the old, worn, leather sofa, while he perched on the edge of Burt's favorite recliner, which he had pulled over to face them in the front room. Skyler was asleep in the back bedroom, which they always shared when they came to visit. He and Melody used to stay in her old room across the hall, but Matt hadn't been able to go in there since her disappearance.

"I'm sorry I didn't tell you sooner, but I wanted to wait until I knew where she was and what was going on . . ." The excuse sounded lame as Matt spoke it, so he let his voice trail off. Neither Burt nor Carol spoke. Their faces were frozen, eyes wide, mouths agape. Matt was silent.

"What are you talking about?" Carol finally found her voice.

Matt took a deep breath. "Melody was in an accident and lost her memory. This crazy older couple rescued her and took her to California, where they claimed her as their daughter, and that's where she's been living."

Burt leapt to his feet, eyes wild, fists clenched at his sides. "Where are they? You tell me right now and I'll let them know in no uncertain terms whose daughter she is."

Matt motioned for him to sit down. "Relax, Burt. She's not there anymore."

"What do you mean? Where is she now?" Carol's voice squeaked. Her eyes filled with tears.

Matt felt his throat constrict and eyes grow moist as he considered what to say next.

"That's the problem," he rasped. "I don't know."

Burt plopped down on the couch, and Carol grabbed his hand in hers and squeezed while tears rolled down her cheeks.

"You'd better start explaining, son." Burt's voice was gruff as he patted Carol's hands, his own eyes swimming behind a film.

"Skyler and I didn't go to Arizona. We've been in California, where I confronted these people, but Melody had already left."

"Where did she go?" The anguish in Carol's voice made Matt duck his head and swallow hard before he continued.

"Utah."

"What?" Burt and Carol practically shouted together.

Matt brought his head up. His elbows rested on his knees. "Jack—that's the man who claimed to be her father—" Burt started to rise again, but Carol's grip on his hand pulled him back down. "Well, he's not as loony as the old lady, Esther, Melody's pretend mother." Color rose in Carol's face and her lips were a tight, white line.

Matt continued. "Anyway, apparently he felt bad when he found out Melody was married and finally told her the whole story and gave her my address in Roy."

"How'd he get your address?" Carol's voice seethed with barely controlled anger.

"From the divorce papers."

"Divorce papers? What? Now what are you talking about? Why would they have divorce papers?" Carol's eyes bored into Matt. His gaze dropped and he stared at the floor as he twisted his hands together.

"Matt?" Carol's anguished whisper brought his head up to look at her. "How long have you known she was alive?"

The question he'd dreaded. He sucked in as much of the heavy air as his lungs would hold, then expelled it through pursed lips before he answered. "Since I went to Vegas."

Shock, then anger registered on her face. Matt didn't dare look at Burt.

"But that was a more than six months ago." Anger he could take, but the hurt that laced her words tore at his guts.

"I know, I know." Matt rubbed his eyes with his fingers, then covered his face with his hands.

"I think you'd better explain." Matt recognized Burt's cold, deadly tone, but had only heard it used once before, when Burt had fired a ranch hand who'd tried to steal Carol's wedding ring from the kitchen windowsill.

Matt ran both hands through his hair and sat back in the recliner. His eyes locked with Burt's. "I don't know if you remember me telling you we were going to a show in Vegas when I dropped Skyler off." Burt gave a curt nod. "Well," Matt took a loud breath through his nose. "Melody was there."

"Where? In Vegas? I thought you said she was in California," Carol shot at him.

"She was. Or at least, that's where Jack and Esther took her. Apparently, they're record producers, and they got Melody started in a singing career." Matt's statement only produced blank stares, so he continued.

"When I said she was there, I meant on the stage. Performing. She was the opening act for the concert we went to."

Both their mouths dropped open.

"When I saw her there, like that, singing merrily away after all I'd been through, I went nuts. I thought she'd left me to make a career for herself."

Burt and Carol silently stared. Hurt and confusion clouded their eyes.

"I thought about telling you when I got back, but, forgive me for this, I didn't know if you were somehow involved. You guys were always close, and I knew she didn't keep things from you. I was so hurt that I couldn't think straight. So I took off."

"That explains a lot." Carol quietly voiced.

"That song." Burt's words were haunted as he turned to Carol. "I heard a song on the radio in my truck a while back.

Remember me telling you?"

Carol nodded. "You said it sounded like Melody."

"I listened for the name of the singer, but it never said." Burt looked at Matt, eyebrows arched.

"Andrea Kensington. That's the name Jack and Esther gave her. I thought it was just a stage name, but she really believed that's who she was."

Silence cloaked them like the darkness. Crickets and bullfrogs provided background noise.

"And the divorce?" Carol finally rasped.

Matt met her eyes. The world of sadness he saw there matched his own. "I filed when I got back, after staying in the cabin."

Carol looked at Burt and grabbed his hand, anguish written on her features.

"I'm so sorry. I was hurt and angry and I thought that was the only way to get on with my life." No response was forthcoming, so Matt continued.

"Anyway, after moping around for a month, I decided to come home and start a new life. The divorce became final a few weeks ago."

Silence gripped the small group, and heaviness filled the air as they contemplated the fact that Matt and Melody were no longer married.

"So . . ." Matt broke the silence.

"So what happens when she gets to Roy and finds you're no longer there?" Burt put words to the question that was burned into Matt's mind.

"Precisely," was all he could say.

The air became so thick Matt found it hard to draw a breath as he watched the war of emotions rage across his ex-in-laws' faces. Feeble light from the cactus-shaped lamp on the end table was all that penetrated the darkness of the room. The musky scent of old carpet and wood-smoke filtered drapes filled Matt's nose.

"So what do we do now?" Carol asked, always the practical one.

Matt's jaw set in determination. "Find her."

Chapter Fifty-nine

Melody started the car as she waved at Karen and Wes on the front porch. Wes, who was holding Jessica, took her tiny hand in his and waved it up and down. Jessica giggled and flapped her other arm and kicked her legs. Steven poked his head out from between Wes and Karen while he clung to each of their legs. A Spiderman T-shirt and jeans had replaced his Spiderman jammies. His feet were bare, his blond hair tousled.

"What a precious little family," Melody mumbled to herself as she put the car in gear, gave a final wave, and eased away from the curb, wiping tears with the back of her hand. Her search for lost love had, instead, netted her enduring friendship and strengthened her resolve to recover what she'd lost. Families were what it was all about. She hadn't been wrong to give up a lonely life on the road to seek a deep and fulfilling relationship.

Glancing over her shoulder, she pulled into the lane before a long line of cars approached. The top was down on her convertible, and the June sun soaked into her shoulders, warming her like a favorite sweater.

Karen had talked her into spending the night so she'd be well rested before driving to Kanab, but sleep had been sporadic. Her mind had refused to shut down as images danced and flickered. Only blinding flashes, but nothing concrete: a dark-haired boy, an older couple, and Matt, always Matt. But only outlines and silhouettes, shadow dancers on a white screen.

Lifting her sunglasses, she checked her reflection in the rearview mirror and was shocked to see the dark circles under her eyes. According to the light in the bathroom, she'd managed to cover them with makeup this morning, but the harsh light of the sun mocked her efforts. Not how she wanted to look for a reunion with a lost love. She dropped the sunglasses back in place. Her hair was going to be a windblown mess, too, but she was enjoying the fresh air and sunshine too much to put the top up. Well, the air was filled with exhaust at the moment as she sat in a line of cars waiting to get on the freeway, but that was temporary.

The light turned green and cars inched forward, most of them going straight to Hill Air Force Base, but many turned onto I-15. Soon, Melody had merged with the traffic heading south and was speeding toward her past, and she hoped, her future.

The divorce was final. Jack had shown her the papers from Esther's safe, and they'd only given her three months to protest something she'd known nothing about. The thought evoked mixed emotions. Melancholy at the thought of a wasted marriage she hadn't known existed, and relief that if her meeting with Matt, when she finally caught up to him, didn't go well, she'd walk away with no legal entanglements. Her stomach plummeted at that thought. Walk away to what? Other than Karen, who had a life and family of her own, she had no one.

A tiny flutter of hope ignited in her heart. That was no longer true. She had her parents. Her real parents. Even if she didn't remember them, they'd remember her. And help her. She glanced at the piece of paper she'd printed off the Internet that was secured on the passenger seat by her purse. With Karen's help, they'd found an address for Burt and Carol Anderson in Kanab. A phone number, too, which she'd dialed with shaky fingers, but a tinny voice had said the number was temporarily out of service. So she and Karen had pulled up a rough map with complicated directions off the Web. Near as she could tell, the ranch was sixty or so miles outside of Kanab.

Melody's mind flashed on the ravine where she'd first awakened. Jack had said it was in southern Utah. Maybe it was somewhere on her parents' ranch. Not that she cared to revisit that nightmare.

An enormous ferris wheel and roller coaster came into view, and a brief image of her and Matt walking through an amusement park with a small boy between them snapped into her brain and then was gone. Memories teased her but offered no satisfaction. She switched on the radio to block the frustration, and the past she did remember rushed over her. Her own voice blared at her over the wind.

California was still a viable option. After all, she had a budding career. Her flight had been so swift and full of anguish that she hadn't discussed royalties on her music, but she knew Jack would be fair. Esther was another story, but now that Melody knew her for what she was, she'd deal with her on her own terms. She had plenty of money for right now, but the future was uncertain and she didn't want to kill any golden geese.

Her song quieted her mind, and she relaxed to listen and enjoy the sunshine and fresh air. At least Wes had assured her that no redhead had been around in any of his dealings with Matt. Whoever she was, and whatever she'd been to Matt, she no longer seemed to be in the picture. That was one less obstacle.

However, the path was far from smooth. What if her parents didn't know where he was or how to get in touch with him? And, once she did find him, could he forgive her? Would he still love her? And . . . a thought that terrified Melody so much she constantly kept it shoved to the back of her mind . . . would she love him? If her memory never returned, would she still fall in love with Matt again?

Chapter Sixty

Matt and Skyler were on the road again. All his paperwork on the house was packed in a box somewhere in the back of his truck, and he wasn't about to unload the whole thing to look for it, so he had no way to get in touch with the people who bought it. Burt and Carol's phone service had been knocked out by a recent storm, and no one had gotten around to come out and fix it yet. And, like an idiot, he'd packed the charger to his cell phone away in one of the boxes, too, or he'd at least try to call one of his neighbors and have them keep an eye out for Melody.

So, he might be headed on a wild goose chase, but he was too antsy to sit at Burt and Carol's for another day. At least while driving, he felt like he was doing something. Melody had probably already stopped by looking for him, and what was that guy's name? Wes, yeah, Wes might know where she went. It was a long shot, but it was all he had.

Carol had given him the names of a couple of Melody's girlfriends from college who lived in the Salt Lake area, but it was useless information if Melody had no memory. He wished she still had her cell phone. He would have called her long ago, but Jack said the cell phone she'd used for the past year was in Esther's name and so Melody had left it behind.

Skyler sat quietly in his booster seat and stared out the window. Unusual for him.

"What ya thinkin' about, son?" Matt broke the silence.

"Nuthin'," came his mumbled reply.

"Are you sad?"

Silence.

"What's the matter, big guy?"

Again there was no reply, and Matt noticed a tear on Skyler's cheek. He reached over to brush it off with the back of his finger.

"Hey, come on, little man. You know you can tell your ole' dad anything, right? Let me help you." Matt had a hard time concentrating on the road. Skyler's tears were like drops of acid to his soul.

"It's Mommy."

Matt's breath stopped. "What about her, Skyler?" His tone was gentle.

Skyler turned to look at him, and Matt's heart constricted at the sight of his green eyes drowning in huge puddles of tears.

"I'm starting to forget her."

Matt choked. He stared at the road ahead while his blood turned to rivers of ice. Placing both hands on the wheel, he negotiated the winding curves of Highway 20 while he took deep breaths to calm himself and decide how to comfort his son.

"Well . . ." Matt had no idea how to proceed.

A deer darted onto the road and Matt swerved to miss it.

"Whoa, that was a close one." His voice shook a bit as he spoke.

"That was fun, Daddy." Skyler leaned forward in his booster seat as far as the seat belt allowed. "Can we do it again?"

Matt gave a nervous chuckle. "I don't think so. At least, I sure hope not."

"Look, Daddy, there's another deer," Skyler shouted excitedly, pointing out the window. "And another one!"

"Yup, there sure are." Examining both sides of the road, there were, indeed, several more deer scattered across the meadow they were passing through. Matt tightened his grip on the wheel even though they were several hundred yards away. He'd driven this road enough to know how unpredictable the darn critters could be. At least they'd taken Skyler's mind off his momma. Matt hadn't mentioned the possibility of finding her to Skyler. There were too many question marks. Kids dealt in here and now. Abstract future promises or hopes were more than their minds could grasp.

When Skyler had asked where they were going, Matt had told him he'd forgotten something from their old house and had to go back and get it. Not entirely a lie, if that something was Melody. Excited about seeing their house again, Skyler hadn't even complained about the long drive.

"I'm hungry, Daddy."

"Well, let's just see what we've got here." Digging through the sack Carol had sent, Matt came up with a fruit snack, which he tore open with his teeth and handed to Skyler.

"Thanks." Skyler went to quietly munching.

"Grandma packed sandwiches, too. Maybe we can pull over somewhere and have a picnic."

"Yeah," came Skyler's enthusiastic reply.

Matt fished an apple from the sack and crunched into it as he pulled off Highway 20 onto I-15, glad to be off the narrow, winding road onto the freeway, where he sped up to seventy-five miles per hour. He glanced at his fuel gauge. Wouldn't hurt to fuel up, either. He'd be glad to stretch his legs a bit and get one of Carol's delicious sandwiches under his belt.

Matt glanced at Skyler, who popped fruit snacks into his mouth while staring out the window. How could Matt help him remember his mom without the memories being too painful? And without getting his hopes up about finding her? The white line ticked in front of Matt's vision. His stomach growled.

Cove Fort. That was it. They'd stopped there several times as a family on the way to Kanab. Melody's ancestors had helped build the fort as protection against the Indians when they'd first settled in Utah. Skyler loved to peek out the rifle holes and pretend he was warding off savages. They hadn't been there since Melody had vanished. She'd regaled them with stories of Skyler's sixth-great-grandpa while they wandered through the fort or ate lunch at the picnic tables across the street.

A service station was off the same exit as the fort, too. Perfect. Matt pressed on the gas.

Chapter Sixty-one

Melody's stomach growled. The bowl of cereal she'd eaten at Karen's had long since fled the scene, but no food establishments interrupted the vast expanse of cedar trees and grassy fields cradled between mountains.

A blue billboard on top of a small hill announced Cove Fort in ten miles. Something stirred in Melody's mind. What was Cove Fort? Was it a town? The name hadn't appeared on the usual green highway signs that stated how many miles and what exit, so she ruled out a town. Perhaps a landmark? Was it really a fort? Did such things still exist?

That something writhed in Melody's mind like a butterfly trying to free itself from a cocoon. What was Cove Fort to her? Her eyes begged to squeeze shut and allow her brain quiet and darkness to break from its web, but her survival instinct forbade her to do it.

The boy. Skyler. His filmy image, green eyes shining, chubby cheeks flushed with pleasure, smiled at her, then his gaze turned to the high rock walls of a genuine fort right out of the old West. The vision faded before solidifying. Melody pounded the steering wheel in frustration.

Another blue sign appeared: Cove Fort, two miles. She had to stop. Her stomach would have to wait, unless they served food at the fort. Signs for a rest area and gas station at the same exit appeared. Good. If her curiosity led her on a wild goose chase, at least she could refuel and grab a snack.

As she exited the freeway, she turned left and saw another sign that said Cove Fort was in two miles. What was the deal? The road wound down through cedar trees to a rest area and gas station on her right. Her tummy gave another loud growl, so she decided to stop before exploring the fort.

Several motor homes, trucks, and travel trailers crowded the pumps, but Melody found an empty one. She stretched and yawned, breathing in the cedar-scented air, before fishing her credit card from her wallet. Checking the rearview mirror, she removed her sunglasses, wiped black smudges from beneath her eyes, and tried to run her fingers through her hair, but it was a lost cause, so she put her glasses back on, opened her door, and stepped out of the car.

A black truck a couple of pumps over caught her eye as she swiped her credit card and removed the gas nozzle. An image of Matt climbing out of a similar truck flashed in her mind. The back was covered with a tarp. Thoughts of the truck wiggled in the back of her mind while she inserted the nozzle and began fueling.

While her car drank the gas, she grabbed her purse and keys and headed inside to find a restroom and food. She glanced back at the truck several times as she went. Nobody was in it, so the owner must be inside. Could it be Matt? Melody shook the thought off as ridiculous. She'd driven from California to look for him. No way she would find him at a gas station on the side of the highway. So why did her insides continue to flutter?

Melody chided herself for her silliness and entered the women's restroom, where she had to wait in line for several minutes. This filled her with inexplicable anxiety, and when she finally rushed from the bathroom and looked out the window, the truck was gone.

Pushing past a clump of people, Melody burst through the doors to the parking lot and frantically scanned the area. *I must be losing my mind,* she thought, but couldn't stop her legs from running to her car when she glimpsed the tail end of the truck headed in the direction of the fort.

Yanking the nozzle from her gas tank and jamming it back into the pump, she cursed her fingers for being so slow as she fumbled with the gas cap and finally replaced it. Not waiting for her receipt or bothering with the car door, she leapt over the side of her convertible, tossed her purse onto the passenger seat, and shoved the keys in the ignition. Gravel flew as she tore out of the gas station in the direction she'd seen the truck go.

What if she didn't find it? Did it matter? Her mind was a jumble of questions.

The truck was no longer in sight on the narrow, two-lane road and Melody felt like bursting into tears, but wasn't sure why. This was crazy.

"Dear Lord, help me find that truck," she found herself mumbling.

Her spontaneous prayer sent Melody into reflection. Prayer hadn't been part of her life with Jack and Esther, yet she'd turned to it quite naturally on several occasions over the past year and a half, speaking to an unknown being like He was a long-lost friend.

Mrs. Brown had mentioned seeing Melody's mother at church with her. Discussing it with Karen later, they'd determined Melody was a member of The Church of Jesus Christ of Latter-day Saints, better as the Mormon Church. Karen also belonged to the LDS Church—maybe that was why she'd felt such an instant bond with her.

Apparently, it was a rather strict religion in comparison with the lifestyles she'd witnessed in California and elsewhere she'd traveled. Melody wondered if she'd be held responsible for living the tenets of religion she knew nothing about. She'd discussed some of the Church's standards with Karen, and Melody's own values lined up anyway. Now she knew why drinking, drugs, smoking, and illicit sex had held no appeal for her despite their prevalence in the world she'd been immersed in. Some things seemed to be ingrained despite a loss of memory.

A large sign announced her arrival at Cove Fort and Melody let her foot off the gas. The words "The Church of Jesus Christ of Latter-day Saints" were under the name of the fort, and her insides did a little jig. A huge barn was on the right next to some corrals and then, an honest-to-goodness fort. A sign for parking guided her attention to the left and her breath caught in her throat when she saw the black truck parked behind an expanse of green grass lined by a white fence.

Melody pulled in the parking lot past a row of small houses. No one was in the truck. With a pounding heart, she parked next to it, picked up her purse, and climbed out of her car on shaky legs. Feeling like a peeping Tom, she looked in the cab of the truck, and her heart nearly stopped at the sight of a child's booster seat strapped to the passenger side. She could almost see Skyler sitting there, grinning up at her.

Her eyes scanned the area, but no child was in sight. Or anyone else, for that matter, until an elderly couple, who looked like they were dressed for church, came out of a small building at the edge of the parking lot and started in her direction. Melody fled across the street toward the fort. Glancing over her shoulder, she saw the couple retreat to the building. Not that she'd expected them to give chase, but she still felt relieved as she slowed her step. Melody had no words to explain the roiling emotions she was experiencing, and idle chit-chat was beyond her capacity.

Melody's nerves quivered as she approached the fort. A large garden area was to the left of it. The fort didn't seem very big, but what did she know about forts? The stone walls rose in front of her like the image that had materialized in her mind when she'd first seen the sign. She'd been here before.

Her feet crunched on gravel as she approached the large, wooden gates. Birds twittered in the trees, and dust and the smell of manure from the corrals choked her lungs. Her heart pounded in her chest. Was she going insane?

Melody stepped gingerly through the gates of the fort and studied the doorways that lined either side of the rectangular enclosure. Three huge trees grew in the grassy middle area of the fort. Melody walked to the rope that divided the sidewalk from the grass.

She froze in place when she heard voices coming from a room to her left. A white-haired gentleman stepped onto the cement walkway and Melody held her breath as he beckoned for whomever was inside to follow.

A young couple came out of the room, followed by an older lady. The man had a little girl on his shoulders. Melody's heart turned to lead and slid to the pit of her stomach.

What had she expected? Did she really think Matt and Skyler would appear on the side of the road and her search would be over? She realized how ridiculous her girlish fantasies had been. Maybe Matt had owned a black truck somewhere in her past. Maybe she had been to this fort with Skyler. But they weren't here now, and she'd lost valuable time chasing ghosts when she could be closer to her parents' ranch where real answers waited.

The older gentleman waved at her. "Would you like to join us? We've just started the tour."

"No thank you," Melody spoke loudly, spying the hearing aid behind his ear. She turned to go.

"Mommy?"

Melody froze. Tingles danced along her spine, and cracks spidered the glass prison that held her mind. Her breath caught in her lungs and held as she slowly turned toward the sound that had swelled her heart to bursting.

"Skyler?" Her eyes frantically searched for the source. No one was there. Had she imagined it?

"Melody?"

Melody looked up. Standing behind a wooden rail on a balcony above her were Matt and Skyler. The glass shattered as memories poured in. Her family. Tears blurred their image.

"Oh, Matt. Skyler," she choked, as she took a stumbling step forward and raised her arms toward them.

Matt scooped Skyler into his arms and ran along the balcony to a stairway on the side. His footsteps pounded on wood as he hurried down them. Melody bounded toward the stairs. All the hurt and loneliness from the past year and a half seeped from her veins as her eyes locked on the people who meant the most to her in the whole world.

Matt set Skyler down and he dove into Melody's arms as she crouched down to receive him. Their tears mixed as their cheeks met and they held each other tightly.

Melody slowly opened her eyes to see a pair of boots in front of her. Her gaze drifted up the jeaned legs and T-shirt to the face of her dreams, tears streaming down his cheeks. Still clutching Skyler, she rose to her feet and stared into the eyes of the man she loved. Every thought and feeling she'd ever had of him and for him pulsed through her veins and was reflected in his eyes.

"Matt," she whispered.

Skyler lifted his head and looked from one to the other then held out one arm to Matt. Matt's arms flew around Skyler and Melody and he crushed them to him.

"Oh, Mel." Matt's anguished utterance clawed at Melody's heart.

"I'm so sorry," she choked, raising her head to look from Matt to Skyler. "I didn't know . . . I lost my memory and I . . ."

"I know, I know. I went to find you and you were gone. But now you're here . . . And you remember?" Melody nodded, unable to speak past the huge lump in her throat. Matt kissed her forehead, her cheek, her neck.

Melody swallowed hard and looked tentatively into Matt's eyes. "But what about the divorce? Do you still want to be with me?"

"Forever and ever, Melody."

"I'll never leave you again." Her voice reverberated with fierce determination as she breathed in the beautifully familiar scent of him.

Skyler smiled an endearing grin and wiped his eyes with the back of his hand. Matt cupped her chin with his hand and captured her eyes with his.

"I'll never let you." The fervency of his words infused her with warmth. His lips found hers and breathed life into her soul.

Epilogue

Fourteen Months Later

 Melody stared out the window overlooking Snow Canyon, then back at the oil painting she was working on. Tapping her chin with the stick end of her brush, she contemplated the desert scene she was trying to capture. The smell of turpentine tickled her nose and a sigh of contentment escaped. She reached for her water bottle on a small table nearby and took a swig while her eyes wandered around the room.

This was her favorite part of the house she and Matt had bought in St. George. Encased by windows, the vista of red cliffs and pink sandstone sculptured by Mother Nature was breathtaking. Her easel and paints were set up where she could enjoy the view and dabble in her renewed hobby. White wicker furniture with blue and yellow cushions surrounded a glass coffee table in a conversation area at the other end of the room. The floor was laid with white ceramic tiles, and the walls were painted a pale, sky blue. Potted green plants gave a tropical feel. Melody smiled. Happiness seeped from every pore.

Her diamond sparkled in the early morning sun as she set the water bottle down. Matt had bought her a new ring when they'd been married in Kanab a week after their reunion at Cove Fort. What a long, yet busy week that had been.

Tears came to Melody's eyes as she remembered seeing her parents again. How her mom had cried and fussed over her. Her stoic dad had been unable to talk as tears streamed down his face. Home. Where the memories were tangible.

As agonizing as it had been for both of them, her mom had insisted that Melody and Matt stay in separate rooms until after the wedding, even though they'd been married before.

"Not married is not married, and we'll have no fornicating in this house," she'd insisted.

Matt had wanted to get the bishop there that same afternoon, but her mom had prevailed on him to let her throw "a halfway decent affair," as she'd put it. A week was all the time he'd allow.

The ranch house had been bursting at the seams with ward members from their church and well-wishers. Karen and Wes had come down with their kids, and Skyler had been thrilled to be reunited with Steven, who, as it turned out, was his buddy from pre-school.

Of course, the ranch hands had all been in attendance, and Melody still shuddered when she thought about their tale of Skyler getting lost and his eventual rescue. Melody set the paintbrush down and rubbed her arms, shaking off the "what-ifs" that always clouded her mind at that memory.

She forced her mind to better thoughts. Matt had taken the missionary discussions and been baptized into The Church of Jesus Christ of Latter-day Saints three weeks after the wedding. Melody's dad baptized him. They'd stayed with her parents until after his baptism, then decided to settle in St. George, since they'd met at college there and had many happy memories of the place. Karen and Wes had attended the baptism and been there a year later when they were sealed in the St. George temple for time and all eternity. Melody sighed again with happiness and watched her ring sparkle in the sunshine.

"Mel?" Matt called from another room.

"In here, babe," Melody answered, setting her brush on the palette.

"I should have known," Matt grinned at her as he padded in on bare feet, wearing pajama bottoms and a white T-shirt, and planted a kiss on her mouth, grabbing her around the waist with one arm.

"Good morning," he murmured next to her lips.

"Good morning to you. What's in your hand?" Melody asked, her arms sliding around his neck.

"You."

"No, your other hand." Her nose rubbed against his in an Eskimo kiss.

Matt stepped back and shook out the newspaper he'd been clutching, and Melody's arms dropped to her sides.

"You're never gonna believe this," he said, as he walked over, sat on the wicker loveseat, and patted the cushion next to him. Melody joined him.

"Do you remember my old boss, Rick?"

An involuntary shiver ran the length of her. "Yes, unfortunately. What about him?"

Matt laid the paper on the table and leafed through to the page he wanted. "He's in jail," Matt pronounced, pointing to an article that took up half the page.

"No kidding?" Melody looked closer at the paper and a picture of Rick leered at her from the page. "What's he in for?"

"Fraud and tax evasion. A lot went on at that dealership I had no idea about."

"Poor Kristy and Jared."

"They'll be okay. One thing I did know is that Rick had a secret bank account in Switzerland. He used to send his parents on trips there to make deposits for him, and I overheard them talking about it once."

"Will Kristy be able to access the money? Knowing him, I'd be surprised if she knows about that account."

"Well, we might just have to give her a call." Matt gave her a sly wink and draped his arm on the back of the loveseat behind her. "I wouldn't mind checking up on her, anyway. She's better off without him, you know."

"I know. I always hated how he treated her. But oddly enough, I think she really loves him."

Their silent reverie was interrupted by the phone on a little wicker stand next to the love seat. Matt picked up the receiver.

"Hello . . . Oh, hi, Jack. Yeah, she's sitting right here." Matt handed the phone to Melody.

"Hi, Jack. How ya doin'?" A pause ensued while she listened into the phone. Matt tickled her leg with a mischievous glint in his eye, and she playfully swatted his hand away while she stifled a giggle.

"That sounds great. Let me talk to Matt and I'll get back with you, okay? . . . Love you, too. Bye."

"What was that all about?" Matt asked.

"He wants me to come to L.A. next week to record my new CD. We can bring Skyler and have one last summer fling before he starts school. Maybe squeeze in a trip to Disneyland."

Matt groaned. "You had me 'til that last part."

Melody laughed. "He might be just as happy playing in the pool for a few days. I'll let you decide. Jack will need you to go over the books with him and plan our promotional strategy for the next year, too. With Esther out of commission, he relies heavily on your help and advice."

"How is Esther?" Matt's voice was full of compassion.

"She's as well as can be expected under the circumstances. Just keeps to her room mostly." Melody patted Matt's leg.

He'd told her about his meeting with Esther and how she'd gone crazy when Martin told her Jack was on his way home. When Jack arrived and found Matt there, he refuted all the lies Esther had told him, and Esther had slipped away into another world and hadn't returned. Jack refused to institutionalize her, though, so he hired a live-in nurse who gave her constant care.

"It wasn't your fault, you know," Melody reassured him for the umpteenth time.

"I know. I just wish I hadn't witnessed it. I mean, she was obviously a few cookies short of a pack to begin with, but my visit pushed her over the edge." His head bowed as he stared at his clasped hands.

Melody's heart swelled as she ran her fingers through Matt's hair. The fact that he felt so bad over the plight of a woman who had caused him untold grief made her love him even more, if that were possible.

As traumatic as her disappearance had been for all of them, things truly had worked out for the best. Matt escaped Rick's clutches. Not a moment too soon, by the sound of it. Now they were able to work together in her music career, which she never would have had if it had not been for Esther and Jack. And, the most important thing, Matt had joined the Church, and their family had been sealed forever. *The Lord works in mysterious ways.*

Skyler came into the room wearing Batman PJs and rubbing his eyes with one fist. Melody smiled at the sight of her old pal, Gus the bear, clutched in Skyler's other hand.

"Good morning, sleepyhead." Melody held her arms out and he ran into them. She lifted him onto her lap.

"Morning, Mommy." Skyler snuggled against her.

Matt ruffled Skyler's hair. "What about me, pal? Am I chopped liver?"

Skyler giggled. "Morning, Daddy."

Matt wrapped his arms around both of them.

My family. So much love crowded Melody's chest she felt ready to burst. Her eyes moistened. Her handsome prince had come. And instead of a white charger, he'd brought a green-eyed bundle of bliss.

About the Author

Kara has been published in the Ensign and in international Liahona magazines. She served as the president of her local chapter of the League of Utah Writers before moving to Mesa, Arizona, in 1992, where she currently lives with her husband, Jeff. She has four children: Jeff, Josh, Jennifer, and Jace; two daughters-in-law, Mindy and Jamie; and one granddaughter, Grace.

Besides writing, she enjoys reading, painting, Yoga, singing with a group called The Reflections, dancing with her husband, and doing puzzles and playing games with her family. She loves everything to do with Christmas, especially the music.